Praise for

holly hepburn

'Like a ray of sunshine on a cloudy day, this sparkling story will sweep you away and leave your heart full of love'
CATHY BRAMLEY

'Irresistible love stories in gorgeous locations with characters that feel like friends. A Holly Hepburn novel is a heartwarming treat!'
MIRANDA DICKINSON

'Losing yourself in a Holly Hepburn book is one of life's pleasures – they're the perfect escape'
MILLY JOHNSON

'Wholly satisfying reads – a warm glow is guaranteed when you snuggle up with a HH book!'
HEIDI SWAIN

Holly Hepburn is the author of seven novels including *The Little Shop of Hidden Treasures*, *Coming Home to Brightwater Bay*, and *A Year at the Star and Sixpence*. Follow her on twitter at @HollyH_Author.

holly hepburn

Escape to Darling Cove

**SIMON &
SCHUSTER**

London · New York · Sydney · Toronto · New Delhi

First published in Great Britain by Simon & Schuster UK Ltd, 2023

Copyright © Tamsyn Murray, 2023

The right of Tamsyn Murray to be identified as author
of this work has been asserted in accordance with the
Copyright, Designs and Patents Act, 1988.

1 3 5 7 9 10 8 6 4 2

Simon & Schuster UK Ltd
1st Floor
222 Gray's Inn Road
London WC1X 8HB

Simon & Schuster Australia, Sydney
Simon & Schuster India, New Delhi

www.simonandschuster.co.uk
www.simonandschuster.com.au
www.simonandschuster.co.in

A CIP catalogue record for this book
is available from the British Library

Paperback ISBN: 978-1-3985-1192-7
eBook ISBN: 978-1-3985-1193-4
Audio ISBN: 978-1-3985-2215-2

This book is a work of fiction.
Names, characters, places and incidents are either a product of the
author's imagination or are used fictitiously. Any resemblance to actual
people living or dead, events or locales is entirely coincidental.

Typeset in Bembo by M Rules
Printed and bound using 100% Renewable
Electricity at CPI Group (UK) Ltd

MIX
Paper | Supporting
responsible forestry
FSC® C171272

*To anyone whose dog has ever
rolled in something yucky.*

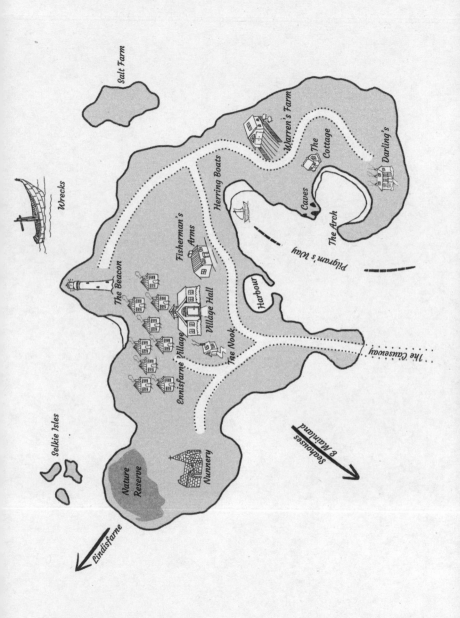

PART ONE

New Horizons

Chapter One

Logan

It looked like the road to the edge of the world.

Logan Silk leaned against the bonnet of the second-hand Toyota Hilux he'd bought especially for this trip and considered the view before him. Tide-rippled sands stretched towards the gunmetal grey horizon, split by the narrow causeway – a black ribbon of road flecked with green algae and the occasional flash of silvery sea water left behind by the tide. Dotted on either side were algae-strewn rocks and boulders that might have been carelessly abandoned by the North Sea, or placed there with more precision by the engineers who had constructed the road decades ago. The tarmac curved away from where Logan stood, cutting across the vast expanse of dull brown sand towards the distant smudged outline of Ennisfarne, a mile and a half from the Northumberland coast. Gusts of salt-laden wind whipped strands of dark hair across Logan's face as he contemplated the road, and his breath misted on the freezing February air. No cars came towards him and there were none behind. Apart from the birds circling overhead, he was entirely alone.

The light wasn't bad, Logan observed with professional detachment, in spite of the wintry sky. A few determined sunbeams had broken through to illuminate a patch of far-off sea – crepuscular rays that set the clouds ablaze with gold – and Logan was tempted to unpack one of his cameras. It was the promise of Northumberland's extraordinary light that had lured the artist Turner to the neighbouring island of Lindisfarne centuries earlier, and it was what brought Logan to Ennisfarne now. That and the anticipation of solitude; being cut off from the mainland for most of the day, at least by road, was appealing. And since the island was home to only two hundred and fifty people, he was very much hoping to keep himself to himself during the coming months. But for now, his cameras would remain in the car. Instead, he removed his gloves and captured the scene with his phone camera, then cast a critical eye over the pictures. The light was better than he'd expected – as always, the camera had caught more than the eye could see and the clouds on the screen had a majestic, almost ethereal quality to them, as though the sky had split open and heaven's glory had burst through.

Logan looked up at the road again and had the sudden irrational idea that he was facing some kind of test; he'd be examined as he crossed the causeway and be found wanting somehow. The waves would roar up from either side and crash down, washing both him and his sturdy car away. Then he smiled, because he was pretty sure he'd stolen the sequence from a movie. And actually, being washed away by the sea wasn't at all unlikely here – plenty of visitors to Ennisfarne and Lindisfarne thought they could beat the incoming tide and had been caught out. There was even a wooden refuge hut part way across each island's causeway, perched high above the level of the waves, so that stranded motorists could abandon their vehicles and climb out of reach of the pitiless ocean to await rescue.

The thought galvanized Logan into action. Pushing himself off the bonnet of the Hilux, he climbed back into the cab and started the engine. The window of time for safe crossing grew smaller with every minute he spent gazing at the sky and he wasn't about to risk becoming the laughing stock of the Seahouses lifeboat team, especially not when there was a chance he'd be recognized. He could imagine the tabloid headlines now:

WASHED UP! Superstar Snapper Silk Left High and Dry After Split

It wouldn't matter that his decision to come to the Farne Islands had nothing to do with the break-up with Suki – that had happened a month ago and they'd split on pretty amicable terms, by celebrity standards. But the tabloid journalists didn't care about the facts – there were no column inches in drama-free break-ups – and all Logan's carefully laid plans for staying under the radar on Ennisfarne would be in tatters. And besides, the Hilux was packed with some of his favourite cameras – old friends he'd used for most of his career. There was no way he was giving them up to the sea.

Gunning the engine, Logan set off along the causeway. As he got nearer to the island, its features spread themselves in a panoramic view. The northernmost tip loomed high above sea level – all forbidding cliffs and crags that were home to an incredibly varied bird population. It also boasted one of the most photographed ruins in England – the dramatic remains of Ennisfarne Nunnery, sister to the similarly desecrated priory on Lindisfarne, and the setting of more gothic horror films and Eighties music videos than Logan could remember. He'd done a shoot there for *Vogue* once and the stark beauty of the ruins had almost upstaged the models. But it was the other end of the island that drew his eye now – the distant limestone arch that curved off the southern tip, forming a doorway to the ocean beyond. That would be his view every morning for the foreseeable future, albeit at much closer range, and he couldn't imagine he'd ever grow bored of it.

The causeway curled round to the left, leading Logan from the flat expanse of sand and onto firm land, although he knew this part of the road would soon be covered by the tide too. And when he checked his rear-view mirror, he wasn't surprised to see light glinting on water behind him. There was no going back now – not for the next seven or eight hours at least. He glanced at the satnav, which was telling him he would reach his destination – Darling Cove – in seventeen minutes. But he'd pass through Ennisfarne village before then, with its tiny harbour and narrow lanes and palpable sense of stepping back in time. He'd be able to grab some basic supplies at the village store before continuing on to the cottage that would be his home until the summer.

The Nook was nestled in between the Fisherman's Arms pub and a cheerful-looking café on Long Street, facing the small harbour with its bobbing fishing boats and haphazard piles of lobster pots. Logan parked in one of the spaces outside the shop and pulled a baseball cap onto his head before heading inside. The owner of the cottage had explained in one of her emails that several supermarkets on the mainland delivered to Ennisfarne so he'd be able to shop online but deliveries had to be carefully timed to give the drivers time to get on and off the island. And he wanted to at least get through the front door of the cottage before he started thinking about practicalities like that, especially when The Nook would serve his immediate needs.

Logan's expectations weren't high as he entered the shop. His career had taken him to some remote locations in the past, where the nearest there'd been to a shop was a cabin-shaped wooden container with no staff and an app to gain access, or an isolated roadhouse where the closest neighbours were 135 miles away, so he understood the vital role small local shops played in their communities. But he was still surprised by the variety of goods on the Nook's shelves; it wasn't exactly London's Borough Market but there was a lot more than the basics. Beside the instant coffee he found Taylor's of Harrogate ground beans, an assortment of high-end fruit teas and some Green and Black's hot chocolate powder. Among the jars of pickled onions and gherkins, he spotted preserved lemons and pimento stuffed olives. And then he reached the end of the aisle and was presented with an entirely unexpected deli counter, stocked with everything from white-coated Spanish sausage to sun-dried tomatoes.

His surprise must have shown on his face because the stocky, middle-aged woman behind the counter looked amused. 'Welcome to The Nook. Is there something in particular you're looking for?'

Her words were coloured by the same Northumbrian accent he recalled hearing on his previous visit to Ennisfarne, distinctly north-eastern but not quite Geordie. At least he could understand her – he was sure there'd been a few island residents he'd struggled with the last time round, although he suspected they'd been messing with him and the rest of the shoot crew for their own entertainment.

'Not really,' he said now. 'Tea, coffee, bread and milk – that kind of thing.'

Now her gaze was curious above her rosy cheeks, as she identified he was more than just a day-tripper. 'You'll find everything you need here. How long are you staying?'

It was a perfectly reasonable question but Logan still had to fight the urge to reply that it was none of her business. 'I'm not sure,' he said, as neutrally as he could. And then, because it was inevitable he'd be shopping there over the coming months, he dredged up a warmer smile. 'A while, I think.'

She nodded. 'I'd better introduce myself, then. I'm Freda, owner of The Nook. If you don't see what you need on the shelves, all you have to do is ask – we're here to help.'

'Thanks, I'll keep that in mind,' he said, and glanced down at the array of tasty morsels beneath the glass counter. 'But it looks as though you have most of the bases covered.'

Freda raised her eyebrows. 'You'd be amazed at some of the things people expect us to have in stock.' She gave him an openly appraising once-over. 'Or maybes you wouldn't. From London, are you?'

Again, he knew there was no point in denying it although he wasn't sure what gave him away; his accent wasn't typically London, more a mishmash honed by all the places he'd lived over the years, but he supposed it was predominantly southern. And she wasn't wrong in any case – he owned a flat in Pimlico that he thought of as home, even though he rarely spent more than a few days there at a time. 'Yes,' he said.

'You'll find the pace of life a bit different here,' she observed. 'Maybes even too quiet, at least until you get used to things. But everyone looks out for each other and you can usually find a friendly face in the pub next door if you're in need of some company.'

Company was the last thing Logan wanted – he wasn't on Ennisfarne to make friends – but it felt rude to say so. Once again, he aimed for a politely non-committal reply. 'Great,' he said and pointed through the glass counter. 'I'll take some of your smoked ham.'

Freda pulled on some gloves and reached for a carving knife. 'Goes well with this Doddington cheese from the mainland,' she said as she sliced the ham. 'Just the thing for your first night on the island.'

He glanced at the smooth yellow cheese surrounded by a deep red rind. It looked delicious. 'Some of that too, then. Thanks.'

Freda gave a satisfied nod, as though he'd passed a little test. 'You'll find fresh sourdough loaves down the aisle, or there should be some farmhouse left if you prefer it. And we've a nice Rioja to wash it all down with.'

Logan couldn't help a wry smile at the sales push, although he knew he'd follow all of her suggestions. The cottage he'd booked listed a wood burner among its attractions and he could picture himself eating this supper by firelight, while listening to the sea crashing against the shore. His mouth was already watering. 'Sold,' he said.

He was browsing the shelves, picking up a few more essentials to get him through the next day or so, when the bell over the shop door tinkled, indicating another customer had entered. Logan looked up automatically and got a jumbled impression of grey hair and an impressive beard, ruddy cheeks and battered yellow waterproofs. But it was his nose that reacted fastest – the reek of fish was so overpowering that his hand was covering his face before he could stop it. If the man's appearance hadn't given it away, the stench would have – this was one of the island's fishermen.

Loitering near the deli counter once more, Logan waited until the other customer had completed his purchase and left the shop before heading towards the till at the front. The fishy top notes lingered, with more than a hint of body odour, and his distaste must have shown on his face because Freda threw him a sympathetic look. 'That's George. The pong's a bit pungent at first but you get used to it. Just don't sit too near him in the pub.'

Logan blinked. 'He smells like that when he's not working?'

'He smells like that all the time.' Freda pursed her lips as she packed his purchases into a sturdy brown paper bag. 'But he has no idea. He lost his sense of smell in an accident a few years ago – fell off the boat and took a bang to the head. Can't taste much either but that's less of an issue for the people around him.'

That certainly made sense, Logan thought, trying not wrinkle his nose again; surely no one would consciously smell so bad. 'Hasn't anyone told him?'

Now Freda's gaze met his and there was a faint hint of coolness that hadn't been present before. 'Of course. But he forgets, which is understandable – no one thinks about the things they can't smell.'

And that was logical too; for most people, life was full enough of sensory input without having to consider aromas they weren't even aware of. 'I suppose not,' he conceded. 'It must be quite difficult for him.'

The shopkeeper shrugged. 'Aye, but on the other hand it wouldn't hurt him to take a shower more often.' She placed the wrapped ham at the top of the bag and nodded. 'That'll be thirty-three pounds and ninety-eight pence, please.'

Logan tapped his card on the reader and hefted the paper bag into his arms. 'Thank you.'

'It's no bother at all,' Freda replied. 'We'll be seeing you again soon, no doubt, once you've settled in and that.'

Logan's thoughts strayed back to the well-stocked deli counter; it seemed Ennisfarne wasn't quite the end of the world after all. 'I'm sure you will. Thanks again.'

On the outskirts of the village, he passed a number of large, upturned boats, their prows pointing to the waves, and remembered they were used as sheds once their life at sea was over. They reminded him of hulking dragons, guarding their hoard and poised to take flight. He could imagine them soaring over the headland where the ruined nunnery now stood, vast wings outstretched against the brooding leaden sky as they circled their roost. The thought made him smile; Ennisfarne was famous for its bird and seal colonies but no one had yet discovered dragons.

The road forked and Logan took a moment to study the sign. Left would take him towards the eastern edge of the island, towards the beacon that had been there for thousands of years, an early warning of sea-faring invaders. The right-hand fork wound south-west, to the dune cottage that overlooked the horseshoe beach he'd seen from the causeway, and past it to Darling Cove itself. A flutter of weariness

prickled his eyelids; it had been a long day and he was looking forward to the end of his journey. Turning right, he
headed for the cove.

The magnificent limestone arch came into view as soon as
he crested the top of the road. Logan slowed the car, taking
in the spectacular natural structure and admiring the sweep
of pale sand that curved away from it. His hands twitched on
the steering wheel, his photographer's instincts tingling, but
there would be plenty of time to take pictures of the cove and
he nudged the car onwards. Further along the road, another
sign pointed the way to the cottage and he glanced right
to see a flash of grey slate rooftop peeping above the single
lane track, the sea glittering beyond it. There were no other
houses in view, which was part of the reason he'd chosen this
particular cottage, but he knew there was some kind of café-
bar at the end of the road. Its presence didn't trouble him; he
doubted it was going be busy at this time of year.

He turned the Hilux into a spacious, gravel-filled car
park and studied the white-washed cottage. Clusters of
snowdrops nestled beneath the windows, with lilac crocuses
as their neighbours, a reminder that spring was on the way
in spite of the sombre skies. The door had cornflower blue
paintwork that looked fresh and a key safe on the wall beside
it. Tapping in the code, Logan retrieved the key and went
inside. The décor was as pleasingly minimalist as the website had suggested – white stone walls, pale wooden floors
and an absence of the sort of seafaring nick-nacks that some
landlords felt added ambience to their properties. But it was

the view that pleased Logan the most – the large windows framed an undulation of buttery sand dunes, topped with lush green marram grass that swayed in the wind. Beyond them, to the left, the arch curled into the sky. Logan stood gazing at the scene for a moment and some of the tiredness fell from his shoulders. This was a view he could get used to.

Eventually, he dragged his eyes away to survey the rest of the cottage. The kitchen was small but had all the basics – his host had left a welcome pack beside the kettle that duplicated a few of the items he'd bought at The Nook – and the bedroom looked comfortable enough, with an array of cosy throws and cushions in blues and greys spread over the pristine white duvet cover. But it was the living room he liked the most; a plush two-seater sofa faced the wood burner, piled high with cushions and thick woollen blankets, and Logan could imagine spending many contented evenings watching the flames lick the smoky glass. Someone had also thought to place an armchair beside the window, facing the enticing view of the dunes. All in all, he decided there were worse places to live. And with luck, the perpetual rhythm of the waves would soothe the restlessness that seemed to have taken over his soul since he'd walked out of his last photoshoot at New York Fashion Week.

It didn't take long to unpack the Hilux. Logan was used to travelling light and the largest items he'd brought all related to his work – camera boxes and lighting, although he had no plans to take any photographs where he might need anything other than natural light. But experience had taught him to be prepared and so he stashed as much of his equipment as he could under the bed and stacked the rest in the corner of the bedroom.

The sun was starting to sink in the sky by the time Logan settled in the armchair by the window, a cup of black coffee in his hands. The sullen clouds from earlier had dissipated, revealing a pale blue sky laced with delicate lemon wisps. His eyes narrowed as he contemplated the late afternoon light – even in winter, the hour or so before dusk often produced the most extraordinary golden blaze and here he suspected the sun itself might be framed by the arch before dropping below the distant mainland. With a bit of luck, it would be a decent sunset. One worthy of a picture or two.

Finishing the coffee in two mouthfuls, Logan levered himself out of the armchair. Five minutes later he was making his way between the dunes, his trusted Nikon camera around his neck as he navigated the gaps in the spiky marram grass. The fine sand shifted treacherously beneath his hiking boots, forcing him to focus on maintaining his balance rather than the view ahead of him and so he was gazing down at his feet as he finally cleared the maze of dunes. A gust of salty air greeted him, along with the suddenly loud crash of waves, causing him to look up and take in Darling Cove for the first time.

He had the beach to himself. To his right, the sand curled round and petered out at the base of the headland that made up one prong of the horseshoe. A jumble of jagged rocks jutted above the incoming tide, sending sea water spraying into the air as the waves hit. Logan made out several dark recesses in the cliffs and assumed they were caves, although it was impossible to tell how deep they were. He turned to his left and surveyed the wide expanse of yellow that wound in a deep curve to the other prong of the horseshoe. The cliffs on this side also stretched out into the sea but ended in the spectacular arch, beyond which the sky was a myriad of delicate amber, blue and pink. And nestled at the base of the cliffs, a safe distance from where the sand met the sea, he saw a large building that he guessed must be Darling's, the bar belonging to his landlord.

Mindful of how fast the sky would change, Logan began to make his way towards the western end of the cove. The sand was easier to navigate here – no less fine but more damp, so his boots didn't sink as deep. The surface was dotted with water-worn pebbles and shells, with a rainbow sprinkling of opaque sea glass that caught and flamed in the last of the sun's rays. The air was crisp and clean, laced with salt and chilled by the impending nightfall. Logan turned up the collar of his coat and wished he'd brought the black cashmere scarf that was draped across the bed in the cottage. He should have known the wind on the beach would be cold but there was no time to go back. Instead, he sped up and used the briskness of his pace to warm him.

He reached the far end of the beach and gave the bar a cursory once over. It was a split-level building, painted in pale blue and yellow, with a large first-floor balcony that overlooked the enviable view and he supposed it would be popular in the warmer months. The ground floor had what looked like floor to ceiling glass doors that led to a low wooden platform jutting out across the beach, with shallow steps that led down to the sand, and he could imagine this crowded with people too. But his attention was soon reclaimed by the glorious sky reflected in the windows. Turning around, he unhooked his camera and strode purposefully towards the shoreline.

The sun seemed determined to impress him as it dipped to the horizon. The colours which had been delicate only moments earlier had deepened; the rose pink was blossoming into cerise, the amber was laced with strands of saffron and orange, and the pale blue had become a wash of lavender, smudged here and there with indigo. The heart of the arch was a luminous burst of gold. Shading his eyes with one hand, Logan unclipped the lens cap and fired off several experimental shots. Frowning at the small screen, he took a few steps to his left and snapped a couple more pictures. Satisfied with the angle, he began work in earnest and was soon absorbed in his task. The colours were already changing again and the sun was dipping fast – he had minutes to capture the scene.

A distant shout pierced his concentration. Logan pushed the distraction away, focusing on the view through the camera lens. Part of his brain registered the incoming tide as the swash bubbled perilously close to his boots; without lowering the camera, he moved backwards. Another shout rang out – he couldn't make out the words but it sounded like a name. A harassed parent summoning a child, he surmised vaguely without looking around. None of his business. And then he became aware of something else, a faint but rhythmic vibration thudding through the sand. A third shout carried across the beach, closer now so he could hear the words. 'Huxley! Huxley, no!'

His concentration now broken, Logan cursed under his breath and began to turn around. But at that exact moment, something low and fast barrelled into the back of his legs. The sky lurched crazily as he felt himself flip into the air; the camera flew from his grip and the next thing Logan knew, both he and the Nikon were tumbling towards the wet sand.

Chapter Two

Eve

Eve Darling watched in horror as the man hit the beach with a wet thump she was sure she felt reverberate through the soles of her wellies.

'Bloody hell!' she muttered through clenched teeth, aghast at the scene. 'Huxley, get back here!'

In typically exuberant fashion, the chocolate Labrador ignored her. Instead, he circled around and began to lope back towards the man, who had got to his feet and seemed to be looking for something. Eve started to run. By the time she reached the man, Huxley was bounding around him in boisterous circles, his mouth split into a friendly grin.

'I'm so sorry,' she called, slowing to a hurried walk as her cheeks flamed with mortification. 'Are you okay?'

The man didn't look up. His attention was fixed on something in his hands, which she now saw was a camera. A big, expensive-looking camera, with a large lens that also had more than a hint of high end about it. Eve felt her heart sink as she realized he must have been carrying it when the dog had hit him. 'Is it broken?'

He flashed her a dark look. 'The lens is cracked. I don't know about the rest of it,' he said in a curt voice. 'You should keep that animal on a lead.'

He sounded furious and Eve could hardly blame him. She eyed his sodden jeans and dripping wax jacket and fought the urge to cringe. 'He's usually better behaved,' she offered apologetically and bit her lip. 'Sort of. Are you hurt at all? It was quite a tumble you took.'

'I'm fine,' he snapped before returning his gaze to the camera. 'Which is more than can be said for this.'

Eve wished the sand would open up beneath her feet. 'Sorry,' she said again. 'I'll pay for the damage.'

And now the man snorted dismissively, turning his attention to Huxley, who was snuffling happily among a cluster of glistening bladderwrack seaweed. 'Are dogs even allowed on the beach?'

Eve regarded him evenly for a moment, taking in the dark hair whipping across his face, the almost black eyes framed with long lashes and the unseasonal tanned skin. He'd be quite good-looking if it wasn't for the attitude, she thought, and wondered who he was. A day-tripper from the mainland, probably, thinking he was David Bailey. Taking in a calming breath, she snapped her fingers at Huxley. 'Here, boy,' she commanded sternly. After a few more enthusiastic sniffs, the dog obeyed and Eve exhaled in silent relief. 'The rules vary depending on the time of year and the beach,' she told the man. 'But on this beach, dogs are always welcome.'

He glowered at her. 'Then they should be kept under control.'

She felt her temper start to slip. Of course, the man had every right to be angry – Huxley had knocked him over and damaged his camera. But it had been an accident; she'd apologized and offered to pay for the damage. Surely a little graciousness on his part wouldn't go amiss. 'Point taken,' she said coolly and drew herself up to meet his glare. 'Although since you're clearly a visitor to Ennisfarne, perhaps you don't know that Darling Cove is actually a private beach. Technically, you're trespassing right now.'

The man blinked. 'Trespassing?' he echoed slowly, raising a black eyebrow. 'I see. That certainly wasn't made clear when I booked.'

Now it was Eve's turn to blink. Booked? What did he mean by that? Unless . . .

The truth hit her with all the force of the waves crashing against the nearby rocks. He wasn't a day-tripper at all. This must be the new tenant of Dune Cottage, the man with whom she'd exchanged a dozen or more emails to sort out the terms of his stay, and who'd paid three months' rent up front to secure the cottage into the summer months. That unexpected income during the off-season had allowed her to employ Petr from the village to patch the leaking roof of the bar, something that would otherwise have had to wait until the money from the tourist season began to flow in. Another hot rush of embarrassment crawled over Eve as she replayed her own words in her head. Had she really just accused her new tenant of trespassing?

She took a deep breath. 'You're Mr Cotton.'

Understanding flickered across his face but his tone didn't grow any warmer as he studied her dispassionately, then gave a short nod. 'And you're Ms Darling. Is this how you greet all your guests? By accusing them of trespassing?'

A searing blush travelled across Eve's cheeks. 'Of course not,' she said stiffly. 'I didn't realize who you were. Is – is everything okay with the cottage?'

'The cottage is fine,' he replied and waved his camera irritably. 'Unfortunately, the same can't be said of this.'

The idiot really did think he was David Bailey, Eve realized. 'I've apologized and offered to pay for it to be repaired,' she said as neutrally as she could. 'I'm not sure what else you want me to do.'

'You can keep your dog away from me, for a start,' he retorted. 'I'll send you an invoice for the replacement camera lens.'

With a final withering glance that encompassed both Eve and Huxley, he turned on his heel and stalked across the sand towards the distant dunes. Eve watched him go and puffed out a heavy sigh. If today was anything to go by, it was going to be a long three months.

*

'Good walk?'

Aiden was leaning against the counter in the kitchen when Eve walked in, Huxley trotting at her side. She grimaced as she shrugged off her coat. 'Not exactly. I met our new tenant and let's just say we didn't make the best impression.'

Her brother picked up a mug of tea from the counter and offered it to her. 'Sounds like you need this. What happened?'

Eve took the tea gratefully and cast a rueful glance at their dog, who was slurping enthusiastically from his water bowl. 'Huxley happened.'

She described the passage of events on the beach, feeling yet another burning rush of embarrassment when she thought about the moment James Cotton had hit the sand, and the way she'd made everything so much worse by declaring he was trespassing. Aiden hid his mouth, his blue eyes dancing. 'I shouldn't laugh.'

'No, you shouldn't,' Eve said, regarding him with stern disapproval. 'What if he'd been hurt?'

To his credit, Aiden's amusement lessened. 'Was he?'

'Only his pride, I think,' Eve conceded, then something else occurred to her. 'But he really wasn't impressed and made no effort to hide it. What if he decides to leave early?'

Her brother shrugged. 'He's paid in advance. But I'm sure he'll come to see the funny side of it soon enough.'

Eve recalled the imperious fury on the face of James Cotton and shook her head gloomily. 'He doesn't strike me as the kind of man who finds anything funny.'

'Then nothing you can say or do will help,' Aiden said. 'Best just to leave him alone to get over it.'

He was right, Eve knew, but it didn't stop her from fretting. She took a long sip of tea and did her best to shake off her lingering mortification and unease. 'Okay,' she said and glanced around for a distraction. Her gaze came to settle on the calendar that adorned one of the walls. 'Did you manage to get hold of the band for next week? I'm slightly worried we'll have an audience with no act to entertain them and George will get his pipes out again.'

The band in question was The Wreckers – a popular sea shanty band from Cornwall who'd been taking social media by storm. Eve had booked them for the bar's monthly music night, which was a movable event carefully planned to coincide with the safe crossing times over the causeway, but they'd proved a little hard to get hold of in recent days and she had a real fear that the one hundred and fifty or so tickets she had sold would need to be refunded. Or, worse, George would insist on plugging the gap; Eve had nothing against the Northumbrian pipes in the hands of a skilled musician, but the fisherman had more enthusiasm than talent and she still wasn't over the last time she'd heard him play. Hamish, the landlord of the Fisherman's Arms, said he'd never seen the pub empty so fast.

Aiden shook his head. 'I left another message. But I'm sure there's nothing to worry about – they're probably just busy touring.'

And that was the biggest difference between her and her

younger brother, Eve thought as she surveyed the placid expression beneath his thatch of wavy blond hair – he didn't worry about anything. At twenty-nine, Aiden was four years her junior but it wasn't the gap in age that made them so different, it was their outlook. Eve was a planner, a committed list-maker who liked to know everything was in hand. As well as the café and bar, they also had a variety of regular bookings – yoga classes, a local art club and dancing – and frequently played host to intimate beach weddings. That was part of the reason Eve usually declined bookings of Dune Cottage in the winter months; the business of running Darling Cove was like spinning plates. If she got distracted, something was bound to come crashing down and she needed the off-season to recharge her own batteries. Whereas Aiden didn't concern himself with the nitty-gritty of details or to-do lists and checking everything was under control. He was endlessly optimistic that things would work out fine without unnecessary worry and rarely acknowledged or even seemed to notice that the reason things usually did turn out well was down to Eve's attention to detail behind the scenes.

'Even so, I'd like to get everything squared up,' Eve said with a frown. 'Apart from anything else, if they don't know the crossing times they won't get here at all.'

'Relax, Eve,' Aiden soothed. 'You warned them about the causeway when you first made the booking. They're professionals – they'll be here.'

Reluctantly, Eve nodded and made a mental note to

find out whether The Wreckers had a manager she might contact. 'Did you finish clearing the tables in the bar? It's Sunrise Yoga in the morning and you know Gemma will need the space.'

'All done,' he assured her. He waved a hand at Eve's phone on the worktop, where she'd left it to take Huxley for his walk. 'And I think you missed a call from Selina.'

Selina Heron was Eve's oldest friend – they'd been insep-arable since their first day of nursery at the tiny island school and had shared everything that followed as part of growing up on Ennisfarne, including boarding away from home during the week to attend secondary school. It had been an impossible wrench when Selina had left the island to attend university in Newcastle but now she was back, running her family's salt farm on a small uninhabited isle off the south-east tip of Ennisfarne. She was closer than a sister to Eve and not a day went by that didn't involve a phone conversation or meet-up.

'I need your practical skills,' Selina said without preamble when Eve called her a few minutes later. 'One of the pipes in the graduation tower is leaking. Can you spare me an hour tomorrow to take a look?'

The graduation tower was a tall and narrow construction of wood and blackthorn through which sea water was fil-tered and reduced to produce the fine Heron's salt that had achieved cult status with celebrity and amateur chefs up and down the country. A leaking pipe could cause a significant reduction in efficiency and potentially affect the quality of the salt. 'Of course,' Eve told her friend and consulted the tide table stuck to the door of a kitchen cupboard. 'Meet you at the harbour at 2.30pm?'

'You're a life-saver,' Selina said, her voice warm with gratitude. 'I'll treat you to cake at the Sea Shell afterwards.'

'Deal,' Eve replied, feeling her spirits lift at the thought of the delicious confections on offer at the cosy café in the village. 'See you tomorrow.'

Aiden gave her a knowing look once she'd rung off. 'Don't tell me – she needs a plumber.'

Eve laughed. 'How did you guess?'

Her brother tipped his head. 'You should set up a side hustle – Darling Plumbing Services, no job too small.'

'Being handy with a spanner doesn't make me a plumber,' Eve objected. 'And it's a job that potentially involves getting up close and personal with blocked toilets, with no one to delegate to. I think I'll stick to hospitality, thanks.'

'Just a suggestion,' he said, holding up his hands. 'At least then you'd be getting paid.'

Eve considered the island community, which often tended to run on reciprocal favours rather than cash. 'Selina is my best friend – I'm hardly going to send her an invoice. Besides, she is paying me.'

'Cake doesn't count,' Aiden replied wryly. 'Not even triple chocolate gateau.'

'So, you won't want me to bring you a slice back from the café, then?' Eve said, raising her eyebrows.

'I didn't say that,' he said. 'Look, Selina aside, I don't want people taking advantage of your good nature. You work too hard, Eve, and it wouldn't hurt you to say no once in a while.'

It was on the tip of her tongue to point out that part of the reason she worked so hard was because he left so much of the business admin to her but she knew from experience that there was no point. Aiden was Aiden and, if Eve was honest, she preferred knowing everything was in hand. 'I'll bear that in mind,' she said diplomatically.

Aiden winked. 'I'll definitely take you up on that offer of cake tomorrow, though. Thanks, sis.'

Eve smiled. Clearly her brother didn't feel saying no extended to him.

'So?' Selina called as Eve steadied herself on the ladder to study the wooden taps that topped the salt graduation tower. 'Can you see anything wrong?'

Some twenty metres up, at the highest point of the gigantic oblong structure, Eve balanced herself against a chill gust of wintry wind and ran a hand along the base of the nearest tap. There should be a steady drip of sea water flowing from the hole, hand-adjusted by Selina each day to allow for the weather conditions, seeping into the thick layers of twigs and thorn below. But the tap was dry and so were its nearest neighbours. She slid her fingers underneath the wood to feel the pipe beneath – also dry. 'The leak definitely isn't up here,' she answered. 'Must be in the lower pipes. I'll come down and take a look.'

Once she was safely on the ground, she set about checking

each of the pipes that drew the salt water to the top of the tower. And there she found the problem. The connector on the penultimate pipe had become loose, allowing water to bubble out instead of sending it upwards. Eve took a wrench from her tool bag and gently tightened the fitting until the bubbling flow of water ceased from around the connector.

She squinted up the ladder, where Selina was now studying the taps. 'How's that?' she asked.

'You're amazing.' Her best friend's voice rang with satisfaction. 'It's all systems go again up here.'

She spent a few more moments carefully adjusting the flow from the taps, then climbed down to join Eve. 'Thank you,' Selina said. 'I really appreciate this.'

Eve shrugged away her thanks. 'It was nothing, honestly. I can show you exactly what I did, if you like, so you'll know for next time.'

Selina shook her head vigorously, sending the red bobble on her woollen hat wobbling. 'Ooh, no. I tinkered with the pipes once before and ended up over-tightening something so badly it damaged the connector and had to be replaced. I leave that kind of thing to the experts now.'

Eve replaced the wrench in her tool bag and smiled. 'I'm hardly an expert. Any skills I do have are all born from necessity rather than training.'

'Don't put yourself down,' Selina said, frowning. 'I bet practical experience is just as useful as a qualification. And as well as being brilliant, you come with the added bonus of being one of my favourite people – I definitely wouldn't invite any of the plumbers from the mainland to the Sea Shell for cake.'

Eve recalled the last time she'd needed to call in a professional, to replace a burst pipe in the ladies' toilets at Darling's. She'd had to wait until the crossing allowed him to come to Ennisfarne and when he'd finally arrived, he had aired some distinctly unpleasant views as he'd worked. Eve had added his name to her list of tradesmen not to call again. 'I'm glad I was able to help you out,' she told Selina. 'The cake is just a happy bonus.'

'It certainly is,' her friend agreed. 'Now, give me a minute to check a couple of things in the tower and then we can head back.'

Ten minutes later, they were aboard Selina's boat and on their way back to the harbour. During the journey, Eve confided what had happened with James Cotton the previous day. A good night's sleep hadn't lessened the embarrassment she felt.

'I'm sure he'll get over it,' Selina said, echoing Aiden's sentiments. 'But enough about that – tell me what he looks like. I heard from Freda he's quite easy on the eye.'

Eve frowned, recalling the irritated, almost supercilious way her tenant had addressed her. If she hadn't been so desperate to make amends for Huxley's behaviour, the man would probably have annoyed her as much as she'd evidently annoyed him. But she could see why Freda had been impressed; James Cotton was tall, dark and would probably be handsome if he ever stopped scowling.

'I was too busy cringing to notice,' she told Selina. 'But I got the impression he's the kind of man who's used to other people jumping to his commands.'

'A business type?'

'Maybe,' Eve replied doubtfully as she pictured the slightly too long black hair whipping around the man's face. 'It was just a feeling I had. We really didn't talk for long.'

Selina's forehead creased with curiosity as she steered the boat over the waves. 'I wonder what he's doing on Ennisfarne.'

Eve had wondered the same thing – three months was an odd amount of time, too long to be a holiday but not long enough to be starting over. 'I'm sure we'll find out soon enough,' she observed. 'Freda has his scent and you know what she's like.'

The owner of The Nook was famously inquisitive and perfectly placed to keep her finger on the pulse of everything that happened on the island. 'That's true,' Selina said, grinning. 'The mysterious Mr Cotton won't keep his secrets for long.'

'Whatever his reasons for coming here, I'm going to try and keep out of his way,' Eve replied with a delicate shudder. 'And so is Huxley.'

Although that might be easier said than done, she thought, given he was staying in Dune Cottage. But she had the definite vibe her tenant wasn't the kind to seek out company and that suited her perfectly. With a bit of luck, their paths wouldn't cross more often than they had to.

Chapter Three

Logan

It took Logan several days to get used to the silence. At first, he couldn't quite put his finger on the reason for his unease. He had stayed in far more remote places – he'd once slept in a tent suspended from a sheer mountainside in order to capture the sunrise as it broke over the neighbouring peaks – but there seemed to be a particularly deep quality to the quiet on Ennisfarne. It managed to be somehow reflective and attentive, as though the island itself was listening, and Logan was reminded of his fanciful notions as he'd stood at the far end of the causeway on Friday. He'd felt the same sense of watchfulness then, although his imagined idea of being judged hadn't lingered. He knew at least part of it was caused by standing still after constantly moving for so long but Logan hoped the unsettled feeling would pass. Perhaps then his nerves would be soothed by the peacefulness, rather than being nettled.

His prickly encounter with Eve Darling hadn't helped, either. Once his temper had cooled, he'd been able to appreciate that it hadn't entirely been her fault but the cracked lens made it harder for him to entirely dismiss the run-in. On Saturday, he'd driven to a camera specialist in Gosforth, on the outskirts of Newcastle, to see whether a repair might be possible but he knew even before the owner whistled through his teeth that it was a lost cause.

'I've got a second-hand Nikon in stock that might do you,' Mr Robertson had offered. 'It's a bit battered around the outside but still in tip-top shape otherwise.'

Logan had politely declined. 'Probably time I upgraded anyway,' he'd said, and given the broken lens a nostalgic pat. 'But this one has been a good friend over the years.'

Mr Robertson nodded sympathetically. 'I know what you mean. It takes time to adjust to any new kit, doesn't it? Even the professionals must find that.'

'I'm sure they do,' Logan agreed solemnly.

'I can order you a replacement lens, if you like,' the other man went on. 'Should be here by Wednesday.'

Logan had accepted the offer, even though it meant a return trip to Gosforth. He could easily have ordered it online but it felt right to give his custom to the camera shop. He'd listened to Mr Robertson's well-meaning advice about which lens would be best, handed over his card for payment and gave his email address so the shop owner could let him know once the lens was ready for collection. And then he'd driven back to Ennisfarne, where the silence was all the more noticeable after the bustle of the city.

His mind strayed to Eve once more as he returned to Dune Cottage. He hadn't seen her since that first explosive meeting and now found it hard to picture her. She'd been much smaller than him – almost petite – and he thought the hair poking out from beneath the chunky bobble hat had been blonde. Her coat had been waxed and her wellington boots were scruffy. Beyond that, he had no idea how she looked. Her dog, on the other hand, was etched on his memory, particularly the expression of cheerful insolence as he'd loped across the sand after dumping Logan on his backside. But now that most of his annoyance had evaporated, Logan had decided not to invoice his landlord for the broken lens. It didn't seem fair, somehow, and it certainly wouldn't help to foster a professionally cordial relationship for the duration of his stay. Much better to swallow the cost himself; if nothing else, it meant one less reason for interaction.

Once he was inside, he saw he'd missed a call from his agent while he'd been driving. In typically efficient fashion, Phoebe had followed up with an email:

I know you're taking a break but GQ mag really want you for a Nick Borrowdale shoot in Monaco at the start of March. Are you tempted or shall I tell them no?

Not even remotely tempted, Logan thought. A few weeks ago, he would have leapt at the chance of an all-expenses paid trip to Monte Carlo, especially with one of his closest friends. Apart from anything else, it would be an easy job – Nick was a total pro and the camera loved him. But now the idea of jetting off to a notorious party town left Logan cold. He couldn't summon any enthusiasm for the photography, either – GQ would almost certainly offer him creative control of the shoot but he'd be running on empty, lacking his usual inspiration, and even Nick's magic touch wouldn't be enough. Whatever the cause of the strange malaise that had seeped into Logan's work and his heart, it wasn't going to be cured by yet another job aboard a luxury yacht.

He tapped out a short response to Phoebe's email, then began to unpack the supplies he'd picked up from a supermarket on the mainland. It wasn't that he was avoiding The Nook, more that he wanted the freedom of shopping without the sensation of Freda's gimlet gaze watching his every purchase. She'd want to engage him in friendly conversation too and he wasn't interested in that. Conversation made it more likely someone might work out who he was and he'd rather keep his identity under wraps. That meant maintaining his distance from the residents of Ennisfarne as much as possible.

But it didn't follow that he had to hide inside the cottage. The tide had come in and the siren song of the waves was tugging at Logan's subconscious. Once he'd put the shopping away, he gave in to the call and headed out again to take advantage of the afternoon light.

It was a blustery day. The waves were silver-crowned monsters throwing themselves towards land and the north wind whipped at the Hilux as Logan made his way towards the highest point of the island – the headland on the eastern edge, facing out into the sea. There was a white granite beacon there that he had a mind to photograph against the rolling clouds, knowing his mind would be settled by the business of composing the best shot and discovering the angle that would elevate the picture into something extraordinary. But he also wanted to simply stand on the headland, gazing out to the horizon while the wind scoured the disquiet from his soul.

As he navigated the narrow road to the headland, Logan's eye was drawn by a black oblong structure some distance from the shore. He slowed the car for a closer look and saw it occupied a small island, with a cluster of low buildings off to one side. The structure was too far away for him to make out any detail but he couldn't imagine what it might be; some kind of hide, perhaps, for observing the birds and sea life around the island? Although he'd thought the northern tip of Ennisfarne was better known for wildlife watching – it played host to a nature reserve and there were several rocky islets that were home to the island's thriving seal population. He stared at the odd collection of buildings for a few more seconds, frowning thoughtfully, then resumed his journey. He'd have to remember to look it up when he got home.

The beacon itself was a perfect four-sided obelisk that gleamed white against the moody sky. Logan's professional instincts were already stirring as he parked up and reached for his camera case. He spent a few minutes gauging the scene, walking around the beacon and taking in the view, deciding what he wanted to capture. The wind made things harder – it whipped at his hands and face, forcing him to concentrate hard and work fast. High overhead, gulls wheeled across the clouds. Logan shifted his position again to include them. A squall of rain spattered against the ground, growing more persistent as he worked, but it was only when he was satisfied that he'd caught a sense of the lonely obelisk standing tall and implacable against the sullen elements that he put the camera back in its box and allowed his concentration to lessen. Taking himself as near to the edge of the headland as he deemed safe, he raised his face to the wind and the rain and gazed at the unbroken sea, stretching all the way to the horizon and beyond. His cheeks stung as the icy rain hit, driven into his skin by the bluster of the wind, and he rocked back on his heels once or twice as the gusts hit him. Rivulets of water trickled from his hair and down his neck, making him shiver. But being battered by the elements didn't make him long for the protection of his car. Instead, the experience brought a rawness, a feeling of purity that penetrated his skin and curled deep into his lungs. Right at that moment, there was no lethargy in his soul. He felt clean and renewed and capable of anything. It wouldn't last, of course, but he knew this was in part what he'd come to Ennisfarne seeking – a reminder that it was possible to feel this way, invigorated and alive.

He stood for longer than he should, so long that the shivering became constant. But before leaving, Logan stopped to place a hand on the smooth, wet granite, admiring its strength and solitude and soaking up its history. It had endured for over two hundred years, warning ships of the rocks ahead if they strayed too close, but previous incarnations had served another purpose – part of a chain of beacons built to warn of impending attack from enemies across the sea. There had been many such invasions, to both Ennisfarne and Lindisfarne, but although blood had been shed, the islands had somehow absorbed the marauders and turned their pillaging to peace. In time, they'd grown to love the islands and had become part of their story. Logan looked around, taking in the lush green headland glistening in the rain, with the wind-tossed steel wool clouds rolling above, hearing the faint cry of the gulls over the thunderous crash of the waves below, and thought he understood why. Ennisfarne seemed to be an easy place to fall in love with. He might even be halfway there himself.

Chapter Four

Eve

Eve's heart sank when she saw the email from James Cotton in her inbox first thing on Thursday morning. She was sitting with her laptop at one of the tables in the bar, facing towards the sun-dappled sand and working through a backlog of admin. It wasn't so much the thought of the invoice he would undoubtedly have attached that made her groan — she'd accepted she needed to reimburse him — but his surliness on their first meeting turned the thought of dealing with him into a headache and it was bound to spoil her mood. In fact, she was almost tempted to leave the email until the afternoon, or even the next day, but she knew it would only hang over her and niggle at her nerves. Better to take her usual approach and get the unpleasant tasks out of the way first, she decided, then cast a speculative look at the shiny coffee machine behind the bar. Everything was easier after coffee. Surely the five minutes it would take to make a latte didn't count as procrastination . . .

Armed with a mug brimming with deliciously aromatic froth, and several chocolate Hobnobs, Eve took a seat at the table again and pulled her laptop resolutely forward. But when she opened the email, there was no mention of the camera. Instead, it appeared the cold tap in the kitchen wouldn't turn off and had a constant stream of water bubbling into the sink. Another tap, she thought wryly, remembering Aiden's joking suggestion that she start her own plumbing business, but she was glad she hadn't ignored the message – she'd learned from experience that any issues at the cottage were best resolved speedily and the tone of the email was polite, with no hint of irritation. She tapped out a quick reply, asking for a convenient time to call round and investigate, then turned her attention to the rest of her inbox. Aiden had finally managed to get hold of The Wreckers and confirmed they'd be attending – ticket sales had increased and Eve was starting to wonder about getting a temporary member of staff in for the evening to help keep things running smoothly. Most of the audience would be islanders and fairly relaxed if the bar was obviously busy but she'd rather not have the problem in the first place. She fired off a quick message to Freda's granddaughter, Tish, asking if she was happy to work that evening.

Huxley padded in, his claws clicking on the wooden flooring. He stopped at Eve's table and dropped a rubber ball at her feet, sniffing at the biscuit crumbs beside the laptop.

'Hello,' she said, fondly ruffling his ears. 'Is this a subtle hint you want to play?'

He grinned at her, his tongue lolling from the side of his mouth. With a sigh of mock reluctance, she reached down and picked up the ball. 'Come on, then. Just a quick game on the beach.'

The day had dawned clear and bright, with sunshine pouring over the sand and a bite to the air that Eve always found invigorating. Sometimes she wondered what it would be like to live somewhere else – a city or even just somewhere inland, away from the constant music of the ocean. Whenever visitors to the bar or guests at Dune Cottage discovered she had lived on Ennisfarne her whole life, they were surprised and she understood why; few people stayed in the place they were born now. Modern life tempted them away and even Selina hadn't been immune, although she'd come back to the island after a time. But for Eve, descended from the same Darlings who'd famously rescued nine shipwrecked passengers from a foundering ship in 1838, Ennisfarne was in her bones and always had been. She'd left school and started to work full-time at the bar with her father, as had always been expected, learning everything he had to teach, from balancing the books to rewiring an electrical circuit. When he'd passed away five years ago, there had never been any doubt that she would take over Darling's. Aiden had come back from the mainland to help and now Eve couldn't imagine living anywhere else. She took a bracing breath of briny air and gazed around, taking in the glistening sand and azure sky shimmering through the arch; how could she leave when she was surrounded by so much beauty?

Aiden's shout interrupted her musing. Turning, she saw him waving at her and knew it was time to get back to work. She whistled for Huxley, who pretended not to hear, and began to make her way towards her brother.

'Mr Grumpy has replied to your email,' he said, as Eve stamped her sandy boots on the decking. 'He says he's available now and will be home until early afternoon.'

Eve mentally reviewed her diary. She had planned to meet Selina for coffee but the cottage took priority. She nodded. 'Okay. I'll grab my tools and head over.'

Aiden's eyebrows lifted. 'He also wanted to know why you were coming instead of a plumber,' he said, unable to hide his amusement. 'Shall we decide now where to put his body?'

'Ha ha,' Eve replied, although she didn't find it the least bit funny. 'It's a good thing I'm too professional to rise to that sort of comment, isn't it?'

But it didn't surprise her that their tenant wouldn't be able to get his head around a woman having the skill to fix a leaking tap. And that was another thing she loved about Ennisfarne – everyone knew and respected her capabilities. A man like James Cotton – good-looking and arrogant – probably struggled to see women as anything more than decorative. Eve squared her shoulders. He was about to have his 1950s attitude challenged.

The Hilux outside Dune Cottage surprised her. She hadn't thought about what kind of car he would drive but, if she had, she would almost certainly have envisaged him in an Audi. Perhaps he was more practical than she'd imagined. And then she gave herself a mental shake because she didn't actually know anything about the man renting the cottage – which meant she was just as guilty of judging a book by its cover as he was.

Her intention to be professionally courteous was put to the test when he opened the door, however. He was dressed casually in a chunky knitted sweater and jeans, with a few days' worth of stubble covering his chin, exuding a chilled-out vibe. But his face was anything but relaxed; his dark eyes appraised her coolly and his mouth pressed into a hard flat line. 'Oh. Didn't you see my email? No disrespect to you, Ms Darling, but I asked for a plumber.'

Eve dredged up a polite smile. 'It'll be a while before a plumber can get over from the mainland. Why don't I take a look in the meantime?'

For a moment, she thought he might refuse to let her in. Then he stepped back, his expression still unwelcoming, and allowed her into the tiny hallway.

'As I said in my email, it's the cold tap,' he said, leading the way through the living room to the kitchen. 'I've tightened it as much as I can but, as you'll see, it's still leaking.'

Eve's gaze slid around as she followed him – James might be rude but he was tidy enough. A paperback sat on the armchair by the window, pages splayed and its spine facing the ceiling, but she didn't have time to catch the title. A half-empty cup sat on the windowsill and she could smell the unmistakeable scent of freshly ground coffee beans in the air. Her mouth started to water, reminding her of the coffee with Selina she'd given up; she'd love a cup now but there was zero chance James was going to offer. As far as he was concerned, Eve was wasting his time and the sooner she was out of his hair the better.

The tap was just as he described – water was trickling steadily from the spout into the white ceramic sink. Eve lowered her tool bag to the kitchen floor and nodded. 'No problem. I'll just isolate the water supply to the sink and then I'll take a look.'

He stared at her doubtfully. 'Is that wise? I know this is your property but it seems to me we'd be better off waiting for an expert.'

His attitude was exactly as she'd expected but she still felt a stab of annoyance. 'Don't worry, I can handle it,' she said, flashing a breezy smile that cost her a lot. 'It's probably just a washer that needs replacing but I'll have a better idea in a few minutes.'

His eyes remained fixed on her, black brows beetled together in obvious scepticism. 'I think you're making a mistake,' he said, folding his arms. 'Plumbing is a skilled job.'

Eve drew in a long, slow breath and let it out again. His determination to believe she was incapable of solving the issue was quite something. 'I know. But I promise I'm not about to flood the kitchen. In fact, it might be better if you leave me to it.'

James gave her one final look, then shrugged. 'Like I said,

it's your place.' He moved to the small kitchen table and waved at a heavy, very expensive-looking camera and lens attached to a sleek MacBook. 'You won't mind if I put these away, though.'

Eve resisted the urge to grind her teeth as she watched him leave and forced her indignation down. She didn't know much about photographic kit but it seemed to her the camera James had just taken out of the kitchen was a significant step up from the one he'd been using the first time they'd met. And not for him the usual laptop; a MacBook Pro was high-end too. All in all, it looked like the kind of equipment a professional would use. Curiosity piqued, she took advantage of his absence to glance around the kitchen but there were no further clues. Maybe there was more to James Cotton than surliness and self-importance. It was a shame his personality wasn't as classy as his kit.

He didn't return to the kitchen, at least. Instead, Eve heard him take a seat in the armchair. Then there was a faint whisper of paper and she guessed he'd picked up the book he'd been reading. And finally there was a genteel sipping sound, as though someone had just taken a mouthful of coffee. She turned back to survey the sink, relieved James didn't intend to peer over her shoulder as she worked. That really would have sent her temper soaring.

She located the small switch that cut off the water to the taps and twisted it. Then she turned the faulty tap, allowing a gush of cold water to flow into the sink. As soon as it had slowed to a trickle, she reached into her bag and began to dismantle the tap. It didn't take long to establish the problem – as she suspected, one of the rubber washers had perished. Eve rummaged in her bag for a replacement and rolled it into place. Once everything was back together, she turned the switch to allow the water supply to resume and felt no small surge of satisfaction at the complete absence of leaking water. Eve glanced over her shoulder to the living room; it had actually been a simple fix and she was tempted to say as much to James, to underline the fact that he hadn't been able to deal with it, but decided with some regret that discretion was the better part of customer service, if not quite valour.

The bedroom door was open as Eve passed. She caught a glimpse of the neatly made bed, the large camera resting on the white cover, and several sturdy black cases stacked in a corner. But there was no time to dawdle – James had evidently heard her approach and was studying her, eyebrows raised, from the armchair. It wasn't immediately clear to Eve whether he realized she'd resolved the problem or not but she decided not to give him the opportunity to insult her again.

'It's fixed,' she said, without preamble. 'Shouldn't give you any more trouble.'

His gaze flickered towards the kitchen, as though he didn't know whether to believe her. 'I'm impressed. Thank you.'

There was an element of grudging respect in his voice that Eve ignored. 'No problem. Is there anything else that needs attention, while I'm here?'

James shook his head. 'I don't think so.'

'I'll leave you in peace, then,' Eve replied coolly. She hefted her bag and took a few steps towards the front door. 'Oh, did you get your camera fixed? I've kept an eye out for your invoice.'

He stood. 'The lens couldn't be repaired. I bought a replacement but I'm not expecting you to pay anything towards it. My insurance will cover it.'

Eve frowned. 'You must have to pay an excess on your claim. Perhaps you'd like us to cover that.'

'Forget it,' he said brusquely. 'Accidents happen.'

If it had been anyone else, she might have argued. There was no escaping the fact that Huxley had been responsible for James falling over, if not for the actual damage to the camera, but she found the man so insufferable that she didn't want to prolong the conversation with her insistence. And besides, she had better things to do. 'Fine,' she said, her own tone equally flat. 'If there's nothing else, I'll be on my way.'

She didn't wait for him to respond. He followed her to the door but she was through it before he spoke again. 'Thank you for coming out so quickly.'

Eve waved a hand, making for her car without looking back. 'All part of the service, Mr Cotton. Enjoy the rest of your day.'

She kept her gaze resolutely facing forwards as she drove away and had no idea whether he stayed to watch her leave. His comments replayed in her head as she drove the short distance back to Darling's and she grew more and more indignant with every metre – short of insulting her appearance, it was hard to imagine how James could have been ruder. His rent money might have paid for the repairs to the bar roof but Eve was more certain than ever that she would be glad when James Cotton was gone.

Chapter Five

Logan

'So how are you settling in?'

Freda's gaze was bright with curiosity as she surveyed Logan over the glass dome of the deli counter. The village shop had to be Gossip HQ and he strongly suspected she already knew about his encounter with Eve and Huxley on the beach. 'It's been smashing so far,' he replied.

Her eyes danced as she nodded. 'So I've heard. Still, it's impossible to hold anything against Huxley. One glance from those gorgeous brown eyes and I'm sure you forgave him.'

Logan pictured his replacement camera lens, which he was actually starting to enjoy, and smiled. 'I did.'

The shopkeeper focused on wrapping the cheese he'd chosen. 'We've not seen you in the pub, though. I hope the thought of running into George hasn't put you off.'

In actual fact, Logan had forgotten all about George and

his pungent aroma but the idea of finding himself sitting next to the fisherman wasn't an enticing one. It probably wasn't polite to say so, however. 'Not at all. It's more that I came to Ennisfarne to recharge, spend some time on my own, so that's what I've been doing.'

'You came to the right place, then,' Freda said, then eyed him shrewdly. 'Although you can have too much of a good thing.'

Outwardly, Logan made sure his expression didn't change but inside his head, a tiny bell rang. He'd arrived on the island craving solitude and respite from his hectic lifestyle, and that was exactly what he'd found. The week he'd spent in Dune Cottage curled up with a book or watching the marram grass wave on top of the dunes had soothed his too-busy brain and calmed the crackling of frazzled nerves, and the beauty of Ennisfarne had done much to ease the vague but growing dissatisfaction that had threatened to overwhelm him on that final photoshoot almost three weeks ago. But while he now felt better in many ways, the truth was he was beginning to miss people. His career had been built on capturing their stories on film, albeit often in a way that had been manipulated to fit the brief, and he had always striven to capture the person behind the clothes or the make-up or the glamour they'd woven around themselves. It had meant forging a genuine bond, however brief; that ability had been a cornerstone of his professional success and he was surprised to discover now that it hadn't simply been a tool of his trade. Being alone had made him realize he missed those opportunities for connection – meeting someone's eyes, listening as they talked, smiling at a memory or laughing at a shared joke, myriad fleeting interactions that Logan had taken for granted. He'd thought he craved solitude. Now he was starting to suspect he'd been wrong. Although quite how Freda had also arrived at this conclusion was anyone's guess.

'I could never have too much of Ennisfarne,' he said, hoping to deflect her. 'It's so beautiful.'

'Can't argue with that,' she agreed. 'Especially with spring just around the corner. But it can be a bit lonely, living here. I'm sure you know yourself best but like I said before, there's always a warm welcome at the pub. Or, if you'd prefer something a little closer to home, there's a gig at Darling's Bar tomorrow evening.'

She waved a hand at a flyer pinned to a cork noticeboard. Logan glanced at it – a band called The Wreckers were playing from 8pm. The name sounded familiar. 'Must be tricky to get acts to play here,' he observed. 'Because of the tide, I mean.'

'Sometimes,' Freda said, nodding sagely. 'All the more reason to come along and support them, I'd say. There are still a few tickets available – I can add one to your order today if you like? Or I'm sure Eve can sort one out for you.'

Logan hid a smile – Freda was quite the saleswoman. 'I don't think I need one. But thanks for the suggestion.'

'No bother, it was just an idea,' she replied. 'Now, can I get you anything else? Some of this fresh crab for your lunch, maybes?'

*

Logan genuinely had no intention of going to the gig Freda had mentioned. He drove home after his trip to The Nook, passenger seat once again laden with more than he'd intended to buy, and settled in for an afternoon beside the wood burner. But his thoughts kept returning to his conversation with the shopkeeper, to the knowing look in her eyes as she'd commented on how lonely island life could be, and he found himself remembering the pleasures of good music in small venues. His work had meant he'd often been backstage at huge concerts or attended intimate gigs with rock stars and household names but he'd always enjoyed the events with lesser-known musicians too. And, sometimes, they'd been the best nights – packed rooms rich with camaraderie, tapping his foot to tunes that thudded through his whisky-warmed bones. He had never regretted taking a risk on a band or artist he'd never seen before and he was sure The Wreckers would be the same. There was no need to get tangled up in conversation with anyone – he could slip in at the back, enjoy the music and escape quickly afterwards. Eve certainly wouldn't be in a hurry to talk to him. He still winced as he recalled the polite but cool disdain with which she'd regarded him the last time they'd met. Nor could he blame her – he'd been an idiot, assuming she lacked the capability to fix the tap when she was clearly more skilled and resourceful than he'd known. Perhaps that was another reason to go to the gig – he'd be able to apologize for his ignorance. Or perhaps it might make things worse and he was better off avoiding further excruci-ating awkwardness. He couldn't decide.

The intangible disquiet was still there on Saturday afternoon, when Logan took a stroll along the beach. High tide
had left brown-black seaweed and driftwood strewn across
the pebble-dotted sand, glistening in the weak sunlight. The
sky was grey and cheerless, the sea flat, and even the craggy
majesty of the arch wasn't enough to dispel his restlessness.
More than once, his gaze was drawn towards the bar at the
end of the beach and as he got nearer, he took a seat on
a small cluster of boulders to study it in more depth. The
rooftop area was deserted, unsurprisingly on a cold and drab
winter's day, but the tall windows beneath glowed invitingly
amid the gloom. There seemed to be a class taking place
inside – Logan could see sleek figures bending and stretching.
A yoga class, or maybe Pilates, he decided, and wondered
whether teaching was yet another string to Eve's bow. He'd
paid more attention to her appearance when she'd come to
Dune Cottage, mostly wondering how she could possibly
have the strength required to wrestle indoor plumbing, and
she definitely looked as though she kept herself in shape. But
the room behind the windows looked like the kind of space
that might easily be rented out, so perhaps Eve was simply
an astute businesswoman making the most of her premises.
He could easily believe that of her too.

His phone vibrated in his pocket. He pulled it out to see
Suki's name on the screen. Surprised, he opened the message – they'd barely spoken since January, when they had
finally closed the door on their on-off relationship. Both had
careers that involved jetting off at short notice and Logan had

thought her silence must be due to modelling assignments. He hadn't been tempted to contact her – once they'd agreed things weren't going to work out, there didn't seem to be anything more to say.

You weren't at London and now you're not in Milan.
Where the hell are you?

Of course, he thought with a jolt, it was Milan Fashion Week – how had he forgotten? Normally he would be there, capturing the trends for the new season but Phoebe had cancelled all of his bookings for the foreseeable future, absorbing the wrath of his clients in the process. The message itself was typical Suki, demanding and direct. Logan could picture her typing the words, full lips pouting, dark brows knitted, her perfectly proportioned, glorious features pulled into a furious frown. He knew that face better than he knew his own – they'd worked together on countless fashion shoots, catwalk shows and exhibitions. She was a photographer's dream, with a luminosity the camera loved and an instinctive understanding of what made a good photograph great. Even on their first shoots, Logan hadn't needed to direct her. She'd just seemed to know what he wanted and before long, they'd become professionally entwined; if Logan was booked for a magazine spread, he requested Suki as one of the models. No one was surprised when they took their relationship a step further and started dating. And that was when the trouble had begun. Punishing work schedules meant they were rarely in the same country, let alone city, and when they did manage to snatch some time together, their individual artistic temperaments had often led to misunderstandings and arguments. Occasionally, these had happened in public, within snapping distance of the piranha-like paparazzi, and Suki Simpson was always front-page news. Even so, they'd spent eighteen months trying to make it work, until finally accepting the truth: they were happier apart.

On impulse, Logan raised his phone and snapped a picture of the arch. Taking a break, he typed. Getting back to nature.

Her reply was fast. Bloody hell. Where is that?!

He smiled, remembering a seaside shoot they'd done once. Suki was most definitely a city girl. Wildest Northumberland. Wish you were here?

Logan didn't expect a positive reply but she surprised him again. Right now I'd rather be anywhere but here. It's not the same without you xx

He was still uncomfortably contemplating the meaning of the two kisses when her next message arrived:

Want me to fly over once I'm done here? Not due in Paris until 3rd March. I'm sure we could entertain ourselves xx

For a moment, Logan was tempted. There'd never been any shortage of physical attraction between Suki and him – not being able to keep their hands off each other had been part of the reason they'd taken so long to finally call it a day. But he'd come to realize that he needed more than that – they'd been great in bed but the happiness was always fleeting. Sooner or later jealousy would raise its ugly head and the fights would begin. They might manage a few idyllic days if Suki came to Ennisfarne but it wouldn't last once reality crashed back in. And then they'd have to break up all over again and the tranquillity of Logan's island escape would be shattered.

Steeling himself, he tapped out a response. It's not a good idea to go back there. We agreed not to do that, remember?

When his phone buzzed again, it was because she was calling him. Knowing it wouldn't do any good to reject the call, he answered. Her face filled his screen, as beautiful as ever. 'You know, I wasn't suggesting we get married,' she said lightly, her expression playful. 'Just a few days of fun, for old times' sake. You can't tell me you're not interested.'

He was – of course he was. Suki was one of the most sought-after models in the world, her beauty was undisputed, and she was smart and fun too. The trouble was that the fun couldn't last and they'd proved time and again that they didn't work as a couple. 'We can't do no strings, Sook,' he reminded her gently. 'Or friends with benefits, or whatever you want to call it. We'll just end up fighting again. That's why we decided a clean break was the only way.'

She frowned. 'No, you decided that. I don't remember it being my idea.'

That was true too – the initial push to break up had come from Logan. But he'd thought Suki had come to agree. She'd seemed okay with it at the time but perhaps she hadn't realized he meant it; they'd broken up so many times in the past, after all, only to get back together. Maybe she'd assumed this was a temporary split too. In which case, she was about to come face to face with reality.

Logan took a deep breath. 'It's over, Suki. That means no hook-ups if we're working the same shoot, no late-night calls when one of us feels lonely, no getting together for old times' sake. You're an amazing woman who deserves someone who can make you happy, but that isn't me.'

Her mouth fell open a little. 'You don't mean that.'

'I do,' he said, and paused for emphasis. 'I really do. We have to stop this now – it's not good for either of us.'

She looked away from the camera then, staring at something Logan couldn't see. When she turned back to him, her eyes were brimming with tears. 'Why are you doing this?' she demanded, her tone bewildered and hurt. 'We're great together – everyone says so. Not perfect, but who the hell is?'

Logan puffed out a breath and gazed at the arch without really seeing it. 'That's the thing, though – we weren't great. Sure, we're good at parties and even better in bed, but there was nothing underneath that.' He hesitated, fumbling for the right words to express a sentiment he wasn't even sure he understood himself. 'I couldn't imagine our life away from the party scene, Sook. I couldn't picture us getting old together.'

She recoiled as though she'd been slapped. 'You think I'm old? Is that it?'

'No,' he said quickly, 'God, no – you're as perfect as

you've always been, getting better with each year, in fact. But I suppose that's what I mean ... it's not enough just being together. I'm tired of pretending to be happy. I want something real.'

Suki's eyes glittered. 'And, of course, I'm not real,' she said, the words so brittle they hurt his ears. 'I'm just a doll you can pose for your pictures.'

'That's not it,' Logan insisted, running an exasperated hand through his hair. 'You're real. But you have to admit our lives are pretty superficial – neither of us has anything rooting us in place. And unfortunately, that made our relationship shallow too.'

She stared at him for a long time, her lips pressed into a thin hard line. 'Let me get this straight,' she said eventually. 'You think I'm shallow and fake and getting old, so not worth any more of your time. Does that sum it up?'

He closed his eyes; her wilful misunderstanding was a familiar pattern in their arguments. 'That's not what I—'

'Don't try to backtrack now,' Suki cut across him and let out an incredulous laugh. 'I suppose I should be grateful you've finally been honest with me. But you're right about one thing – it is over between us. And don't come crawling back when you need me to save your dying career – without me you're nothing, Logan. As you're about to find out.'

She cut the call, turning his screen black and his mood even darker. He sat in silence for a few seconds, then sighed heavily. Maybe it had been a mistake to answer her call but he'd genuinely thought they'd been on the same page when they'd agreed to split in January; clearly, he'd been wrong. In which case, the conversation they'd just had was one that had to happen sooner or later. Remembering her tearful gaze, Logan groaned. He probably could have handled it better, which was a sentiment that applied to their whole relationship.

Besieged by guilt and self-recrimination, he glanced towards the golden glow of Darling's, where it seemed the exercise class had come to an end. The figures inside were rolling up mats and standing in clusters, presumably chatting and sharing jokes. The contrast between the bright scene inside and Logan's gloomy mood was not lost on him; he lifted his phone and took a picture. It would make a decent painting, he thought, the light and shade accentuated with textured oil or acrylic, but he wasn't much of an artist. Photography was all he was good at and even that seemed unable to excite him lately. Perhaps it was time to look for another career – one that wouldn't bring him into contact with an evidently furious Suki.

With one final glance at the bar, Logan got to his feet and started to trudge back to Dune Cottage. The thought of a long evening loomed large, filled with replays and recriminations of his argument with Suki; he'd have to find a film or a book to distract himself. And then he remembered Freda's comments of the day before, and suddenly a friendly face was exactly what he wanted to see. Googling the phone number of The Nook, he called her.

'Aye, we've a ticket or two left,' she said, once he'd

identified himself and explained what he wanted. 'But no need to drive here to collect it – I'll just let Eve know you're coming and you can pay on the door.'

'Thanks,' Logan said, his spirits lifting. 'That would be great.'

'No bother,' Freda said warmly. 'Should be a cracking evening. I hope you brought your dancing shoes!'

Chapter Six

Eve

Freda had called Eve to say James Cotton was coming to the gig but she still swallowed a groan when she saw him walk through the door. So much for keeping her distance, she thought irritably as she surveyed his unsmiling expression. But Freda had also shared her belief that he was finding his time on Ennisfarne more isolating than he'd expected.

'Just a feeling I have,' the older woman had said. 'So be friendly.'

'I'm always friendly,' Eve had objected, even as she scowled at the very idea.

There'd been a snort on the other end of the phone. 'I've known you since the day you were born, Eve Darling, and you could freeze lava with that smile of yours if you've a mind to. There's more to being welcoming than saying the right words.'

That was the trouble with living on a tiny island, Eve thought – everyone knew each other far too well, although her glacial good manners were usually reserved for the most truculent of tourists. 'Point taken,' she'd conceded. 'I'll put some bunting out, shall I?'

'No need for that,' Freda replied mildly. 'But he's a good-looking man – if I was twenty years younger, I'd be making eyes at him myself. Have you asked if he's single?'

Eve had rolled her eyes; her resolutely single status was another thing she knew was frequently discussed among her fellow islanders. 'No, because he's a sexist pig. I'd rather crack on with George than spend more than two minutes with James Cotton.'

'I'll be sure to let George know,' Freda said. 'He'll think it's Christmas and his birthday all rolled into one, though I'm not sure Hettie will approve.'

Hettie was George's long-suffering lady friend and Eve often thought she must have the patience of St Hilda to tolerate George's less than scrupulous personal hygiene. 'Ha ha,' Eve said dryly. 'I'll do my best to be friendly to James tonight but I can't say I expect him to return the favour. I don't think sociable is in his repertoire.'

And now here he was in front of Eve, apparently as grumpy as ever and proving her point. Squaring her shoulders, she dug up the kind of smile even Freda couldn't have found fault with. 'Hello, nice to see you again. Welcome to Darling's.'

Was it her imagination or did his grumpiness diminish

slightly? 'Thank you. Freda said there'd be tickets for the gig on the door – is that right?'

Eve hesitated. Here was her get-out clause – would she be a terrible person if she said no? Maybe not but Freda would undoubtedly find out and she'd take a dim view of such behaviour. 'Yes, that's right,' she told James. 'Twelve pounds.'

He paid without comment and Eve handed him a pale green raffle ticket. 'For the meat raffle,' she explained when she saw his blank expression. 'It'll be drawn at the end of the gig. You'll need your ticket if you're the winner.'

James's eyebrows shot up. 'The meat raffle? Is that— wow, I didn't know they were an actual thing.'

Once again, Eve felt the first bristling of irritation. 'It's supplied by a really good butcher on the mainland.'

There must have been something in her tone because his expression changed. 'Oh, I'm sure it's fantastic. It just isn't something I've encountered before, that's all.'

I bet you haven't, Eve thought, and made a conscious effort to force her annoyance down as Freda's words echoed again in her mind. 'You can always decline if yours is the winning ticket.' She pointed to the double doors to their left. 'The bar's through there, the gig starts at eight.' And then, because she couldn't resist, she added, 'Just follow the bunting.'

'Thanks,' he said, then paused as though there was something else he wanted to say. Eve dipped her head and busied herself with writing his name on the corresponding raffle ticket. After a moment or two, she heard him move away, the doors swishing as they opened and closed, and slowly let out the breath she'd been holding. She had to concede she hadn't been as friendly as she'd intended. What was it about him that got under her skin every time they met? True, he was arrogant and snobbish, not to mention sexist and sullen, but she'd had plenty of customers who had behaved worse and she'd managed to maintain a veneer of bonhomie and professionalism with them, at least to their faces. James seemed to bypass all her good intentions, however, and go straight to Exasperation Central.

She was spared having to dwell on it further by the arrival of more villagers, including Hamish, who'd closed the Fisherman's Arms for the evening so he and his staff could catch The Wreckers' performance.

'Wouldn't miss it for anything,' he told Eve as he collected his raffle ticket. 'And let's face it, everyone will be here. There's no point in opening up.'

By seven-thirty, she decided everyone who was coming had arrived. There was an outside chance a stranger or two might turn up but she could keep an eye out from the bar and she really needed to check everything was under control. Aiden was a great host and loved working the bar but he often got caught up in conversation and failed to notice thirsty customers waiting to be served. And she didn't want to give James the satisfaction of having a reason to complain, although she wasn't entirely sure why his good opinion mattered. Maybe it was professional pride, she mused as she pushed back the door of the bar.

The evening was already in full swing. The bar was

packed, spilling out through the glass doors onto the veranda, although there was a noticeable circle of space around George and Hettie's table. On the stage, Eve could see the warm-up act, Near and Farne, who were a local folk group made up of her friends and neighbours who often played at music nights both at Darling's and the Fisherman's Arms. The lead singer, Noah, gave her a wave when she glanced over, reassuring her everything was in hand there. Aiden and Tish seemed to be holding their own behind the bar too; Eve slid beneath the wooden flap and immediately spotted Freda waiting to be served.

'A G and T?' she asked, purely out of politeness because the last time Freda had ordered anything else Eve had been too young to serve alcohol.

'Yes, please,' Freda replied. 'And a pint of Thirsty Bishop for Len.'

Eve nodded, because that was entirely expected too, and reached for a glass. Hamish was next – professional pride was at stake there as well so she made sure she took his order fast. Aiden saw her serving and went to collect glasses, although Eve knew it was also an excuse for a chinwag with friends. She didn't mind; he'd earned a break.

She worked through a steady stream of customers until inevitably, she found herself facing James. 'What can I get you?'

'A glass of Malbec, please,' he said, leaning forward to make himself heard over a melodious burst of harmonica. 'And a vodka and coke.'

Eve fought the urge to look over his shoulder to see who he might be buying a drink for. She wasn't entirely surprised someone had pinned him down in conversation – news travelled fast in such a small community and Freda's curiosity about the tenant of Dune Cottage meant everyone was curious. Eve had lost count of the number of times she'd been asked what James was doing on Ennisfarne. He'd been spotted taking photographs of the boats on the edge of the village, as well as around the beacon, so she was fairly certain that was at least part of the reason he was here but she'd had to admit she didn't know much more. He'd probably be sorry he'd come to the gig.

'No Huxley tonight?' James asked as she reached for the wine.

Eve couldn't decide whether he was having a dig or simply making conversation. 'Not when there's a meat raffle,' she said evenly. 'He stole the sausages last time.'

There was a flicker of amusement behind his dark eyes. 'Ah.'

She placed the drinks on the bar and took the payment without further comment. Once again, she had the feeling he had something more to say so she flashed a brisk smile and turned away to serve Nora from the bakery. When she glanced back, James was gone. She put him out of her mind and concentrated on making sure no one was waiting long for a drink.

The queue at the bar slowed down once Near and Farne started to play. Eve leaned against the fridges, tapping her foot in time to the music and watching the crowd enjoying themselves. Aiden leaned beside her, arms folded. 'Our tenant is certainly getting people talking,' he said, his gaze fixed on the band. 'I don't think I've ever been asked so many questions I couldn't answer.'

'I can imagine,' Eve replied, glancing over to where James was sharing a table with Freda and Len.

'But I'm sure we'll know a lot more by the end of this evening. Freda could winkle information out of a brick.'

It was on the tip of Eve's tongue to respond that a brick would probably be more interesting but that wasn't strictly true. For all his faults, she didn't think boring was an accusation that could be levelled at James. She had to admit she'd spent more time wondering about him than any previous residents at the cottage. Although she hadn't had quite the same excruciating first meeting with any of them.

'Selina will have got some dirt too,' Aiden went on. 'She was grilling him earlier. He seemed to be holding his own, though – I think I even heard him laugh at one point.'

Eve fired another covert look at James, outlined against the twinkling fairy lights on the decking outside the tall windows. He appeared to be smiling and she realized it transformed his face. Freda was right, he was good-looking. Strikingly so, in fact. As the song came to an end, he broke into animated applause and leaned towards Freda to say something, who nodded and laughed, with an expression that Eve could only describe as girlish. 'Perhaps he's not as charmless as he seems,' she said, raising her eyebrows.

Aiden grinned. 'I'm sure Selina would agree. She might even have been flirting with him.'

'I doubt it,' Eve said with a snort. 'She's far too sensible to be taken in by a pretty face.'

Her brother gave her an appraising look. 'You've changed your tune. Yesterday, you called him an arrogant throwback to the 1950s.'

Eve shifted uneasily, feeling warmth crawl across her cheeks. 'I still think that. I've just decided he's a good-looking, arrogant throwback, that's all.'

'You're not the only one,' Aiden observed. 'Judging from the way they keep glancing over, I think half the women in the village agree with you.'

Frowning, Eve surveyed the crowd and saw that he was right. Most of the audience had their attention fixed on the performance on the small stage at one end of the bar. But every now and then, someone would steal a glance backwards or sideways at James, and Eve couldn't help noticing it was almost always the women. 'More fool them,' she said.

It was another forty toe-tapping minutes before the folk band played their final song, a thumping, raucous rendition of a traditional Northumberland tune that had the crowd up on their feet. Eve nodded to Aiden and Tish. 'Brace yourselves for the stampede.'

The Wreckers were due to start their set at nine-thirty. Once Eve had checked they had everything they needed, she slipped behind the bar once more and barely had time to think as she poured pint after pint. The room was filled with warmth, both from the number of bodies inside the bar and the obvious enjoyment they'd got from Near and Farne's performance. It gave Eve a warm glow of her own; this was what Darling's was all about – bringing people together.

By the time The Wreckers were ready to begin, the atmosphere was alive with anticipation but the noise level dropped the moment the lead singer held up a hand. 'We'd like to start with a song that's been sung for generations where we're from,' he said, the words rounded by an instantly recognizable Cornish burr. 'It's called "The Song of the Western Men" and it goes something like this.'

Without accompaniment, he began to sing. 'A good sword and a trusty hand, a merry heart and true, King James's men shall understand what Cornish men can do.'

There was a fractional pause before the thud of a skintopped drum kicked in and the hum of an accordion sent a sombre melody into the room. The lead singer repeated his original refrain, joined by two of his fellow bandmates, and the three of them sang in harmony. The tune swelled and grew, casting a spell over the crowd so that they swayed and bobbed and stomped their feet in unison. When they finished, the applause was tumultuous and Eve grinned at her brother. 'Amazing,' she said. 'Who knew sea shanties could be so sexy?'

Aiden winked. 'Wait until the end. I bet even old Mrs Purkiss will be swooning.'

It wasn't a surprise when the dancing started – the music was utterly infectious and demanded the heart and soul of the audience. The Wreckers played song after song, sometimes taking the mood and the volume down but mostly filling the bar with pounding beats and soaring harmonies. Eve had never heard anything quite like it, even though she recognized more of the melodies than she expected. These were songs that had been sung for centuries, written into the collective consciousness without most people realizing they knew them. Some of the crowd joined in, especially as the drinks flowed, which only encouraged The Wreckers to play louder and faster. When they finished, with an intoxicating whirl of a shanty that told of fearless smugglers and desperate sailors who'd battled to put food on the table and protect the land they loved, the bar was thrumming. Eve knew the lyrics would resonate with many of the islanders present, all of whom came from seafaring families; her own ancestor, Grace Darling, had risked her young life to save nine souls from a terrible shipwreck. The Wreckers' music summoned up the ghosts of the past and invited them to dance once more among the living and Eve was sure she wasn't the only one who was overcome with breathless joy when the last notes had died away.

There was a brief moment of appreciative silence, then the bar erupted into cheers and whoops. Beside Eve, Aidan bellowed his appreciation and she thought the noise might actually lift the newly repaired roof. Grinning and waving, the band quit the stage and a flood of thirsty drinkers surged towards the bar again.

It was long past midnight when the crowd began to thin.

Many of the islanders wanted to buy the band members a drink, or at least clap them on the back by way of thanks, and Eve wasn't about to deny them the opportunity. She took her own chance to thank them before they left and made sure they knew they were welcome back any time.

'Thanks for having us,' Jasper, the lead singer, said as they packed up their equipment. 'We haven't had much time to explore but Ennisfarne has amazing energy – I'm not surprised you've got a celebrity in residence.'

Eve blinked at him. 'Sorry? I don't know who you mean.'

Jasper winked. 'Got you. Least said and all that. Don't worry, we won't tell anyone.'

'Oi, Jas,' his drummer called. 'That amp ain't going to load itself into the van.'

'All right, mate, I'm coming,' Jasper called back, and gave Eve an apologetic shrug. 'Sorry. He gets a proper face ache if he thinks I'm getting too lah-dee-dah to help with the gear.'

Eve was forced to let him go without finding out what he meant by celebrity. Once The Wreckers had gone, Eve's customers started to disperse and she forgot all about the baffling comment. She stood at the door, thanking everyone for coming and reminding them about the March music night, when Near and Farne would be playing again. James Cotton was one of the last to leave – she saw him hanging back and she knew he was waiting for a moment to say whatever he'd been considering earlier in the evening. Pushing her tiredness to one side, Eve took a deep breath and summoned up some friendliness.

'Did you enjoy the music?' she asked as he drew near. 'Not quite Wembley or Glastonbury but you don't get to chat to the band afterwards there, do you?'

His mouth twisted in a wry smile. 'Not always, no. But I enjoyed myself very much, thanks. Both bands were brilliant, although I think The Wreckers are destined for the big time, if they haven't already hit it.'

'I'm just grateful they came,' Eve admitted. 'It was a good night all round. One of the best we've had.'

James nodded. 'Glad to hear it.' There was an uncomfortable pause. 'Listen, this is long overdue but I wanted to apologize for the way I acted when you came round to fix the tap. I shouldn't have doubted your ability, it was unforgivably sexist and unfair. I'm sorry.'

The sincerity in his voice caught Eve by surprise, as did his honesty. Whatever she'd been expecting, it hadn't been this. He wasn't going through the motions of an apology, he genuinely appeared to mean it.

'Oh,' she said, wrong-footed. 'Erm . . . thank you.'

He watched her for a moment and she had the distinct impression he was seeing her properly for the first time. His gaze seemed to linger on her no-nonsense pony tail and bare face and she supposed he disapproved, if his attitude towards her plumbing skills was anything to go by. She caught the prickle of annoyance before it could erupt into anything more. 'Sorry you didn't win the meat raffle.'

'Me too, now I know the sausages are endorsed by Huxley,' he said and this time she knew he wasn't having a dig. 'But maybe next time. Do you know who's going to be headlining yet?'

Eve shook her head. 'Not a clue. It can be hard to get acts to come here sometimes – we're not exactly on the beaten track.'

'No,' he agreed. 'But that's what I like most about Ennisfarne.'

What did that mean, she wondered, trying hard not to stare. Was he hiding from something? Or recovering? He appeared to be in perfect health but she knew illness wasn't always outwardly visible. There was no way to ask without seeming horribly nosy and besides, she wasn't giving him the satisfaction of knowing she was interested. 'As I said earlier, our next music night is in March – Freda will have the details if you'd like to join us again.'

'I'll keep it in mind,' he said and once again, she felt his sincerity. 'Thanks again for a great night.'

Eve watched him leave, trying to subdue the burn of curiosity he had kindled, then turned and went back into the bar, where Selina was waiting. 'That seemed to go with an almighty bang,' she said, grinning at Eve. 'I might have to set up a sea shanty playlist on Spotify.'

'Glad you enjoyed it,' Eve said, gathering up a few stray glasses from a nearby table and stacking them on the bar. 'I always expect something to go wrong – remember the time we had that power cut and none of the electric guitars were playable?'

'I do,' Selina replied. 'It's one of the best acoustic gigs I've ever been to. But nothing went wrong tonight, did it?'

Eve sighed. 'Not really, no. Unless you count Mr Grumpy turning up.'

Her best friend nodded slowly. 'Ah, yes. The mysterious Mr Cotton. You know, he wasn't half as bad as you made him out to be. I enjoyed talking to him.'

'Not you as well,' Eve protested, eyeing her with raised eyebrows. 'Freda's a big fan too.'

Selina snorted. 'I'm not surprised – fresh meat isn't something we get too often in these parts, if you don't count the raffle.'

'You sound almost as sexist as him,' Eve said, with a playful roll of her eyes.

'But you have to admit he's attractive,' Selina said, giving her a sidelong look. Then she frowned thoughtfully. 'Although he reminds me of someone – I can't quite put my finger on who it is.'

'Maybe he looks like someone famous,' Eve suggested. 'One of the lads from the band said pretty much the same thing. At least, I assume he meant James – I can't see anyone else being mistaken for a celebrity.'

'George is a dead ringer for Captain Birdseye, maybe that's it,' Selina joked. Her frown deepened. 'But I wish I could remember who it was. It's been nagging at me all evening.'

Eve shook her head. 'I wouldn't lose any sleep over it.'

Her friend stared at her. 'You really don't like him, do you?'

Eve hesitated for a fraction of a second, remembering the olive branch James had offered her. 'Not much, no,' she said.

'But I'm sure the feeling is mutual and he'll be gone in a few months. We can avoid each other until then.'

'You do remember we live on an island, don't you?' Selina asked, her tone doubtful. 'It's impossible to avoid anyone and you are his landlord.'

Freda's admonishment rang in Eve's ears once again. 'I'll be friendly. Doesn't mean we have to be friends.'

'Heaven forbid,' Selina said, sounding amused. 'You don't mind if I make friends with him, though?'

'Of course not,' Eve said and shot her a mischievous look. 'I'm relying on you and Freda to find out all the gossip.'

Selina winked. 'Mission most definitely accepted.'

Chapter Seven

Logan

Logan awoke on Sunday morning to four missed calls from his agent and numerous calls from unknown numbers. He stared blearily at the screen for a moment, uneasiness chasing the soft warmth of sleep away. What on earth could be so important to make Phoebe call him four times before eight o'clock on a Sunday? Whatever it was, he doubted it was anything good – only bad news arrived with such insistence – but he couldn't face finding out for sure without coffee to fortify him. It was only when he was nestled in the armchair, with a piping hot mug at his side and a view of the grey-blue sky dotted with wispy clouds above the dunes, that he checked his messages. The first was timed at 6.47am.

We need to talk. Call me as soon as you get this.

Then, ten minutes later: I mean it, Logan. Please answer your phone or call me ASAP.

And finally, time-stamped 7.16am: IT'S URGENT. CALL ME. DO NOT SPEAK TO THE PRESS.

He read the last line three times, a heavy sinking sensation settling into the pit of his stomach. He'd never been one to court fame, it was simply a consequence of his success, but Phoebe hadn't ever felt the need to warn him about talking to the press before, not even when he'd been dating Suki and the tabloid column inches had really started to stack up. Since then, he'd tried to keep out of the limelight, before finally dropping off their radar completely when he'd come to Ennisfarne. For his agent to explicitly mention it now meant something had shifted to make him journalist fodder again, a notion that didn't exactly thrill him. He took a long sip of coffee, watched the gulls wheeling over the dunes for a moment, then called Phoebe back.

She answered on the second ring. 'Thank god,' she said, without greeting. 'Please tell me I'm the first person you've spoken to this morning.'

Logan raised his eyebrows. 'You're the first person I've spoken to. Why, what's happened?'

'Have you seen the papers yet?'

The leaden feeling in his stomach worsened. 'You know I don't read them,' he said. 'What's going on, Phoebe?'

He heard her sigh. 'Suki's done a kiss and tell – an exclusive, no-holds-barred account of – and I quote – her heartbreak hell with snapper Silk.'

Logan's jaw dropped. 'She's what?'

'It's all over the front page – they're calling you Love Rat Logan.' She paused and gave a delicate cough. 'We've known each other a long time and you can tell me this is none of my business but I'm assuming you didn't really bed two models while Suki was nursing her invalid mother.'

'No, I bloody well didn't,' Logan said grimly, after taking a second or two to process the words. He thought of Suki's incredulity when he'd turned her down the day before. This was her revenge for that rejection and he had to give her credit – she hadn't wasted any time. 'Which paper did she go to?'

Phoebe let out a snort of derision. 'You already know the answer – the worst one, of course.'

He closed his eyes. Whatever story Suki had concocted wasn't true. He'd never cheated on her and certainly not when her mother was undergoing chemotherapy; he'd been there as often as he could. In fact, the worst accusation Suki could level at him was that he'd been so rarely available. But he supposed that was why she'd chosen this particular fabrication – it was both plausible and hard to disprove. And the truth didn't matter where a story like this was concerned – the public wouldn't care whether it was an utter work of fiction or not. They'd be calling him Love Rat Logan for the rest of his career.

'What's the damage so far?' he asked, opening his eyes to stare once more at the view.

'Too early to say, especially since you're taking a break at the moment. But it could be bad – the US publications are particularly squeamish when it comes to this kind of thing and involving her mother was a masterstroke. There will be repercussions, I'm afraid.'

She was right, of course; if he'd had any upcoming photo-shoots they would almost certainly be cancelled once other publications picked up on the story. In many ways it was a good thing he wasn't working right now. 'So, what do we do? Ride it out – wait for something else to knock it off the front page?'

'We could do that,' Phoebe said, matter-of-factly. 'I can talk to a few of the big editors, let them know you've been stitched up by Suki and see what they think. But – I'm sorry to say this – I'd need to know if any of her allegations are true before I approach any of them. And whether there's any more to come.'

He ran a hand wearily over his chin. 'I have no idea what she's accusing me of but I do know I was never unfaithful to her. When we spoke yesterday she told me I was nothing without her, so I imagine this is her way of proving that.'

When Phoebe spoke, her voice was tight with anger. 'Then she's a stupid girl. I suggest you read the story and see if there's any truth behind her claims. If not, we hit her hard and fast with a defamation lawsuit.'

Logan puffed out his cheeks. 'Great. Can't wait to read what a monster I am.'

'The sooner you look, the faster we can act,' she said, sympathetic but firm. 'And look on the bright side, at least you're not going to have the paparazzi camped out on your doorstep. No one knows where you are.'

'The benefits of being at the edge of the world,' he replied, as a faint smile tugged at his lips. 'Thanks for your support, Phoebe. I had no idea Suki could be so vindictive.'

'We'll get through it,' she said. 'But maybe steer clear of highly strung supermodels next time you're looking for love, okay?'

Logan shuddered. 'Believe me, I intend to. In fact, I'm going to steer clear of love altogether.'

'Sensible. Consider getting a dog if you want a companion who'll never let you down.'

Logan managed a hollow laugh, remembering the way Huxley had swept his legs from under him on the beach. 'I think I'll just go it alone for now.'

His laughter was long gone by the time the call ended. He brooded in the chair for a while, watching the grass swaying on the dunes without really seeing it, trying to dredge up the strength of mind to google the tabloid headlines. The trouble was, he knew he was going to be incensed by what he found, which made him loathe to go looking for it. But by the same token, his peace of mind was already ruined – he might as well know the worst of it. Although there was nothing to say he had to do it there and then, in Dune Cottage. He could take his phone along the beach and kick pebbles into the sea once he'd finished reading. As long as he wasn't tempted to lob the phone into the waves too . . .

The morning breeze was bracing as he picked his way

through the dunes, snatching his dragon breath the moment it left his mouth and scattering it to the sky. The tide was roaring back in, the wind whipping spray from the top of the waves like candyfloss as they crashed against the shore. Logan breathed deeply, gasping at the cold sting of the salt air as it hit his lungs, and forced himself to release the breath slowly. Instead of walking parallel to the shoreline, he headed towards the waves and allowed the bubbling breakers to wash over his wellies. The sand shifted beneath his feet as the water surged and ebbed away. There was something cleansing about watching the water flow over the rubber of his boots, he decided, as the breeze buffeted his face. He felt fresh, scrubbed clean of his shock and anger at Suki's betrayal and the thought of reading the lies she'd told was more manageable. Slowly, he made his way towards the boulders he'd rested on yesterday. There was no exercise class behind the glass windows of Darling's today; the lights were off. But it wasn't yet nine o'clock on a Sunday morning, Logan reminded himself. Most sensible people were still in bed, or at the very least having a leisurely breakfast, and Eve had proved herself very sensible indeed. The polar opposite of Suki, in fact.

With a grimace of reluctance, Logan decided he'd prevaricated enough and pulled out his phone. No sooner had he typed his name than the headline jumped out at him:

LOVE RAT LOGAN!

Suki Simpson Bares All

He stared at the screen for a moment, taking in the accompanying photo of a beautifully stricken Suki, then savagely stabbed at the link and began to read.

It seemed she hadn't held back but the story was so comically over the top that Logan almost laughed. No wonder it had made the front page – the gossip-hungry editor must have thought he'd won the lottery when the scoop came in. Suki had clearly borrowed heavily from the world of fiction – she'd portrayed Logan as a serial cheat whose frequent indiscretions had finally become too much, leading her to end their tempestuous relationship. According to the newspaper, he was charming and affectionate on the outside but it hid a narcissistic streak that had him craving one-night-stands:

> Logan Silk is on a mission to self-destruct. I tried
> my hardest to love him but in the end, he was
> determined to hurt us both. One day I hope I'll
> stop crying.

He read all the way to the end, observing with grudging admiration the thoroughness with which Suki had got his attention. The allegations were ridiculous – if he'd cheated as much as she claimed he wouldn't have time for anything else – but plenty of people would believe Suki's claims, or at least some of them. He suspected that was what she was banking on, either that he'd be so furious he would contact her to ask what the hell she was playing at, or that he'd be forced to defend himself, thus forging a connection between them that would rumble on for months. Perhaps she was hoping for both.

He wasn't sure how long he'd been sitting there when he heard the footsteps. Tearing his gaze away from the waves erupting around the base of the arch, he turned to see Eve picking her way towards him.

'Good morning,' she said once she was within earshot. 'You've been out here for ages. Aiden thought you might need this.'

She was holding out a cardboard cup with a white lid. A faint curl of steam was issuing from a hole at the top. Her expression was carefully neutral, neither welcoming nor unwelcoming. 'We weren't sure whether you'd want milk or sugar,' she went on. 'I brought some just in case.'

Logan cleared his throat and took both the drink and the small paper bag. 'Thanks. That's kind of you.'

Eve shrugged. 'Like I said, you've been out here ages.' She eyed his bare head and gloveless hands dispassionately. 'Aren't you cold?'

'A bit,' he admitted warily, trying to work out whether she'd seen Suki's accusations. She would undoubtedly have questions if she had – she'd want to know why he'd lied about his name, for a start. But her expression wasn't angry or even curious. There was a hint of pity around the extraordinarily blue eyes he'd found himself admiring the previous night but that might easily be down to his stupidity at venturing onto the beach in late February without a hat or gloves.

Eve nodded, as though his reply had been exactly what she'd expected. 'It's a good spot to sit and think,' she said, fixing her gaze on the arch. 'But maybe wrap up a bit more next time.'

She turned away and began walking back towards the bar. 'I will,' Logan called after her. 'And thanks again.'

Raising a hand in acknowledgement, she kept going. Logan watched her until she disappeared through the tall glass doors and decided nothing about her demeanour suggested she'd seen the headlines – she hadn't gawped or grinned in a knowing fashion or refused to look him in the eye. She had simply seen him sitting on the beach and had been both kind and practical. But his speculation did present him with an unhappy truth – someone on the island was bound to read the paper in question, or at the very least see the story online, and it was quite likely to be Freda, who stocked the papers. Once the news broke on Ennisfarne, his cover would be well and truly blown. It wasn't that he minded them knowing his real identity as such, more that he didn't want them to believe Suki's accusations were true. And there was always the outside possibility that one of them would tip off the newspaper that had run the story and he'd find himself knee-deep in paparazzi after all. But there was very little he could do about that, he reasoned, and took a swig of coffee. He'd just have to hope the people of Ennisfarne were as decent and compassionate as they seemed.

Chapter Eight

Eve

'So?' Selina demanded through the mobile when Eve called her back.

'It's him,' Eve confirmed and shook her head incredulously. 'You know, this explains a lot. Why he has so many cameras, for a start.'

'And why he was so annoyed when Huxley broke one,' Selina replied. 'Just think about all the celebrities that camera has captured.'

'Don't,' Eve said, groaning. She'd googled Logan Silk the moment Selina had rung earlier that morning to say she'd realized why James Cotton seemed so familiar. There had been an extensive, star-studded list of famous faces he had photographed, from rock 'n' roll royalty to actual royalty. She'd also discovered the many column inches devoted to his relationship with Suki Simpson, along with the lurid headline of a certain Sunday tabloid. She hadn't bothered with the article itself – the newspaper wasn't one she had much time for and it had a reputation for printing first and establishing the facts later. Besides, it felt horribly intrusive to delve into the private life of someone she actually knew. It had been three years since her last relationship but she knew she'd hate to find the details of her love life splashed across the pages of a newspaper or magazine.

'Do you think it's true?' Selina asked, clearly feeling no such scruples. 'He doesn't come across as the type but you can never really tell what people are like behind closed doors, can you?'

Eve considered what she knew of James – or Logan, as she supposed she ought to call him now – and pursed her lips. He might be arrogant, taciturn and decidedly old-fashioned when it came to gender roles but he didn't deserve to be humiliated in the national press – no one did. And Freda liked him – that counted for a lot with Eve. 'It doesn't matter one way or the other,' she said stoutly. 'But to be honest, there's only one reason someone like Suki Simpson would sell her story and that's revenge. It's not like she needs the money, is it?'

'Good point,' Selina agreed, sounding thoughtful. 'Maybe that's why he's here, to escape the fallout, and why he used a fake name.'

It sounded depressingly plausible, Eve thought. Break-ups so often turned nasty, especially when one half of the couple was hurt and didn't want to let go. It was part of the reason she'd decided to stay single after things had ended with Michael, in spite of well-meaning pressure from her friends. Love was a risky business and Eve was in no hurry to get her heart trampled again. 'Could be. He did say his favourite thing about Ennisfarne was the isolation.'

'Poor guy,' Selina said. 'I wonder if he knew Suki was going to sell out.'

There was no way to tell – Eve doubted Logan would be discussing the allegations with anyone on the island and she certainly wasn't about to ask him. 'Who knows?' she said. 'But I imagine it will be old news in a day or two and at least he can lie low at Dune Cottage.'

'Exactly,' Selina replied and her tone brightened. 'And on the plus side, now we know he's definitely single.'

'Selina!' Eve laughed, with a mixture of disbelief and amusement.

'What?' her best friend said. 'I'm just pointing out that it's not every day we get hot celebrities hiding away on Ennisfarne. Maybe he needs some help to nurse his broken heart.'

Eve shook her head, still smiling. 'And you're the woman for the job, I suppose?'

Selina didn't hesitate. 'I'd give it a go. Unless you were interested, of course.'

'Absolutely not,' Eve said, equally fast. 'You know I'm happily single and even if I wasn't, James Cott – sorry, Logan Silk – isn't my type. He might be easy on the eye but he's got an attitude the size of Newcastle.'

It wasn't until she'd put the phone down that she appreciated there had been a very good reason for her tenant's ill-temper – whether he was the heartbreaker or the heartbroken, the end of a relationship was deeply affecting. Freda had been right when she'd suggested Eve should cut him some slack, although she couldn't have suspected the motive behind Logan's escape to the island. But it did remind Eve of a universal truth, that you rarely knew about the struggles of others and everyone should be a bit kinder as a result, and she was glad she'd given in to the spur of the moment impulse to take him the coffee. He'd managed a passable pretence at being okay and if she hadn't already known about the kiss and tell, she might have been fooled. But beneath the game face, Eve thought he had looked utterly dispirited and weary. Maybe it was time for a fresh start where Logan was concerned, she thought, glancing out at the now empty beach. Perhaps it was time to extend an olive branch of her own.

'Oh, thank goodness you're here,' Freda said, the moment Eve walked into The Nook. 'I've just tried to call you at the bar – Aiden said you were already on your way over.'

She looked as calm and composed as ever but Eve could tell she was agitated. 'What's wrong?'

The shopkeeper folded her arms behind the counter. 'I can't be totally sure but I think there's a journalist sniffing around.' She waved a hand at the Sunday papers, laid out on a shelf by the door, and pursed her lips. 'He pretended to be a day-tripper, had a photo of the arch and wanted to know how to get there, but he didn't look like a tourist. Too flash, for a start, and he had something weaselly about the eyes. Even so I might have believed him if he hadn't asked whether we'd had any newcomers moving to Ennisfarne lately. What kind of tourist wants to know something like that?'

'The kind who isn't a tourist at all,' Eve said uneasily. Her gaze flickered to the newspapers and she saw there were no copies with the LOVE RAT LOGAN headline.

Freda saw her looking. 'I put them out the back, in case he came in,' she said, with a sniff of disapproval. 'Load of old tosh. And nobody's business, anyways.'

'So, who do you think it was?' Eve asked. 'A journalist looking for James – I mean, Logan?'

'I reckon so,' Freda said. 'Might as well have had a big sign over his head flashing "Dirty Nosy Parker".'

The image made Eve smile. 'What did you tell him?'

She shrugged. 'There wasn't much I could say about the arch – told him to follow the road out of the village and go right at the fork. That's why I called – to warn you he might turn up at the bar.'

'Aiden can handle him, or Huxley can lick him to death,' Eve said, then paused. 'But the road to the arch leads right past Dune Cottage. What if the journalist decides to knock there?'

'He won't be doing anything for a while,' Freda replied, with evident satisfaction. 'I told him to stop by the Fisherman's Arms and ask there. George was drafted in to keep him occupied and according to Hamish, he's been talking about barnacles for twenty-five minutes.'

Eve wasn't sure who to feel most sorry for – George for having to talk to a tabloid journalist, the stranger for having to ride the wave of George's aroma through unaccustomed nostrils while listening to almost half an hour of crustacean chat, or Hamish for having to handle both of them. But as delaying tactics went, she had to concede it was pretty effective. 'Excellent,' she said, grinning at Freda. 'I actually came in to get some supplies for Logan – milk, bread, that kind of thing in case he didn't feel like showing his face for a few days. If I grab them quickly, I can be at Dune Cottage before our friend Nosy Parker has recovered his senses.'

'Very thoughtful of you,' Freda said approvingly. She stepped out from behind the cash till. 'I know exactly what he'd like.'

Forty minutes later, Eve was approaching the entrance to Dune Cottage. The late afternoon sun was glowing on the white walls as she drove into the gravel car park, illuminating it against the grey clouds so that it seemed the little building was on fire. The Hilux was parked in the same spot it had been on her previous visit. It wouldn't have been the end of the world if he'd been out – she'd have left the sturdy box of groceries on the doorstep – but she'd rather explain Freda's news face to face. Always assuming Logan opened the door, of course. If Eve had been in his shoes, she'd prefer to never face anyone again.

She was preparing to lower the box to the ground when

the door finally opened and Logan stared out. From his startled expression, he was surprised to see her. 'Sorry, I wasn't expecting anyone to knock.'

Eve nodded. 'Ordinarily, I wouldn't just drop in but – well, something's come up.' She hefted the box in her arms. 'Do you mind if I come in for a minute?'

He frowned and studied her. 'Can it wait? It's not really the best time.'

'I know,' she said, her mouth twisting into what she hoped was a sympathetic smile. 'I've seen the headlines.'

Logan's jaw tightened. 'Right. Only to be expected, I suppose.'

'I'm not here to gawp or pry,' Eve reassured him. 'We only want to help.'

Now there was a flash of steel in his gaze. 'We? Did you have a village meeting about it?'

Eve felt her own hackles start to rise and took a deep calming breath. Surely they could manage at least one conversation without rubbing each other up the wrong way. 'Of course not.' She sighed and sought another way to prove she was trying to do a good deed. 'Look, this box is full of things from The Nook that Freda and I thought you might need. It's quite heavy so if you're not going to let me in, could you at least take it off me?'

Blinking, Logan glanced briefly at the box and then back at Eve. He shook his head wearily and reached for the box. 'Sorry, I'm being an arse. Come in.'

With a relieved glance over her shoulder, Eve followed

him into the cottage. It was as tidy as on her previous visit; his MacBook was open on the coffee table in front of the glowing wood burner and his mobile phone was next to it. Had he been trying to work or was that out of the question, she wondered.

'Can I offer you a coffee?' Logan said as he headed for the kitchen. 'Or tea?'

Eve hesitated. Her gut instinct was to deliver the news and leave him in peace. But there was also a chance Logan needed a friendly ear, no matter how unwelcoming he appeared on the surface. She was beginning to appreciate that aloofness was his default position and now that she knew who he really was, she supposed it made sense. 'That sounds lovely. Tea with milk, please. No sugar.'

She hovered in the living room for a moment and then realized he might suspect she was nosing around, so followed him into the kitchen and watched him filling the kettle. Once it was rumbling gently, he turned his attention to the box. 'This was really kind of you. Thanks.'

'You're welcome,' she said. 'It's nothing really, just a few essentials to get you through the next few days. In case you don't feel like going out or getting a delivery.'

Logan pulled out a large bar of Dairy Milk and raised a dark eyebrow. 'Essentials?'

'Absolutely,' Eve replied. 'Chocolate is medicinal in moments of extreme stress. I thought everyone knew that.'

'I see,' he said, and held up a bottle of Malbec. 'Now this is definitely medicinal. I'm tempted to open it now.'

Eve grimaced. 'You might need it once you're heard what I have to tell you.'

The look he gave her was measured. 'Sounds ominous. I assume it's got something to do with my ex-girlfriend's front-page hatchet job?'

'I'm afraid so.'

'Tea first, then,' Logan said, wheeling away to slot the milk into the fridge. 'Bad news is always easier to take when there's tea.'

It wasn't until they were back in the living room that Eve remembered how small the sofa was. The warmth of the wood burner was inviting but she didn't want to sit right next to Logan. But he had evidently seen the problem too because he waved her towards the sofa and fetched the armchair from beside the window. It meant she had a clear view of his mobile phone as it lit up on the coffee table: Unknown Caller.

Logan saw it too but made no move to answer. 'Okay,' he said in a resigned tone of voice. 'Hit me with it.'

Eve did as he asked, passing on everything Freda had told her. He listened in silence, watching his phone light up twice more, then let out a low growl of disgust. 'I'm sure Freda's instincts are right – it'll be a journalist. I don't know how they knew where to find me – I've only told my agent and my mother, and I don't think either of them will have tipped the papers off.'

'They had a photo of the arch,' Eve said, sipping her tea. 'Have you posted any pictures on your social media?'

'No. I haven't shared any of the pictures I've taken here — they're not my usual style,' he said. Then he slapped a hand to his forehead. 'Wait, I'm an idiot. I sent a photo of the arch to Suki, right before we had the argument that started all of this. She must have handed it over when she sold the story so they'd be able to find me and really rattle my cage.'

Eve stared at him, open-mouthed. She was really starting to dislike Suki Simpson. 'Wow. That's terrible.'

He managed a mirthless smile. 'Hell hath no fury like a scorned supermodel. I assume she also gave them my mobile number, which is why my phone has been blowing up all day. I'm waiting for a call from my solicitor, otherwise I'd switch it off.'

Sympathy welled up inside Eve. She could only imagine how wretched he must feel. 'They won't find out where you're staying,' she said quietly. 'Not from anyone on the island, at least. We stick together here, protect our own.'

As he opened his mouth to reply, there was a sharp knock at the door. Logan grew suddenly still. 'Sounds like you and Freda were right,' he murmured.

Eve stood up. 'I'll get rid of him. You stay here, out of sight.'

She didn't wait to see if he would argue but headed to the tiny hallway. A quick peek through the spyhole told her it was a man matching the description Freda had given her earlier. Arranging her expression into look of surprised enquiry, Eve opened the door. 'Hello. Can I help you?'

The man smiled in a way that reminded her of a

crocodile. 'I'm looking for someone called Logan Silk. Is he staying here?'

Her heart suddenly thumping, Eve pretended to consider the question. 'No, this is my cottage. There's no one here by that name.'

The man peered over her shoulder. 'Is that right? What's your name, if you don't mind me asking?'

She couldn't see a reason to lie – if the man was any kind of journalist he'd probably be able to dig up the land registry details. 'Eve Darling. Who are you?'

'Charlie Ford,' he said, eyeing her inquisitively. 'The bar up the road is called Darling's – any relation?'

Again, Eve took refuge in the truth. 'I run it with my brother. We're closed today but Monday night is Two-for-One on cocktails, if you're interested.'

He grinned, baring too many teeth again. 'Maybe I will, if I can find somewhere to sleep. I asked in the village but all the hotels seem to be closed. I don't suppose your place does rooms, does it?'

'It's off-season,' Eve said coolly. 'And no, we don't do rooms. Sorry.'

Charlie nodded, then glanced speculatively at the Hilux, parked next to Eve's Prius. 'Did you say you live here alone?'

'No,' Eve replied, her mind racing for a plausible explanation for the extra car. 'My boyfriend lives here too. He's called James. That's his car.'

Inwardly, she cursed – giving a name and mentioning the car had been too much, unsolicited details that screamed she was lying. But Charlie didn't seem to notice. Instead, he reached into his coat pocket and pulled out a business card. 'Logan Silk is a friend of a friend. If you do happen to run into him, can you let him know I'd love to have a chat?' He smiled in a way that went nowhere near his eyes. 'See how he's doing, that kind of thing.'

Eve glanced down at the card, which bore the name Charlie Ford and a phone number, nothing more. 'Sure,' she said, aiming for casual uninterest. 'Watch out for the tide, if you're not staying on the island. You wouldn't want to leave too late and get caught out on the causeway.'

He tipped his head, studying her as though he was committing her to memory. 'Good tip. Thanks very much, Eve, and sorry to have bothered you.'

'Bye,' Eve said, closing the door firmly. She leaned against the wood, willing her racing heart to slow down, and then went back to Logan.

'Charlie Ford,' she said, handing him the business card before crossing to the window overlooking the dunes and lowering the blind. 'He said he's the friend of a friend.'

'That's one way of putting it,' Logan said grimly as he tossed the card onto the coffee table. 'Although I think it's safe to say Suki and I are definitely not friends.'

Eve puffed out a long, slow breath and sat on the sofa. 'I don't know if he's been to the bar or that's his next stop but hopefully I was convincing enough to send him back to the mainland.' She let out a tiny huff of amusement. 'He said he couldn't find anywhere to stay.'

Logan frowned. 'I thought there were a couple of bed and breakfasts, as well as the hotel.'

'There are,' Eve said, smiling wryly. 'But they're all mysteriously closed tonight. So, unless Charlie wants to sleep in his car, he'll have to leave Ennisfarne this evening.'

The penny seemed to drop. 'Oh,' Logan said, and paused. 'That's extraordinarily good of them.'

'I told you, we look after our own here,' Eve said. 'And since you've paid to stay at Dune Cottage for the next few months, that makes you one of us, at least temporarily.'

Logan was silent for another moment. 'Thank you,' he said eventually. 'I think that's the kindest thing anyone has said to me for a long time.'

There was something in his voice, the merest hint of a catch, that made Eve believe his words were absolutely the truth. And she found herself wanting to say something that might make him feel better, if that was possible. 'Then I'm glad you found your way here. It sounds like you're in dire need of some friends.'

A rueful smile crossed his face. 'Probably. There are a lot of people who would call themselves friends but there's only one I'd trust to totally have my back and he's filming in Antarctica right now. So, do you know how many friends I've called since this nightmare began this morning?'

She pursed her lips. 'Is it zero?'

'It is,' he said, with a huff of self-deprecation. 'Apart from my agent and my mother, you're the only person I've spoken to about it.'

Eve stared at him for a long moment. She'd known he was an attractive man from the first moment they'd met, but it had been a purely objective observation; she hadn't been at all attracted to him. And she'd agreed with both Selina and Freda when they'd described him as good-looking — hot, even — but again, she hadn't felt the pull of attraction herself. Sitting here with him now, however, she felt as though she was seeing beneath the physical attributes and assuredness that drew in most people and catching a glimpse of a vulnerability she suspected few others got to see. He was still the most infuriating man she'd ever met, and there was always the possibility Suki's accusations hadn't been entirely untrue, but she was starting to appreciate how much more there was to him. 'Well, then,' she said, smiling. 'I guess that makes me your friend.'

He studied her thoughtfully. 'I guess it does. But I don't think we've been formally introduced. I'm Logan Silk.'

She shook his hand, noticing his long artistic fingers for the first time, and played the game. 'It's good to meet you, Logan Silk. I'm Eve Horsley Darling.'

If Logan thought anything of her odd middle name, a throwback to her famous ancestor, he didn't show it. 'Nice to meet you too.' Raising his half-drunk cup of tea, he touched it against hers. 'To new friends.'

Eve's gaze met his and she felt a shiver of something that might have been anticipation run down her spine. 'Absolutely. Here's to being friends.'

PART TWO

Hidden Depths

Chapter Nine

Eve

Eve Darling wasn't sure what was worse – the stink coming from Huxley, the slimy brown substance oozing down his chocolate fur or his air of utter satisfaction at a job well done. She wrinkled her nose and fanned her watering eyes. 'Is that—'

Warren turned his gaze from Eve to contemplate the Labrador, sitting in the centre of the cobbled farmyard like a king surveying his domain. 'Aye, it's cow pat,' he confirmed. 'More than one, if I'm any judge. The crusty bits dangling from his tail are a few days old, whereas the stuff sliding down his haunches is fresh today.'

Not for the first time, Eve wondered what she'd done to deserve a dog whose idea of heaven was rolling in the most disgusting things he could find. He was so thoroughly coated it was hard to tell where the slime ended and his fur began.

And was it her imagination or was he steaming in the chilly morning air? 'I'm sorry about this, Warren,' she said, with the same toe-curling embarrassment she usually felt when apologizing for Huxley. 'Is Mildred okay?'

Her neighbour shrugged. 'She's a five-hundred-kilo Highland Cow – I don't think Huxley here is much of a threat to her. But it was lucky we had her calf in the barn for a check-up with the vet. You don't need me to tell you mothers are very protective of their young and it might have been a different story if Dora had been in the field.'

The thought of an enraged cow lashing out at Huxley made Eve's blood run cold. Mildred was normally docile and friendly as she watched the world from beneath her russet red fringe but Eve could easily imagine the cow's protective instincts being ignited by a boisterous Labrador bouncing around her eight-month-old baby. And what made things all the more excruciating was that this wasn't the first time Huxley had escaped to the neighbouring farm. Eve had no idea how he'd managed it this time – she was sure all the doors and gates had been closed – but somehow he had evaded all her security efforts and made a bid for freedom. Warren was an understanding and good-natured neighbour but Eve was well aware he was also a farmer, with all the hard-nosed pragmatism that came with the job. Sooner or later, his patience was going to run out.

'I know,' she said. 'And I'm sorry. I've enrolled in some training classes, to try and curb his wanderlust. We start next week.'

'That might work,' Warren said, nodding. 'Although some dogs are too set in their ways to learn.'

It was a thought that had crossed Eve's mind; Huxley had come to her aged eight months, a rescue dog given up by a family who hadn't understood how much care and exercise a growing Labrador needed. Living beside a private beach had enabled Eve to give him plenty of space to run but, four months on, Huxley continued to resist her efforts to curb his desire to roam further afield. She could only hope professional training would help. 'He's bright. I just need to persuade him that home is where the heart is.'

Warren eyed Huxley, who was sniffing his own hindquarters with the air of a diner about to tuck into a gourmet meal. 'I know it's bitter but I expect you'll be wanting to hose him down before you go.'

'I don't think I've got much choice,' she said with a rueful sigh. 'There's a good chance I'll pass out at the wheel if I don't.'

The process of cleaning Huxley up would have been much quicker if he hadn't been so hellbent on biting the water squirting from the hose. Its coldness didn't seem to trouble him, nor the sharp easterly wind whistling across the yard, but he was so busy joyously snapping at the water Eve was sluicing over him that she supposed he didn't have time to get cold. It was only when the water was running clean and his brown fur was slick and sparse against his skin that his enthusiasm for the impromptu bath seemed to wane.

'Maybe that will teach you not to roll in cow poo,' Eve

told him as she rubbed him dry with the tatty old towel Warren had given her.

Another icy gust tore across the yard, making Eve glad of her thick coat and the woolly hat jammed over her blonde hair. Warren glanced speculatively at the sky, which was clothed in a purple-grey blanket so dense that the feeble March sunlight stood no chance. 'The wind is picking up. You'd best be on your way.'

Eve shivered and it was only partly due to the wintry blast. The weather forecasters had been warning the whole country of another Beast from the East cold front for days, supposedly more ferocious than the last, but Eve had been hoping Ennisfarne might escape the worst of the snow, at least, if not the wind. That morning's shipping forecast had put paid to her optimism – gale force winds and Siberian temperatures were imminent, predicted to last the whole weekend, and the islanders were preparing to batten down the hatches. 'Come on, Hux,' she commanded, as the dog gave himself another vigorous shake. 'Time to get you into the warm.'

Having thanked Warren again, Eve secured Huxley in the back of the old Land Rover she shared with Aiden and navigated her way along the narrow roads. She heard the roar of the waves just as the craggy limestone arch at the end of Darling Cove came into view and Eve was struck once again by the bruised, foreboding skies. The tide was already battering the base of the arch, further in than usual for the time of day, which often happened during particularly high winds, and the waves were topped by thunderous white horses galloping wildly towards the beach. To her right, a pale flash caught Eve's eye – Dune Cottage – and she risked a quick glance towards it as she passed the entrance to the little car park, reassuring herself all was well with the holiday home. Not that she expected any problems – the little white-washed cottage had withstood everything the weather could throw against it for almost two hundred years and Eve took care to make sure it was well maintained. Barring a freak accident, she felt confident her tenant would remain snug and safe within its walls. The thought brought a sardonic twist to Eve's mouth; snug was not a word she imagined anyone associated with Logan Silk. Cool, mysterious and edgy were more his style, with more than a hint of moodiness, and Eve would be the first to admit she'd actively disliked him when he had first arrived on Ennisfarne. But once she'd got to know Logan a little and, more importantly, begun to understand the reasons behind his prickly manner, much of her dislike had ebbed away. Her brother, Aiden, had playfully suggested the turnaround had a lot to do with the revelation that their tenant was a world-famous photographer and Eve couldn't deny the discovery had ignited her curiosity. But it was sympathy, after a scurrilous kiss and tell had made the headlines, which had really changed her opinion. And now she caught herself watching out for him on the beach and resisting the temptation to check in under the pretext of being his landlord, something else that hadn't escaped the notice of her brother.

'Ask him out,' he'd suggested the last time he'd spotted

Eve gazing absently out of the windows at the yellow sand. 'What's the worst that can happen?'

Eve had given him a level stare. 'Oh, I don't know – he laughs in my face?'

Aiden shook his head. 'I bet he wouldn't. He'd probably be flattered.'

It was typical of her younger brother, who Eve was certain had never suffered a moment of self-doubt in his life. 'Ha ha,' she'd replied, trying to shake an image of Logan's scornful expression. 'Firstly, he's used to dating supermodels. Secondly, he's on Ennisfarne to recover from a break-up. And lastly, also most importantly, I'm not interested.'

And Aiden had smiled in the same way that had been infuriating Eve for most of their lives. 'Of course you're not. Oh, is that him on the beach now?'

Eve had turned her head so fast she almost gave herself whiplash. 'Where?'

'The defence rests, m'lud,' her brother had said, with a grin so smug Eve had wanted to pinch him.

The memory of that exchange encouraged Eve to press a little harder on the accelerator as she passed Dune Cottage, in case her subconscious used the coming storm as a pretext to drop in. Keeping her eyes on the road, she followed the curve round to Darling's. The building hunched at the base of the cliffs, as though weighed down by the oppressive skies, its glass frontage impassive against the crashing waves further down the beach. A few brave gulls were riding the gusting wind but Eve was certain most of the wildlife would have taken shelter amid the craggy shoreline that surrounded the islands. There would be no soaring above the sea once the stronger gales and snow flurries hit.

Aiden met her at the door of the house that backed onto the bar. He glanced down at Huxley, amusement dancing in his blue eyes. 'Looks like someone had a good time. I'd pat your head, Hux, but there's a definite whiff of Eau de Poo about you.'

'Got it in one,' Eve sighed. 'I'll give him a bath but it's the kind of smell that lingers.'

'All the best perfumes do,' Aiden replied, utterly straight-faced. 'Good thing we're not going to be stuck indoors with him for the next twelve hours.'

'Don't,' Eve said, groaning. 'And speaking of being stuck indoors, we should close the storm shutters on the windows. The Shipping Forecast mentioned force nine gales.'

Her brother raised his eyebrows. 'That's the strongest we've had for a while, although the bitter temperatures sound like a bugger too. I brought a big stash of logs in from the shed so at least the fire won't burn out.'

'Thanks,' Eve said gratefully, even as her thoughts strayed to Logan once again. Would he have known to stock up on fuel in case the power went down? The undersea pipes that supplied Ennisfarne were usually reliable but if there was a problem on the mainland ... Perhaps she would send a quick message before the weather started to deteriorate, to set her mind at rest.

'No bother,' Aiden said. 'Why don't I sort out the shutters while you're bathing Mr Stinky?'

'My favourite job,' Eve said, with a long-suffering look at Huxley. 'Come on, then. Let's get this over with.'

It could have been worse, she reflected as blobs of brown-tinged soap suds dripped from the Labrador – she could be doing this in the same bath she had to use. It wasn't the first time she was grateful for the wet room at the back of the house she and Aiden had inherited from their father. Until Huxley's arrival, it had mostly been used after she'd been scuba diving among the wrecks that proliferated the waters around Ennisfarne, or when her brother had taken his surfboard out. Now it seemed to be Huxley's private bathroom but Eve didn't mind. At the very least it saved sand and seaweed being tracked into the rest of the house.

By the time she'd towelled Huxley dry and settled him to gently steam in front of the fireplace, the daylight had dimmed dramatically. Eve stood beside the double doors that led out onto the first-floor balcony of the bar, her hands wrapped around a mug of coffee as she peered through a gap in the storm shutters to assess the conditions outside. The wind was already rattling the wood but it wasn't anywhere near the speed predicted by the Met Office. Keen to get a sense of its strength, Eve unlocked the doors and eased aside one of the shutters. The first thing she noticed when she stepped onto the wooden boards was the drop in temperature – her coffee instantly bloomed petals of steam that were snatched away by the wind and her cheeks stung with the cold. On the sand below, the tide continued its assault – the wave crests were being whipped into tendrils of spindrift that grasped greedily at the air. But beneath the tumultuous urgency of the wind and thundering sea there was a strange stillness, an odd sense of expectation that thrummed on Eve's nerves. It wasn't the calm before the storm because the conditions were anything but calm, more a certainty that something else was coming. And sure enough, as Eve stood there with the chill nipping all the way down to her lungs, a soft white snowflake whirled past the end of her nose. She held out a hand and another flake landed on her palm, instantly melting. It was replaced by another, which met the same fate, and Eve raised her face to allow the swirling snowflakes to pepper her skin. Each delivered a tiny pinprick of ice before thawing and joining its fellows to form rivulets than ran down her cheeks, but the flurries kept coming and when Eve looked across to the sea, the arch was obscured behind a curtain of white. The crash of the waves was dampened too, even as the whistling wind grew louder. A sudden gust scoured the wooden floorboards and sent the tumbling flakes skywards. With a hurried step backwards, Eve closed the shutters and took refuge inside the bar. It looked as though this Beast from the East planned to be just as ferocious as its predecessor.

'And so it begins,' Aiden said, his tone matter of fact, when Eve made her way downstairs and into the kitchen. He was standing next to the window above the sink, watching the snow being driven hard across the yard by the wind. 'Think it's going to settle?'

Eve recalled the dense grey clouds looming above the cliffs, so laden with moisture, and nodded. 'It's certainly cold enough. We're in for a lot of snow, some of it is bound to stick.'

'Maybe we'll finally have time for that game of Battleships you've been avoiding,' Aiden replied, grinning mischievously.

'Maybe,' Eve said, laughing. 'Although I'm sure there's a boxset or two we could binge.'

Her brother cocked his head in playful challenge. 'You just don't want to lose.'

Which was true, Eve had to concede. There had always been a competitive edge to her relationship with Aiden and although it had subsided significantly as they'd grown up, there were times when it still showed. It didn't help that Aiden was an unbearable winner – magnanimity was definitely not his strong suit. Most of the time Eve smiled and let him have his moment but that might prove more difficult if the weather meant she couldn't escape for a stroll on the beach. At least he didn't cheat the way he had when they were younger. 'I don't mind losing.'

'I'm going to remind you of that when I sink your battleship,' he said, looking far too enthusiastic at the prospect.

'Bring it on,' Eve said with a grimace. 'Nothing helps me through a storm like scuttling a fleet.'

A faint shiver travelled down her spine as she spoke. The ocean floor around Ennisfarne had more than its fair share of shipwrecks already, some centuries old, but it had thankfully been a long time since a large vessel had foundered anywhere nearby. The lifeboat service was still a vital service; both Eve and Aidan had volunteered with the Seahouses crew in the past and had friends manning the boathouse. She sent out a silent prayer to the sea, asking that the lifeboats wouldn't be called out over the weekend. The only safe place in a storm like this was inside.

As if reading her mind, a blast of hailstones rattled against the kitchen window. At Eve's feet, Huxley let out a soft whine and looked up at her. 'You're right, boy,' she said, reaching down to ruffle his now mercifully clean ears. 'It's time to stoke the fire. Whatever the Beast has to throw at us, we won't be cold.'

Chapter Ten

Logan

Logan Silk had seen worse storms than the one currently battering Ennisfarne but there hadn't been many. He'd once been caught in Nova Scotia during a blizzard that had delivered a side order of thundersnow and caused him to spend an unscheduled two days snowed in with the infamous rock band XXX. Although since it had yielded a series of brilliantly relaxed, natural photos of the band members that had thrilled the magazine Logan had been working for, it hadn't been much of a problem and he still met up with the lead singer for drinks every now and then. And then there'd been a typhoon in Manila that had sent thousands of people, Logan included, hurrying to storm shelters to wait out the weather. That had been considerably less enjoyable than the blizzard. He was sure he'd be safe enough inside Dune Cottage – he had food and plenty of books to read, a boxset if he got really bored – but the creak of the old stonework as it withstood the howling wind and hail being dashed against the windows was enough to tug at some primal instinct for danger. When Logan looked outside, the marram grass that topped the sand dunes was horizontal against the sand, flattened by the force of the gale and weighed down by snow. He'd wondered whether any would settle so close to the sea but while there was a much thicker layer of white covering the ground behind the cottage, piling in drifts against his Hilux and the stone wall beside the narrow road, he could also see a decent amount topping the dunes. It was a good thing he'd stocked up on food – it was entirely possible he'd be snowed in again, with no outrageous rock stars to entertain him this time.

He was engrossed in a book about the turbulent history of the Farne Islands when the table lamp at his elbow went off, plunging the living room into sudden gloom. The music Logan had been playing to soften the noise of the storm abruptly stopped too, causing him to frown and check his phone – he no longer had a wifi connection. Further investigation revealed the reason for that – he had no electricity. The storm must have caused a power cut.

It didn't take long to light some of the candles from the box he found in one of the kitchen cupboards. Their light joined the glow of the wood burner, creating flickering shadows that danced across the white walls. Being without power was inconvenient but Logan had to admit there was a charm and romance to the candlelight, especially when coupled with the raging storm outside. His Danish friends would nod approvingly and call it *hygge*, although Logan felt he probably needed more blankets and cushions, plus fancier candles, to properly achieve that vibe. And perhaps some company, although he'd come to Ennisfarne in search of solitude so he could hardly complain about being alone now. In fact, the islanders had turned out to be friendlier and kinder than he'd expected, welcoming him into their community at a time when he'd unexpectedly needed support. They looked out for each other, he'd been assured by Freda, the owner of the village shop, an observation that was underlined when the cottage landline rang shortly after the power went off.

A burst of static crackled through the receiver when he held it to his ear. 'Logan, it's Eve.'

He wasn't surprised it was his landlord – he hadn't given the cottage number to anyone so the possibilities were few. 'Hi, Eve. Everything okay?'

'Apart from the storm wiping out Netflix, you mean?' The static cleared enough for him to detect the rueful amusement in her voice. 'Yeah, we're good. I just wanted to check you're all right for food and fuel. Last time the power went down the energy company sent generators over to keep us going but obviously that's not going to happen in this weather.'

Logan glanced outside at the blanket of white swirling past the window. The sea was hidden from view but he could imagine both the causeway and the waves were unnavigable. 'No, I can appreciate that.' He looked at the pile of logs in the basket beside the wood burner. 'I should be fine for a few hours. Caffeine withdrawal might kick in at some point but I suppose I can open a bottle of wine instead, since I'm not going anywhere for a while.'

There was a silence, during which Logan wondered if the phone lines had gone down too, but then Eve spoke again. 'Thing is, the power could be down for a lot longer than a few hours. I don't imagine things will get sorted before tomorrow morning and that's if the storm dies down – have you got enough fuel to last until then?'

He visualized the almost empty bag of logs in the storage box to the side of the cottage. He'd meant to pick up another bag but hadn't managed it and perhaps naively, he hadn't anticipated there might be a power cut, which would also take out the boiler controlling the central heating and hot water. A long evening of watching the fire burn stretched ahead of him, with the accompanying soundtrack of the wind whipping around the cottage – not the most riveting Saturday night he'd ever had. But at least he had four walls and a roof to protect him, and a couple of cold meals wouldn't do him any harm. 'I'll be okay,' he told Eve stoutly. 'If it gets really cold I can put on some more layers.'

There was another pause, shorter this time. 'You could always come here. We've got an Aga, there's a stew bubbling inside it now, and the kitchen is really cosy. There's coffee too. And just one or two bottles of wine, of course.'

Logan's mouth watered at the mention of stew but he didn't want to impose on Eve's hospitality, least of all because they'd had a bumpy start to their relationship as tenant and landlord. He strongly suspected she was only offering out of neighbourly duty and the last thing she wanted was for him to say yes. 'That's very kind of you but I have everything I need here.'

Eve snorted. 'It's not kindness, it's self-preservation. Aiden has already beaten me at Battleships and is suggesting Twister next. You'd be doing me a favour.'

The thought of practical, no-nonsense Eve trying to contort herself to satisfy the physically impossible demands of the Twister needle made Logan smile. 'Does he play poker? I've played a few times, I could challenge him to a hand or two.'

'Anything,' Eve replied, sounding grateful. 'Although I can't promise Huxley won't try to eat the cards.'

Logan grimaced. He and Huxley had an even bumpier history; the dog had knocked him over on their first meeting, sending Logan and his expensive camera tumbling to the sand. But they'd met since then and Huxley had been a little less boisterous with his hello. 'How is he coping with being stuck indoors?'

She laughed. 'Oh, he's mostly been sleeping off his morning's adventures. But he's been out briefly this afternoon and came over all puppyish in the snow.'

Once again, the image created by Eve's words made Logan smile. 'I bet. I'm surprised by how much it's settled.'

'I think there's more to come, according to the shipping forecast,' Eve said. 'Do you have snow tyres on your car?'

He pictured the second-hand Hilux, which he'd bought especially for his extended stay on Ennisfarne, and frowned.

'I'd be extremely surprised if I do. Apart from anything else, I wasn't expecting to need them.'

'No problem. We've got an old Land Rover with tyres that can cope with anything. It's probably best if I come and pick you up.'

'I can't ask you to take a risk like that.' The words were out before Logan could stop them and he knew from the huff on the other end of the phone that he'd managed to annoy her.

'The *risk* would be you getting into a vehicle without the right tyres and driving on a road you don't know in a blizzard,' Eve replied in a clipped tone. 'And if you did have an accident, I'd have to come out and rescue you anyway.'

It was a fair point, Logan thought, and wondered yet again what it was about Eve Darling that made him constantly underestimate her. She was small in stature — most of the models he worked with would dwarf her — but she more than made up for it in capability, tenacity and practical skill.

'So I'll come and get you,' Eve went on, then paused. 'Unless you really don't trust my driving.'

That was when Logan realized he'd backed himself into a corner. Doubtless he would be perfectly fine at Dune Cottage; the storm would blow itself out eventually, the energy company would be able to reach Ennisfarne with emergency generators if they couldn't restore power sooner and he wasn't about to starve or succumb to hypothermia. But if he said no now, it would look very much as though he didn't trust Eve's driving and he'd managed to come across as sexist once already, when she had come round to fix the tap; he didn't need to reinforce that reputation. And besides, he had to admit the picture Eve had painted was inviting: a cosy kitchen scented by delicious cooking smells and filled with the promise of conversation and laughter. Logan was sure his Danish friends would tell him that was more *hyggelig* than spending the night shivering on his own.

'I've got a bottle of Argentinian red and a deck of cards,' he said. 'Anything else I need to bring?'

'Your wallet,' Eve said, without missing a beat. 'I play poker too.'

A blast of warmth and the rich smell of the stew enveloped Logan like a hug as soon as he stepped into the small, dimly lit kitchen. He stood in the doorway for a moment, taking in the scene; the source of both the heat and the cooking aroma was a cherry-red Aga that dominated one wall of the room. Silver lanterns stood on the worktop to either side, sending a golden glow across the room to mingle with that from the candles on the ancient-looking oak table in the centre of the room. Aiden was sitting there, a freshly started jigsaw puzzle in front of him. He raised a hand in greeting just as Huxley came hurrying over to Logan, his tail sweeping back and forth with unbridled enthusiasm.

'Down, boy,' Eve commanded in a stern voice that the Labrador completely ignored. 'Huxley, get down!'

'It's okay,' Logan reassured her, ruffling the dog's ears. 'I left my camera at the cottage.'

It wasn't true – his favourite Nikon was safely cocooned

in the hastily stuffed rucksack on his shoulder, along with a toothbrush and a change of clothes, in case the weather allowed him the opportunity to photograph the cove's arch in the storm. He'd never been the kind of photographer who chased extreme weather, seeking to capture the fury of the elements, but that didn't mean he'd ignore the chance if it presented itself.

'He has to learn some manners,' Eve said, glaring at Huxley. 'Those obedience classes can't come soon enough.'

The dog licked Logan's hand and gazed up at him with laughing brown eyes, apparently unconcerned at his owner's disapproval, and Logan recalled Freda telling him it was hard to hold a grudge where Huxley was concerned. 'He's still young, isn't he?'

'That's what I keep telling her,' Aiden put in mildly. 'He's only just turned one – still a puppy in a lot of ways.'

Eve folded her arms. 'A puppy who weighs thirty-five kilograms and doesn't know his own strength. Not an ideal combination.'

Logan could certainly vouch for that. 'I'm sure he'll learn.'

'He'd better,' Eve said, letting out an affectionate sigh. 'But at least you're still on your feet. Shall I show you to the spare room so you can drop your bag? It's not quite as cosy as in here, I'm afraid.'

The difference in temperature once they left the kitchen was noticeable. Eve waved a hand at a closed door off the hallway as they approached the stairs. 'There's a fire lit in the living room so we're not limited to the kitchen but upstairs depends on the central heating for warmth.' She glanced sideways at Logan. 'I hope you brought warm pyjamas.'

He couldn't tell if she was joking. Did anyone under sixty actually own pyjamas? He usually slept naked. 'Of course,' he said gravely. 'Sheepskin slippers too.'

She nodded. 'Keep those away from Huxley. He loves a slipper, the fluffier the better.'

Perhaps she had been serious, Logan thought, and wondered why he'd ever doubted it. Eve was practicality personified – of course she'd have the right clothes to stay warm. 'I'll leave mine upstairs.'

The spare room was small and, it had to be said, quite cold. But there was a thick duvet on the single bed and a sunny yellow blanket that looked big enough to cover Logan twice over. If the wind kept up its howling he was going to need it, he thought, eyeing the impenetrable whiteness outside the window.

'I realize it's probably not quite what you're used to,' Eve said, a delicate flush creeping up her cheeks. 'There's definitely no en suite.'

It was true that he'd stayed in some of the world's most prestigious hotels but Logan had also once camped in the heart of the Australian Bush for three days to capture the gloriously changeable colours of Uluru at different times, and spent a cold and lonely night in a tent on the very edge of the Arctic Circle in search of the aurora borealis. Compared to those trips, a single bed with pillows and a duvet was luxury. 'It suits me perfectly,' he told Eve, lowering his rucksack.

'And thank you for coming to collect me. I'm sure I would have ended up in the hedge if I'd tried to drive.'

He thought she looked pleased but it wasn't false praise. The journey had been short but treacherous, with poor visibility amid the swirling snow, and even the chunky tyres of the Land Rover had struggled for grip. Eve had handled it like a pro, however, steering the vehicle expertly along the narrow road. 'No problem,' she said. 'Now, let me show you where the bathroom is and then we can get back to the warmth of the kitchen.'

Almost on cue, Logan's stomach rumbled. 'Sorry,' he said. 'Your stew smells so delicious and I've lost track of when I last ate.'

Eve nodded as she led him back along the landing. 'It's weird when there's a storm – time seems to stand still.' She pushed back a door to reveal a spacious white bathroom. 'But I can't take the credit for the stew – I can cook if I need to but Aiden's the real chef. I'm comfortable with a monkey wrench but not at all creative.'

In Logan's view everyone was born with creativity inbuilt – it simply got buried as they grew up – but he didn't argue the point. 'I'm looking forward to tucking in, whoever made it.'

'Then let's not waste any more time staring at the bathroom,' Eve replied, making for the stairs. 'With a bit of luck Aiden remembered to add the dumplings.'

He had and the resulting meal, served with creamy mashed potato and warm crusty bread, was so satisfying that

Logan knew he'd remember it with fondness for a long time. Aiden made him laugh with stories about growing up on Ennisfarne, his wilder recollections tempered occasionally by Eve, and Logan enjoyed the opportunity to observe the relationship between them. Eve was firmly set in her role as big sister and it was clear she did a lot to make Aiden's life easier, while he sat back and let her. But the affection between them was obvious, even as they bickered.

'Have you always lived on Ennisfarne?' he asked Eve, during a brief lull in the conversation.

She nodded. 'We're Farne Islanders through and through, born and bred here.'

Logan tried to imagine spending his whole life in the place he'd grown up – a small, unremarkable town in Hampshire – and failed. 'But you've travelled, right?'

'We went to secondary school on the mainland, in Berwick-upon-Tweed,' she replied. 'The tides mean all the island kids have to board during the week once they're old enough. And obviously I go to Berwick or Newcastle pretty often now, and to places like the Lake District for holidays. But I've never been tempted to live anywhere else.'

'You've never left the UK?' Logan asked, trying to disguise his incredulity.

She crossed her arms. 'I'm perfectly happy – Ennisfarne has everything I need so why would I go anywhere else?'

'But there's so much to see,' Logan protested. 'Travel opens your eyes. It—'

'Broadens your horizons?' Eve cut in, raising her eyebrows.

Aiden was watching the conversation as though he was spectating the final at Wimbledon. He didn't interject, however, leaving Logan to tip his head in acknowledgement of Eve's point. 'Okay, it's a cliché but only because it's true. There's something extraordinary about experiencing new places and different cultures, seeing how other people live. It makes you feel alien and small, while somehow expanding your understanding of the world and your place in it at the same time.'

She held up her hands, blue eyes flashing. 'I get it – you like to travel. I've just never felt the urge.'

There was a faint warning note in Eve's voice but Logan still couldn't help regarding her as though she had said something entirely incomprehensible. 'You've never wanted to watch the sun set behind the Pyramids? See the Northern Lights dancing across a Nordic sky? Dive in the Great Barrier Reef?'

Eve hesitated, toying with her wine glass. 'Of course those things sound wonderfully tempting. But they're brief moments in time – highlights, I suppose, rather than real life. I guess what I'm saying is I've never wanted more than Ennisfarne had to offer.'

'Then you're very lucky,' Logan said, after a moment's silent consideration. 'I don't think I've ever known contentment like that.'

There was a pause, during which Eve's gaze rested on Logan and something passed between them – a flicker of understanding, perhaps – and then Aiden spoke. 'I couldn't wait to leave,' he said cheerfully. 'But the old place dragged me back and now Eve keeps me chained to the bar so I can't run away again.'

The outrageous accusation eased the tension on Eve's face. 'I do not. You know perfectly well you're free to go whenever you want to.'

Aiden winked at Logan. 'She says that but she'd be lost without me.'

A snort of derision escaped Eve. 'It's the other way round. And you're just not organized enough to get past the day-dreaming stage.'

'Fair point,' Aiden said, with an unconcerned shrug. 'That's why I need you to come with me, so you can take care of the planning.'

'Exactly. I do enough of that here, thanks.' She glanced at Logan. 'It's a long way from the Great Barrier Reef but there's no shortage of wrecks around the Farnes if you've a hankering to dive. Assuming you're a good enough diver.'

'I used to do underwater photography but it's been a long time since I did any proper diving,' Logan said, shaking his head. 'I bet I've forgotten what to do.'

'Eve's a qualified instructor,' Aiden said. 'She'd be able to sort out a refresher course for you.'

Her eyebrows shot up as she looked first at her brother, then at Logan. 'In theory, yes. But it would depend on how experienced you were to start with, when you wanted to do it and—' she hesitated then ploughed on. 'Well, you might prefer someone else. I could recommend another instructor if you'd rather.'

It took Logan a moment to work out the reason for her hesitation – either she assumed he would doubt her competence or she didn't want the hassle of teaching him. He wasn't sure which was worse. 'I'm not sure I'll have time,' he said, diplomatically dodging the issue. 'But I should have known you'd be drawn to shipwrecks, with a surname like yours. Are you related to Grace Darling?'

Eve nodded. 'An aunt, going back several generations, obviously. She died young, of tuberculosis, without any direct descendants of her own. It was quite tragic.'

Not long after arriving on Ennisfarne, Logan's curiosity had been piqued by a faint memory of a Victorian heroine with the same surname as Aiden and Eve. A quick google had fleshed out his hazy recollection of a death-defying sea rescue; Grace had become a national sensation in 1838 after risking her life to save survivors of a terrible shipwreck in stormy seas near one of the smaller Farne Islands. It wasn't a huge leap for Logan to assume there could be a link between Darling Cove and Grace herself, and Eve's confirmation that he'd been right made her attachment to Ennisfarne easier to understand – her roots on these islands must run deep.

'It must be wonderful to have such an illustrious ancestor,' he observed. 'Children learn about her bravery in school, don't they?'

'They do in the local schools, at least,' Eve replied. 'She's buried in the graveyard of St Aidan's Church in Bamburgh and there's a museum dedicated to her as well.'

Aiden leaned forwards. 'She got all kinds of attention once people found out about the rescue. She was a proper celebrity – artists turned up at Longstone Lighthouse, demanding to paint her. Wordsworth wrote a poem about her and Queen Victoria gave her fifty pounds.'

'There were quite a few marriage proposals too,' Eve added, shaking her head. 'Not that she accepted any of them – she was far too canny for that.'

Logan tried to imagine how bewildering it must have been for Grace, being catapulted into stardom without even seeking it. 'Glory hunters?' he suggested.

'Fortune hunters, more like,' Aiden answered. 'Fame brought a decent wedge of cash with it. Grace suddenly found herself quite the catch.'

'Obviously things were different back then,' Eve said. 'Women had fewer options in life. But what sort of idiot proposes to someone they've never met, on the strength of a newspaper story? It makes me admire Grace all the more, knowing she refused to entertain such shenanigans.'

Logan smiled. 'You don't find it romantic, then? Imagine all logic and reason being swept away in the face of someone's incredible courage, compelling you to reach out to them. Isn't that sense of connection part of what makes us human?'

She eyed him silently for a moment, a frown creasing her forehead. 'It might be romantic in a book or a movie. But in real life it's just creepy. Even by Victorian standards.'

'You'll never persuade my sensible sister to view anything

through rose-coloured glasses, Logan,' Aiden said, with an amused shake of his head. 'She never lets her heart rule her head.'

'Hey,' Eve objected, batting her brother's arm. 'That's not true – I enjoy a good love story just as much as anyone. But being expected to marry a complete stranger isn't romantic, no matter what reality TV suggests.' She shook her head as another thought occurred to her. 'And the entitlement of those men, expecting Grace to say yes! You can bet none of them were Prince Charming.'

The flash in her eyes was unmistakeable now; this was clearly a subject she was passionate about. Logan sipped his wine, trying not to notice the way the candlelight caught the gold of her hair. 'I'm not disagreeing,' he said mildly. 'But you said yourself, things were different then. It doesn't always work to view historical actions through a modern filter. And Grace didn't marry anyone, so perhaps the weight of expectation wasn't as heavy as we assume.'

'Or she simply had the strength to say no,' Eve countered. 'And was lucky enough to have a financial cushion that made it possible. I don't think many Victorian women had the same options.'

Logan couldn't argue with that, either. Not that he was inclined to – Eve put her points across well and she had a low enough opinion of him as it was. 'I'm sure you're right,' he said and raised his almost empty glass in a toast. 'Here's to strong women, past and present.'

Eve smiled and Logan thought perhaps some of the ice in

her blue eyes had thawed a little. 'Now that's something we can agree on,' she said as she touched her glass first to his and then to her brother's. 'Cheers, boys. Now, who's up for a game of poker?'

Chapter Eleven

Eve

The first thing Eve noticed when she woke up on Sunday morning was that the wind no longer sounded as though it was trying to remove the roof. The second thing she noticed was a delicate but insistent throbbing at her temples, the tell-tale sign that she might have had one glass too many the night before. She lay still for a moment, gauging the strength of both the storm and her hangover; the wind was still loudly proclaiming its presence, even if it wasn't quite as ferocious as it had been, and a too bright gleam against the curtains suggested the snow had continued to fall. The headache was nothing a brisk walk on the beach wouldn't fix but it didn't sound like that was going to be an option for some time yet. Painkillers first, she decided, followed by a decent cooked breakfast.

Swinging her feet over the side of the bed, Eve probed

her memories of the previous evening. From what she could recall, the poker game was to blame for her sore head – it had lasted much longer than anyone had expected, meaning more wine had flowed as they'd eyed each other across the kitchen table. She remembered laughing a lot; it turned out Logan's cool exterior hid a robust sense of humour. He'd been very good at poker too – there had been several hands he'd whisked out from underneath her nose – but ultimately, he hadn't quite been good enough to beat her. The recollection gave Eve a small surge of satisfaction. She'd anticipated Logan might underestimate her and it gave her a perverse pleasure to use that against him. Although she doubted he'd make the same mistake again, at least where poker was concerned.

The landing was almost as cold as Eve's bedroom. She hurried down the stairs as fast as she could, heading for the sanctuary of the kitchen. The warmth from the Aga had dissipated overnight but the room was still a much better temperature than upstairs. Huxley raised his head as she entered, his tail thumping against the stone floor.

'Morning, boy,' Eve said, opening the back door to let him out and wincing as a gust of icy air blew a flurry of snow-flakes into her face. Hurriedly, she pulled the door to, leaving a crack to observe Huxley. The sight of him frisking around the yard, snuffling happily in the snow, made her headache lessen but the wind was tugging at the door and she was glad when he finished his morning business. 'Looks like another indoor day,' she told the Labrador as she wiped the dusting of snow from his wavy brown fur. 'Sorry about that.'

In response, the dog padded across to his bed near the Aga and settled into the softness once more, closing his eyes with a huff of contentment. Eve smiled to herself; even Huxley wasn't crazy enough to hang around outside in a blizzard.

Pulling her thick dressing gown around her a little more tightly, she placed a heavy black kettle on the hob and lit the gas burner beneath it. Then she surveyed the table, which bore silent witness to their late night – wine glasses with ruby dregs glistening in the bottom, two empty bottles standing sentinel beside them and the remains of some cheese and biscuits she now remembered they'd eaten mid game. The plates from the meal they'd shared were piled beside the sink. Eve cast a wistful look at the dishwasher, powerless beneath the worktop, and set about filling the sink with hot water.

She had the table clear and wiped down, and was halfway through the washing up when the kitchen door creaked open. Expecting it to be Aiden, she reached for a tea towel and waved it in his general direction. 'About time. Help me get this lot cleared up before Logan comes down, will you?'

'I'm afraid it's a bit late for that.'

The voice did not belong to Eve's brother. She turned fast, embarrassed without really understanding why, and managed an apologetic grimace. 'Sorry,' she said, dropping the tea towel onto the worktop. 'I wasn't expecting you to be up this early.'

'Nor was I,' Logan replied as he paused to ruffle Huxley's ears, then crossed the kitchen and took the tea towel. 'But the wind woke me up and then I couldn't get back to sleep, so I came in search of tea.'

Eve waved at the almost boiling kettle on the hob. 'On the way.' She eyed Logan, who was reaching for a dripping plate on the draining board. 'You really don't have to do that. You're a guest.'

Logan shook his dark head. 'A guest you kindly took in and fed during a storm. Drying the dishes is the least I can do.'

She shifted her weight from one foot to the other, uncomfortably aware it would be ungracious to press the point. And really, would it be any less awkward for him to sit at the table watching her? 'Okay,' she said, after a few seconds of internal tussling. 'Thank you.'

Returning her attention to the washing up, Eve began to scrub at the burnt-on gravy along the sides of the casserole dish. 'Did you sleep well? I hope the storm didn't keep you awake.'

'It didn't bother me at all,' Logan replied. 'Although the wine probably helped there. But it doesn't sound quite as bad out there now.'

Eve nodded. 'No, I think things have calmed down a bit.' She glanced through the kitchen window at the snow-covered yard. 'It's still blowing a hoolie, mind. I doubt the power will be back on today if it goes on like this.'

'And no emergency generators,' Logan observed. 'Do you know how the other islanders are getting on?'

Again, Eve nodded. 'The Nook is our emergency

HQ – anyone who needs help will contact Freda and she'll muster support. But Hamish has a generator at the Fisherman's Arms, so most of the more vulnerable villagers went there yesterday.' She paused. 'I imagine there are a few sore heads this morning.'

Logan pulled a face. 'At least they weren't hustled at poker. How much did you take me for in the end?'

She pursed her lips, mentally totting up her winnings. 'I think it was a cool ten grand.'

Wincing, Logan shook his head. 'That royal flush in the last hand finished me off. It's good thing we were only playing with matchsticks.' He lifted up the casserole dish and began to dry it. 'Have you ever considered playing professionally? You've got quite the poker face.'

'Ha!' Eve said, allowing the water to drain from the sink. 'If you think I'm good, you should play George. He's the poker king of Ennisfarne, although Hettie has banned him from hustling the tourists. She says it's cruel to ruin their holidays.'

'I bet,' Logan said with a laugh, and Eve was reminded how different he looked when he smiled. And then she gave herself a mental shake, because it was quite likely Aiden would appear at any minute and the last thing she needed was for him to catch her staring at Logan like she was thirteen.

She lifted the kettle from the Aga and carried it to the table. 'Anyway, we've all learned how to lose to George. If he ever goes to Vegas it will be carnage.'

Logan's mouth quirked as he sat down. 'I think I'd actually pay good money to see that happen.'

'Don't tell him that, whatever you do,' Eve warned. 'He's been trying to persuade Hettie it's the perfect honeymoon destination. She'll have your guts for garters if she finds out you encouraged him.'

'Got it,' Logan said. 'When's the big day?'

Too soon, Eve was tempted to say as she poured steaming water into the chunky brown teapot that had belonged to her father. As far as she knew, George and Hettie hadn't even considered having their ceremony anywhere but Ennisfarne and in spite of the island's long religious history, neither had been keen on a church wedding. Darling's was the obvious choice – Eve and Aiden played host to a handful of intimate weddings every year so it was no hardship, as long as the registrar could make it across the causeway to officiate. But most couples opted for the summer season, when the weather was more reliable and the beach was looking its best. The first weekend of April was an altogether different prospect and Eve was worried for several reasons, not least of which was that April was rushing towards them with terrifying haste. But of course she hadn't been able to say no when George had asked. 'It's the date Hettie's parents got wed, years back,' he'd said, fixing her with a hopeful look. 'Would mean a lot to her – to both of us – if you'd consider it.'

And Eve had known there was no possibility she could say no. George had been a confirmed bachelor for as long as she could remember and most of the islanders had assumed he'd be single for the rest of his days. After all, who would marry a set in his ways fisherman whose personal hygiene had been questionable even before he lost his sense of smell? But then something entirely unexpected had happened – George had met Hettie, a widow who had moved to Ennisfarne after her son emigrated to Australia, and an unlikely but charming friendship had developed. Somehow, Hettie saw past the unkempt grey beard and grubby yellow waterproofs to the generous and clever soul beneath. And George had blossomed under the sunshine of her attention, going as far as getting a haircut and even attempting to trim his beard, albeit with more enthusiasm than skill. Hamish had done a double-take when George had walked into the Fisherman's Arms for his first date with Hettie wearing a chunky cream jumper and a pair of fairly clean jeans – it had been the first time anyone had seen him out of his work clothes in years. Before long, they were an established couple, helped hugely by the fact that Hettie's own sense of smell had been damaged by an illness some years earlier. They were, as Freda had observed with delighted satisfaction, perfect for each other and the whole island was looking forward to the wedding.

'They're all set for early April,' Eve told Logan. 'In exactly four weeks' time, they'll be married. Everyone on the island is coming – it should be quite the party.'

He smiled and Eve realized her mistake. 'I'm sure you'd be welcome. It's just that the invitations went out before you arrived on Ennisfarne.' She nodded encouragingly. 'The more the merrier, if I know those two.'

Logan looked far from convinced. 'Will there be a stag do?'

The question conjured up a few mental images Eve couldn't get rid of fast enough. 'At the Fisherman's Arms, I believe. You'd be welcome there too, I expect, although there'll be a lot of seafaring humour.'

'But a stag do is different to a wedding,' he said. 'It's more personal, with only the groom's closest friends. I couldn't just invite myself.'

'This one won't be like that,' Eve replied firmly. 'We don't stand on ceremony here. When there's a party, everyone is invited. You could even come to Hettie's hen do if you wanted, no one would bat an eye.'

'Thanks,' Logan said, his eyebrows raised in amusement. 'Are you going?'

'To Hettie's, yes,' Eve said, stirring milk into her tea. 'Wild seahorses couldn't drag me to George's.'

He laughed. 'Fair enough. I've never been to a stag do so I can't really comment.'

'Oh.' Eve stirred her tea, pondering his words. Was it odd that a mid-thirties man hadn't been to a stag do? Surely some of his friends must be married.

'It's partly a side-effect of the job,' he said, shrugging. 'I never seemed to be in the right place when they were happening. And like I said, they're different to weddings – no one invites you to a stag do to help snag a four-page spread in *Hello*.'

There was no bitterness in his voice – his tone hadn't varied – but Eve picked up the subtext. Until Logan had arrived on Ennisfarne, she'd never really considered what it must be like to be a celebrity but she was beginning to appreciate there were considerable downsides. Being invited to a wedding simply so that your name could be dropped as a guest had to feel a little crappy. Then again, celebrity weddings were so glamorous that most people wouldn't care why they'd been invited – they'd be happy just to attend. 'Well, I can promise you George and Hettie's wedding won't be featured in *Hello*.' She paused. 'Obviously, they signed an exclusive with *Sailors Weekly*.'

Again, Logan laughed. 'Obviously.'

They sipped their tea in companionable silence for a moment. It still sometimes caught Eve by surprise that the Logan who was her tenant, living in Dune Cottage and chatting with Freda in The Nook, was the same man famous for photographing every celebrity she could think of, from Prince William to actual Prince. And here he was, sitting at her kitchen table and drinking a cup of tea she had made. It was somehow surreal and absolutely normal at the same time. 'Don't you miss it?' she asked, after observing him over the rim of her cup for a few more seconds. Logan gave her a slightly puzzled look and she hurried to explain. 'Your work – all the travel and exotic locations. I know you came here to get away for a bit but it's such a big change. You must miss the photography part, at least.'

Logan's eyes were fixed on the grainy surface of the table for so long that Eve began to worry she had offended him. 'You don't have to answer,' she said, as the silence stretched. 'I honestly wasn't being nosy.'

His gaze returned to her suddenly, as though he'd almost forgotten she was there. 'No, it's okay. I know you're not.' He puffed out his cheeks and sighed. 'I do miss it – some of it, anyway. I miss reading people's stories through the lens of the camera, capturing something the naked eye can't detect – a momentary lowering of their guard when they think I'm not looking, perhaps revealing the glint of a long-hidden secret or an emotion they don't even realize they feel. I guess most people think I just point the camera and click but there's a lot more to it than that.'

He stopped abruptly, as though he had said more than he'd intended. Eve shook her head in wonderment. 'I don't think that. I've seen some of your pictures and anyone can see the skill behind them. They're beautiful – a real testament to your talent.' She hesitated, then ploughed on. 'But if you miss photography so much, why have you stopped working? Surely not because of Suki?'

The words hung in the air and this time, Eve really did think she'd gone too far. She knew the break-up with supermodel Suki Simpson had been another part of the reason he'd come to Ennisfarne – the whole island knew, since she'd sold her story to a Sunday tabloid and brought a journalist sniffing around in search of Logan – but he hadn't exactly poured his heart out to Eve. It was really none of her business.

'No, not because of Suki,' Logan said, and suddenly looked tired. 'It just got hard. Every shoot seemed to take more effort – I had to dig deeper to find the magic. Sometimes it wouldn't come at all and I'd look at the pictures afterwards with embarrassment, waiting for someone to call me out. No one ever did but I knew.'

He ran a hand over his face. Eve waited, breathing as softly as she could.

'Then I was at New York Fashion Week, doing a shoot for a high-end magazine. The model was proficient, the location was great, the lighting was good … everything I needed was in place. In body I was there, lining up the shots and clicking the shutter.' He took a long draught of tea. 'But in spirit, I was somewhere else – don't ask me where. I just know I wasn't present. I felt … adrift.'

'You burned out,' Eve said quietly.

Logan nodded. 'As soon as I had the shots I needed, I walked off the set and told my agent to cancel everything I had coming up. I haven't worked since.'

It wasn't what Eve had expected to hear but his explanation made perfect sense. 'It sounds rough,' she said. 'Selina – my best friend – had something similar when she was in her late twenties. Eventually, she quit her high-pressure job and came back here to take over the family salt farm. She says it's the best thing she ever did.'

'Salt farm,' he repeated thoughtfully. 'Would that be the tall weird-looking thing off the coast towards the beacon?'

'That's right,' Eve said. 'The graduation tower is made from blackthorn and the salt is distilled as sea water trickles through. I'd say it's at least as temperamental as any human employer but Selina says the wood has more empathy than her last boss.'

That coaxed a smile from Logan. 'It definitely sounds like she made the right move. I would never have guessed it was a salt farm, though – it looks more like the wall of an impenetrable fortress.'

'I can see that,' Eve said, picturing the oblong structure she'd crawled across any number of times in search of leaks. 'It's a really clever design. The nuns of St Hilda used to pan the salt centuries ago, before the nunnery was destroyed, and the tradition was handed down from generation to generation. Then Selina's dad learned about the graduation towers in Germany and installed one here – the business has been growing ever since.'

Logan looked impressed. 'I'll have to track some down.'

Eve smiled. 'Most of their sales are wholesale – to restaurants and the like. But it's on sale in The Nook and I expect Selina would be happy to give you a tour, if you're interested in seeing how it works.'

Logan opened his mouth to reply but was interrupted by a blast of cold air from the door to the hallway. Aiden hurried inside, rubbing his arms vigorously. 'Bloody hell, it's like the Arctic upstairs.'

Huxley jumped up and bounded across to him. He bent to make a fuss of the dog, then glanced up at Eve. 'What's for breakfast? Please say a big greasy fry-up.'

Eve looked at Logan. 'How does that sound to you?'

'Like heaven,' Logan said. 'As long as you let me help. My egg poaching skills are pretty legendary.'

Eve tried to ignore the look of dismay on her brother's

face; he liked his eggs liberally fried in butter. 'Perfect,' she said, before he could object to the healthier option. 'Three full Northumberland breakfasts, then.'

Huxley raised his head to stare at her, letting out a gentle whine that caused Eve to grin. 'Sorry, boy. *Four* full Northumberlands coming right up.'

Chapter Twelve

Logan

By early afternoon, the storm had more or less blown itself out. The wind had lost most of its ferocity, although the occasional gust still sent snow hurtling across the windows, as though reminding everyone of its might. On the horizon, the sky had lightened from forbidding lead to dove grey, suggesting the sun hadn't stopped shining after all. The temperature was still bitterly cold but Logan didn't mind that, especially when the view was so spectacular. He stood on the balcony overlooking Darling Cove, snugly wrapped in several warm layers, and marvelled at the beauty of the snowy landscape. There was something magical about snow, Logan thought as he admired the white-speckled arch and silvery sand contrasting with the blue-green sea, a transformative power that lent a sparkling purity and freshness to everything it touched. It changed Logan, too – awakened the sense of wonder and excitement he'd felt as a child the first time it had snowed enough to change his world. And it didn't matter how many times he crunched his boots against the powdery whiteness, or reached out to gather a handful of flakes – it never got old.

'Get any good pictures?' Eve said as she stepped out to join him on the balcony. She let out a small, self-deprecating laugh. 'What am I saying? Of course you did.'

Logan touched the top of the camera hanging from his neck. 'I don't imagine I've done the scene justice but I can send you the best ones, if you like. For your website.'

Her eyes widened. 'Yes please. Although I'm not sure we can actually afford your licence fee.'

'No charge,' Logan said, holding up a hand. 'Consider it a down-payment for your hospitality.'

'I'm not going to argue,' Eve replied, sounding surprised and pleased at the same time. 'But you don't owe us anything. I've – *we've* – enjoyed having you here.'

Her words caught Logan a little by surprise. He'd noticed her attitude towards him had become less prickly, especially once she'd fleeced him at poker, and there'd been a moment that morning, when he'd shared the real reason he'd come to Ennisfarne, that he'd felt they were on exactly the same wavelength. But perhaps she was just being polite, in the same way that she'd agreed to help refresh his scuba diving qualification without actually wanting to. It was hard to tell – he found her so very difficult to read. 'Thank you for keeping me warm, fed and entertained. I learned a useful lesson too.'

'Oh?' Eve said, looking intrigued. 'What's that?'

Logan grinned. 'Next time I feel like gambling, I'll go to Vegas.'

The power was restored not long after they'd retreated back inside, announcing its arrival with a burst of illumination and beeps as various machines and devices came back to life. Not wishing to outstay his welcome, Logan turned down Eve's offer to stay another night, and her follow-up offer to drive him home. 'I can easily walk along the beach. The snow isn't thick there and it will give me the chance to take some more photographs.' He glanced out of the kitchen window to the snow drifts piled up in the yard. 'Much easier than digging out your Land Rover.'

Eve pulled a face. 'It'll probably have to be done at some point. But Huxley could do with stretching his legs – maybe we could walk part of the way with you.'

'Sure,' Logan said. 'Let me grab my bag and say thanks to Aiden.'

'Just don't invite him to join us,' she warned ruefully. 'Unless you want things to degenerate into a snowball fight within thirty seconds.'

Now that the drama of the storm had passed, Logan could appreciate another extraordinary effect of the snow – the way it dampened sound and laid a soothing tranquillity on the landscape. He'd observed the phenomena many times, in the forests of Siberia, the Canadian Rockies, New York's Central Park – in fact anywhere that experienced a significant amount of snowfall – but Ennisfarne was one of the quietest places he had ever been, there wasn't much noise to muffle. It was more than just the absence of sound, however; it felt to Logan as though he was enclosed in a bubble, part of a real-life snow globe scene shielded from the wider world. A few birds circled high above, their cries out of earshot, and even the sea seemed muted. The incoming tide was partially responsible for that – the waves were still far enough away to offer a distant rumble instead of the thunderous crash the storm had provoked – but the snow's magic seemed to calm even the untameable ocean. Logan took a long, deep breath of freezing air and released it slowly. As much as he'd enjoyed the warmth of Eve's kitchen, it was good to be outside again.

Beside him, Eve unclipped Huxley's lead and watched the Labrador tear off across the sand. The lower half of the beach, leading down to the far-off water, was its usual sea-washed bronze. In stark contrast, the upper half was buried beneath a layer of white. Patches of gold peeped through here and there where the snow had drifted, and there were several humps which Logan assumed were the boulders where he often sat to watch the sun set behind the arch. And further around the horseshoe cove, just visible against the pale grey sky, he could make out the hunched shape of Dune Cottage.

'It's not a bad view, is it?' Eve said, starting to walk. 'Not as spectacular as a lot of places you've been to, I expect, but it isn't the worst.'

'Far from it,' Logan said. 'It's glorious. I can see why you've never wanted to leave.'

She glanced sideways at him. 'Can you? Or do you secretly think I'm a right country bumpkin?'

Logan hesitated. His own wanderlust had always been so strong that he found it hard to understand how anyone could stay in the same place their whole life. But, gazing at the snow-dusted arch, absorbing the fresh stillness of the land, accompanied by the constancy of the sea, he did at least appreciate what kept Eve at Darling Cove. 'Definitely not. I admire anyone who knows exactly what they want out of life.'

Eve let out a sharp burst of laughter. 'I've got no idea what I want, apart from waking up to this view each day.' She paused, as though considering. 'A lottery win might help, so I can expand the bar and offer more to the community. A brother who doesn't leave his wetsuit in a puddle on the floor when he's finished surfing. And I'd quite like a dog who doesn't eat my socks.'

Logan didn't smile, even though he knew she was trying to be funny. Instead, he kept his gaze fixed on the cliffs at the far end of the cove, the caves at the base like black buttons on a sparkling white coat. Once again, he was struck by the differences between Eve and Suki. He remembered a drunken conversation along the same lines, back when he and Suki talked more than they'd argued; she'd wanted an apartment in Monte Carlo, more *Vogue* covers than supermodel Lauren Hutton, and an engagement ring bigger than Beyoncé's. 'I think you're out of luck with the socks,' he said.

'Probably,' Eve agreed peaceably. 'But you can't have everything. How about you – what do you want?'

He should have seen the question coming but it still caught him unprepared. A glib reply popped into his head, something that would deflect her without really answering, but he forced it down, puffing out his cheeks as he thought. 'I'd like to feel passion again,' he said, after a momentary silence. 'Not in a romantic sense, although that would be perfectly acceptable too, but in here.' He placed a hand on the centre of his chest. 'The kind that lights you up inside, makes you see the beauty in everything. I used to get it through my work but it's been a long time since I felt anything like that.'

He didn't expect her to understand but she nodded. 'That's how I feel about diving. I haven't been out for ages but there's something so exhilarating about being underwater – even seaweed is transformed into something beautiful, waving in the current.'

'I can see that,' Logan said, surprised yet again. 'Why did you stop?'

Eve shrugged, staring at the horizon. 'No time. The bar keeps me pretty busy, even in the winter, and there's always someone who needs something. Aiden says I'm not very good at saying no but I like helping people.' She sighed. 'Something had to give, anyway, and diving isn't something you can really do spontaneously.'

'Not in my experience,' Logan agreed, recalling the significant amount of planning involved in his underwater shoots. The equipment prep alone was time consuming enough and that was before sorting out boat hire and contemplating the weather or the tides. 'But it's a shame you don't get to go out any more, especially when you're working so hard. There's nothing quite like the peace you get fifteen metres down.'

Her nod was thoughtful. 'True. Maybe I need a reason – something to get me back into the water.'

Logan thought about the conversation the night before, when Aiden had volunteered his sister to help Logan himself get back to diving. Eve hadn't seemed massively enthusiastic but then he supposed that was understandable. She would want to enjoy the dive rather than hold the hand of someone who was relearning the ropes. 'I could offer you a trade,' he suggested. 'You help me do the refresher I need to do and I'll teach you some photography skills.'

Was it his imagination or did she look tempted? But seconds later, she shook her head. 'I really don't have the time right for either now,' she said, sounding genuinely regretful. 'But I can help you find a dive school on the mainland if you'd like? There's a guy called Billy who'll sort you out pretty quickly and he knows all the best wrecks too, when you're ready to go out.'

'Thanks, I'd appreciate that,' Logan said. 'And the offer stands – let me know if there's anything you'd like to know about photography.'

'I will,' she said. 'Although I'd be a terrible pupil. I wasn't lying when I said I don't have a creative bone in my body.'

Logan raised his eyebrows. 'I don't believe that.'

She smiled. 'That's kind of you but my secondary school art teacher would disagree. *Eve has plenty of enthusiasm but unfortunately no discernible talent*, I think she wrote on my report.'

Her tone was light but Logan still felt a little surge of indignant anger on her behalf. 'Wow. Teacher of the Year.'

'She wasn't wrong,' Eve said, shrugging. 'And she did teach me to accept my limitations. I'm practical, not arty. And that's okay.'

Logan scuffed the snow with one booted foot, still irritated by the unnamed teacher who had narrowed Eve's creativity. 'Maybe you just haven't found the right artistic outlet yet.'

'Maybe.' She didn't sound convinced. 'Or it might just be that some of us are destined to take wonderful photographs or paint brilliant landscapes and others are meant to make sure they hang straight on the wall.'

He opened his mouth to argue and then closed it again. There wasn't anything he could say that would change Eve's mind. The only way to unpick the damage done by her teacher's criticism would be to show her she could be creative. And perhaps that was something else he could do to repay her hospitality, something that would give her joy long after he had moved on from Ennisfarne. But it wasn't something he could achieve today; he'd have to think about ways to overcome her firm belief that her skills were purely practical. 'That is definitely a talent I lack. My flat in London would give you nightmares.' He shook his head in mock-sorrow. 'Not a single straight picture frame to be found.'

Eve tipped her head. 'There you go. We make a good team.' She stopped talking, fixing her gaze on Huxley, who was snuffling at something buried beneath the snow. When Logan looked at her, he saw she was blushing a little. 'Anyways, you'll be wanting to get on and I'm dying for a coffee. Let me know if there are any problems at the cottage, won't you?'

'Of course,' Logan said. 'Thanks again for rescuing me. You and Aiden were great company.'

'No bother at all,' Eve said. She whistled for Huxley, who completely ignored her. 'Take care, now. Mind the dunes.'

Logan nodded. 'I will. See you around, Eve.'

He walked briskly away, leaving her glaring at Huxley, and when he glanced back, he saw she was hurrying towards the disobedient Labrador. The dog stood waiting, tail wagging in greeting, until she got close and then bounded away up the beach. Logan couldn't help grinning to himself as he made for the path between the dunes. It looked like it might be a while yet before Eve would get her coffee.

It took another twenty-four hours for the snow to melt, helped on its way by a gentle but steady rain that arrived on Monday afternoon and lasted most of the day. Someone had taken the trouble to clear the road past the cottage; he'd heard the rumble of a tractor passing by early on Monday morning, and that allowed him to drive to The Nook to stock up on logs. He had stopped along the way to snap some pictures of the upturned boats along the shore, their pastel hulls dusted with icing sugar white. And since he was already out, he'd pushed on to the ruined nunnery on the north-eastern tip of the island, hoping to capture the crumbling ruins in their frosted finery. He hadn't been disappointed. The roofless sandstone walls and empty arched windows stood in austere desolation amid the snow, surrounded by half-buried tombstones, reminding Logan that the island had once been a haven for pilgrims. It was fitting that it now formed the gateway to a sanctuary of a different kind, he decided as he wandered among the tumbledown graves; the vast headland beyond the ruins was a nature reserve, with an abundance of carefully protected flora, birds and sea life. Logan hadn't gone further than the nunnery, however. Wildlife photography required time, patience and a great deal of sitting very still – he'd come back when the ground wasn't frozen solid.

And then the rain had started, raising the temperature by several degrees, and the snow was gone. On one hand, Logan was glad the storm's disruption was over but he also had to admit he missed the stark beauty of Darling Cove in its wintry coat. He'd been lucky to see it, even though it had meant imposing on Eve and Aiden.

Over the days that followed, he was careful to avoid the times when he anticipated Eve might be walking Huxley on the beach. It wasn't that he didn't want to see her, more a vague feeling that she'd earned some space. Which was nonsense when he really thought about it, but the notion persisted and he'd taken the opportunity to explore the caves at the other end of the cove. They'd proved to be a treasure trove of rock pools and dark tunnels, occasionally punctuated by fissures in the stone that allowed daylight to pour inside and illuminate the mineral-rich walls. Logan knew without looking that the images he'd caught were good but it seemed on Ennisfarne, all he had to do was point his camera and click to capture something spectacular.

He'd just finished editing the cave pictures, late on Thursday evening, when his mobile vibrated on the coffee table. Glancing at it, Logan saw it was Nick, who was the closest Logan had to a best friend. Meet-ups were rare – Nick was an actor whose career had scaled the heady heights of Hollywood and his schedule made even Logan wince – but occasionally their paths crossed professionally and both knew the other was only ever a phone call away. Somehow, their friendship had survived in spite of their busyness.

'Nick,' Logan said, swiping to accept the call. 'Good to hear from you. What's up?'

'Not much,' Nick replied, through a faint crackle of static. 'I'm in Buenos Aires, we've just finishing filming the Antarctic thriller I've been working on. How are things with you?'

Logan smiled. 'You could have done some of your scenes here last weekend. It's been pretty cold and snowy. In fact, we got snowed in.'

'We?' Nick repeated. 'Is there something I should know? I thought you were keeping a low profile after Suki's hatchet job.'

'I am,' Logan said. 'But the weather had other ideas.'

Briefly, he explained what had happened over the previous weekend. When he'd finished, Nick sounded impressed. 'So

Eve drank you under the table and beat you at poker? Sounds like my kind of woman.'

'She's far too sensible for you,' Logan said, grinning as he imagined Eve's unimpressed reaction to Nick's charm offensive.

His friend laughed. 'But maybe sensible is what I need – someone down to earth and settled. I'm tired of drama and relationships that don't last longer than a few months.'

Logan nodded to himself. A large part of the reason Nick struggled to find a long-term romantic partner was that his work took him all over the world, much like Logan's had done. And that meant he often dated women in the film business, who were often equally busy. It was a mirror image of Logan's relationship with Suki, although as far as he knew, none of Nick's ex-girlfriends had sold a mostly fabricated revenge story to a tabloid. 'Eve is certainly settled,' he said, and paused. 'I don't think I've met anyone quite like her.'

'Now I am intrigued,' Nick said, his tone teasing. 'Is she single?'

'As far as I know,' Logan answered, trying to remember whether Eve had ever mentioned her relationship status. 'But like I said, she's too level-headed for the likes of us.'

'Shame,' Nick said. 'But still, I've got some downtime to come, now that filming is wrapped up, and I was going to suggest dropping by your island retreat for a few days. Maybe I could meet this paragon of good sense while I'm there.'

The sudden pleasure Logan felt at the thought of seeing his friend was tempered by something he couldn't quite define, a faint flash that came and went before he could identify what caused it. 'Sure,' he said, dismissing the rogue emotion. 'When do you want to come?'

'Is next week too soon?'

Logan mentally reviewed his sparsely populated diary. Other than the scuba diving refresher course he had booked for the coming Saturday and Sunday, he had no concrete plans. They hammered out a rough itinerary, open to change in case Nick was suddenly called away to do something else. 'Make sure you stick to the crossing times on the causeway,' Logan warned. 'You're not actually a superhero and I'm not coming to rescue you if you get stranded. That will be down to the lifeboat volunteers or the coastguard and I don't think either would be sympathetic, no matter how much you flash that famous smile.'

'Noted.'

'And leave the Lamborghini at home,' Logan went on, recalling his friend's relaxed attitude to timekeeping. 'I'd hate to see that washed away by the North Sea.'

'Helpful, thanks,' Nick said, with a smile in his voice. 'It'll be good to see you. It's been too long.'

Logan found he was smiling too. 'It has. Although I have to warn you, it's quiet here. No flashy nightclubs or Michelin starred restaurants.'

Nick laughed. 'I've just spent a month filming in Antarctica. Believe me, anywhere is going to feel lively after that. But I'll bring some whisky, just in case.'

They wrapped up the call, with promises to firm up plans

after the weekend. Replacing his phone on the table, Logan made a mental note to ask Eve about the best place for Nick to stay – Dune Cottage wasn't big enough to share. He found his spirits were lifted at the thought of seeing Nick and showing him around Ennisfarne. Logan wasn't sure what the islanders would make of having a movie star in their midst but there was one thing he did know – they'd make Nick as welcome as they'd made him. He reached for his laptop once more, still smiling at the thought of Freda's face when Nick walked into The Nook. Next week was suddenly looking a whole lot more interesting.

Chapter Thirteen

Eve

It was amazing what a bag of cocktails sausages could do. Eve looked at Huxley, whose gaze was fixed on her as though she was the only person in existence, and shook her head in wonderment. Why hadn't she thought of using sausages as bribery before? They were much more effective than any shop-bought treat she'd tried.

It had taken the dog trainer less than a minute to point out Eve's mistake. 'You want something tastier than that,' she'd said, casting an unfavourable look at the yellow bag of dried dog treats. 'You need something he doesn't get every day.'

She trotted over to her van, parked at the edge of the field where the training session was held, and returned with a small freezer bag filled with chopped up sausage. 'Here,' she said, thrusting it at Eve. 'Try this.'

The transformation in Huxley had been instant. His nose

had quivered and his ears had cocked as he stared at the bag. 'Now you've got his attention,' the trainer said in satisfaction. 'Let's see if you can get him to walk on the lead without wrenching your arm from its socket.'

It was definitely a work in progress, Eve thought as they half walked, half jerked around the field. Her only consolation was that some of the other owners were clearly struggling too. There was a bulldog called Frank who refused to walk at all, a West Highland terrier who seemed to have springs instead of paws, and a beautiful fox-red Cocker Spaniel puppy called Molly who joyfully scampered in circles around her owner's wheelchair and tangled the long lead around his wheels. Huxley was particularly keen to play with her and it took at least half the bag of sausages to distract him. But then they moved on to the sit command, which Huxley could do, and from there to stay, and Eve felt a tiny bit better. Huxley might be one of the oldest dogs there but he did seem to be learning.

'You're doing great,' Selina called from the sidelines, where she'd been observing the class. 'Well done, Huxley!'

The Labrador's head jerked around at the sound of his name and he lurched sideways towards Selina, hauling Eve with him.

'Sorry,' Selina said, as Eve tried to free a morsel of sausage from the little bag. 'You're going to need more than a coffee after this.'

Gritting her teeth, Eve concentrated on regaining Huxley's attention. The plan had been to find a nice café in nearby Morpeth after the class, and perhaps even a slice of cake, but Selina was right – the way things were going, Eve was going to be in sore need of a beer garden.

'Well done, everyone,' the trainer called. 'Now let's practise our recall off the lead. If you're afraid your dog won't come back, we can use a long line. The main thing is to sound excited so they ignore all the other dogs and come back to you.'

At least there were no cow pats, Eve thought as she watched a German Shepherd called Zeus zoom across the grass to his owner. Molly did beautifully too, although she stopped to eat a dandelion clock along the way. Frank refused to budge, even when tempted by a sausage, and Bonnie the Westie bounced straight past her owner to pounce on Molly.

'Now, who do we have left?' the trainer asked, gazing around the small circle of dogs and owners. 'Ah, Huxley. Let's see how you do.'

Eve dutifully brought him over. 'Will he come if you call him?' the trainer asked.

'Yes,' Eve replied. 'Probably.'

'We'll use the long line, just to be safe,' the trainer said, attaching the yellow nylon lead to Huxley's collar. With some trepidation, Eve left her dog standing beside the woman and hurried away, making for the canal path at the far side of the field. She stopped and turned to see Huxley straining on the lead, with the trainer holding him firmly in front of her.

'Now call him,' the trainer shouted. 'Lots of excitement and enthusiasm.'

Eve took a deep breath. 'Huxley!' she bellowed as brightly as she could. 'Here, boy! Here, Huxley!'

The trainer let go of the lead and the dog leapt forwards, tearing towards Eve with his ears streaming behind him and his tongue lolling from one side of his mouth.

'Come on, boy!' Eve called, holding out her arms. 'That's it, come to me.'

Except that he didn't seem to be slowing down. For a split second, she thought he would barrel straight into her, knocking her into the air the way he had Logan on their first meeting. But at the last moment, the dog switched course and bounded past her. The long line yanked from the trainer's hands to bump along the ground after Huxley. Eve spun around in consternation and waved the almost empty freezer bag helplessly. 'Huxley! Get back here!'

He paid absolutely no attention and, with a sinking feeling, Eve realized what had caught his eye: the canal. She should have known, she thought, breaking into a run. If there was one thing Huxley loved more than cow poo, it was water.

She could only watch as he leapt majestically from the bank, sailing through the air with all four legs splayed in unbridled anticipation of the joy that was to come, and hit the water with an almighty splash. Several ducks took flight with loud, indignant quacks. Puffing, Eve arrived at the canal edge, to see him paddling in pursuit of a grey and black goose. 'Huxley,' she groaned, feeling a hot tide of embarrassment flood her face. 'Come here, you absolute nightmare.'

But he was having far too much fun to pay attention to

anything Eve might say. It took the combined efforts of Selina, the trainer and Eve to eventually tempt the dog out of the water.

'I'm so sorry,' Eve said to both women, as Huxley shook himself vigorously, spraying canal water everywhere. 'He just loves swimming.'

'He's a gun dog,' the trainer replied, coiling the soggy nylon lead. 'They often love a dip. But next time, we'll send you to the other side of the field, away from temptation.'

'Looking on the bright side, at least you won't have to give him any lunch,' Selina said, laughter dancing in her eyes as they walked back to the Land Rover.

Eve couldn't argue with that – it had taken another full bag of sausages to persuade Huxley to abandon his game of tag with the canal's bird population. 'I'm so embarrassed. Everyone was laughing – there's no way we can come back next week.'

Selina grinned. 'I think they were all sympathetic, to be honest, and grateful it wasn't them. In fact, you've probably made them all appreciate their dogs a little bit more.'

Eve glared down at Huxley, who was trotting at her side as though he wasn't dripping canal water and pond weed. 'You're a bad dog.'

'He's a character,' Selina corrected. 'Would you rather he was like Frank and didn't move at all?'

'Yes,' Eve said, although she didn't mean it.

'He'll learn,' Selina said and linked her arm through Eve's. 'Come on. I'll buy you brunch to make up for the trauma.'

They stopped at the Land Rover to rub Huxley down

using an old blanket and then walked into Morpeth town centre in search of a café with an outside seating area. It was only once Eve was presented with a large coffee and a stack of waffles that her mood began to improve. She listened as Selina described the repairs at the salt farm following the storm – some of the blackthorn filtration system had been damaged by the wind and needed to be replaced, but the worst of the issues had stemmed from the freezing temperatures. The snow had caused a number of wooden taps to swell and warp as they froze, which meant split tap heads and leaks. 'Jakob will be able to replace them,' she said, referring to Ennisfarne's resident boatbuilder. 'But they have to be hand-crafted and that takes time. Production is going to be affected for the next few weeks.'

'Are you going to be able to fulfil your orders?' Eve asked, chasing some banana and maple syrup around her plate.

'Hopefully, we've got enough stock to cover everything. As long as there's no sudden hike in demand.' Selina paused to sip her coffee. 'I ran into our resident celebrity yesterday, at The Nook.'

'Logan?'

Selina nodded. 'He asked about a tour of the salt farm, said you'd been describing how the process works.'

'It came up in conversation during the storm,' Eve explained.

Her best friend blinked. 'Did you run out of things to talk about? I mean, obviously I'm passionate about salt but it's a far cry from the glamour of the fashion industry, isn't it?'

Eve chewed a mouthful of waffle, remembering the laughter and conversation that had flowed throughout Logan's impromptu stay. 'No, we had plenty to talk about.' She considered his description of the graduation tower as a fortress, which had made her view the structure with fresh eyes. 'But he sees things in an interesting way. I suppose that's what makes him so good at his job.'

'I'm quite happy to show him around,' Selina said, shrugging. 'And if he wants to buy me a drink afterwards, to say thank you, I wouldn't mind that, either.'

The words caused a niggle of uneasiness to worm through Eve and she took a moment to examine the feeling. It wasn't that she couldn't see Logan's appeal – quite a few of the island's residents would jump at the opportunity to spend time with him – but she was also aware that he was only on Ennisfarne for another two months. Getting to know him and becoming friends was one thing, pursuing a romantic agenda was another, and Eve had a shrewd idea where her best friend's interest lay.

Her reservations must have shown on her face because Selina raised her eyebrows. 'You haven't changed your mind about him, have you? I don't want to tread on your toes if you've decided to have a crack at him.'

'No,' Eve said instantly. 'It's just – well, you said it yourself, his real life is totally different to ours. You only have to google him to see the kind of woman he usually dates.'

Selina threw her a mock-affronted look. 'Are you saying he's out of my league?'

'Of course not!' Eve took a deep breath. 'I'm saying you inhabit different worlds. And at the end of his tenancy, when his batteries are recharged, he's going to leave Ennisfarne without a backwards glance. I don't want you to get hurt when that happens.'

Her best friend studied her for several long seconds, then reached out to squeeze her hand. 'Not every man is like Michael,' she said quietly.

Instinctively, Eve opened her mouth to deny there was any connection and then closed it when she realized Selina knew her too well. And there was no doubt that her break-up with Michael was still colouring the way she viewed romantic entanglements, even two and a half years on. The end had come out of the blue – a shock announcement one evening that he didn't see a future on Ennisfarne – and had left Eve reeling. He hadn't tried to convince her to go with him, had simply explained that he'd taken a job in Glasgow and would be leaving the following week. 'I know you love it here,' he'd said, refusing to meet her stricken gaze. 'But it's not enough for me. There's more to life than a quiz night at the Fisherman's, with the same faces week in, week out.'

'But you could come back for weekends,' she'd argued, struggling to believe he could have had such a seismic change of heart. 'I could come to visit.'

He'd picked awkwardly at a jagged fingernail. 'The thing is, I want someone who isn't afraid to dream big and reach for the stars.' He had looked at her then and she'd known there was no hope. 'And that someone isn't you.'

She hadn't begged, at least. It had taken every bit of self-control she could muster but she managed to wish him well through her tears, even as she wondered what she'd done wrong. Once Selina stopped cursing him, she had tried to reassure Eve the problem was Michael, not her.

'Any man who uses *reaching for the stars* as the reason to end a four-year relationship has got issues,' she'd growled but it hadn't made Eve feel any better. She'd thought their dreams had been the same – building a life together on Ennisfarne and perhaps, in time, starting a family of their own. But it turned out those had just been her dreams. Slowly, she'd picked herself up and tried to avoid running into his mother in the village. She hadn't heard from Michael since.

Sighing, Eve fixed Selina with a wary look. 'I know. But my point still stands. You'd have to be crazy to start something with Logan when there's no chance of him sticking around.'

Her best friend raised her chin. 'Who says I want him to? Maybe I'm in the market for something short and sweet, with no strings.' She lifted one hand, ready to tick items off on her fingers. 'One, he's good-looking. Two, he's single. Three, we're both adults and four, I think it would be fun.'

They were all fair observations, Eve realized. Selina had never been governed by the same caution that ruled Eve, in love or anything else. She held up her hands in surrender. 'In that case, be my guest.'

'Really?' Selina said, giving her a searching look.

Eve summoned up a smile, pushing her reservations to the back of her mind. 'Really.'

'Good.' Selina drained her coffee. 'It's about time someone showed him there's more to Ennisfarne than peace and quiet and a gorgeous beach.'

Eve nodded, even though she was fairly sure Logan had discovered that already. 'Absolutely,' she said, recognizing the determined gleam in her friend's eye. 'Go for it.'

The conversation moved on to the preparations for George's wedding but Eve was only half listening. She pushed the last of her waffle around her plate in absent-minded distraction, replaying the previous exchange in her head. When Selina set her sights on something, she went all out to get it and, as she had so convincingly explained, there was nothing to stop her getting to know Logan better. So why did Eve suddenly feel as though a stone had settled in the pit of her stomach?

Chapter Fourteen

Logan

When Logan pulled into the car park beside the Fisherman's Arms on Thursday, there was no sign of a supercar. Instead, there was a top of the range Audi, spattered with droplets of sea water from the journey across the causeway that shimmered in the midday sunshine. There was no sign of its driver but Logan knew without a doubt who it belonged to: in typical Nick Borrowdale style, his best friend had made it across the causeway with minutes to spare.

He found Nick at the bar, talking to a dazed-looking Hamish. No need to ask whether he'd recognized his latest customer, Logan thought, suppressing a smile. It wasn't that Nick threw his reputation around – he often used an assumed name when he wanted to travel under the radar – but his face was regularly plastered across the sides of buses or advertising hoardings, which made him almost instantly recognizable.

Even if that hadn't been the case, like a lot of celebrities he gave off a certain aura that drew the eye without him even trying. It was partly what made him so easy to photograph, Logan reflected as he crossed the pub. And definitely what was causing the three or four regulars dotted around the bar to stare.

'Is he giving you trouble, Hamish?' Logan called, crossing the dark wood floor. 'He really doesn't need gold taps in the bathroom, no matter what he claims.'

Nick turned around, his dark eyes crinkling with warmth as he surveyed Logan. 'I wasn't demanding gold taps, actually,' he said mildly. 'We were just discussing what colour M&Ms I wanted, if you must know.'

Laughing, Logan pulled his best friend into a hug. 'It's good to see you. How was the journey?'

'Mostly smooth,' Nick replied, then arched one eyebrow. 'But you weren't kidding about the incoming tide – it felt like I was being chased across the causeway by a vengeful sea god.'

Logan shook his head wryly. 'That's because you almost left it too late. When I said you needed to get to the coast before twelve, it wasn't supposed to be a challenge to see how fine you could cut it.'

Nick shrugged with good-natured acceptance. 'I made it, didn't I?'

Behind the bar, Hamish cleared his throat and pushed a heavy iron key across the wood. 'Room Three, at the top of the stairs,' he said, in an abashed tone that was a far cry from his usual bonhomie. 'It's the best room I've got, with a nice view of the harbour.'

'Perfect,' Nick said, taking the key and glancing at Logan. 'I'll drop my bag off and you can give me the grand tour.'

To Freda's credit, she didn't so much as blink when Nick walked into The Nook. She greeted Logan, nodded at Nick as though he was just another tourist, and resumed stacking the shelves but Logan wasn't fooled. The Nook was the nerve centre of the island – nothing happened on Ennisfarne that wasn't relayed to Freda – and he was certain Hamish would have reported in the very second Logan and Nick had left the pub. And sure enough, when Logan glanced over at Freda again, he saw she was peering over the top of the aisle.

Nick had noticed too, because he winked at Logan. 'Is this the famous deli counter you've been banging on about for the past month?' he said, loud enough for Freda to hear.

Instantly, she stopped what she was doing and beetled over, her eyes bright and her cheeks flushed. She slid behind the counter and beamed at both Nick and Logan. 'We aim to please,' she said, with a fluttery little giggle that almost caused Logan to lose his own composure. There was no doubt about it – Freda was every bit as starstruck as Hamish had been.

'This is my good friend, Nick,' Logan said. 'And this is Freda, who has saved me from a sad supper of Pot Noodle on many occasions.'

Freda lost a little of her reserve as she rolled her eyes. 'As if you've ever eaten a Pot Noodle.' Her gaze travelled back to Nick and Logan saw her smile widen. 'Hello, anyways. It's very nice to meet you, Nick. Although I feel like I already know you – I have to confess I am a huge fan. I loved you in that World War Two film last year, the one set on Orkney. Made me cry like a bairn but I forgive you.'

She stopped, as though aware she was gushing, and then plunged on. 'Are you here for work? Maybes scouting out a location or getting into character?'

The last question was laced with undisguised hope. Nick shook his head. 'Just a long overdue catch-up with a very good friend. He's made life on Ennisfarne sound so idyllic that I had to come and see it for myself.'

He added just enough charm to offset any disappointment his answer might cause. Freda took the bait. Her face glowed with pride. 'Oh, he's one of us now, right enough. I don't suppose there's any chance we might persuade you to settle down here too, is there?'

Logan laughed. 'He's only been here half an hour. Give me a chance to show him round first.'

'Aye, I suppose you've got a point,' she conceded. Her expression sharpened as she glanced down at the counter. 'But I daresay you'll be after some delicious snacks to keep your strength up on your travels. What can I get you?'

Twenty minutes later, they were loading Logan's Hilux with three bags of cheese, meat and wine. 'She's quite the saleswoman,' Nick observed as he climbed into the passenger seat. 'I'm amazed she didn't sell us a bridge.'

Logan grinned. 'Believe me, if she had one, she'd try. The trouble is, everything she sells is really good. I'm hooked.'

'There are worse things to be addicted to,' Nick replied.

Logan started the engine. 'It does mean we should stop by the cottage first, to stash this lot in the fridge. But any preference after that?'

Nick waved a hand. 'None whatsoever. This is your manor – lead on, Macduff, as Shakespeare never actually said.'

It felt strange to hear Nick describe Ennisfarne as his territory but Logan supposed it was, albeit temporarily. He certainly took a quiet pleasure from his friend's enthusiastic appreciation of Darling Cove when it swung into view.

'Bloody hell,' Nick said, staring at the golden sand curving round to meet the imposing limestone arch. 'That's not a view, it's an out-of-body experience.'

Logan slowed the car a little, taking in the glittering silvery sea beneath the forget-me-not sky. Waves leapt lazily around the base of the arch, sending bouquets of spray into the air before tumbling down to start all over again. It was a scene he knew he'd never tire of seeing, not if he woke up to it every day for the rest of his life. But of course that wasn't going to happen; in two months' time, he'd be leaving Ennisfarne and life would return to its old frantic pace. All the more reason to appreciate it now, Logan decided.

'You should have seen it in the snow,' he said, speeding up again. 'I've got photos I can show you but obviously it's not quite the same.'

Nick grimaced. 'Like I said, I've had enough of snow for the time being. Give me amber sands and crashing waves and a breeze that catches your breath every time.'

'I'm pretty sure I can promise you all of those things,'

Logan replied, easing the Hilux into the little car park alongside Dune Cottage. 'But before that, tea.'

Forty-five minutes later, they were exploring the devastated glory of the nunnery. 'Local legend says some of the nuns threw themselves off the cliffs to avoid the invading Vikings,' Logan said as they strolled among the roofless ruins. 'St Hilda took pity on them and turned them into seals so they wouldn't drown.'

'Very good of her,' Nick said dryly. 'I can't help thinking that an army of Godzillas might have been more practical, though.'

Logan laughed. 'Just be polite if you run into any seals. It's bad luck to displease them.'

The next stop on Logan's itinerary was the white granite beacon that stood on the headland on the other side of the island. He and Nick sprawled on the lush grass, soaking up the spring sunshine and watching gulls and guillemots drifting on the thermals overhead.

'I suppose there can't be a lighthouse on every island,' Nick said, when Logan described the beacon's purpose in warding off ships from the rocks. 'But I guess that means there are plenty of shipwrecks down there. Good for diving.'

'Funny you should say that,' Logan replied. 'Eve told me exactly the same thing so I did a scuba refresher course last weekend. I'm hoping to go exploring as soon as the weather allows.'

'Ah, the enigmatic Eve. Does she dive too?'

Logan nodded. 'She's a qualified instructor.'

'Perfect,' Nick said, looking impressed. 'She'll know all the best wrecks.'

'I expect so,' Logan said, tipping his head back to stare at the cloudless sky. 'But there are a few boats on the mainland that go out all year round, weather permitting. I'll book with one of those.'

If Nick thought there was anything odd in Logan's plan, he didn't show it. 'I look forward to seeing the pictures.'

They drove back to Dune Cottage and took the path through the dunes to Darling Cove. Nick whistled when they reached the sand, glancing up and down the horseshoe beach with an appreciative gaze. 'I can see why you're in no hurry to leave.'

Logan checked the time as they walked. 'I saved the best for last. In around thirty minutes, the sun is going to drop behind the arch. We're in for a treat this evening, I think.'

Nick turned to study him, his eyes speculative. 'You've gone native.'

'I have not,' Logan snorted.

'You have,' Nick insisted. 'You've shared several island folk stories, waxed lyrical about the wildlife and bird population, and the locals describe you as one of them. If that isn't going native, I don't know what is.'

Logan had to concede that most of Nick's observations were true. But he'd been on Ennisfarne for a month now — surely it was inevitable he'd soak up some of the history and be on friendly terms with his neighbours? 'Maybe,' he said doubtfully.

'It suits you.' Nick shook his head, eyeing him more closely. 'You've always been such a city lover that I half expected you to be like a fish out of water but you seem really comfortable. Like you're at home.'

Logan was about to argue that London was definitely still his home when a movement in the distance caught his eye. A small dark dot was speeding over the sand towards them and, as it grew nearer, he knew what it was. 'Brace yourself,' he told Nick with a grin. 'You're about to meet Huxley.'

The Labrador was as effusive as ever in his greeting, bouncing between Logan and Nick with his tail wagging so hard that he looked as though he might take off. Nick sank to his knees in delight, allowing Huxley to slobber all over him as he rubbed the dog's ears, and Logan looked up to see Eve hurrying towards them.

'I'm so sorry,' she puffed, once she was near enough for them to hear. 'The little bugger snuck out when Aiden opened the balcony doors.'

Logan glanced at Nick, who was now rubbing Huxley's tummy. 'No harm done. I assume the training is ongoing?'

Eve groaned. 'Don't even ask. But yes, as you can see, we're still working on a few things.' Her gazed rested on Nick. 'At least you're both still on your feet.'

There was a subtle hint of a question beneath the words. 'Oh, sorry. This is my friend, Nick Borrowdale – he's visiting the island for a few days. Nick, this is Eve Darling – my landlord and the owner of Darling's Bar.'

Nick stood up, brushing sand from his hands as Huxley bounded away. 'Hello. Nice to meet you at last.'

Eve looked a little taken aback. 'At last?'

'Absolutely,' Nick said, smiling. 'Logan has told me a lot about you. And everyone else, of course.'

Logan waited for the smile to have its usual effect but Eve simply nodded. 'Got you,' she said. 'You must be his only friend. He's mentioned you too.'

She wasn't wrong – Logan had once told her he considered himself to have just one true friend – but hearing it repeated back to him sounded so tragic. Nick evidently agreed because his smile had a wicked edge as he glanced at Logan. 'We all have our crosses to bear.'

'Where are you staying?' Eve asked. 'Not at the cottage, surely?'

Her cheeks grew slightly pink as she looked from Logan to Nick. 'I took your recommendation and booked him in at the Fisherman's,' Logan said. 'He'll be Hamish's problem tonight.'

Eve tilted her head. 'It's more likely to be the other way round. Hamish is so excited to have an actual movie star staying at his pub that he'll probably have installed a blue plaque by the time you get back this evening.' She pursed her lips. 'Or at the very least started charging people to come in.'

Nick laughed. 'I'm not sure he'll have many takers.'

'You must be joking,' Eve said. 'Your arrival is the most interesting thing to happen here since – well, since Logan moved in.' She turned an enquiring look his way. 'I hope you've invited Nick to the stag do on Saturday.'

Logan hesitated, mostly because he'd been planning to use Nick's visit as an excuse to avoid the party. 'Not yet, no.'

'What's this?' Nick said, looking interested. 'A stag do? Who's getting married?'

'George,' Logan said, and decided to save further description until later. 'I meant to mention it – the pub is hosting things, so there's a good chance you might be kept awake.'

'All the more reason to join in,' Nick said promptly, and glanced at Eve. 'As long as you think George won't mind.'

'Mind?' Eve shook her head in amusement. 'He'll be dining out on it for years, believe me.'

'Great,' Nick said, with obvious enthusiasm. He fixed Logan with a mock-accusatory stare. 'And you said there'd be no parties.'

'I said no nightclubs,' Logan corrected. 'So at least it won't be an all-nighter.'

Eve let out a hollow laugh. 'You've clearly never seen sailors drink.' She paused and met Logan's eyes. 'But seriously, it would mean a lot to him if you went along, even if it's just for an hour or so.'

Swallowing a philosophical sigh, Logan accepted his fate. 'I'm sure we can manage that.'

'Excellent,' Eve said, her eyes dancing. 'Now all we have to do is stop Hettie from finding out and joining you.'

*

'The thing about being a fisherman is . . . is . . . it's a lot like being an actor.'

The Fisherman's Arms was as full as Logan had ever seen it; plenty of George's friends from the island and the mainland had come to celebrate the end of his bachelor status. Seats were hard to come by but Logan and Nick were wedged around a wobbly table in the window with George in between them. The music hadn't begun but the noise levels were on the rise, fuelled by a steady flow of alcohol, and they had to lean in close to maintain a conversation. Logan was relieved to note that George had showered in honour of the party – there was only a hint of brine and fish about him.

To his credit, Nick gave George's slightly slurred comparison of fishing and acting due consideration. 'They both involve a lot of lines?' he suggested, utterly straight-faced.

Logan hid a grin as George blinked owlishly. 'S'right.' He raised an unsteady hand, waving one calloused finger in Nick's face. 'But what I mean is, we both have cruel mistresses. Mine is the sea and yours is . . .'

He trailed off, his gaze slightly unfocused as he tried to remember what he'd been about to say. 'What's yours again?'

'The fickleness of humanity,' Nick said solemnly. 'And sometimes my agent.'

George shook his head. 'No, no, no, s'not what I meant.' He swayed a little, then clumsily snapped his fingers. 'Your moos! She's just as cruel as the sea, right?'

Nick thought about that too. 'I think you've got it worse.

A muse doesn't try to drown the artist when she's having a bad day.'

'True enough,' George said, and puffed out a long beery breath that caused both Logan and Nick to shift subtly backwards. 'But we're hooked just the same. The sea might be cruel but she's the keeper of my soul.'

His last sentence was so unexpectedly poetic that Logan smiled. 'But not your heart,' he said.

That roused George from his looming introspection. 'No. That belongs to Hettie,' he said, baring surprisingly white teeth in a smile. He turned to Nick. 'Have you met her? A fine woman, she is. Knows what to do with a pollock, if you catch my drift.'

Logan took a hurried sip of his pint to hide a snort but Nick was made of sterner stuff. 'Not yet but she sounds very much like a keeper,' he said.

George gave a vigorous nod, somehow managing not to spill his beer. 'She is. 'M a lucky man.'

He lapsed into silence, clearly lost in happy thoughts of his bride-to-be. Logan took the opportunity to fire a meaningful look Nick's way. 'Didn't you want to talk to Hamish about the taps in your room?'

Nick frowned for a moment, then his brow cleared. 'I did. Would you excuse us for a minute, George?'

They eased out of their seats and Logan wove his way through the crowd to the bar. The buzz of conversation dimmed as they passed each cluster of men; Logan caught several curious looks and a number of outright stares, which he supposed was understandable, but there was no hostility or resentment that an outsider had breached their midst. Ennisfarne simply wasn't that kind of place.

'How's the stag holding up?' Hamish asked when they reached the bar. 'Started reciting "The Rime of the Ancient Mariner" yet?'

'Not so far,' Logan replied.

Hamish glanced towards the window, where George was now in conversation with Jakob. 'It won't be long. And then Jakob will counter with some Skaldic poetry. I'd better tell the lads to get the music going.'

The band for the evening was Near and Farne, who Logan had last heard play during the monthly music night at Darling's. Logan and Nick found an unoccupied corner of the bar and settled back to listen. It wasn't long before the band's infectious melodies and thumping beats had everyone nodding along, and Logan wasn't surprised when the dancing started, although George turned out to be considerably steadier on his feet than he'd expected.

'He's got some decent moves,' Nick observed, as the crowd made some space for the stag to strut his stuff.

'Apparently, he's a man of many talents,' Logan replied. 'But like most people here, he's got a heart of gold.'

Nick turned to study him. 'Why do I get the feeling you're never going to leave?'

Logan shrugged. 'I don't know. Maybe because this is the longest you've ever known me to stay in one place?'

'No, it's more than that,' Nick said thoughtfully. 'There's

something different about you here – I think it might be contentment.'

Again, Logan started to martial a denial and then stopped. The truth was he did feel contented on Ennisfarne, whether that was a result of cancelling his work and slowing down, or spending time with ordinary people and remembering the things that made up normal life. But it didn't necessarily follow that he was planning to stay. His intention had always been to go back to London when his three months were up and that hadn't changed.

'I like it here,' he acknowledged. 'There's something about it that soothes my soul and calms me down. Maybe it's the sea, or the way the light flows across the sand and over the headland or just the silence – I can't put my finger on it.'

Nick raised a questioning eyebrow, because the pub was currently a long way from being silent. 'It's probably all of those things and a bit of something else,' he said, and he took a mouthful of his pint. 'Connection.'

As soon as he said it, Logan knew he was right. Photography had taken him all over the world, allowing him the privilege of working with some incredibly talented people, but it was rare for him to form much more than a fleeting connection with anyone and it was almost always through the lens of his camera. He supposed that was why he'd subconsciously clung onto his relationship with Suki for so long, even though he'd known it wasn't good for either of them; he'd craved a more substantial connection. And although he hadn't formed anything resembling a deep bond with anyone on Ennisfarne, he saw the same people on a regular basis, knew enough about the rhythm of their lives to develop a genuine interest. That interest had been reciprocated, along with kindness and warmth and generosity, so that Logan's days had become rich with micro-connections. And it had all happened without him really noticing.

'Possibly,' he said. 'But that doesn't mean I'm never going to leave.'

'Unless you make a stronger connection,' Nick replied evenly. 'With an extremely attractive local businesswoman, for example.'

So that was what he was getting at, Logan thought wryly. 'I told you before, Eve wouldn't give the likes of you or me a second glance.'

His best friend gave him a knowing look. 'Ah, but she did give you a second glance. A third too, if I'm not mistaken.' He paused to smirk at Logan. 'You probably didn't notice because you were desperately trying not to look at *her*.'

Was Nick right, Logan wondered? Had he been trying to avoid looking at Eve? Or was his friend simply trying to win the argument? 'You're making this up.'

'Am I?' Nick said. 'I'm only telling you what I saw and that was two people pointedly *not* looking at each other.'

'Eve doesn't like me,' Logan said, his tone flat. 'She makes an effort to be friendly because she's a nice person and probably thinks I'm lonely but that's as far as it goes.'

Nick considered this for a moment. 'But you like her?'

'No!' Logan said in exasperation. 'Obviously yes, as a person, but that's all. Stop trying to turn this into a movie.'

Whatever Nick was about to say next was lost when the music came to a sudden tumultuous end. As the applause died down, George steadied himself against the nearest chair and looked around with the determined air of a man who had something to say. He raised both hands to quieten the last of the applause and took hold of the microphone. Gazing blearily around at his friends, a beatific smile crossed his face. Logan and Nick exchanged glances; any speech was likely to be long and rambling, if their previous conversation with George was anything to go by. But there was no escape – the bar was too full to allow a discreet exit. With silent resignation, Logan caught Hamish's eye and signalled two more pints. George cleared his throat and paused, then opened his mouth to speak.

'*It is an ancient Mariner,*' he proclaimed, '*and he stoppeth one of three. By thy long grey beard and glittering eye, now wherefore stopp'st thou me?*'

Beside Logan, Nick let out a barely audible groan. 'I wish thou wouldst stoppeth,' he muttered and beckoned Hamish over. 'We're going to need the best whisky you've got.'

Noticing Jakob watching George with an air of anticipation, Logan leaned across the dark wood bar. 'Better bring the bottle, Hamish. Something tells me it's going to be a long night.'

Chapter Fifteen

Eve

Eve didn't think she'd ever watched the weather with more apprehension than in the week leading up to George and Hettie's wedding. Darling's had hosted plenty of ceremonies before – small and intimate affairs because they weren't set up to accommodate hundreds of guests – but the couples tying the knot had always been strangers, at least until they'd exchanged their vows on the beach in front of the arch and danced the night away on the sand. But Hettie and George were so much more than that – they were like family, and it mattered to Eve that their day was perfect. She'd been a little surprised that they hadn't opted for a church wedding but George had been adamant he wanted to make his commitment in the presence of his other great love, and Hettie hadn't argued.

'Saves me looking like a meringue too,' she'd confided to

Eve at her hen party. 'I'm too old to play the blushing bride and besides, I've been there and done that.'

All of which meant Eve felt the weight of responsibility even more than usual as the big day approached.

'You really don't have to micro-manage every detail,' Aiden had remarked when she'd insisted on checking the order he'd placed for beer, wine and the all-important champagne. 'What's next, watching Esther bake the cake to make sure she gets it exactly right? Standing over Lucia while she makes the canapés?'

The comment had stung but it hadn't lessened Eve's anxiety. 'I don't want anything to go wrong, that's all.'

Aiden had smiled in his usual laid-back manner. 'Relax, Eve. Nothing is going to go wrong.'

It seemed his optimism was well founded. By Wednesday, the newspapers were predicting a mini heatwave for the coming weekend, with temperatures that were set to rival Ibiza, and as the skies dawned clear and blue on Thursday and Friday, Eve cautiously began to believe the Met Office might have it right. The weather was going to be glorious.

She was up early on Saturday morning, before the sun had risen. Huxley had no complaints about a pre-dawn run along the beach – he snuffled happily amid the seaweed deposited by the tide and raced through the breakers with every bit of his usual enjoyment. Eve took the opportunity to soak up the tranquillity of the morning. Once the causeway was safe to cross, just after eight o'clock, suppliers would begin to arrive and the day would begin in earnest; after that, Eve very much doubted she would have time to breathe until the last wedding guest had staggered away in the early hours of Sunday morning.

The florist, Paulina, arrived first, laden with vases of delicate blue hydrangea and white roses for the tables. There'd been talk at one point of a flower arch on the decking but Hettie had felt the cove's limestone counterpart would simply upstage any floral decoration. Instead, she had asked for the seats to be placed on the sand facing the arch and Eve had been glad, because she wholeheartedly agreed that the view could not be improved. She left Paulina dressing the tables in the downstairs bar and went in search of Aiden to help her set the beach chairs out.

Other suppliers came and went. The seats around the tables in the bar were dressed in white with sea-blue organza ribbons. Esther delivered the wedding cake – a three-tier masterpiece covered in waves of Italian buttercream icing that looked just like the ocean – and then hurried home to get changed. The DJ arrived with his decks for later in the evening – George had wanted to play his Northumbrian pipes but Hettie had overruled him. As the morning wore on and the plans started to become a reality, Eve felt some of her worries melt away. Everything appeared to be under control.

'Oh, Eve, it looks wonderful,' Hettie exclaimed when she arrived, just after ten-thirty. Her grey hair was set in large rollers that wobbled as she glanced around the bar, and she wore a hot pink hoodie that proclaimed her MRS POTTS TO BE. 'Just like I imagined it.'

'I'm glad,' Eve said warmly, and checked the time. 'Now, let's get you settled in the house so you can finish getting ready in peace.'

She led Hettie and her bridesmaid, Mabel, into the house and upstairs, to her own room which she'd given up to act as the bridal dressing room. 'There's some champagne in the ice bucket there,' she said, pointing to a silver stand. 'Glasses are here, or we can rustle you up some tea if you prefer, and Esther left some cookies in case you get hungry.'

Hettie patted her stomach conscientiously. 'I'd better not,' she said, glancing towards the shrouded dress Mabel was carrying. 'It's not a figure-hugging frock but even so . . .'

Eve smiled. 'I understand. I'll be running around, getting things ready, but message me if there's anything you need.'

She left the two women alone, promising to send the hairdresser along as soon as she arrived, and hurried back to the bar to see how Aiden and Tish were getting on with the setting the tables.

'Ninety minutes to go until blast off,' Aiden noted, as Eve consulted the seating plan and began to lay out place names. 'Have you heard from the registrar?'

'She's on her way,' Eve replied. 'Providing everything runs to time, she should be able to get back across the causeway before the tide comes in.'

Aiden grinned. 'At least we know the bride is going to turn up. I'm not so sure about the groom.'

Hamish had warned them that George had been growing more and more nervous as the week went on. 'I wouldn't say he's got cold feet, exactly, but they're definitely feeling the chill.'

'He'll be here,' Eve reassured her brother. 'I've told Jakob I'm holding him personally responsible for George today – he's to get him here even if he has to carry him. That's what the Best Man is for, after all.'

It was well after eleven o'clock when Eve's phone vibrated insistently in her back pocket. Pulling the handset out, she saw it was Hettie. 'Hello. Everything okay?'

She was not prepared for the loud wail that bore into her ear. 'Noooooooo, it's not!'

Wincing, Eve held the phone several centimetres away. 'What's wrong, Hettie? Is there a problem with your hair? Your dress? Try not to panic, I'm sure we can fix whatever it is.'

On the other end of the line, Hettie took a deep breath. 'It's not my hair or the dress. It's the photographer. He's got a family emergency and can't come.'

Eve squeezed her eyes shut. 'Okay. Try to breathe. Is he sending someone else?'

'That's just it – he can't! He's a one-man-band and everyone else he knows is already booked. What are we going to do?'

The hysteria in her voice rose again. Eve tried to stem the tide. 'Try to stay calm, Hettie.' She ran through their options. 'Freda's husband is a keen photographer, could we ask him to step in?'

There was a silence on the other end of the phone that was somehow worse than the panicked wails. Eve thought back to previous weddings Darling's had hosted, all beautifully recorded by professional photographers, and imagined suggesting to any of those brides that their big day be captured by an enthusiastic amateur. 'Or maybe not,' she conceded.

'I know you're trying to help,' Hettie said, her tone more dignified than it had been. 'But George and I are only going to have one wedding day. Photographs are like memories you can hold in your hand – I don't think I'm being a diva by wanting pictures that are professionally taken. No offence to Len, who I'm sure takes a very nice photo.'

'Of course you aren't,' Eve said. 'But unfortunately we don't have that option. Unless—'

She broke off, biting her lip. Of course they had another option – it just wasn't one Hettie or George or anyone on Ennisfarne could afford. She didn't dare think what Logan Silk charged for a photoshoot and there was no point in suggesting it to Hettie. 'It's a disaster but I'm afraid we don't have much choice,' she said, as gently as she could. 'Look at it this way – any photographs are better than none at all.'

But it was too late, Hettie had worked out what Eve had backed away from saying. 'Could we ask Logan?'

Eve pinched the bridge of her nose. How could she explain that while Ennisfarne's close-knit community often ran on an economy of favours and skills-exchange, the outside world was different. It wasn't acceptable to expect ordinary people to work on that basis, much less world-famous, top photographers. She wasn't even sure Ennisfarne had anything to offer Logan in return. 'I don't think we can afford him.'

'Oh,' Hettie said, sounding taken aback. 'But I'll get my deposit back from our original photographer, surely Logan will give us a bit of a discount. Mates-rates, or whatever it's called.'

Eve pictured some of the lavish pictures she'd found online, back when she'd been curious about who Logan really was, and cringed even more at the idea of asking him to photograph George and Hettie's modest wedding. It was like asking Leonardo da Vinci to paint a bathroom. Hettie had really had no idea what she was asking. 'I'm not sure it's fair to put him in that position.'

'Fine,' Hettie said, after a second or two of silence. 'Give me his number and I'll do it. George says he's a good man, I'm sure he'll want to help.'

Her words made Eve pause. In her mind, there were two Logan Silks – the one who photographed royalty and A-listers and rock stars, and the man who had sat in her kitchen, laughing and joking as he lost to her at poker. The Logan she knew was kind and generous with his talent – he'd offered his pictures of Darling Cove for free. Perhaps Hettie was right; perhaps Eve was doing him a disservice by deciding he wouldn't want to help.

'No, you concentrate on getting ready,' she said at last. 'I'll call Logan now, before he sets off.'

Anxiety coiled like a baleful viper in the pit of her stomach as she pulled up Logan's number. Heart thudding, she checked the time as she waited for him to answer – 11.20. Surely he couldn't be on his way already?

'Hi Eve.' His voice was faintly muffled, as though she'd caught him pulling on a coat. 'Everything okay?'

She took a deep breath. 'Not really. We've got a bit of a problem and I'm really hoping you might be able to save the day.'

She spilled the story out. When she'd finished, there was a split second when she wished she could rewind the clock and decide not to ask him after all but the impulse was washed away by Logan's reply. 'Absolutely. I'll pack everything in the car now. Can you save me a parking space in your yard? It'll make life easier.'

The breath Eve hadn't realized she'd been holding whooshed out. 'Oh, thank you. I'll tell Hettie – she's going to be so happy.' She hesitated. 'One last thing, I'm not sure they'll be able to pay what you're used to, although they'll get a refund from the photographer who couldn't make it—'

'Eve,' Logan cut in mildly. 'There won't be a fee. After everything you and everyone else on Ennisfarne have done for me, it will be my pleasure and honour to photograph Hettie and George's wedding free of charge.'

She frowned. 'But—'

'No buts,' he said, sounding utterly resolute. 'I'm happy to be able to help out.'

She wanted to argue, to explain that it hadn't been her

intention that he wouldn't be paid. Perhaps the amount George and Hettie had been paying the previous photographer was insultingly low for someone of Logan's experience and status but she hoped he knew no one expected him to sacrifice his day and work for free.

'Even so,' Eve said, equally determined. 'They'll want to show you their respect and gratitude.'

A thoughtful pause ensued. 'Well, if they really insist, they can make a donation to charity in lieu of a fee. How's that?'

It wasn't ideal, Eve thought, but she was acutely aware of the ticking clock edging ever closer to twelve-thirty. Guests would start arriving soon. She didn't have the time to make an argument out of something that wasn't strictly speaking her business. 'That's very kind of you,' she said. 'I'm sure Hettie and George will thank you themselves but I want you to know how much I appreciate this.'

'Like I said, it's my pleasure,' Logan said briskly. 'Now, I'd better pack the car. See you in ten minutes.'

Resisting the temptation to thank him again, Eve went to give Hettie the good news. On the way back, she checked the registrar had arrived and that the catering was on track, and glanced once more at the pristine blue skies over the arch for any sign of clouds. The weather might be beyond her control but nothing else was going to go wrong – not if she could help it.

Everyone agreed it was the most beautiful wedding. George had scrubbed up remarkably well, dressed in a fresh from the hanger navy blue suit, aquamarine tie and with his beard neatly trimmed. He'd stood beside Jakob, waiting on the sand in front of the registrar with nerves that were almost palpable. His fidgeting had only stopped when Hettie appeared at double doors of the bar and began to make her way along the makeshift aisle. She looked amazing in her sea-green shift dress, her feet bare and her hair laced with silver flowers. An appreciative murmur rippled across the guests in their seats and George looked as though he might implode with happiness as she walked towards him. They exchanged their bespoke vows beneath the beaming spring sunshine, framed by the arch and with the thunder of the waves as a fitting backdrop. And then the registrar had declared them husband and wife, and Darling Cove had rung with whoops and cheers and enthusiastic applause. At the start of the ceremony, Eve had been aware of Logan, moving deftly around with his camera hiding most of his face, but his movements had been so careful and respectful that she'd soon ceased to notice him.

Afterwards, the newlyweds had posed on the beach for photographs, as near to the arch as the tide and shadows would allow. Eve had been circulating among the guests on the decking, topping up glasses, but it was hard not to watch Logan work. He moved with an economical grace, weaving left and right, pausing to adjust the camera or check the screen before shifting again, calling out the occasional instruction. Eve hadn't been close enough to hear what was being said but George and Hettie were relaxed and beaming, apparently loving their moment of stardom. A smile tugged at Eve's lips as she watched; if this was how Logan worked all the time, it was no wonder he got such wonderful results. She couldn't wait to see the pictures.

It was one of those joyful spring days when the sun was so warm it could almost be the start of summer. Light sparkled on the waves and the sky was a cloudless cornflower blue. Children raced across the sand, chasing balls and playing tag, the sounds of laughter and chatter filled the air. The atmosphere was so pleasant that Eve had been loathe to summon everyone inside to eat, but the enticing aromas floating out of the kitchen had helped.

'Hettie fell on her feet,' Selina observed to Eve as she came in from the balcony. 'Having Logan Silk as your wedding photographer is the kind of thing money can't buy.'

Eve cringed inwardly, reminded all over again just what a favour she'd demanded. 'I know. I felt awful asking him but he agreed immediately.' She glanced outside, where Logan was taking pictures of the guests. 'I don't think he's sat down since he got here.'

Selina followed the direction of her gaze. 'There's something very sexy about a man totally absorbed in his craft, don't you think? Aside from the whole tall, dark and handsome thing he's got going on, obviously.'

Eve shifted uncomfortably, although she wasn't sure what it was that made her uneasy. 'I suppose so.'

Her best friend shook her head in amusement. 'I know you don't see it. But I'm looking forward to this evening, when he lets his hair down.'

'I'm not sure he will,' Eve said. 'He's taking his responsibilities pretty seriously at the moment.'

'Ah, but he has to put the camera down at some point,' Selina said with a wink. 'And when he does, I'll swoop.'

Eve looked outside again. 'Actually, you might not have to wait that long. Here he comes now.'

A flash of panic crossed Selina's face. 'Is he? Do I look okay?' She pulled her teeth back in a hurried grimace. 'Lipstick on my teeth?'

'You look great,' Eve reassured her under her breath, as Logan drew near. She caught his eye. 'You look like you need a drink. What can I get you?'

'Just some water, if you don't mind,' he replied. 'I totally believe it's hotter than Ibiza out there.'

Selina moved ever so slightly forward. 'That's because you've been working so hard,' she said, and slipped her arm through his. 'Why don't you let me help you find your seat? Eve can bring some water over to you.'

Logan gave her a grateful look. 'Sure. Thank you.'

Eve watched them make their way through the throng towards the table plan, a wry smile tugging at her mouth; Selina certainly wasn't wasting any time. Shaking her head a little, she headed for the bar to find Logan some water. When today was over, she'd have to find some way to make things up to him properly.

The meal led into the speeches, which were considerably more PG-rated than Eve had been anticipating. Jakob managed to weave some Icelandic poetry into his, mercifully one of the shorter versions. Hettie's brother, Roger, stood up in lieu of the traditional Father of the Bride speech, and talked about how wonderful it was that she'd found George.

'I only have to look at my sister today to see how happy she is,' he said, glancing back and forth between the newlyweds. 'And I know Eddie would be delighted too, knowing Hettie has found love again. I'm sure he's watching and raising a heavenly glass.'

George reached across to squeeze his new wife's hand and Eve felt tears prick the back of her eyes. What was it about weddings that turned even the least romantic person into an emotional wreck?

'And with that,' Roger went on, 'I'd like to ask you all to do the same and join me in a toast to the happy couple. To Hettie and George.'

The other guests lifted their glasses. 'To Hettie and George!'

The next hour flew by. Eve managed to grab a quick break while dessert and coffee were being served, popping back into the house to let Huxley out. Guilt wrenched at her heart as she left him again but there was no way she could keep an eye on him and ensure the wedding guests were looked after at the same time. He'd probably end up on the other side of the island, or at the very least in a compromising position with the wedding cake.

'I'll make it up to you, Hux,' she promised as he watched her go. 'Sorry, boy.'

There was a lull after the meal as people let their food

settle. Even so, it wasn't long before the dancing began. Hettie and George surprised everyone with a beautiful waltz to Ed Sheeran's 'Perfect' and Eve saw several friends dabbing at their eyes. She caught sight of Logan slipping in and out of the guests around the edge of the dancefloor, camera working hard as he captured the moment.

'Did you know George could dance?' Aiden whispered, passing Eve as he unobtrusively collected empty glasses.

'Not a clue,' Eve said. 'He's proving to be a bit of a dark horse, our George. Next stop, *Strictly*!'

The dancing got going in earnest after that, as the infectious joy of the day took hold and alcohol lowered inhibitions. Eve was kept busy behind the bar and lost track of Logan but she hoped he'd finally put his camera down and was enjoying the celebrations. Outside, the sky had darkened to a velvety dark blue and the first stars were beginning to glimmer overhead. Laughter rang out across the beach as guests spilled out onto the decking and the first-floor balcony, lit by the cheering glow of the fairy lights.

And eventually, Eve started to notice tired eyes and barely hidden yawns among the revellers. In small clusters, or one-by-one, they began to find their way to Hettie and George to make their farewells. By midnight, the newlyweds had gone too and the crowd thinned to a few die-hard party animals. Eve let Tish and the other bar staff go, pressing hefty tips into their hands as they left, and set about gathering up the many empty glasses dotted about the decking. She was just about to step onto the upstairs balcony when she overheard the low hum of conversation beyond the glass doors and saw there was a couple occupying one shadowy corner. Eve paused, trying to work out whether she could interrupt, and then she heard a soft laugh that she recognized as Selina's. The rumble of a male voice followed and Selina laughed again. Feeling as though she was eavesdropping, Eve peered around the edge of the door and realized who her best friend was with: Logan.

Their dark heads were very close, gleaming faintly under the fairy lights. As Eve watched, they grew closer still. There was no sound, other than the distant rush of the sea. Transfixed, Eve watched, her heart thumping uncomfortably in her chest. They were kissing, she thought numbly. Logan and Selina were kissing.

Suddenly aware she was intruding in the most horrible way, Eve stumbled backwards and made for the stairs. She met Aiden at the bottom, who took one look at her frozen expression and frowned. 'Eve? Are you okay?'

The question brought Eve up short. Why shouldn't she be okay? Selina had made her intentions clear, after all, and Logan was perfectly free to kiss whoever he chose. So why did Eve feel as though something had fractured inside her?

She swallowed down a burst of acid and dug deep for a breezy smile. 'I'm fine.' She thrust a stack of glasses into her brother's hands. 'Stick these in the dishwasher, if you don't mind. I need to grab some air.'

On the decking, she took several long breaths and gazed up at the starry sky, trying to sift through her jumbled emotions. She ought to be glad Selina had got what she wanted but that wasn't what she felt at all. For the first time in her life, Eve was jealous of her best friend's happiness; miserably, shamefully jealous. It was the shock of walking in on them, she told herself as she struggled to dampen the churning in her stomach. Once it had passed she would be fine with the idea of Logan and Selina – happy for them, even. Eve bit her lip, determined to make it so. Because really, what choice did she have?

PART THREE

Stormy Seas

Chapter Sixteen

Logan

'So, I hear you're stepping out with Selina Heron.'

Freda's gaze was bright and openly mischievous as she studied Logan across the narrow aisle of The Nook. He supposed he shouldn't be surprised – on an island the size of Ennisfarne, he didn't imagine there were many secrets – but the statement still irked him. He squashed down the niggle and kept his expression blank. 'What makes you say that?' he said, dropping a sourdough loaf into his shopping basket and moving along to study a neighbouring row of jars.

The shopkeeper pursed her lips and squinted thoughtfully at the ceiling. 'Well, I can't be totally sure but I think it's probably got something to do with Selina announcing it in the pub last night.'

He wanted to groan. It hadn't been that long ago that his love life had been of vital interest to most of the tabloids and while Freda's curiosity wasn't in the same league as the lurid headlines, it still made him feel flat. 'Right.'

'Of course, she didn't put it like that,' Freda went on. 'What was it she said? Not Netflix and chill – that was Hettie's suggestion.'

Logan's hand paused halfway towards the green pesto. He was almost sure she was joking; he couldn't imagine sixty-something Hettie coming out with such a phrase, even if she did know what it meant.

'Not friends with benefits, either,' Freda mused, then snapped her fingers. '*Seeing each other*, that was it. Which seems a ridiculous way to describe it to me. I see you most days and we're not romantically intertwined.'

Laughter danced in her eyes when Logan looked at her again, perhaps because stepping out was an equally ridiculous euphemism, and it was impossible for him to stay annoyed. It was hardly Freda's fault if Selina was revealing details of her and Logan's sole date so far. And the shopkeeper's playfulness was a little endearing; it suggested she was comfortable enough to tease him, the kind of thing friends did to one another. Teasing and leg-pulling weren't things that regularly happened to Logan, which wasn't a surprise given that he rarely settled anywhere long enough to make friends. Or at least he hadn't until now.

'I imagine Len would have something to say if we were,' Logan replied, picturing Freda's friendly but generally taciturn husband. 'But it's too early to put a label on things with Selina. Let's just say we enjoy each other's company and leave it at that.'

Freda opened her mouth to reply, but whatever she was about to say was forestalled by the tinkling of the bell over the door and a burst of loud chatter as a group of bobble-hatted tourists clattered into the shop. Instinctively, Logan ducked his head. The arrival of spring and the accompanying warmer weather had brought a sharp increase in visitors to Ennisfarne, meaning the village and roads surrounding it were much busier, especially during the periods when the causeway was covered and tourists were effectively trapped on the island. There'd been an increase in traffic on the road past Dune Cottage too, heading for Darling's Bar with its spectacular view of the magnificent limestone arch that dominated the cove, and consequently more people on the beach that curved around from the bar. The upturn in visitors hadn't caused Logan any major problems so far, apart from making it harder to find a parking space in the village, but it did make him a little more wary when he was out and about, and he'd taken to wearing a baseball cap. It had been almost two months since he'd last been splashed across the front page of the papers and the news cycle had definitely moved on but that didn't mean some eagle-eyed tourist wouldn't recognize him. It wouldn't be the end of the world, of course, but he'd come to Ennisfarne to keep a low profile and it was a position he'd like to maintain.

Freda bustled over to the new customers, pointing them towards the deli counter with the practised air of a born saleswoman. Logan smiled as he finished making his own grocery selections and headed for the till beside the door. He was sure she'd been a hypnotist in a previous life – no one ever left The Nook empty-handed.

Two more clusters came in while Freda packed Logan's purchases into the bag he'd brought with him. 'You're going to need some help if it carries on like this,' he observed, tapping his card on the reader.

'This is nothing,' she replied, her tone cheerful. 'Wait until Thursday, when the Easter crowds arrive. You won't be able to move for visitors then – luckily, they're usually hungry and thirsty, especially if they've just finished the St Hilda's Pilgrimage.'

He frowned. 'What's that? Something to do with the nunnery?'

One tip of Ennisfarne boasted the ruined magnificence of a seventh-century nunnery, founded by St Hilda and maintained for centuries until Henry VIII ordered it to be suppressed during his power and land grab from the church in 1537. Logan was aware that the towering remains of the building were popular with tourists but he hadn't realized they were a site of religious pilgrimage.

Freda nodded. 'It's a walk from Whitby Abbey to Ennisfarne, a bit like St Cuthbert's Way, except that runs from Melrose in the Scottish Borders to Lindisfarne.'

That made sense, Logan thought, given that St Hilda had been Abbess of Whitby until her death. Her remains had rested briefly on Ennisfarne, during which time a number of miracles were said to have occurred, and there was an abundance of half-hidden carvings and symbols in her honour dotted about the island for those who knew what to look out for. Perhaps it would be more surprising if there weren't pilgrimages in her honour, he reflected.

Casting an eye over the browsing tourists, Freda pushed the bag of groceries towards Logan. 'The walk can be done at any time of year but on Good Friday, we get some pilgrims arriving carrying big wooden crosses. You can see them crossing the sands once the tide is out – we had almost a hundred one year.' She shook her head in cheerful contemplation. 'Mad buggers.'

It was perfectly possible to walk across the sands from the mainland – for centuries it had been the only way to reach both Ennisfarne and her sister island, Lindisfarne, on foot. The path was marked by a series of tall wooden poles and it didn't shift like other, more treacherous, coastal crossings. But, as with the modern tarmac causeway, the tide was merciless to unwary travellers and timing was everything. 'They must have to set off walking as soon as the tide is low enough,' he observed, wondering how much a large wooden cross might weigh. 'Rather them than me.'

'Takes about seventy-five minutes,' Freda said. 'It's quite the sight when they first appear, a bit like travelling back in time.'

Logan pictured the poles stretching out across the sands beyond the weathered, tar-covered hulls of the upturned herring boats now repurposed to store fishing gear and other essential kit. He could see Freda's point. 'It might make a good picture, if the light is right.'

'I'm sure it would, if you're the one wielding the camera,' Freda agreed. 'I know Hettie and George are thrilled with their wedding pictures. If you ever get bored of photographing royalty, I reckon you could make it as a wedding photographer.'

'Thank you,' Logan said gravely. 'I'll keep that in mind.'

The shopkeeper winked. 'Just in case you and Selina decide to go *Instagram official*.'

The last two words were laced with an exaggerated reverence that made Logan grin in spite of himself. But Freda was glancing over towards her other customers once more and her expression had become business-like. 'Duty calls,' she told him. 'But you're coming to the movie night on Saturday, right?'

There was no cinema on Ennisfarne and the tides made it difficult to catch a film on the mainland so the islanders had improvised. This weekend, Darling's was showing *Top Gun* via a big screen on the beach. Or possibly on a big screen inside the bar, if the weather had other ideas. 'Wouldn't miss it for anything,' Logan said. 'See you then.'

There were two cars waiting for his parking space when he reversed out, each driver apparently determined that the spot belonged to them. Logan watched the stand-off through his rear-view mirror as he drove away and decided to avoid the village as much as possible over the coming Easter weekend. The road that led to the south-west tip of the island had more traffic than usual, although it was still a million miles away from the rush hours Logan had experienced in every city he'd visited. As he passed the upturned boats, nestling along the shore like slumbering sea monsters, a sudden whim came over him. He pulled in to the side of the road and got out of the car.

The tide was in, stretching towards the distant mainland in a silvered grey expanse and gulls wheeled low overhead, making the most of the meagre thermals of an overcast day. A few were perched on the slender poles of the Pilgrim's Path, more still scattered along the fins of each boat, all watching Logan's approach with calculated caution and doubtless assessing the probability of food, although they didn't move when he stopped beside the boats.

It always struck Logan that such care was taken to maintain the hulls of the long-retired, upcycled vessels. It made sense, of course – they were protecting valuable goods, after all – but it was more than that. The islanders had a make-do-and-mend approach that was both refreshing and grounding at the same time, and Logan felt the contrast all the more since the demands of his work meant so many elements of his life were transitory. It wasn't about saving money, either. Turning the worn-out boats into sheds was undoubtedly thrifty but he knew from his conversations with the islanders that they were proud to preserve the traditions that had crafted the boats too. He placed one hand flat against the side of the nearest boat and stood for a moment, marvelling at the solidity of the tar-patched wood, imagining the prow cutting through the glistening waves with a cargo of freshly caught herring. Logan was no sailor but he could still picture these stalwarts of the sea in their glory days, masts as tall and proud as the men steering them, their sails whiter than the cotton wool clouds. It was an arresting image – he could almost smell the pungent scent of the fish.

'If you're hoping for a ferry you'll have a long wait.'

The voice startled Logan from his daydream. He turned to see Eve standing three boats along, turning the key in the lock of a cornflower blue door that was exactly the same colour as the one of Dune Cottage. Her blonde hair was tied back in its usual no-nonsense ponytail and she wore a battered, navy-blue wax jacket that was fraying at the cuffs. In her arms, she held a pair of long black flippers and she was gazing over the top of them with undisguised curiosity.

Realizing he'd had his eyes closed, Logan stepped quickly away from the boat. 'Just trying to absorb some history,' he explained, pushing down an unaccustomed surge of something that felt a lot like embarrassment. 'I bet these boats have a few stories to tell.'

Eve pursed her lips thoughtfully. 'Almost certainly. Although I imagine there'd be quite a lot of boring bits about barnacles and the like. It's not all high drama.'

Logan hid a smile; she was as practical-minded as ever. 'No, I suppose not.' He eyed the door she'd just locked. 'Is this yours?'

'Mine and Aiden's,' she replied. 'She belonged to my dad, and to his dad before him.'

'A grand old lady of the sea,' Logan said, smiling. 'Does she have a name?'

She regarded him quizzically. 'Not many people ask that.

My grandfather called her *Cecily*, after my grandmother, but Dad decided on *Lookfar* when he inherited her.' She patted the tar-covered hull. 'It's painted under here, if you know where to look.'

'Two very different names,' Logan said, then frowned. '*Lookfar* sounds familiar but I can't put my finger on why.'

Eve smiled. 'You must have read *A Wizard of Earthsea* by Ursula le Guin – that's where Dad got the name. He was a big fantasy fan. Darling's was almost called The Prancing Pony after the pub in *The Lord of the Rings* but Mum put her foot down.'

The little insight into Eve's childhood made Logan smile too, even as he tried to recall reading the book she'd mentioned. '*A Wizard of Earthsea*,' he repeated slowly. 'A boy from a tiny island fights off invaders and becomes the greatest mage ever known, is that the one?'

'Sounds like the plot of a lot of books but yes, that's the one,' she said. 'I think Dad identified with the small island bit and secretly hoped he'd turn out to be a wizard too but that didn't happen, as far as I know. Although he did argue with the tourists from time to time.'

The last sentence made Logan grin. 'Perhaps he was a secret wizard.'

'Perhaps,' Eve said. 'He was certainly a magical sailor, hence the boat name. He was heartbroken when she was no longer seaworthy.'

'At least she got a new lease of life here,' Logan offered. 'It's a great idea to reuse them as sheds.'

'Ours is a relative newcomer – she's only been here twenty or so years.' Eve waved a hand towards the sheds behind them. 'But a couple date back to the 1900s. It's amazing they've survived this long.'

Logan took another look at the line of upturned boats, astonished that some of them might be more than a hundred years old. 'The preservation is extraordinary. But surely they belong in a museum rather than out here, exposed to the elements.'

Eve's mouth twisted wryly as she glanced at him. 'They're our heritage, part of the island's traditions. What good would they be stuck in a museum, miles from here with no context or background to give the full picture? As long as they're here they can serve a dual purpose, keeping things dry and pulling in the tourists.'

Logan could see the sense of what she was saying but couldn't prevent himself from arguing. 'But what will happen when the weather and salt water cause too much damage?'

'Then we'll let them go,' Eve said simply. 'Not everything is meant to last for ever. I thought you'd understand that, being artistic and all.'

There was a definite hint of rebuke in her voice and once again, Logan knew he'd inadvertently managed to irritate her. Would they ever have a conversation where he didn't? 'I do understand,' he said, holding his hands up in apology. 'And I didn't mean to teach you your business. The fact that the boats have survived as long as they have shows you and the other islanders know everything you need to about wood preservation. I'm sorry.'

The flinty look in her eyes softened. 'I know you meant well. But they're more than just old boats or sheds to us – they're a link to our past and the people we've lost. Their history is our history.'

He nodded. 'Of course. I suppose that's where my particular speciality comes into its own. Photography is a form of preservation, not quite the same as having the original but a way of remembering it when it's gone.'

Eve appeared to consider this. 'That makes sense,' she conceded. 'Maybe you could photograph the boats, so we'll have something to look back on when the inevitable happens.'

Logan glanced at the boats, recalling how he'd imagined them as hulking dragons when he'd first arrived on Ennisfarne, and his brain immediately began to compose the shots. It would need a brighter day, one where the sun sparkled on the high tide, and if he could time it to the last hour before sunset, he'd benefit from the extraordinary golden light that lifted even the most humdrum subject and made it remarkable. With luck and a little forethought, he might capture the scene before him in a way that would ensure these pieces of Ennisfarne's history were never truly lost to the ravages of time. 'Sure.'

'You don't have to, obviously,' Eve said. 'All I seem to do is ask you to take pictures.'

She looked embarrassed. Logan shook his head. 'I'd love to photograph the boats,' he said. 'Leave it with me.'

Eve hoisted the flippers in her arms and pulled a face. 'I'd better get back to the bar. I left Aiden in charge of Huxley – who knows what trouble the pair of them will have cooked up.'

Logan smiled; Eve's brother was marginally more responsible than her year-old chocolate Labrador. 'Are the fins for you or Aiden?'

She shook her head. 'He's a surfer, not a diver. All the talk of diving last month gave me a hankering to get out there but I've been too busy, what with George and Hettie's wedding and the tourist season getting going. I thought the least I could do was check my gear.' There was a brief pause, during which she looked as though she was debating her next words. 'Billy's running a dive in a week or so, once the Easter rush is over, if you want to come. It won't be anything fancy, just fifteen metres or so to one of the wrecks off the east coast.'

A flicker of surprise sent Logan's eyebrows shooting up. His imagination had been captured by Eve's description of the many shipwrecks around Ennisfarne and he'd taken a scuba dive refresher course as a result. But she hadn't seemed keen on diving with him then – in fact, she'd actively discouraged the notion. Inviting him to join her on Billy's dive was unexpected. He spent a moment wondering what had brought about her change of heart and then decided it didn't really matter. 'I'd love to. As long as you don't mind a little rustiness in my technique – I'd forgotten how tricky it is to swim wearing the tanks and fins.'

'I'm sure it will come back to you,' Eve said. 'We won't

be doing anything too strenuous. There's a World War Two wreck just off the nature reserve that's always fun to explore. Good for seal spotting too.'

'Sounds wonderful, thanks,' Logan said. 'I'll bring my camera.'

Eve favoured him with a wry smile. 'I thought you'd say that. The exact day depends on the tides and the weather, obviously, so it might be short notice. Is that okay?'

Logan mentally reviewed his diary, which remained satisfyingly empty, and tipped his head. 'Fine by me. I don't have much on over the next few weeks.'

The look she gave him was envious. 'Lucky you. I'll let you know the plan as soon as Billy and I work things out.'

'Sounds perfect,' Logan answered. 'But I'll see you on Saturday, for the movie night. How's the planning coming along – anything I can do to help?'

She pursed her lips. 'I think everything is under control, apart from the weather. Do you have any contacts who can sort out an evening of balmy sunshine for me?'

'Sadly not,' Logan said, laughing. 'Sorry.'

'We'll just have to cross our fingers, then,' she replied. 'And on that note, I'd better get back. See you at the weekend.'

'Looking forward to it,' he said warmly.

It wasn't until after Eve had gone and Logan was left alone with his thoughts that he considered her words in more detail. People had often commented on his luck; he was lucky to travel the world, working in glamorous locations with A-listers and royalty and more. Lucky to have reached the pinnacle of his career, so his diary was never empty and his agent was always happy. Lucky to be dating one of the most beautiful models in the world. But when Eve called him lucky, she did so precisely because none of those things were now true. She envied his empty schedule and freedom. And as Logan watched the grey and white gulls soaring over his head, he appreciated his good fortune all over again. It wasn't luck that had made him turn his back on his glittering career, it had been a serious case of burnout that had robbed him of his creativity and zest for life. But it might just be luck that had brought him to Ennisfarne.

Chapter Seventeen

Eve

The view from the balcony of Darling's was spectacular, even if Eve did say so herself.

The sun was dipping towards the horizon, bathing the beach in a hazy amber glow as it laced the sky with delicate fronds of raspberry and lemon. Retro bulbs hung from temporary lampposts, lighting the way to the deckchairs laid out before the giant screen just beyond the tideline. It was 7.30pm – thirty minutes from the advertised start time for the film – but the bar was already busy with movie-goers. Some had taken their seats and were chatting in small groups, others were lingering on the decking below the balcony or sitting on the golden sand. And presiding over everything, in dignified contrast to the sun's showy display, was the crowning glory of Darling Cove – the sea-worn limestone arch reached from the headland into the sea and made the beach one of the most breath-taking in Northumberland. It was almost a perfect evening, Eve thought, pulling her jacket a little closer to her body. If the temperature had been a few degrees warmer, she'd have won the outdoor cinema lottery.

The crowd didn't seem to mind the chill in the air as night fell but she supposed that was because they were mostly islanders, and almost everyone who'd come over from the mainland was of hardy Northumbrian stock. She'd marketed the event as BYOB – not 'Bring Your Own Booze' but 'Bring Your Own Blanket' – and most people had done just that. One or two people had brought sleeping bags and their determination to enjoy the movie was something Eve whole-heartedly admired. As she'd heard numerous Scandinavian visitors to Ennisfarne say in the past, there was no such thing as bad weather, only bad clothes.

Switching her attention from the audience to the pro-jector beside her on the balcony, she checked for the tenth time that the power cable was connected. Darling's had run several movie nights in the past and they had always gone smoothly; Eve was keen for that success to continue, which meant double-checking everything. Satisfied everything was in order, she fastened the black cloth cover around the kit and went downstairs to see how Aiden and Tish were coping behind the bar.

'How's it going?' she murmured to her brother as he filled a cardboard carton with delicious-smelling popcorn from the machine they'd hired for the night. 'Any problems?'

He threw her a look that was as close to being harassed as he ever got. 'Apart from having a corn kernel somewhere unmentionable, you mean?'

Eve bit her lip, trying not to laugh. 'Oh dear. Where do you need me?'

Aiden glanced over towards Freda's granddaughter, Tish, who was doing her best to work through a line of hungry and thirsty customers, and pulled a face. 'Just dive in,' he suggested, lifting three overflowing popcorn boxes and balancing them between his hands. 'I think we might need some more ice cream in a minute but that can wait.'

Eve didn't argue. The mood in the bar was cheerful – no one seemed to be complaining that the service was slower than usual – but it mattered to Eve that her customers were kept happy and with less than half an hour until show time, she needed everyone in their seats sooner rather than later. Plastering on a professional smile, she caught Freda's eye and asked what she could get her.

'Two honeycomb gelato, a large G&T and a bottomless coke, please,' Freda said.

Nodding, Eve set about getting the drinks.

'Good turnout tonight,' Freda said conversationally, glancing round. 'You obviously made a good choice with this film.'

'It's a classic,' Eve said as she turned to reach into the freezer behind her. 'Who doesn't love an aeronautical adrenaline rush?'

'Not me,' Freda replied. 'George and Hamish were all for

re-enacting the volleyball scene on the beach just now but I think they decided it was a bit too chilly to go topless.'

Eve almost dropped the tubs of Ferrelli's ice cream she'd just taken from the freezer. George and Hamish were a long way from having the buff, tanned physiques of the fighter pilots in the movie and she didn't dare think about the injuries they might sustain diving onto the cold, damp sand. 'Probably for the best,' she replied with a shudder.

'Oh, I don't know,' Freda said, her eyes twinkling. 'They were talking about roping Logan in. I wouldn't mind seeing him shirtless.'

The shopkeeper made no secret of her admiration for Logan and had occasionally suggested he'd be a good match for Eve, although not since he'd got together with Selina. Eve wasn't sure whether there was anything behind Freda's comment now, other than her fevered imagination, and decided not to dignify it with an answer. 'Can I get you anything else?'

Freda cast a speculative look towards the popcorn cart, then shook her head regretfully. 'That'll do for now, thanks.'

A whirlwind twenty minutes later, they'd run out of popcorn and the queue at the bar had dwindled to a handful of customers. Eve had spotted Logan in the line, standing next to Selina, and had managed to ensure she was serving someone else when they reached the front. It wasn't that she wanted to avoid either of them, exactly, more that Freda's volleyball comment was proving hard to dislodge and Eve wasn't sure she'd be able to look Logan

in the eye without blushing. Much easier to be busy else-
where and hope the mental image was gone by the time
she next saw him.

But she'd reckoned without the actual scene in the film.
She watched from her position on the balcony, next to the
projector, and was glad she was nowhere near Freda as the
sun-drenched game played out on screen. The truth was she
couldn't imagine Logan indulging in such macho postur-
ing – she had no doubt he took care of himself and would
probably look the part, but he didn't seem the type who
needed to win. Then again, she'd considered him every bit
as arrogant as Maverick when they'd first met and though
that opinion had changed as she had got to know him better,
Eve was well aware she could hardly claim to be an expert on
Logan Silk. Perhaps he did play beach volleyball in his spare
time. His work must have taken him to enough glamorous
locations to offer the opportunity and he knew plenty of
beautiful people to achieve the same aesthetic as the movie.
She just felt he'd be more likely capturing it on camera rather
than joining in.

Night had well and truly fallen by the time the closing
credits rolled. A contented muttering broke out below as the
audience stretched and shifted in their seats. Some got to their
feet to head inside where Aiden and Tish would be ready to
serve them. Waiting for the final credits, Eve allowed her
gaze to roam the heads of her friends and neighbours, still
lit by the glow from the screen and the lights strung across
the beach. Freda was chatting animatedly to Hettie. Hamish

had turned in his seat and was deep in conversation with Warren, the farmer who was the nearest Eve and Aiden had to a next-door neighbour, with George hovering nearby. And Selina was saying something to Logan that made him smile. Suddenly feeling like she was spying, Eve turned her attention back to the projector. The moment the film had ended, she shut the equipment down and hurried to help Aiden and Tish in the bar.

The mood was buoyant downstairs – everyone seemed to have enjoyed the film, which made Eve happy too. Darling's barely made a profit from these movie nights, once licence costs and equipment hire had been taken into account, but that wasn't why she arranged them. Ennisfarne's isolated location meant its residents couldn't easily enjoy films on the big screen – it pleased Eve to bring some of the joy of a cinema visit to them. Seeing so many smiling, relaxed faces was payment enough, she felt, although she doubted her accountant would agree.

'Inspired movie choice, Eve.' Selina beamed at her from the other side of the bar, two empty glasses in her hands. 'Do you remember the first time we saw it? I almost applied to join the Navy so I could be a fighter pilot too.'

She had, Eve recalled, and a brief obsession with all things aeronautical and the Armed Forces had followed before common sense kicked in. They'd watched the film too many times that summer and had been able to quote large chunks of the dialogue, although Eve had realized during the course of this evening that she only remembered the most famous lines now. 'Things probably worked out for the best,' she said, smiling. 'Did you want another drink?'

'Absolutely,' Serena said. 'I feel the need.'

'The need for gin?' Eve replied, cocking her head.

Her best friend nodded. 'And a whisky for Logan. Neither offers quite the adrenaline rush of a dog fight with a Russian Mig but we have to take our fun where we can.'

'How's it going?' Eve asked as she placed the drinks in front of Selina. 'With Logan, I mean.'

Selina puffed out her cheeks. 'You know how it is – it's still early days. He's a bit quieter than I expected, given his party animal reputation.'

Eve raised both eyebrows. 'You know better than to believe everything you read on the internet.'

'True,' Selina conceded. 'And it's quite hard to be rock and roll on Ennisfarne. Maybe I'll lure him to Newcastle for a big night out and see what he's like when he lets his hair down.'

Eve thought back to the evening she and Aiden had spent with Logan, snowed in during the storm in March. He'd shared plenty of star-studded anecdotes but she'd got the impression he'd been more of an observer than a participant in any excessive partying, a perception that was backed up by the way he'd acted since arriving on Ennisfarne. If Logan was a party animal, he'd done an excellent job of hiding it. 'He might not be up for it, given he's trying to keep a low profile.'

Selina gathered up the drinks and winked. 'I'll just have to find a way to persuade him, then.'

Eve watched her slip through the crowd, heading back to Logan, and pushed away a tiny dart of unease. She still wasn't totally convinced Selina's interest in Logan was a good thing, given he'd be leaving the island in just over six weeks' time, but she'd learned long ago not to argue with her best friend once she'd set her heart on something. The difficulty this time was that she'd come to like and respect Logan, and, as his landlord, she felt a peculiar sense of responsibility that his time on Ennisfarne was positive. But the bottom line was that what he did, and with whom, was none of Eve's business. All she could do was hope that neither her oldest nor her newest friend got hurt.

The remainder of the Easter break zoomed by in an exhausting flurry of rushes and lulls that frequently saw Darling's jammed with customers. None of them were islanders – those who ran businesses that relied on the tourist trade were just as busy and had little time to visit the cove. Eve wasn't surprised that Logan seemed to be avoiding the bar too; she'd grown used to seeing him wandering along the beach around sunset, camera in hand, but he was conspicuously absent. But Eve was too run off her feet to give it much thought and it wasn't until the crowds thinned after the long Easter weekend that she started to think about her invitation to go diving. The weather looked settled for several days, which hopefully meant visibility might be good below the waves. Eve wasn't sure she'd ever encountered perfect diving conditions – those were reserved for more tropical waters – but calm seas and warmer temperatures usually made for an enjoyable dive. After a quick consultation with Billy about his commitments, she messaged Logan.

Are you free on Thursday afternoon? Looks like the best day for diving.

His reply was swift. Absolutely. What time?

Eve checked the tide tables again — diving at high tide usually offered the best visibility and the location of the shipwreck she had selected meant that there shouldn't be much interference from strong currents. With some wrecks it made sense to aim for a window of slack water, when the change of tidal flow meant there was no current pulling one way or another, but the sunken ship Eve had in mind wasn't usually affected by the pull of the tide.

How does 1pm sound? she typed. I'll pick you up on the way past, save a bit of fuel.

Her phone pinged a moment later. Perfect, thank you. I'll remind Billy what size wetsuit I need. And thanks for arranging this — really appreciate it.

Thursday dawned bright and clear, exactly as the Met Office had predicted, and Eve was pleased to observe the surface of the sea was smooth as the tide rolled in. A gentle breeze ruffled her hair as she pulled up outside Logan's cottage, and she could see the grass undulating on top of the dunes beyond the small, white-washed house. Logan appeared in the doorway almost immediately, gave her a quick wave and briefly vanished before slamming the corn-flower blue door behind him and crossing the yard to Eve's Land Rover.

'It looks like you picked a good day to dive,' he observed as she navigated the lane that led towards Ennisfarne village and the harbour.

Eve nodded. 'It doesn't get much better than this. We should get to see plenty of wildlife from the boat – if we're really lucky we might spot some dolphins or even a whale.'

He patted the camera case in the footwell. 'I've come prepared. I'm looking forward to getting some underwater shots if the visibility is good enough.'

'It should be,' Eve said, and hesitated. Scuba diving was a complicated activity at the best of times and Logan had already admitted it had been some time since his last open water dive. She wasn't sure he should be adding another layer of complexity to what would be his first dive outside a pool since his refresher course. But, on the other hand, he was Logan Silk and photography came as naturally to him as breathing. There was no way she was going to tell him to leave his camera on the boat.

As though reading her thoughts, Logan pulled a wry face. 'Don't worry, I'm not treating this as photoshoot. I'm not actually sure I remember how to work the camera so it will be a miracle if I get any pictures that aren't a blurry mess.'

She glanced sideways. 'Sounds unlikely to happen. Just make sure you don't take any risks. The conditions may be good but there are still dangers down there. No wandering off after the perfect shot, okay?'

For a nanosecond, she thought she'd gone too far, but Logan simply dipped his head. 'You're the boss. I'm just glad you're letting me tag along. Who else is diving?'

'Em Davey and Sam Hopwood,' Eve replied. 'They're both seasoned divers and used to diving together, which leaves me free to be your dive partner.'

'And Billy will be manning the boat and managing the dive,' Logan said. 'Have you worked with him much?'

Eve eased the Land Rover around the left turn that would take them to the village. 'Yeah. He's the best – utterly unflappable and he knows these waters better than anyone. It makes me feel safer, knowing Billy has my back while I'm below the surface.'

Logan nodded. 'Having a good support team is critical.' He rubbed his hands together in anticipation. 'I can't wait to see what else your island has to show me.'

Billy's boat, *Serendipity*, was waiting in the harbour when Eve and Logan arrived. Her clean white lines stood out against the grey-blue of the lapping water. Ordinarily, there would be an assortment of other vessels to welcome her but for now she pretty much had the harbour to herself – all the working boats were out at sea, bringing in the harvest that was a large part of the island's economy.

'Afternoon,' Billy said as Eve and Logan crossed the gangplank. 'Welcome aboard *Serendipity*.'

'Hi Billy,' Eve said, nodding to the grizzled,

fifty-something captain she'd known most of her life. 'I'm sure you remember Logan.'

'I do,' Billy replied, his gaze transferring to Logan. 'Glad you could join us, lad. Sam and Em are in the prow, checking the kit, if you want to say hello and get yourself sorted. We'll get underway shortly.'

Eve picked her way around the side of the boat to where Em and Sam were bent over an assortment of tanks, vests and masks. Both were already wearing wetsuits and they straightened as she and Logan approached, smiling as introductions were made.

'Your wetsuit is here, Logan,' Em said, pointing to a folded black bundle. 'And your fins are next to it, with your mask and vest. They should all fit but we've got spares down below if not.'

'Great, thanks,' Logan said, and reached down to unfold the wetsuit.

Eve lowered her backpack, which held her own wetsuit and mask. 'Need me to do anything? Check the tanks, weigh down the vests?'

Sam waved a hand towards four sets of gas tanks on the other side of the deck. 'All done. You know Billy, he's Mr Organized.'

'True,' Eve said, laughing as she pulled her wetsuit out of her rucksack. 'That's why I like diving with him.'

Em glanced at Logan, who also had an armful of neoprene wetsuit. 'You should try that on. There's plenty of room to change downstairs.'

He shook his head. 'I've tried that before and ended up a hot, sweaty mess. Much better to put a wetsuit on in the open air, which is why I've got swimming trunks on underneath my jeans.'

Eve approved of his practicality; she'd done the same with her swimming costume. She watched as Logan shook out his wetsuit and then focused on getting into her own electric blue suit, reaching behind to tug the zip up towards her neck and adjusting the ankles and cuffs to fit snugly. Curiosity got the better of her as she straightened up from tugging on her neoprene shoes and she couldn't resist sneaking a peek at Logan. She caught a glimpse of a tanned chest dappled with black hair that tapered down to his waist and instantly, warmth flooded her cheeks. That was Freda's fault, she told herself as she firmly averted her gaze once more. All that talk at the movie night had clearly stuck in Eve's head and turned her into a Peeping Tom, or whatever the female equivalent was. Concentrating on her own kit, she didn't look up again until she was sure Logan would be fully dressed.

'Everyone ready?' Billy called from behind the wheel.

Sam fired an enquiring look at Eve and Logan, who both nodded. 'All set, Billy.'

The rumble of the engine sent a gentle shudder through the deck and a moment later, the boat was moving away from the quay and aiming for the gap in the grey harbour walls. Em and Sam took themselves below deck, leaving Eve alone with Logan and she saw him studying the brightly coloured buoys that bobbed on the swell of the waves – several were acting as perches for seagulls.

'Have you seen the harbour at low tide?' she asked.

Logan considered the question. 'I don't think I have.'

Eve pointed to the rapidly approaching left-hand harbour wall. 'There's a blowhole over there. When the sea hits it at low tide, it sends a huge spray of water across the harbour. My dad used to say someone had angered the dragon that lived underneath the island and made it roar. It took me years to discover it was a natural phenomenon.'

He laughed. 'Parenting 101 – scare your children into behaving.'

She tipped her head in acknowledgement. 'Probably. But I always think of him as such a practical man, really not given to flights of fancy.'

'Except that he read Ursula le Guin,' Logan pointed out. 'I seem to remember one or two dragons in that story.'

'True,' Eve said, smiling. 'But the truth is we never really know our parents, do we? As people in their own right, I mean, rather than simply as the adults in charge of us.'

Logan regarded her thoughtfully for a moment, then transferred his gaze to the harbour wall. 'I suppose so. My father died suddenly not long after I left home. I've always wondered whether we'd have got along, as two grown men.'

It was an unexpected confidence; Eve wasn't sure she'd heard Logan talk about his family before. 'I'm sorry to hear that. Was he creative too?'

The briefest of smiles flickered across Logan's face. 'No, he was an engineer – worked on the railways. I don't think he understood my fascination with photography. He thought it was a hobby, not a job.'

His tone was matter of fact but Eve though she detected a faint sadness behind the words. She felt a stirring of sympathy. 'It's a shame he never got to see how successful you became. I bet he'd be proud of you.'

Logan's mouth twisted wryly. 'Maybe. He'd still have told me to get a proper job, though.' He glanced over her shoulder and nodded. 'I think your dad was onto something. Ennisfarne is the perfect hideaway for dragons.'

Eve grinned. 'Don't tell Freda that. She'll change the name of The Nook and start organizing tours.'

He laughed. 'I have no doubt she would. I'm pretty sure she could have sold sand to the Pharaohs.'

'If they were still around, she'd probably try,' Eve agreed with a fond sigh. 'But we wouldn't have her any other way.'

They fell into a companionable silence as the boat chugged through the opening in the harbour wall and made for the channel between Ennisfarne and the mainland. It was a perfect spring afternoon – the sun sparkled on the water as Billy turned north to navigate the route to their destination and there was barely a cloud in the sky. It was almost too nice to dive, Eve thought, shielding her eyes with one hand, but at least the visibility would be good. She wondered what Logan would make of the wreck she'd chosen – it was a far cry from the Great Barrier Reef but she hoped he'd appreciate the less flashy beauty of the North Sea just as much.

Her thoughts were interrupted by the reappearance of Sam and Em. The three of them spent a few minutes catching up with each other's news before Eve began to wonder whether she should include Logan in the conversation. But he was sitting near the prow of the boat, his gaze fixed on the horizon, and he seemed to have forgotten they were there. After a moment or two, she saw him reach for his camera and she decided to leave him to it. She'd seen him work before and his focus was intense.

But it wasn't until they had neared the north-east tip of the island, where the ruins of the nunnery stood proud and desolate on top of the headland, that Logan's professional instincts really seemed to kick in. She watched from the corner of her eye as he began clicking in earnest and, not for the first time, she wished she could see Ennisfarne through his eyes. The island was her home and she loved every aspect of her life there but there was something intriguing about Logan's creativity behind the lens. Somehow, he took the places she'd seen every day for most of her life and transformed them into something fresh and new. And she had absolutely no idea how he did it.

But it wasn't until they reached the cluster of small islands off the tip of the nature reserve that she crossed the boat to stand beside Logan. 'We call these the Selkie Isles,' she said, pointing to the bare rocky outcrops. 'In the breeding season, they're covered with seal pups.'

Logan lowered the camera to glance at her. 'Selkie Isles?'

Eve nodded. 'After the legend of the nuns who threw

themselves into the sea to escape the invaders. Selkies are mythological creatures who could turn from humans into seals and some of our ancestors thought that was what happened when St Hilda blessed the nuns as they jumped.'

'Better than the reality,' Logan replied, tilting his head. 'And who knows – maybe that's exactly what happened.'

'Maybe,' Eve said with a smile. 'Our dive spot is just beyond them. Probably a good time to get our tanks on.'

By the time the engine stopped, each diver was fully kitted out with buoyancy vest, double gas tank and mask. Billy stood before them and ran through the timings for the dive, reminding them to check their gas supplies and return to the boat if the levels reached 50 bar. 'The conditions should be good down there but make sure you stay safe,' Billy went on. 'Especially since this is a wreck most of you know well. Keep within sight of your buddy at all times and make sure you communicate. Don't forget this is a maritime war grave, so no entering the wreck itself. Outside observation only, please.'

Logan gave Eve a questioning look. 'Some war wrecks are considered the final resting place of the sailors who perished when their ship sank,' she explained. 'We aren't allowed to disturb them or remove any artefacts without a licence.'

'That makes sense,' Logan said. 'How long do we have under the water?'

Billy checked the time. 'It depends how much gas you get through. You should have around twenty minutes of slack water by the time you reach the wreck, and then you'll need to make a judgement call based on current strength.' He scanned the waves with an experienced gaze. 'On a day like today, I'd expect a decent forty-five minutes of dive time but Eve will be in charge. If she thinks the conditions are shifting, she'll make you surface sooner.'

'I'm optimistic we'll last the distance,' Eve said, aiming an encouraging look Logan's way. 'Plenty of time for you to rediscover your scuba skills.'

'Right,' Billy said, with a decisive nod of the head. 'If there are no more questions, we should get you in the water.'

Eve felt the familiar flutter of adrenaline in her stomach as she fastened her mask in place and took her first lungful of the oxygen mix. The thrill of stepping off the boat and plunging into the water never got old, even though it was laced with the ever-present danger that something might go wrong. Sam and Em were both unflappable, experienced divers – she knew she didn't have to worry about their reactions once they were under the waves. But Logan was an unknown quantity. Billy had said he'd been both calm and competent during the refresher course he'd undertaken but Eve knew that a diver's reactions in a swimming pool could be very different to those in open water and she had to acknowledge a small quiver of disquiet at diving with Logan. But it was no different to going out for the first time with anyone new; hope they had a great dive but be prepared for a tricky one.

Billy appeared in her line of vision and made a circle with his thumb and forefinger, the recognized 'Okay?' gesture all divers used. She nodded and made the same shape with her own fingers. Once he'd checked in with the others, Billy tipped his head. 'Stay safe. See you in forty-five.'

Sam and Em went first. Eve allowed a moment or two for them to clear the side of the boat, then caught Logan's eye and waved him forward. She watched as he stepped out and vanished under the water, then took a deep breath and followed.

Chapter Eighteen

Logan

The first thing Logan noticed was the immediate absence of sound from the world above the water, as though someone had abruptly cut the speakers. A cascade of bubbles tickled past him as he sank into the green depths, creating a low gurgling song that merged with a lighter melody of faster-moving bubbles as he exhaled. Everything else was still as the in-out rhythm of breathing dominated his senses, and he spent a second or two marvelling at the total change in sensory input; the water was a mesmerizing mix of emerald and turquoise, deepening to royal blue and jade below him. His arms and legs felt clumsy and alien yet the gas rushing through his body made him feel almost weightless. He moved one hand to wave it in front of his face, trying to ignore the unnerving impression that it belonged to someone else, and squinted around to find Sam or Em. Then he felt a muted impact from above. The water around him swirled and he looked up to see a dark shape descending to his right. A moment later Eve's masked face was opposite his own, checking he was okay. Once he had returned the signal, she gestured at him to follow her. Taking a steady breath, Logan did as he was told.

It took several minutes to reach the wreck, by which time Logan had started to relax. The initial tension in his limbs melted away as they swam and he was starting to enjoy the slow deliberate motion that moving in full scuba kit demanded. The view became a little gloomier and the water temperature dropped as they went deeper. He knew they must be close when they reached the seabed, a reef alive with gracefully dancing anemones, coral and seaweed, but even so, the hull seemed to loom up suddenly. A cluster of tiny silver fish scattered as Logan and Eve approached, leaving wispy swirls of silt in their wake, and Logan felt the breath catch in his throat as he took in the wreck, half submerged beneath the seabed. He'd known it would be huge, of course, but at the same time had somehow managed to fail to visualize the scale of the sunken vessel. It was a submarine, perhaps even a German U-boat, and whatever had caused it to sink had not caused massive damage. In fact, as far as Logan could see, the hull on this side was undamaged.

Reaching out, he brushed the fuzzy silver-black surface with his hand, feeling the roughness of barnacles under his fingertips. A shimmering amber starfish rested just to his left, nestled beside a cluster of purple seaweed fronds and cerise jewel anemones, and a shoal of quicksilver fish darted among the rippling strands. Swathes of vibrant green fur hid the metal from view, dotted with golden sun stars, and the spectacular abundance of marine life that colonized the wreck made it clear the submarine had long since ceased to belong to the men who had built her. She had been claimed by the sea and was irrevocably part of that domain now.

Turning in the water, Logan made eye contact with Eve and touched the camera securely fastened to his vest. Once she'd signalled her agreement, he moved backwards, working out the best angles. Further along the hull, beside the remains of the conning tower, he could see Sam and Em silhouetted against the paler greens and blues of the water overhead. It was too good a shot to miss and he lined it up as fast as he could. Checking the screen, he moved the camera to capture the elegant sway of the plants that had made their home on the vessel, the myriad sea creatures that now adorned the cold metal surface. As he worked, he noticed a subtle change in the movement of the delicate plant fronds – instead of waving aimlessly, they began to drift in one direction which told Logan the tide had turned. Then Eve was beside him again, reminding him to check his gas levels, and he was surprised to see how much he'd used – almost half his supply was gone. He relayed the number to her and she pointed to the other side of the wreck, waggling her hands up and down to mime swimming. Once again, Logan followed her instructions and together, they made for the far side of the submarine.

It became instantly clear what had caused the boat to be wrecked. A jagged hole marred the otherwise intact metal, a metre or so across. The edges had been rubbed smooth by the constant motion of the sea and were edged in green in the same way as the rest of the surface but there was no mistaking the signs of a violent impact. Perhaps a torpedo, Logan thought, or possibly run aground on the rocks around Ennisfarne. There would be records online; he'd have to do some research after the dive. But he could now fully appreciate why the submarine had been designated a maritime war grave. A great many men must have died when she was lost.

Yet here too there was beauty. A riot of colour softened the ugliness of the destruction that had wrecked the vessel. Logan snapped still more pictures, smiling as a red crab edged into the shot to photobomb, and marvelling at nature's absorption of mankind's intrusion. Then Eve was moving on again, heading for what was left of the tower. Along the way, she pointed out the submarine's hatch, which was forever open to allow its new residents to come and go. Kelp and seaweed twisted like wraiths in the hole; briefly, Logan wondered what it would be like to explore the black void inside the hatch but the thought didn't hold much appeal. There was more than enough to see outside and he had no desire to disturb the hard-won peace of the sailors who'd lost their lives.

Sam and Em were waiting on the far side of the ruined conning tower. As soon as Eve reached them, Sam engaged in a series of rapid signals that Logan couldn't quite follow.

Eve responded with some mimed questions of her own, peering in the direction Sam had indicated, before turning to Logan and gesturing at him to swim alongside her. As before, he obeyed her directions without question but it wasn't until they'd left the wrecked submarine and reached clear water that he realized why Sam had appeared so animated. Up ahead, swooping through the emerald depths with a silky grace that took Logan's breath away, was a herd of silver-skinned seals.

His camera was raised almost before he realized, his professional instincts taking over even as his brain processed what he was seeing. The seals were looping around, carving circles and figure-of-eights through the water, snatching panicked fish from a shoal that was darting this way and that in an effort to escape. The acrobatic twists and turns were hypnotic and Logan could only hope the camera was capturing even a fraction of the brilliant display. His fellow divers stayed back as the feeding frenzy ran its course and it was only once the last of the fish was gone that the seals seemed to notice they weren't alone. Most cast curious glances at the divers and then swam away, undoubtedly in search of more food, but one split from the herd and came to investigate. Logan had to fight the urge to hold his breath, continuing to inhale and exhale steadily as a big-eyed, whiskery face nudged the lens of his camera before peering straight into his mask. He couldn't prevent a brief burst of laughter, sending a storm of bubbles upwards, and the seal playfully chased them before swooping around to examine the other divers.

Logan watched as the seal nibbled experimentally at Eve's fin, then circled round to study Sam and Em. Finally, she appeared to conclude they were not fish and whirled away to follow the herd.

All four divers stared at each other for a moment, as though unable to believe what had just happened, and then Eve broke the spell. She signalled to check their gas levels, waiting as each of them responded, and then gestured to the surface. A surge of regret washed through Logan – there was so much more to explore – but his tank gauge told him the dive was over for today. Tucking his camera away, he followed Eve as she led them back the way they'd come. They hadn't gone deep enough to worry about decompression but she made the ascent slow and steady, until they found the guide rope Billy had attached to the marker buoy and finally broke the surface a short distance from the boat.

It felt strange to be above the water, Logan observed as he clambered up the ladder to the deck. Noisy, for a start – the birds circling overhead seemed to have turned the volume of their cries up – and the warmth of the sun on his sea-chilled skin felt like a heat lamp. Billy met him at the top of the ladder, his gaze watchful as he guided him to the prow. 'Are you well, Logan?' he asked.

Logan removed his mouthpiece and lifted the mask from his eyes. 'I'm well. Thank you.'

Nodding, Billy left him to help the others aboard. A few minutes later they were all standing together, dripping onto the wooden planks and grinning at each other. Billy took in their beaming expressions and grunted. 'Good dive, I take it?'

Eve's grin widened. 'A very good dive. We bumped into a herd of grey seals towards the end.' She turned to look at Logan. 'Please tell me you did remember how to use that camera.'

'I hope so,' he said. 'Although I'm not sure the photos will do any justice to the beauty down there. It was extraordinary.'

She almost seemed to glow with pride as she unclipped her tanks and slid them to the deck. 'Not bad for a little island off the north-east coast of England.'

He inclined his head wryly, recalling her assertion that she had no need to travel the world when Ennisfarne had everything she wanted. 'Not bad at all,' he agreed.

'So I hear you made a new friend on Thursday.'

Selina smiled playfully over the top of her wine glass as she leaned back into her chair and regarded Logan across the white-clothed table. It was Saturday evening and Pilgrim's restaurant was around half full; a low buzz of conversation accompanied the usual chink of cutlery and glasses and the tables around Logan and Selina were dotted with other diners. The menu boasted locally sourced, award-winning produce and Logan had no doubt the restaurant would be packed in the summer months – his starter of scallops with creamed potato puree was certainly faultless and the view across the ocean at sunset had to be a draw. But it also helped that it was one of only three restaurants on Ennisfarne. The

Fisherman's Arms served hearty pub grub that was perfect after a hard day's walking, and Mango's was a thriving curry house just off Eastgate, but neither had seemed right for a second date and the tide prevented Logan and Selina from venturing to the mainland. Her suggestion of Pilgrim's had been a good one, although he'd already caught one or two bright-eyed glances their way and knew Date Two would be reported to Freda before the evening was out. It was the price of living in a tiny community and he wasn't the least surprised that Selina had heard the details of the dive on Thursday.

'I did,' he replied mildly. 'And she turned out to be a natural – I'd definitely work with her again.'

Selina laughed. 'It sounds like you really hit it off. How was the rest of the dive?'

Dutifully, Logan described the afternoon, even though he was sure she must have heard all about it from Eve. He praised Billy's efficiency in running the dive, Eve's skill in managing their time under the water and the wild exquisiteness of the wreck itself, but played down how long he'd spent sifting through the photographs afterwards, choosing the best ones and editing them so that they shone from the screen. Like almost every picture he'd taken during his stay on Ennisfarne, the subject was a long way from his usual work but he'd very much enjoyed sitting in Dune Cottage on Thursday evening, reliving the dive with a glass of wine at his elbow and marvelling all over again at the sea's splendour. But he suspected Selina wasn't interested in hearing him describe the satisfaction of a quiet night in. Those were easy to come by on Ennisfarne and he had a feeling she expected more from him.

'Are we about to become famous?' she asked, once he'd finished talking.

He frowned. 'In what way?'

'You have all these photographs of the island. I just thought you might be planning to sell some and turn Ennisfarne into a celebrity hotspot.'

She was smiling as she spoke but Logan thought he detected a hint of seriousness behind her words. He shook his head. 'No, I'm not going to sell any pictures. But I have been toying with the idea of an anonymous exhibition – maybe in the village hall, showcasing the beauty of Ennisfarne. Do you think that might be something the other islanders might be interested in?'

Selina sat forward, her eyes gleaming. 'Are you kidding? Our little island, seen through the eyes of a world-famous photographer – what's not to love about that?'

'It wouldn't have my name attached to it,' Logan reminded her, reaching for his water glass.

'No, but we'd all know it's your work,' she said. 'And I'm sure the photos will be incredible – I can't think of a single objection. It's a wonderful idea.'

'Great,' Logan said, warmed by her enthusiasm. 'I'll speak to Freda about it, see what she thinks.'

Selina pursed her lips thoughtfully. 'I'm going to go out on a limb here and suggest she's going to snap your hand off. Especially if there's a way to make some money for the island's upkeep – she's always keen to boost that.'

He nodded. 'I'd prefer it to be free to enter but perhaps we could ask for donations to cover the use of the hall.'

The waiter materialized at their table, unobtrusively whisking away their empty plates and topping up their glasses. Once he was gone, Selina fixed Logan with a knowing look. 'You're going to have no shortage of models, once word gets out. Everyone is going to want their fifteen minutes of fame.'

Logan gave the observation some thought. The idea of an exhibition hadn't been much more than a fleeting notion until now but he'd had a vague idea of limiting his subject to the landscape of the island, rather than its people. But why shouldn't he include them? Why not make it a celebration of Ennisfarne as a whole? It was the least he could do after they had welcomed him so warmly. 'Do you think so?'

'Definitely,' Selina said. 'Although there is one important stipulation I'm going to have to insist on.'

'Oh?' Logan replied, raising his eyebrows as their main courses arrived. 'What's that?'

She smoothed her dark hair and smiled winningly across the table. 'That you take my picture first, of course.'

Chapter Nineteen

Eve

There was no doubt about it, the village hall was cold. Eve pulled her jacket closer around her ears and tried to ignore the chill in her feet. It was her own fault for wearing a t-shirt; the hall hadn't been used since the weekend, two days ago, and the weather had cooled since then. She should have known it would take an age for the heating to kick in and brought a jumper. Her only consolation was that the parish council meeting was almost finished. She had survived discussions on increasing the visitors' car park fees, the cleaning rota of the island's public toilets and measures to discourage the criminal tendencies of the harbour's seagulls. Now Freda was peering down at the agenda again and, when she looked up, her expression was considerably more enthusiastic than it had been for the previous three items. 'Ah, Item Twelve,' she said, beaming at her fellow committee members. 'Ennisfest. Over to you, Eve.'

Five other faces turned expectantly towards Eve. She cleared her throat and then wondered why she felt suddenly nervous. She'd been arranging the island's annual music festival for the past four years, regularly updating the parish council on the acts she'd booked and tickets sold, as well as leading the administrative team that managed the logistics of welcoming over two thousand festivalgoers to Darling Cove for a weekend of dancing and revelry. This year was no different to any other year – they had a tried and trusted schedule in place, with systems to handle every aspect of the weekend. Every member of the committee – Warren, Hamish, Nina, Petr and Shona, plus Freda as Chair – had known Eve for most of her life. So why did she suddenly feel as though she had something to prove?

Pushing the uncomfortable sensation aside, Eve glanced at her notes. 'As you know, the festival is just two months away now. All the acts have been confirmed, most of the food and drink vendors are agreed and I'm pleased to say tickets are almost sold out.' She looked at Hamish. 'Our usual arrangement with the brewery continues this year, so we'll have lager, cider and several ales on tap from marquees around the festival site. They're also providing a number of non-alcoholic spirits and I've had an enquiry from a mocktail vendor who'd like to join us, which I'm all in favour of.'

Shona sniffed. 'I should hope so. What are you going to do about the beach overnight? We don't want a repeat of last year.'

It was a good question and something that had given Eve a

few sleepless nights. There were always one or two instances of drunken festivalgoers attempting to swim in the sea once the music had finished for the night but the previous year one had got into difficulties and had needed to be rescued. Everyone was keen to avoid a similar risk but it was no small headache.

Eve consulted her notes. 'Access to the beach will be restricted for the duration of the festival,' she said. 'Metal fencing will be in place for the entire length of the cove, preventing anyone from entering from further along the beach and we'll run a fence down to low tide level to bisect the sand. There will be signs warning against swimming and we've assigned additional stewards to try to ensure everyone's safety but I'm afraid, ultimately, we can't stop someone if they're really determined.'

Warren gave her a reassuring nod. 'The bars on the festival site will all close at midnight, an hour after the headline acts finish. That should encourage people to go back to the camp site, where there'll be several food and drink vendors.'

'Thanks, Warren,' Eve said, grateful for his support. The camping area was on his land, as was the car park, and she was aware there would be no Ennisfest without him. 'The vast majority of our festivalgoers are impeccably well behaved and I'm confident that will continue this year.'

Freda leaned forwards. 'I agree. Let's not forget what an important contribution the festival makes to local businesses and the island as a whole – we're all very grateful to you for your tireless hard work, Eve.'

'Thank you, Freda,' Eve replied and some of the tension slipped from her shoulders. 'But it's the whole festival management team that deserves the credit. I couldn't do it without them.'

Across the table, Warren and Hamish smiled; they were Eve's right-hand men and her first port of call when she had a problem. Freda tipped her head in agreement. 'Of course, we're grateful for everyone who makes the festival happen. Now, is there any other business?' She gazed enquiringly around and, when no one spoke, shuffled her papers as though looking for something. 'I have one final item, then. Logan Silk has offered to exhibit some of his photographs of the island next month and would like to use this hall. Are there any objections?'

Eve blinked. It wasn't a surprise that Logan had enough Ennisfarne photos to create an exhibition – finding him without a camera in his hand was rare – but she was surprised he wanted to put them display, much less at the busiest time of the year for visitors to the island. But perhaps he felt media interest in both his personal life and his whereabouts had died down enough that he could risk discovery.

None of the committee members raised their hand so Freda continued. 'Needless to say, it will be anonymous. Logan will cover the costs of keeping the hall open and staffing the exhibition himself, and he's also waived the copyright of all the images so we'll be able to use them ourselves. I think that's very generous.'

There was a general murmur of approval around the table.

'Do you know when he plans to launch?' Eve asked, suddenly aware of a curious gnawing in the pit of her stomach. When Logan had first arrived on Ennisfarne, his three-month tenancy of Dune Cottage had felt lengthy to her but the time had flown by and it came as something of a shock to realize it was less than a month until he was due to leave, in spite of the fact that the cottage had a queue of holidaymakers lined up to take temporary possession across the summer. The thought of not bumping into Logan on the beach made her feel – she wasn't sure what it made her feel. Dismayed, at the very least. And possibly even sad.

'We haven't pinned down the details yet,' Freda said, firing a shrewd look Eve's way. 'But I got the impression he wanted it to happen before he leaves.'

Eve felt her cheeks growing warm even as she reminded herself Freda couldn't know what she was thinking. 'Good,' she said. 'I was wondering whether we could use the pictures for the festival promo materials, that's all.'

'Of course you were. Ever practical, that's our Eve,' Freda replied, with a bland smile that didn't fool Eve for an instant. She could expect an interrogation the next time she went to The Nook. All she had to do before then was convince herself she didn't care that in a month's time, she'd probably never see Logan again.

The meeting over, Eve said her goodbyes and did her best to avoid Freda as she left the hall. Night had fallen and brought with it a cold drizzle that sent her scurrying over the road to the car park of the Fisherman's Arms. Head down as she made for her Land Rover, she almost didn't notice the two people crossing the car park in front of her. Stopping abruptly, she realized with a lurch it was Logan and Selina.

'Woah there,' Selina said, amusement in her voice. 'Have you just come from the parish meeting? Was it that bad?'

'No,' Eve said, hoping her voice wasn't as high-pitched as it felt. She took a deep breath, wondering what on earth was wrong with her. 'Yes, I have but it was fine. The usual stuff.'

'In that case, you'll need a drink.' Selina linked her arm through Logan's and smiled. 'We're just popping in for a couple. Why don't you join us?'

It ought to be a no-brainer – Selina was her best friend and Logan was – well, he was a friend too and hadn't she just been fretting about how little time he had left on Ennisfarne? But there was no way she was going to crash what was quite obviously a date. 'I can't,' she blurted out, then caught herself and summoned up a weak smile of her own. 'Need to get back to Huxley. You know how it is.'

Selina raised her eyebrows. 'He'll be okay for another twenty minutes, won't he? Isn't Aiden at home?'

'He's had to go out,' Eve said, crossing her fingers surreptitiously inside her pocket. 'Unexpectedly. He messaged earlier.'

Logan's forehead creased into a frown as he studied Eve and he looked like he was about to contradict her. Fumbling in her bag for her keys, Eve dredged up what she hoped was a regretful expression. 'I'd better go, anyway. Let's grab a drink some other time.'

She edged past them and headed for the Land Rover, hauling the door open and sliding inside before they could accost her further. Focusing on manoeuvring her way out of the car park, it wasn't until she was out of sight of the pub that Eve released the breath she'd been holding and allowed her shoulders to slump. What had that been about? A reluctance to be a gooseberry was understandable but the clenching of her gut suggested it was more than that. And she couldn't shake the suspicion that it had nothing to do Selina and everything to do with Logan Silk.

The message from Logan arrived shortly after ten-thirty on Wednesday morning, just as Eve was clearing up after the Beach Bums exercise class that used the space in the bar. She gave her phone a cursory glance and saw Logan had a problem with the boiler at Dune Cottage – there was no hot water. Probably the pilot light, Eve decided; it had been occasionally known to go out in the past. She mentally reviewed her schedule. Aiden had taken Huxley for his morning walk but was due back soon and she had nothing that needed her urgent attention, at least not until after lunch. Glancing over at Tish, who was cleaning the coffee machine, she bit her lip; ordinarily, she tried not to leave her to work alone. But a quick message to Aiden established he was less than ten minutes away so Eve grabbed her tool bag and headed to Dune Cottage.

'Thanks for coming so quickly,' Logan said as he answered her knock at the door. 'It's probably something stupid but you could write what I know about boilers on a gas molecule so I thought I'd better leave it to the expert.'

It was a far cry from his attitude towards her when he'd first moved into the cottage, Eve thought ruefully, but she said nothing and followed him through to the kitchen, where he'd clearly been working. His MacBook was open and she saw a photograph of the wrecked submarine on the screen. 'Wow,' she said, pausing to appreciate the riot of colours. 'That's stunning.'

'I know,' Logan said. 'I can't take all the credit, though. If you hadn't taken me down there I'd never have known the wreck was even there. It was a team effort.'

His words caused a ripple of pleasure to flow through Eve, although she shook her head almost immediately. 'I've done that dive a dozen times or more and never taken a single photo, much less one that looks like it could win Wildlife Photographer of the Year. The credit most definitely belongs to you.'

'Team effort,' he repeated firmly. 'Don't argue.'

She gave in gracefully. 'Okay. Now, I'd better take a look at the boiler. I'll try not to disturb you.'

It didn't take long for Eve to establish the problem: there was a build-up of dirt around the pilot light mechanism that was preventing it from relighting. Shutting off both the gas and electricity supply to the boiler, she set about removing the debris. Once it was clean, she twisted the gas knob to restore the supply, then flipped the electricity switch back on. For a heartbeat, nothing happened. Then there was a muted click, followed by a gentle whoosh as the gas ignited and a small but steady blue flame appeared in the pilot light window. Allowing herself a little smile of satisfaction, Eve replaced the white metal cover and turned around. She'd expected Logan to be engrossed in his work. Instead, she found he was watching her.

'Once again, I am impressed,' he said, shaking his head in wonder. 'Is there anything you can't fix?'

'Loads of things,' Eve replied, deflecting his praise again. 'Orchids. Broken hearts. Huxley's determination to roll in cow poo.'

He laughed. 'I'm not sure anyone can fix that last one. And orchids are famous for being divas. I've worked with supermodels who were less highly strung.'

Now it was Eve's turn to laugh. 'But they didn't pretend to be dead if you stood them in the wrong place. At least I hope they didn't.'

'Not so far. Not even Mimi Van Morten and she's the highest maintenance of them all.' He paused and returned his attention to the screen once more. 'I don't miss having to deal with that.'

Here it was, Eve realized, the perfect opportunity to find out what Logan planned to do once his escape to Ennisfarne was over. It didn't sound as though he had any interest in going back to the fashion industry but that was hardly a surprise, given the way he'd walked away from it at the start of the year. A large part of his reason for coming to the island was to recover from career burnout and he'd once confided in Eve that he'd fallen out of love with photography. What did the future hold for him if it didn't involve his camera, Eve wondered, but she didn't quite have the courage to ask. Instead, she focused on packing her tools away.

Logan looked up as she closed her bag. 'There is something else you can help me with, if you're not too busy.'

Eve hesitated, hoping she had the right equipment to deal with whatever else was wrong. 'Sure,' she said, lowering her bag onto the worktop again and reaching for the clasp. 'What's the problem?'

'Oh, it's not with the cottage,' Logan said. 'I suppose it's more of a favour, although hopefully something you'll find enjoyable.'

Mystified, Eve tipped her head. 'Okay,' she said slowly. 'What do you need?'

He turned the MacBook around so she could see the screen, which was now covered with tiny thumbnail images. 'Have you heard that I'm planning an exhibition next month?'

She nodded. 'In the village hall. Freda is very excited about it, she's been googling the Tate Modern for ideas.'

Logan looked amused. 'Why doesn't that surprise me? But before we get to the installation, I need to choose which photos represent the heart of Ennisfarne. I really don't want to get this wrong – would you be able to help?'

It was the last thing Eve had been expecting to hear and it took her a moment to adjust. 'Oh, I thought . . . now?'

He puffed out his cheeks. 'If you can, or whenever works for you. I know how busy you are.'

Eve's doubtful gaze flickered to the screen again, with its neat grid of snapshots. 'I don't know anything about photography, though.'

'But you do know Ennisfarne and the people who live here,' Logan said encouragingly. 'I want to know which images speak to you about the life and history of the island.'

Eve had to admit it was tempting. There were probably people who'd kill to get behind-the-scenes access to the work of such a celebrated photographer and the fact that it was on offer here, on the tiny island she'd spent her whole life on, was actually quite mind-blowing.

She came to a decision. 'I could come back later. Aiden should be able to handle the bar for an hour or two.'

'Thank you, that would be great,' Logan said, gratitude etched onto his features. 'Hopefully it won't take up too much of your time. Let me know when you're leaving and I'll open some wine.'

'Sounds good,' Eve said, smiling, but it wasn't until she was on her way along the road back to Darling's that she realized how much she was looking forward to her unexpected evening plans. Belatedly, it occurred to her that there'd been no trace of the awkwardness she'd felt during her previous encounter with Logan and Selina, just the quiet contentment of a problem solved, with the bonus of some enjoyable conversation and a fascinating opportunity to learn more about Logan's work. She decided not to dwell on the observation, however, and allowed herself a thrill of anticipation for the night to come. A few hours of Logan's company, spent in peaceful Dune Cottage with a glass of wine and nothing more taxing to do than look at incredible pictures of the island that was her world. What could be better than that?

Chapter Twenty

Logan

It was a novel experience for Logan to feel apprehensive when someone was viewing his work and he wasn't sure he liked it. While he was sure Eve wasn't going to throw her hands up in disgust, the way one of his tutors had when he was a student, her approval mattered immensely. Apart from anything else, she was a barometer for the way the rest of the islanders might react and he trusted her judgement. But it had still been a long time since he'd felt anything like this level of nervousness about his pictures. Then again, it had been long time since he'd felt *anything* where his work was concerned. Maybe the anxiety writhing through his gut was a good thing. Maybe, just maybe, it meant he was on the road to recovering his passion for photography.

His gaze travelled to Eve's face as she leaned forward on the sofa to flick through the images on the computer screen.

Absorbed in the task, she was completely unaware that he was watching her, which allowed him more time to study her profile. She had a decent chin and a good nose, he decided; straight but slightly turned up at the end. Her cheekbones were high – not dominant and jutting, like many of the models he worked with, but delicate and feminine. Up close, he could see that the lashes framing her extraordinary blue eyes were long and full, as blonde as her hair. A good make-up artist would make those eyes a focal point for the camera, accentuating their colour and coating the fair lashes in mascara to make them stand out. She might even pass for a model, he thought, narrowing his gaze in professional appraisal – he'd worked with less striking women and the results had graced magazine covers across the world. But he knew with absolute certainty that Eve would laugh if he told her so and besides, she had the kind of natural beauty that shone without make-up. Who was he to suggest she became anything more than she was?

She turned suddenly, catching him staring. A frown knotted her eyebrows and Logan felt his cheeks flush. 'Sorry. Occupational hazard. I was thinking about photographing you.'

Her eyes widened a fraction, then she laughed. 'Not even you could make me look good, Logan. I'm famously bad at having my photograph taken – it's like my face can't decide what to do and I end up gurning like Wurzel Gummidge.'

Now it was Logan's turn to frown. 'I don't believe that for a second.' He reached for the computer and began scanning through the thumbnails. 'I've caught you on camera several times and I'm pretty sure you looked perfectly fine. See?'

The image on the screen had been taken at George and Hettie's wedding. It showed Eve laughing with George at a joke the camera couldn't possibly capture. Her head was thrown back in delight, her eyes dancing with infectious joy. It was an utterly natural shot and Logan found it impossible not to smile when he looked at it.

Beside him, Eve sniffed. 'Okay, I'm not gurning in that one.'

Logan pulled up another picture, this one taken aboard Billy's boat, *Serendipity*. It was after their dive, so Eve's hair was dark and sleek against her head, streaming down her back like silken seaweed. She was half out of her wetsuit which hung like a second skin from her waist as she gazed wistfully out at the lapping waves. The mid-afternoon sunlight conspired with the camera lens to bathe her in gold and the overall effect was so other-worldly that it was almost enough to make Logan believe selkies were real, although perhaps that was another observation he wouldn't share with Eve. 'You're not pulling a face here, either. I'm beginning to think you're making this up.'

She let out a hollow laugh. 'Believe me, there are plenty of terrible photos I could use to prove my point. Luckily for both of us, they're safely locked away at home.' But even as she spoke, her eyes were straying back to the MacBook. 'Although I have to admit this one isn't terrible.'

Logan's lips quirked. 'You're too kind.'

Eve seemed to realize what she'd said and turned pink. 'You know what I mean. It's a wonderful photo, in spite of me being in it.'

He wasn't about to let an opportunity like that go begging. 'So you won't mind if it goes into the exhibition, then.'

'Oh,' she said, hesitating as though wrong-footed. 'I suppose not, if there's space.'

'There's space,' he reassured her. 'Which others did you like?'

She talked him through the images she'd picked out and he was pleased to see a number of his own favourites on her list: the nunnery rendered monochrome by the snow, Hettie and George exchanging rings in front of the limestone arch at Darling Cove, the pilgrims bearing their wooden crosses as they'd crossed the sands and several from their dive the previous week. A lot of portraits made the cut, including one of George at the harbour, dressed in full fisherman's kit and looking like he'd stepped from a fishfinger advert, and another of Freda standing outside The Nook with an irrepressibly cheeky smile. And of course there were some that captured the view from Dune Cottage – the marram grass on the sand dunes with the sun setting on the distant horizon.

'This one could be a piece of wall art,' Eve said, tapping the picture of russet-red Mildred the Highland cow with her baby, Dora. 'Warren will be over the moon.'

Logan smiled. 'And of course the exhibition wouldn't be complete without this lovable rogue.' The screen was filled with Huxley's furry face, his tongue lolling to one side as he cocked his head to stare into the lens.

Eve's laugh was affectionately rueful. 'Of course – just try to keep him out!'

Having moved the files into a separate folder, Logan double-checked how many Eve had selected. 'So I make that thirty-two pictures in all,' he said. 'That should be enough, if all the subjects consent to having their picture on display. Thanks for your help.'

She took a long sip of wine and sat back. 'Don't mention it, I'm honoured you asked. In fact, it's me that should be thanking you, on behalf of everyone on Ennisfarne. The photos I've seen tonight are a real gift to us all and I'm sure those featured will be over the moon to be included.'

'Even you?' he teased.

'Especially me,' she said fervently. 'Like I said, good photos of me are rarer than hen's teeth. If I didn't already know you had talent, I would now.'

He wasn't sure whether it was the way the flickering light from the wood burner played across her hair, or the gentle curve of her lips as she smiled, but Logan suddenly wanted to reach for his camera. 'I'd like to photograph you again.'

She gaped at him in surprise. 'Not now,' he added hurriedly. 'Another time, maybe on the beach. You'd get to keep the pictures, obviously.'

There was a brief pause, during which Eve seemed to be facing some kind of internal struggle. Then she nodded slowly. 'I'd like that too. I mean, you're Logan Silk – does anyone ever say no?'

'Not usually,' he conceded. 'But it's been a while since I asked. Photography has been my job for so long that I'd almost forgotten what it's like to feel inspired.'

Eve blinked. 'Then I'm doubly honoured. Will you promise to delete any that look like Wurzel Gummidge?'

He lifted his eyebrows. 'There won't be any.'

'But if there are,' she persisted.

Laughing, Logan reached for his glass to tap against hers. 'You've got yourself a deal, Eve Darling.'

He stayed on the sofa long after she'd gone home, sifting through the photos she had selected and trying to establish a sense of narrative between them. Slowly, a subtle story emerged, something he hoped would guide the viewer through the images without dictating how they should react. He meant it as a love letter to the island, a thank you for making him so welcome and reminding him how it felt to enjoy taking photographs. He lingered on the pictures of Eve, appreciating the delicate set of her features all over again, and then ran a weary hand over his eyes. It was time for bed, he decided as a yawn crept over him. If he was very lucky, he might dream of a golden-haired selkie with eyes like the sea.

May arrived and seemed determined to impress, continuing April's fine spring weather and hinting at summer just around the corner. The warm air and calm sea allowed another dive window to materialize early the following week. Eve messaged Logan on Tuesday morning, asking if he'd like to explore another wreck, this one deeper and older than the U-boat, and he'd jumped at the chance. He hadn't been disappointed. In 1915, a Norwegian steamship had foundered on rocks off an uninhabited neighbouring island further along the coast. The *Gunhilde* lay half wedged in a gully, about twenty-five metres or so down, and once again Logan found the reef's variety of sea life took his breath away. Sponges snuggled beside soft corals, sea urchins spread their spines in perfectly treacherous globes and he saw more than one eel wriggling through the kelp. But the highlight of the dive was an octopus shyly peeping out from the crevice behind an enormous iron steering wheel; Logan had instantly known that the resulting photo would be going into the exhibition. And there had just been time for a cursory exploration of the sea caves cut into the base of the underwater cliff, although Eve hadn't allowed Logan to enter. Once again, the tide was their enemy; Logan noticed a strong downward current tugging at him as they swam back to the *Serendipity*.

Billy was waiting by the ladder when they returned aboard, uncharacteristically grim-faced as he checked their well-being.

'What's wrong?' Eve asked, as soon as the dive manager had established they were all well and helped them remove their tanks. 'You look worried.'

'I am,' Billy said. 'I picked up a distress call to the coastguard around fifteen minutes ago, a small boat off the south-east tip of Ennisfarne that's taking on water fast. It's Selina, Eve. She's in trouble.'

Eve's face was stricken as she glanced at Logan. 'Have they deployed the lifeboat? It shouldn't take long to reach her from Seahouses.'

Billy shook his head. 'They're out on a call – a cruise ship in trouble further north, with forty passengers on board. It's a major incident and has to take priority. They've sent both lifeboats and the National Coastwatch has deployed too.'

His words caused a knot of anxiety to lodge in Logan's stomach. 'So what now?'

Eve's attention was fixed on Billy. 'You've got Selina's longitude and latitude?'

He nodded. 'We're thirty minutes away.'

'Then let's go,' Eve said, her voice steely with calm. 'You set the course, I'll let her know we're on the way.'

'Is there anything I can do?' Logan asked, as Billy hurried away.

Eve pressed her lips together. 'Go below deck and find the emergency first-aid kit. Bring the blankets up too – if she's been bailing out water, it's likely she'll be cold and wet.' She stopped and he saw her eyes were pinched with worry. 'And stay kitted up – if the boat has gone down by the time we get there, we might need to go into the water.'

Logan did as he was told, a task that occupied him for a measly few minutes. After that, he stayed close to Eve as she waited by the radio. The last contact with Selina had established her boat was still above water but would not be for long. The silence from the radio nipped at Logan's nerves, even though he knew Selina must be too busy bailing out to keep in touch. Eve noticed him fidgeting and managed a brittle smile. 'She's been sailing since before she could walk. She knows what to do in an emergency.'

The reassurance helped a little but Logan couldn't help imagining the worst. Knowing what to do was one thing but would it really help if the boat sank entirely? How long could someone survive in the North Sea, even with a life jacket to keep them afloat? Would Selina be washed out to sea with the tide? At what point did hypothermia set in?

He tried to distract himself by watching the seabirds on the cliffs below the Ennisfarne beacon but nothing could shift the dread that dragged at his spirits. No further radio communication was heard from Selina and Logan could see Eve growing more and more tense as they rounded the island that housed the salt farm. But eventually, a shout went up from Billy. 'She's there! Up ahead, two hundred metres off the starboard side.'

Both Eve and Logan scrambled to their feet and hurried to the prow of the *Serendipity*. Only the tip of Selina's boat was visible, pointing upwards like an uneven monument. As they watched, there was an audible rush of escaping air. With a groan of twisting timbers and a gush of sea water, the boat vanished beneath the waves. 'Oh no,' Eve gasped. 'Where's Selina?'

Squinting, Logan scanned the waves and spotted a flash of orange bobbing on the wash from the wreck, some distance away. An arm waved at them and he heard Eve exhale loudly. 'She's alive. Thank god.'

Relief flooded through him. 'It's a shame we weren't fast enough to save the boat.'

'I know,' Eve replied grimly. 'But it's lucky we were near enough to get here as quickly as we did. The currents are strong – Selina might easily have been carried further out if she'd had to wait for the lifeboat.'

Edging the *Serendipity* as close as he could, Billy cut the engine when they were ten metres away. Eve was in the water the moment he did so, scything her way towards Selina with strong, economical strokes. There was a brief conversation, words exchanged that Logan couldn't hear, and then Eve was towing Selina back towards the ladder. He reached down as soon as they reached the boat, holding out an arm for Selina to grab as Eve guided her onto the metal steps. She gripped the neoprene sleeve fiercely and Logan pulled steadily upwards, bringing Selina with him until she half crawled, half staggered onto the deck. She lay on her back for a moment, shivering and breathing hard, then rolled onto her side and threw up. Eve was beside her in a flash, taking the glass of water Billy was holding and offering it to Selina. 'Rinse your mouth with this,' she said in a gentle voice. 'Then we'll get you out of the lifejacket and into a blanket.'

Selina looked up gratefully. 'Th-thanks,' she said, through chattering teeth. 'I d-don't think I've ever been s-so cold.'

As she sipped the water, Eve set about unbuckling the life-jacket. Once it was fully unfastened, she lifted it over Selina's head and helped her to her feet. 'Let's get you warmed up,' she said, taking the blanket from Logan and draping it around her best friend's shoulders. 'Are you hurt?'

Selina shook her head. 'Just cold.' She looked up and seemed to notice Logan properly for the first time. Her eyes brimmed with sudden tears. 'I'm so glad you're here.'

She took one or two faltering steps towards him. He caught her as she fell, wrapping his arms around her and holding her close as she sobbed. 'It's okay,' he murmured against her dripping hair. 'You're safe.'

Her only response was to cling to him more. Over the top of her head, Logan's eyes sought Eve's. 'What now?'

'We'll take her to Berwick Infirmary,' Eve said, not quite meeting his gaze. She glanced at Billy. 'Have you got enough fuel for that?'

'Plenty,' the older man said gruffly. 'She needs to be checked over. Let's be on our way.'

Eve threw him a grateful look. 'Thanks, Billy. For everything. If you hadn't picked up Selina's call ...' She trailed off, shuddering, then turned back to Logan. 'Do you want us to drop you off at Ennisfarne harbour? There might be a wait at A&E, I'm sure you know how it can be.'

Logan felt Selina shiver harder in his arms, as though protesting. 'No, it's fine. I'll come with you.'

If Eve was surprised, she didn't show it. 'Fair enough,' she said, taking a step towards Selina. 'Come on, Sel. Let's get you downstairs and out of those wet clothes. You'll feel better once you're dry.'

For a moment, Logan thought Selina might refuse to let go. But then her grip loosened and she allowed Eve to lead her away, still quietly sobbing.

'It's the shock,' Billy observed, watching them descend to the cabin below. 'She'll be right after a hot drink and a sit down.'

'I hope so,' Logan said. 'Thank goodness we were nearby.'

'Aye,' Billy said, then glanced sharply at Logan. 'You'd better get dried while I get us back underway. I don't need two cases of hypothermia.'

He bustled off, leaving Logan alone on deck. Now that the adrenaline of the rescue was wearing off, he could feel a chill creeping along his skin. But it was nothing to the icy horror he felt when he thought about what might have happened had they not been out diving that afternoon. A tragedy had been averted and it was due in no small part to Billy and Eve's decisive action. Perhaps she'd inherited more of Grace Darling's bravery than she'd known, Logan thought as he sank to the wooden bench and stared out at the sea. It seemed to him Eve Darling was an absolute hero too.

'How are you feeling?'

It was Monday morning, almost a week after Selina's near-miss, and Logan had stopped by her cottage with flowers and chocolates. Her hospital stay had been brief – they'd kept her in for six hours, observing her heart rate and breathing, but had eventually allowed her to go home, with instructions to rest and report any unusual symptoms. Billy had ferried them all back to Ennisfarne and they were met at the harbour by Selina's worried parents, who whisked her back to the family home. Wanting to allow her time to recuperate, Logan had kept his distance and checked in with messages. But today, Selina had asked him to call round and he was glad to see the colour was back in her cheeks.

She looked up from making tea and offered a brisk shrug. 'I'm fine, I think. No lasting physical effects, as far as I can tell, although the nightmares aren't helping with the whole sleeping thing.'

'I bet,' Logan replied sympathetically. 'But I guess they'll fade, in time.'

'So I'm told,' she said. 'And in the meantime, the salt farm won't run itself. Luckily, my brother has been able to borrow a boat and head over to the island to adjust the water flow each day and check everything is okay but he can't do that for ever. I'm going to need to get back on the proverbial seahorse one of these days.'

Logan had once done a photoshoot with an army captain who'd returned from Afghanistan minus his legs and suffering from severe PTSD. The interview that went with the pictures had been an inspiring lesson about coping with adversity and developing resilience, during which the captain had talked about revisiting the scene of the blast that had almost killed him and how it had helped in his eventual recovery. Selina hadn't faced the same horror but Logan could easily understand her reluctance to set sail on her own again.

'I'd be happy to come with you, if you think it might

help,' he offered. 'I can't promise to do anything practical but I could give you some moral support.'

With a curiously forced smile, she handed him a mug of tea. 'That's really kind of you,' she said, and gestured at the kitchen table. 'Why don't we sit down?'

Logan wasn't sure whether he'd imagined the hint of stiffness in her voice but he took a seat at the table. Sensing she had more to say, he waited for her to go on.

'As you'd imagine, I've been doing a lot of thinking over the past few days,' Selina said, lacing her fingers around her mug. 'Taking stock, I suppose you'd call it. There's nothing quite like the terror of being adrift in the ocean to make your life flash before your eyes, if that's not too much of a cliché.'

Logan nodded but didn't speak, in spite of a looming suspicion he knew where she was going.

'Quite a few things fell into place in the days afterwards too – the usual stuff, I suppose, like what I want out of life and whether I was actively seeking that or just drifting. And I thought about you a lot too.' Her gaze skittered towards him briefly, then she took a long sip of tea and sighed. 'Look, there's really no easy way to say this. I like you, Logan, and I'm really grateful you were there when I needed you on Billy's boat. But one of the things I've realized in the aftermath is that life's too short to waste on something you know isn't right. I want a partner in crime, someone who really gets me and who's in it for the long haul, and as much as I can't believe I'm saying this, I don't think that's you. Sorry.'

Logan managed a wry smile; his suspicion had been bang

on the money. But just as he wasn't surprised, he couldn't blame Selina for deciding to call it a day. She'd told him after the first kiss they'd shared on the balcony of Darling's that what she wanted from Logan was no-strings fun. That had suited him, too – the fact that he'd be leaving Ennisfarne at the end of the month made anything else more difficult, if not impossible. And it had been fun; he'd very much enjoyed spending time with her. But at the same time, he wasn't devastated by her declaration and he certainly understood the reason for her change of heart.

'Don't be sorry,' he said, taking her hand. 'We had a few great dates and I enjoyed your company. No hard feelings here.'

She squeezed his fingers in gratitude. 'I knew you'd understand. Thank you.'

'I can't say it doesn't sting, mind you,' Logan went on, shaking his head in mock self-pity. 'But I'll get over it.'

Selina smiled. 'Ah, stop it. You'll find yourself a gorgeous model the moment you leave the island.' She hesitated, eyeing him thoughtfully. 'Assuming you're still planning to go, that is.'

Logan frowned. What on earth had prompted that comment? 'Of course I am,' he said, nonplussed. 'Apart from anything else, I'd find myself homeless if I stayed – as I understand it, Dune Cottage is fully booked from the start of June to late October.'

Her gaze remained thoughtful. 'There are always options if you wanted to stay out of the limelight for a bit longer – I'm sure we could sort something out.' She paused and reviewed what she'd just said. 'As a village, I mean. Not you and me personally.'

'Of course not,' Logan answered, amused by the hurried clarification. May had seemed ages away when he'd been looking around for somewhere to escape to and time had seemed to slow once he'd arrived, so that he hadn't really registered the days ticking by. He remembered having a similar conversation with his best friend, Nick, during which the actor had questioned whether Logan would actually return to London. The thought of packing up his belongings and leaving Dune Cottage had felt distant at the time, but it was certainly looming on the horizon now. Once the plans for the exhibition were finalized, he'd have to start thinking seriously about what came next. 'I'll keep the offer in mind. Thanks.'

'Please do,' Selina said, beaming in satisfaction. 'Apart from anything else, it's nice having our very own celebrity on Ennisfarne, even if we're not allowed to tell anyone. And yes, I am that shallow and selfish. You've had a lucky escape.'

Logan's thoughts were jumbled as he drove back to Dune Cottage. It hadn't been a lie that Selina's rejection had stung but it was more the prickle of wounded pride than anything else – deep down, he'd known Selina's interest was only superficial. What it had also done was remind him in no uncertain terms that his stay on the island was almost over. Ennisfarne might have been exactly what he'd needed two months ago but it had never been for ever. It was time to face reality and work out where his future lay.

Chapter Twenty-One

Eve

As the tourist season began to kick in, it became more difficult to find the time and space to walk Huxley. Technically, Darling Cove was a private beach but Eve had never tried to enforce that, especially during the island's busiest time, and although it was never jammed with visitors the way mainland beaches often were, it was still popular. And given the Labrador's enthusiasm for literally bowling people over, which obedience classes were slowly curbing, Eve preferred to take him out when the likelihood of running into strangers was lessened. Which often meant early in the morning, while those tourists staying on Ennisfarne were still asleep and the day-trippers were yet to arrive.

She often walked to the beacon, cutting across Warren's fields to avoid the roads. He housed his ewes close to the farm throughout lambing season so the worst thing Eve had to worry about was Huxley's love of cow pats, the supply of which was delivered by Mildred and Dora, the mother and calf pair of Highland cattle Warren kept as pets. But the dog-training classes had helped with that too – now when Eve bellowed at Huxley to stop, he sometimes complied.

The path across the fields also took her past the cottage studio belonging to Morag Chester, the nearest Ennisfarne had to an artist in residence. It had quite an illustrious history: rumour had it that Wordsworth himself had stayed there and it had certainly been host to the famous Romantic painter, William Turner, when he visited the Farne Islands in the nineteenth century. But it had been empty since Morag's illness the previous spring. She'd gone to the mainland to convalesce with her daughter and, from what Eve had heard, the old woman's failing eyesight made it unlikely she would ever be coming back. The squat white building sat facing the distant beacon, the pinnacle of which was just visible over the steady rise of the ground, and the air of melancholy exuded by the shuttered windows and unkempt garden caused Eve to slow. She had often come across Morag up at the beacon in years gone by, her easel planted firmly in the grass and a paintbrush in hand as she stared towards the sea. Sighing, Eve resumed her walk. It was a shame she would never meet Morag that way again.

Her mood was still introspective when she reached the white granite beacon. Even Huxley's joy at discovering a cluster of dandelions couldn't lift her spirits. She wandered towards the obelisk, settling at the base to watch the waves rolling towards the cliffs. It was a scene she'd admired from a different perspective on Logan's computer screen, the camera somehow adding depth to a view she thought she knew well, but today she was trying not to look southwards, where the remains of Selina's boat was now becoming part of the seabed. Eve had relived that day several times in the week since the awful moment Billy had broken the news, washing away the peace and pleasure of the dive. It was sheer luck that they'd been in the right place at the right time to reach Selina before she suffered any physical ill-effects and Eve would always be grateful for the whim and fair weather that had prompted her to arrange the dive. The outcome had the *Serendipity* not been able to race to the rescue didn't bear thinking about.

Shifting restlessly, Eve reached down to pick a fuzzy dandelion head that had somehow escaped Huxley's attention. As a child, her father had persuaded her that dandelions were used instead of clocks in olden times and she'd spent days seeking them out to test their efficiency. Even now, she couldn't resist the urge to tell the time, scattering the seeds on the gentle breeze. Huxley raised his head to watch them.

'Leave,' Eve said in a stern voice and was gratified when the dog made no effort to chase them. A few months earlier he would have pulled her halfway across the headland. 'Good boy.'

His tail thumped the green grass as she rubbed his ears affectionately. 'I suppose we should be getting back,' Eve told him. 'Ennisfest won't organize itself.'

The festival wasn't the only thing on her agenda. An email had arrived from Logan the night before, confirming the date he'd be vacating Dune Cottage and asking for recommendations for local cleaners. She'd been expecting it, of course – her next guests were due to arrive on the first weekend of June – but his email had still caused a jolt of dismay, tinged with something else she couldn't immediately identify, and she suspected it was the root cause of her grumpiness that morning. Now that Logan's departure was looming, she was reminded all over again how much she enjoyed his company; she was going to miss knowing he was just along the beach. But there was nothing to be done. His time on Ennisfarne had only ever been temporary and perhaps she'd still get to see him, if he came back to see Selina. Although the thought of that set Eve's teeth on edge too and she wasn't sure why. She gave herself a mental shake and stood up, doing her best to force her reluctance and restlessness to one side. 'Come on, Hux,' she said, patting her leg to encourage him to abandon his snuffling. 'Time to get on with the day.'

She arrived back at Darling's to find an A5 jiffy bag on the doormat, addressed to her and obviously hand delivered. Frowning, Eve turned it over; there was no return address or other clue. She unclipped Huxley from his lead and grabbed a glass of water before heading out to the decking, the unopened jiffy bag in her hand. Aiden hadn't set up the tables yet so she unfolded one from the stacked pile and dragged a chair towards it. Then she turned her attention to the mystery delivery.

Inside the brown padded bag there was a smaller, expensive-looking white envelope with her and Aiden's names neatly handwritten in black, and a sleek black USB stick. Her gaze rested on the stick for several seconds while she considered what it held and then she put it to one side to slide a finger under the flap of the envelope. The rectangle of card inside felt just as heavy and expensive as the envelope. The surface was grained and embossed with a gold leaf border but the print was a clear, elegant black.

> **YOU ARE CORDIALLY INVITED**
> **TO THE LAUNCH OF**
>
> **EXTRAORDINARY ENNISFARNE**
>
> **ON FRIDAY 20TH MAY**
>
> **6.00PM—8.00PM**
>
> **ENNISFARNE VILLAGE HALL,**
> **LONG STREET, ENNISFARNE**

There was no doubt who the invitation was from but Eve turned it over to see the sender had added a note. It was the same ink that adorned the envelope, although the handwriting here looped and swirled expressively like the flight of a butterfly.

*Please come if you can— I owe so many of the
photographs to you.*
*Hope you like the pictures on the stick. I think they're great.
You're a real natural.*

It was signed with a single L. Eve sat for a moment, staring
at the words. She certainly hadn't felt like a natural during
Sunday's photography session with Logan on the beach. His
instructions had been patient and gentle, asking her to turn
one way, tilt her head another, lift her chin, stroke Huxley ...
Nothing he'd suggested had been tricky but she'd still felt
stiff and wooden. Her smile was a grimace, her movements
lacked grace and Huxley had refused to stay in one place for
more than a few seconds. By the end she was sure her face
resembled a tomato and Logan must be secretly wishing he
hadn't bothered, despite his reassurances that she was doing
brilliantly. And now the resulting photographs were here, all
she had to do was plug the stick into her laptop and her lack
of star quality would be abundantly clear. It was more than
she could bear. Stuffing the USB device back into the jiffy
bag, she went to find Aiden to open negotiations. She might
not want to see her own photographs but she most certainly
wanted to see the exhibition. With a bit of luck and some
gentle persuasion, he'd volunteer to run the bar that night.

'Okay, Eve, what's going on?'

Eve looked up to see Selina standing at the open glass
doors that led from the decking of the bar. Beyond her, the

sea rumbled onto the beach as she surveyed Eve, hands on hips, eyes narrowed. 'You've been off with me for over a week,' her best friend went on, weaving between the tables to close the space between them. 'And don't try to deny it — we've been friends since before we were born. What's the problem?'

Behind the bar, Eve reached for a tea towel and slowly dried her hands, evading Selina's gaze as she wondered what to tell her. She hadn't been consciously avoiding her, any more than she'd avoided the other islanders — she'd genuinely been up to her eyeballs in festival planning and managing all the other plates she kept spinning on a day-to-day basis. But if she was honest, she had felt an unfamiliar reluctance whenever she thought about her best friend — something that had never been there before — and she hadn't wanted to explore what was causing it. Instead, she'd thrown herself into her work even more than usual and now her avoidance was coming home to roost. There was a determined thrust to Selina's chin that warned of a controlled explosion if Eve didn't explain herself. 'I've been busy,' she said.

Selina sniffed. 'You're always busy. That doesn't usually stop you replying to my messages.'

That wasn't fair, Eve thought — she'd never left Selina on read. 'I have replied.'

'One-word answers and emojis don't count,' Selina said. 'You didn't come to last night's Book Club and I know it's not because you haven't read the book.'

Eve felt her cheeks grow warm. She'd fully intended to

join the small group of readers at Freda's house; that month's book was a sexy historical romp through a reimagined Battle of Waterloo and Eve had been looking forward to sitting down with a glass of wine to hear whether the others had loved the brooding Earl of Lamorna as much as she had. But her enthusiasm had been tempered by a creeping disinclination that she'd done her best to dismiss over the course of the afternoon.

'Shouldn't you be going?' her brother, Aiden, asked when the clock crept round to seven o'clock.

Eve had hesitated, weighing up the options before shaking her head. 'I've got so much to do. I'll go next month.'

It hadn't been a lie – she'd worked until almost eleven. Selina had messaged before the club had started, asking which wine Eve was bringing, and then again afterwards, to ask why she hadn't turned up. Eve had replied the following morning – this morning – and clearly her excuses hadn't been convincing enough.

'I got caught up with work,' she said now, squaring her shoulders and forcing herself to meet Selina's gaze. 'The festival is five weeks away.'

'This is about more than you being busy,' Selina insisted. 'Don't fob me off with excuses – I know you.'

Eve felt her temper start to rise. 'It's not an excuse. You've got no idea how much organization something like this takes, plus I've got all the usual stuff to take care of – bookings for the cottage, ordering for the bar.'

Selina raised her eyebrows. 'But you've been doing all of

this for the past however many years, and I've never felt like you're pretending I don't exist. It's like you've put up a wall between us.' She stopped to shake her head. 'There's only one thing that's different and that's Logan Silk.'

'Now you're being ridiculous,' Eve snapped but the accusation hit home. A deep uneasiness began to churn her stomach as she forced herself to consider Selina's words. Was it Logan that had caused her to feel alienated from her best friend? It couldn't be, could it?

'Am I?' Selina studied her, her brow furrowed, and understanding started to dawn in her eyes. 'That's it, isn't it? He's the problem.'

'No,' Eve muttered but she knew the furious glow of her cheeks was giving her away.

'Oh, Eve,' Selina said, her voice softening. 'You've got it bad.'

Eve opened her mouth to issue another denial but a horrible recognition was washing over her – Logan *was* the reason she'd subconsciously stepped back from Selina. She didn't know when it had happened – that day on the boat, perhaps, when she'd watched her best friend throw herself into Logan's arms – but somewhere, somehow, her feelings had got tangled and twisted and jealousy had wound its sinewy roots between the gaps and into her heart. Which made her an even worse person, she thought miserably, because what kind of friend resented someone who'd just narrowly escaped death? The fact that she hadn't known she was doing it didn't matter one bit.

Closing her eyes, she took a deep breath. 'I'm sorry.'

Selina folded her arms. 'You should be,' she said, but she didn't sound angry. 'Of all the people to cut off, Eve. We've always told each other everything.'

Eve gave a wretched shrug. 'I didn't know. I thought I was just overwhelmed with work – I mean, how could I be jealous when I'd told you over and over to go for it with Logan? And I was so sure I didn't feel anything, that he was my tenant and maybe a friend but nothing more.' She swallowed hard as a lump appeared in her throat and hot tears swamped her eyes. 'I'm a terrible friend.'

Selina was at her side in a flash, pulling her into a hug. 'You are not. Admittedly, you've dropped the best friend ball these past few weeks but that's the first time in thirty-odd years. And now I know why, it all makes sense.'

Tears cascaded down Eve's face. 'I'm sorry. Can you ever forgive me?'

Selina held her tight for several long seconds, then drew gently back. 'There's nothing to forgive.'

She was being kind, Eve knew, but the burning acid in her gut told her otherwise. 'There is,' she mumbled. 'I should be happy for you and Logan, not jealous.'

'Ah,' Selina said slowly, her expression suddenly indecipherable. 'Well, perhaps if you hadn't been basically unreachable for the past week, you'd know we're not actually together any more.'

The words hit Eve like a punch, momentarily stunning her and sending her thoughts spiralling into nonsense. 'What?'

'We broke up,' Selina explained patiently. 'After the accident, I realized we were both sort of going through the motions, trying to make something exist that wasn't really there. So I sat him down and told him it wasn't going to work out and that was that.'

Eve knew her mouth was hanging open but she didn't seem to be able close it. 'What?' she said again.

'He took it well,' Selina went on. 'To be honest, he wasn't as much fun as I expected. He was nice but a little too intro-verted for me.' She fixed Eve with a speculative look. 'And I always had the feeling he wasn't totally present, even when he was kissing me. It was like part of him was somewhere else. But now I'm wondering if it's because he has feelings for someone else.'

It took Eve a moment to grasp what she was getting at. 'No,' she said firmly. 'Whatever I feel for Logan, it's defi-nitely a one-way street. He dates internationally acclaimed models, Selina. Not Jacks-of-no-trades from a speck of an island off the Northumberland coast.'

Selina raised her eyebrows but said nothing.

'And even if by some impossible twist of fate he was faintly interested in me, he's leaving Ennisfarne in less than two weeks' time to go back to his glamorous, jet-setting life,' Eve continued, giving a voice to all the objections it seemed her subconscious had been creating for some time. 'I'm sure he's got more sense than to stir up trouble with someone he's never going to see again.'

'All of that is true,' Selina conceded, nodding slowly.

'But you'll never know what could be unless you try. And if there's one thing I've learned about you, Eve Darling, it's that you don't duck out of something just because it's hard.'

Eve stared at her helplessly. 'But this isn't a job or a music night I can organize – it's someone's heart. It's *my* heart.'

'I know,' Selina said, reaching out to squeeze her hand. 'And I know you keep that safely locked away, where no one can reach it, thanks to that bloody idiot Michael. But here's the thing: Logan's already got through. Are you really going to let him walk away without finding out how he feels about you?'

The mere thought of initiating a conversation like that made Eve feel dizzy. What on earth could a man like Logan Silk see in a woman like her? 'Yes,' she said, and almost convinced herself. Except the thought of never seeing Logan again made her palms sweat and her heart race. 'No. I don't know.'

Her best friend eyed her closely for a few seconds, then sighed. 'Well, you've got two weeks to make your mind up. You always did work best with a deadline.'

Eve swallowed, pushing down the familiar sense of panic Logan's departure induced. 'Thanks.'

Selina spread her hands. 'It's true. Although I'm basing that on A Level History essays rather than potentially life-changing decisions you might regret for the rest of your life.'

This time, Eve couldn't prevent a small snort of laughter from escaping her. 'Again, thanks.'

'Don't mention it,' Selina said easily. 'But you and I both know you're already head over heels in love with Logan Silk. Which only leaves us with one question – what are you going to do about it?'

PART FOUR

Christmas Wishes

Chapter Twenty-Two

Logan

'I've got to be honest, Logan, you had me worried for a while.'

Logan Silk eyed his agent, Phoebe, across the pristine, white-clothed table and wondered which of his actions in recent months had troubled her the most. 'Oh?' he said mildly, reaching for his champagne glass. 'In what way?'

Phoebe fixed him with a hard stare. 'Let's see. Could it have been your abrupt cancellation of all professional commitments?' She held up her fingers, ready to tick the items off. 'Your refusal to accept any new work, no matter how glamorous or lucrative? The way you suddenly dropped off the face of the Earth?'

'I came to Northumberland, Phoebe,' Logan pointed out. 'Only a couple of hours away from London. It's hardly Mars.'

She sighed and took a grissini. 'You know what I mean. And Ennisfarne is more than a couple of hours away – most of the time it's cut off from the rest of the country by the sea.' The breadstick wove through the air as though she was conducting an orchestra. 'What is it with you artistic types and remote islands, anyway? Merina ran away to Orkney and I've never been able to tempt her back.'

Logan smiled. Merina Wilde was a supremely successful novelist and another of Phoebe's clients; they'd met on several occasions and Logan had found her smart, charming and funny. She was a friend of Nick's too – he'd starred in an adaptation of her most recent novel which, Logan now recalled, had partly been filmed on Orkney. 'Isn't Merina the reason you're here in Newcastle?' he asked, lifting his eyebrows. 'If she's appearing at the literary festival then she can't have given up leaving her remote island entirely.'

'Yes, she is and no, she hasn't,' Phoebe conceded. 'But this is the exception rather than the rule. And that isn't the point, anyway. A novelist can write wherever they like but world-famous fashion photographers –' She broke off and met his gaze with frank honesty. 'Well, I don't imagine there's much *haute couture* happening on Ennisfarne.'

A mental image of George popped unbidden into Logan's mind, dressed in grubby yellow waterproofs and grinning toothily from beneath his bedraggled grey beard. He was as far away from the models Logan usually photographed as it was possible to get and yet Logan had enjoyed taking his picture much more than any of the stylized fashion shoots he had worked on in the past year. 'Not unless Fisherman Chic has become a thing,' he agreed. 'But that's part of the reason

I went there. Fashion photography just doesn't interest me right now.' He took a deep breath. 'In fact, when I walked out of that shoot in New York, I didn't care if I never took another photo of anything.'

His agent said nothing for a moment, regarding him soberly across the table. 'And now?'

Logan thought of his laptop, which was full of pictures he'd taken since arriving on Ennisfarne. It was as though the island had cast a spell on him as he'd stood at the start of the causeway that first afternoon, watching it snake across the sands, and it was a magic that had kept him bewitched for the duration of his three-month stay. He'd fallen in love with the way the light shifted throughout the day, transform-ing a scene he thought he knew well into something fresh that had him reaching for his camera. And then he'd been asked at the last minute to step in and photograph George and Hettie's wedding, an honour which had reminded him how much pleasure could be found in helping to capture the memories of such a joyful day. There was no doubt that Ennisfarne and her inhabitants had reignited Logan's passion for photography but was that something that would last once he left? He wasn't sure he could say. 'Now is different,' he allowed, after a brief pause. 'But maybe that's because there's no pressure – if I pick up my camera these days, it's because I want to, not because I have to.'

'So where does that leave us, in terms of future work?' Phoebe asked. 'Obviously, you're not feeling fashion at the moment and that's fine – you shouldn't take any job when your heart isn't in it. But it would be helpful to get a feel for what you do want to do.'

And that was the problem, Logan thought gloomily as the waiter appeared with their starters – he didn't actually know. The only thing he was sure of was that he couldn't go back to the way he'd worked before. Phoebe was dancing around another good point, too – his erratic behaviour had been out of character and it had caused her headaches. 'I know I owe you an apology,' he said. 'You got a lot of grief when I bailed on everything.'

Phoebe waved the sentiment aside. 'Oh, forget about that. It's my job to protect my clients and we've worked together long enough for me to know you wouldn't walk away on a whim.' She paused to regard him steadily, surrounded by the clink and chink of cutlery and glasses, the murmured conversation of their fellow diners. 'When I said you had me worried for a while, it wasn't your work commitments or your career that I was fretting about. It was your well-being and mental health, especially after that awful hatchet job by Suki.'

Logan allowed himself a brief grunt of agreement. Hatchet job was exactly the right description for what his ex-girlfriend had done to try to demolish his life and his career. But although it had distressed him at the time, he found it hard to care now. Ennisfarne had muffled the impact and soothed the upset away. It also helped that he hadn't so much as looked at a newspaper for months.

'Of course, now I can see you're rested and relaxed,

practically radiating contentment,' Phoebe went on, shrugging. 'Which brings me back to my previous question – where do you want to go from here?'

'I'm coming back to London soon,' he said, with an answering shrug. 'In less than two weeks, I'll be settling into city life again and who knows – perhaps I'll have an epiphany and things will be clearer. But I don't think I'll really know until then – sorry.'

'Okay, let's pick things up once you're back,' she said, her expression philosophically accepting, then arched a curious eyebrow. 'Now that's the business out of the way, tell me what you've been up to on this island retreat of yours. Has it been all monastic isolation and navel gazing?'

He laughed. 'Not at all. The islanders have been very welcoming – I've had plenty of fun. In fact, I'm putting on an exhibition of some of the photographs I've taken while I've been there – anonymously, of course – as a way of thanking everyone for being so kind to me.'

Phoebe threw him a triumphant look. 'So, you have been taking pictures – I knew you wouldn't be able to resist. Can I see them?'

'Sure. The exhibition launches tomorrow evening, if you're still around,' he said on impulse. 'Although you'll need to factor in the safe crossing times for the causeway so it will mean an overnight stay.'

His agent pursed her lips. 'Merina's event is this evening so I could detour to Ennisfarne tomorrow. I assume there's a hotel?'

There were several, Logan thought, but it had suddenly occurred to him that there was a high probability they would all be fully booked. Nick had taken a room at the Fisherman's Arms when he'd visited the island earlier in the year but Logan wasn't sure what immaculately turned-out Phoebe would make of the no-frills accommodation or the pub's landlord, the equally hale and hearty Hamish. 'They might be busy at this time of year. Would it be easier to send you the photographs instead?' he suggested.

Phoebe tapped a scarlet fingernail on the tablecloth. 'It's not quite the same as seeing them exhibited, though,' she said, frowning. 'No, I'll come to the launch party. Apart from anything else, I'd like to see what you've been up to all these months.'

Even as he nodded, Logan was running through the favours he might pull to find somewhere for Phoebe to stay at such short notice. At a pinch, he could let her have Dune Cottage and see if Hamish had a room he offer could to Logan. But that might entail explaining why the Fisherman's Arms wasn't an option for Phoebe herself and Logan was keen to avoid any slight to Hamish's feelings. He'd pop into The Nook when he got back and consult Freda. He would have asked Eve but she'd been conspicuously absent for the past few days and he assumed she was snowed under with organization for June's music festival. 'Leave it with me,' he told Phoebe, crossing his fingers and hoping Freda would come through. 'I'm sure we can sort something out.'

*

Freda pursed her lips thoughtfully when Logan stopped at The Nook to put his question to her. 'Could be a tall order. You're right in thinking all the usual places will be booked up. I suppose there could be a last-minute cancellation – someone who's misjudged the tide – but I wouldn't want to bank on it meself.'

Logan watched a cluster of tourists hover around the Ennisfarne mead display, discussing how many bottles to buy. 'It's my fault – I should have thought to invite Phoebe long before now but I'd never expect her to come up from London for something like this. It's only because she's already in Newcastle with another client that I suggested she came to the exhibition launch.'

Freda tapped absently on the glass of the deli counter. 'The causeway definitely makes spontaneity harder,' she observed. 'And I don't suppose this agent of yours is the type to cheerfully bunk up on a sofa, is she?'

The mere idea sent a shiver of horrified amusement down Logan's spine. 'Not really, no.'

Whatever the shopkeeper had been about to say next was lost as her attention was caught by the tourists approaching the till at the front of the shop. 'Just give me a moment, Logan. Duty calls.'

She bustled away, leaving him to survey the many delights of the deli counter. He remembered his first visit to The Nook, when he'd been amazed to discover such an array of mouth-watering foods. Freda had reeled him in that day with all the expertise of a born saleswoman and he'd been a regular ever since. He knew he was going to miss it when he left, even though London had plenty to offer in its place. Perhaps what he was really going to miss was Freda's warmth as she skilfully filled his basket with things he hadn't intended to buy but very much enjoyed eating in the cosiness of Dune Cottage.

After a few minutes, the bell over the door tinkled, indicating the tourists had made their purchases, and Freda was back. She gave Logan a business-like nod. 'So, I can ask around and see who's got a spare room they can offer. But if your agent prefers her own space then there's Morag Chester's old place up near the beacon that might be a better bet.'

Logan frowned, trying to work out which property she meant. 'Is there? I've never seen it.'

She shrugged. 'It's tucked away on the edge of Warren's farm – you'd likely only find it if you cross the fields and I imagine you normally drive up to the beacon.' He nodded and she went on. 'Morag's daughter has been sprucing it up to sell, now that Morag herself has moved in with her on the mainland. She left a spare set of keys with me, I'm sure she wouldn't mind Phoebe using it for a night.'

It was definitely an option, Logan thought, turning the idea over in his mind. He could go and take a look, at least, and if it wasn't quite up to Phoebe's standards then he could sleep there himself while she stayed in his cottage. 'That might work,' he said. 'Do you want to check with Morag's daughter and let me know?'

Freda reached for her mobile phone. 'I'll ask her now.'

A short text message exchange followed and then Freda was beaming with satisfaction. 'There, I knew she wouldn't mind. She says the bungalow is clean and tidy but the studio still has quite a few of Morag's paintings lying around so best not to disturb them if you don't mind.'

'Paintings?' Logan repeated, his curiosity piqued. 'Is Morag an artist, then?'

The shopkeeper nodded. 'She was, before her eyesight started to go, and a bloody good one at that. The studio was where she mostly worked, although I used to run into her all over the island, easel set up, paintbrush in her hand.' Freda smiled. 'You'd think she might have got bored with looking at the same places over and over but she once told me the light on Ennisfarne meant she never painted the same picture twice.'

Logan felt his mouth twist in recognition. 'I can certainly understand that,' he said. 'It sounds like I need to look up Morag's work.'

'Absolutely,' Freda said. 'I think there's even a couple of hers in one of the fancy London galleries but don't ask me which one.'

'I'm sure I can find out,' Logan replied, impressed all over again by Morag's evident talent.

'Make sure you do – it'll be a little piece of Ennisfarne to keep you going once you've left us. And in the meantime, I'll give you the keys so you can go and check whether the bungalow will do for your agent.' She flourished a hand at the deli counter in the manner of a magician revealing her latest trick. 'Do you want to buy a few treats to welcome her to Ennisfarne?'

Twenty minutes later, Logan was bumping up the narrow track that led to Morag's bungalow, a brown paper bag of Freda's best delicacies on the passenger seat of his Hilux. He already suspected the remote location would put Phoebe off – she'd mentioned hiring a car in Newcastle to make the trip to Ennisfarne and Logan doubted she would want to risk its bodywork on the craggy, pot-holed surface that was barely a road. Whoever bought Morag's property would need to invest in some repairs if they wanted their vehicle's suspension to have a long and happy life, he mused as he navigated the rugged Hilux across the deeper ruts. After another bone-jolting bump or two, the track twisted sharply around a hairpin bend to reveal a small cluster of trees shadowing a squat white bungalow with a grey slate roof and a gleaming yellow front door. A chimney pointed upwards from one end, as though trying to draw his attention to the peach and lemon cloud wisps drifting across the faded cornflower sky, and the distant cry of seabirds floated on the air. There was no 'For Sale' sign but Logan supposed it didn't need one; everyone on the island knew it was on the market and there would be very few passers-by.

Grappling with the paper bag, he crunched his way up the gravel path to the front door. Efforts had been made to tame the garden – the lawn was mowed, the roses around the door trimmed and the flowerbeds weeded – but there was still a faint whisper of melancholy that no amount of fresh paint on the windowsills could dispel. Past the cheery front door, he found a dim hallway containing several doors, one of which led to a kitchen where he left the bag from The Nook and went to explore further.

The air was still as he returned to the hallway and opened another door, which led him into a living room. He'd expected a stale mustiness, perhaps even the whiff of lavender, but there wasn't a trace of either – just a faint hint of an odour he knew but couldn't quite pin down and a strange sense of expectation, as though the building was holding its breath. Logan shook the notion away and focused on the practicalities. The furniture was well used but serviceable – a sofa that faced an empty fireplace, two armchairs on either side. A rectangular shadow adorned the white paint of one wall, suggesting a picture might have recently hung there. There was the usual chill that came when a room had been unused for a while, and the carpet had definitely seen better days, but it was clean and empty of any personal belongings. The next door he tried took him to a bedroom – once again clean and presentable, with a surprisingly modern-looking bed, freshly made up and scattered with bright cushions. Sunlight slanted through the window, catching dust motes dancing in the stillness and giving the room a warmer, more inviting feel. It was the room Logan liked the most, until he found the studio.

Respectful of Freda's instruction not to disturb anything, he hung back in the doorway and spent a long moment taking in the unexpected hexagonal shape and the floor to ceiling windows. Stacked canvases leant against one of the walls – he couldn't see if they were painted – and there were dust sheets draped over what Logan assumed to be easels. A pair of skylight windows allowed more sun to pour in but Logan also saw a tall, angle-poise lamp on one side of the room and he supposed that was for when the artist had been burning the midnight oil. And there was the mystery smell he hadn't been able to identify earlier. It was much stronger here and now he recognised it instantly – the scent of linseed oil, presumably from Morag's oil paints. It mingled with the pungency of turpentine, as though Morag had been at the small porcelain sink only that morning, cleaning her brushes amid the faint roar of the ocean. Both were distinctive aromas that whisked him back to his student days at art college, although he'd never been any good at painting nor spent much time in the art rooms. Another, older, memory surfaced – his dad's shed at the bottom of their tiny garden, its walls lined with gardening tools and saws, and the shelves creaking with jam jars full of screws, paint brushes soaking in turps and balls of twine. A stack of old paint tins stood in one corner, beside a tatty armchair worn shiny with use. Logan hadn't thought of the shed in years but the odour of turpentine had yanked him back in time faster than he could blink. He'd only ever been allowed as far as the doorway of that sacred space too.

He stood on the threshold of the studio for quite some time, lulled by the sound of the sea and allowing his gaze to wander slowly across the scene, soaking up the peace and tranquillity. Morag was a tangible presence in the room. If Logan lifted the dust sheets and liberated the easels beneath, it might almost feel that she was somewhere nearby, perhaps just out of sight in the garden. He didn't find the notion troubling – Morag was alive and well, as far as he knew, so he guessed it was an echo of her artistry that he sensed, rather than her ghostly presence. In fact he found it soothing. So much creativity had undoubtedly flowed through this place that he could well believe it had seeped into the fabric of the room. He could almost feel it shimmering on the air.

At length, Logan recalled why he was there in the first place and roused himself to close the door of the studio and return to the rest of the house. There was nothing wrong with the bungalow that a blast of heating wouldn't fix but somehow he knew it wasn't the right place for Phoebe. She'd prefer the less isolated, cosier comfort of Dune Cottage, although she'd be reluctant to turf him out of his home if he gave her the choice. But Logan didn't mind spending the night away from the cottage. He'd be spending every night away from it soon enough.

It was with an unsettling mixture of anticipation and apprehension that Logan awoke on the morning of the exhibition launch party. On one hand, he couldn't wait to see the reactions of the islanders to his interpretation of their lives and their home – he was as proud of these images as any he'd taken for prestigious magazines or famous faces and he hoped his admiration for Ennisfarne shone through. But at the same time, he was wracked with unaccustomed nerves that had ebbed and flowed like the tides ever since he'd settled on the idea of exhibiting some of the photographs he'd taken over the past three months. Every artist knew it was impossible to please everyone and yet it mattered enormously to Logan that the exhibition was well received. Then again, he intended it as a gift to them, a tribute to express his gratitude for the sanctuary he'd found with them, so perhaps it wasn't at all strange that he was keen for them to like it. Everyone whose portrait would be included had seen their own picture – Logan had thought it was only fair to show them before asking them to grant him their consent – but very few islanders had viewed the complete exhibition, hanging in the village. And now that he had cut the ribbon and invited the intended audience inside to look, apprehension was in danger of winning out. It really was the most ridiculous thing.

Deciding that what he needed was some impartial feedback, he went in search of Phoebe. He found her standing in front of a large photograph of the shipwrecked *Gunhilde*, a flute of champagne in one hand and her head tilted to one side as she considered the image. 'It's the octopus that makes it,' she said. 'I hope you got him to sign a consent form.'

Logan smiled. The octopus was gazing quizzically from behind a large ship's wheel, eyes fixed on Logan and his camera as though trying to work out what manner of sea creature he was. If cephalopods had eyebrows, Logan thought, they would have been raised in puzzled surprise. 'He tried but we couldn't get the ink to dry.'

Phoebe pulled a face. 'Ha ha. But seriously, it's a wonderful picture. They all are.' She gave him a sidelong look. 'I could probably sell half of them to *National Geographic*.'

'They're not for sale,' Logan replied firmly. 'Apart from anything else, I've given the copyright to the islanders.'

Predictably, Phoebe sighed. 'Shame.' She took a few steps to her right and studied the next photograph, which showed Eve after one of their dives, glistening and golden in the afternoon light. 'This one wouldn't look out of place on the cover of *Wanderlust*. You might not want to sell these but if this is a road you want to go down professionally then I'm sure there'll be a demand.'

The suggestion gave Logan a moment's pause. Although he'd enjoyed taking photographs on Ennisfarne, so far away both physically and conceptually from his usual subject matter, it didn't necessarily follow that he wanted to risk that enjoyment by turning it into work. But he'd known Phoebe a long time and she'd never been one to think small. Part of her brilliance as an agent was her connection to the top editors at the most prestigious publications. Before Logan knew it, he'd be back on the glossy magazine treadmill, flying from location to location and never settling anywhere. Just the idea made him feel weary.

His gaze came to rest on the image of Eve once more. 'I'd have to think about that,' he said slowly. 'Maybe it could work, if we limited the number of commissions.'

A small cluster of islanders were drifting near. Phoebe leaned towards him and lowered her voice. 'Here's the thing,' she said in a kindly but matter-of-fact tone. 'You're Logan Silk. I could offer a picture of your breakfast and there'd be a mad frenzy of bidding for it. So I'm not suggesting you dance to anyone's tune but your own – if you want to take photos of Farne Island women on boats for the rest of your career, or capture the wonder of the deepest shipwrecks, then that's fine with me. We'll make it work.'

Immediately, it was as though a weight had lifted from Logan's heart. 'Thank you,' he said, grateful for her understanding. 'As I said yesterday, I think I'll be in a better position to decide what comes next once I'm back in London.'

Phoebe nodded, then eyed him curiously. 'Is this the same woman as that picture over there – the one with the dog?'

He followed the direction of her gaze. 'Yes. That's Eve. She runs the bar at Darling Cove and she's also my landlord, which makes her your landlord this evening too.'

'Ah, I see,' Phoebe said and then seemed to connect the dots. 'So she's the one who sent the reporter packing, when the Suki story broke? And that's the dog that broke your camera?'

'Both correct,' Logan replied, grinning. 'Would you like to meet her?'

'It would be positively rude not to,' Phoebe answered. 'Apart from anything else, I need to compliment her on her impeccable taste in tenants.'

Logan scanned the room until he spotted Eve chatting with Hamish and Selina over by the door. He'd seen her among the crowd earlier when he was cutting the ribbon but hadn't had the time to say hello. Now he looked properly, he noticed she'd foregone her usual ponytail – her blonde hair was brushing the shoulders of a pretty summer dress that was also a departure from her usual no-nonsense attire. As Logan watched, she tipped her head and laughed at something Hamish had said, and his fingers twitched for his camera. But then he remembered he was standing with Phoebe and turned his attention back to her, only to find her observing him closely. 'She's over there,' he said, wondering how long he'd been staring at Eve. 'Come on, I'll introduce you.'

Phoebe reached out to switch her empty glass for a full one. 'I can't wait,' she replied, something indecipherable in her voice. 'Lead the way.'

Chapter Twenty-Three

Eve

'I'll say this for Logan – he's dynamite with a camera.'

Selina was gazing at a large photograph of herself, taken with the thorny graduation tower of the salt farm in the background. The sky was a sullen grey, the clouds glowering as though they resented being in the picture at all, but it gave the scene a brooding, almost gothic feel. Eve had no doubt the dour weather had been a deliberate choice by Logan; he'd suggested more than once that the tower looked as though it belonged in a Brothers Grimm fairy tale. Selina had more than a hint of magic about her too – her dark hair was streaming to one side as if she was standing her ground amid ferocious winds and a half-smile played around her lips. She looked as though she might summon up an elemental spirit at any moment.

'It's a beautiful picture,' Eve said, and glanced around the village hall at the incredible images that surrounded them. 'But then they all are.'

There were close to forty photographs on display in the *Extraordinary Ennisfarne* exhibition and each one seemed to leap from its frame to demand the viewer's attention. Eve had been lucky enough to help Logan sift through the hundreds of pictures he'd taken during his three-month stay on the island and she knew there were many more wonderful images that could easily have made the cut, if there'd been more display space. But Logan had been adamant that less was more. 'The human brain can only absorb so much,' he'd said, when Eve had suggested squeezing a few more in. 'And there needs to be space between each photo, to allow it to stand out.'

Now that the exhibition was mounted, Eve could see what he'd been driving at. To anyone unfamiliar with Ennisfarne, the images might seem like an eye-catching but random assortment – Mildred and Dora, the island's shaggy-haired Highland cattle, staring into the camera with comical curiosity; Huxley, his tongue dangling as he grinned at the camera; her brother, Aiden, on the balcony of Darling's Bar during one of the recent music nights; Hettie and George exchanging wedding vows in front of the limestone arch that dominated Darling Cove. Then there were the old fishing boats, upturned and repurposed as sheds and caught beneath an azure sky; the harbour dotted with newer boats and illuminated by the sun's dying rays; the hypnotic beauty of the shipwrecks submerged off the island's coast. There seemed no pattern to the order in which the photographs appeared and yet Eve was certain Logan had placed them precisely.

Beside Eve, Selina nodded. 'That's true. Even this one of you, Hamish.'

The publican eyed the image in question, taken at George's stag do with the bar's optics artistically blurry behind him, and rubbed his hairy chin. 'Don't know about that. But it didn't break the camera and that's the main thing.'

Selina took a sip of champagne and cast around the hall. 'I see Hettie has made George trim his beard for the occasion,' she said approvingly. 'Who's that with Logan?'

Eve didn't need to follow her gaze to know who she meant. Freda had told her about the conversation she'd had with Logan the day before and so Eve had clocked the elegantly dressed stranger even before the ribbon cutting, having watched her step from Logan's car and walk across the road from the Fisherman's Arms. 'I think that's his agent,' she told Selina, then nudged her. 'Don't stare.'

'I'm not,' Selina objected but she kept her eyes on the other woman. 'How come she's here? I'm sure Logan told me she was based in London – it's a long way to travel for something like this.'

Taking a sip from her own glass, Eve wondered how to answer. Freda had given her the whole story, of course, but that didn't mean Eve had to admit she knew the details. She tried not to raise the subject of Logan with Selina – all too often it resulted in her best friend trying to push her into telling Logan how she felt about him. And that was something Eve was determined was never going to happen, especially not when there was a living, breathing reminder right under her nose that Logan Silk did not belong on Ennisfarne. 'I don't know,' she told Selina, resolutely turning her attention to the next photograph and hoping she didn't sound as stilted as she felt. 'You'd have to ask Logan.'

'I will,' Selina replied. 'He's heading this way now, with whoever she is right behind him.'

Drawing in a long, steadying breath, Eve steeled herself. In the weeks since Selina had forced her to admit she had feelings for Logan, she'd settled on a plan that would allow her to safely navigate the time he had left on the island without damaging their friendship or giving herself away. For the most part, it meant keeping busy and minimizing contact with him but she hadn't wanted to miss the launch party. And now her defences were about to be tested, under the knowing scrutiny of Selina. She could do this, Eve reminded herself as Logan drew near. All she had to do was smile, be polite and escape at the first opportunity.

'Hello,' Logan said as he approached. 'Can I introduce you to my agent, Phoebe Ward-Hooper? Phoebe, this is Selina, who runs the island's salt farm. And Hamish, the landlord of the Fisherman's Arms.'

Both nodded in greeting as Phoebe smiled. 'Hello,' she said warmly. 'It's lovely to meet you.'

'And this is Eve,' Logan went on, 'who I've come to suspect is Superwoman's more accomplished sister.'

Eve's cheeks grew warm at the praise and she was sure Selina must be aiming an eloquent look her way. Hastily, she fixed her eyes on Phoebe. 'I promise you I'm not. But I am very pleased to meet you. Logan's spoken about you often and it's great you could come to the exhibition.'

Phoebe inclined her head. 'I'm glad I was able to see it. Logan has been a bit of a dark horse about Ennisfarne and now I understand why – it's so gorgeous he wanted to keep it all to himself.'

Eve allowed her gaze to flit briefly to Logan and found he was already watching her. 'You'll get no argument from me,' she said, slightly flustered as she returned her attention to Phoebe.

'He's one of us now,' Hamish rumbled. 'Whether he likes it or not.'

'Oh, I like it,' Logan put in. 'Just try keeping me away. I'll be like the whiff of George's waterproofs – always lingering, never quite disappearing for good.'

Hamish and Selina both laughed at the affectionate nod to George's less than perfect personal hygiene and once again, Eve didn't dare look her best friend's way. Selina would undoubtably consider Logan's words to be some kind of veiled promise that he planned to stick around the island. 'What do you think of the exhibition?' she asked Phoebe, hoping to nudge the conversation into safer waters, and then cringed inside, because this was Logan's agent – she was hardly going to launch into a stinging critique.

'I am a little biased, of course, but I think it's wonderful,' the other woman replied. 'How did you enjoy posing for him? I see you appear in several pictures.'

Eve hesitated before answering, mostly because her instinctive reaction was to downplay her role in creating the photographs Phoebe referred to, placing the credit for how well they'd turned out squarely at Logan's feet. And it was true, for the most part.

Eve hadn't been aware he was taking two of the photos. But the third – the one of her and Huxley together on the sand of Darling Cove – had come from a bona fide photoshoot in which she caught a glimpse of what it might be like to actually model for Logan. And she had to concede he'd been brilliant. Somehow, he had made her feel as though there was no one else on the beach but her – almost like there was no one else in the world. It had been exhausting and exhilarating to be the sole focus of his attention, even for the relatively short amount of time it had taken him to get some images he was happy with. But she had no intention of admitting that now, certainly not with Selina or Logan himself listening. She might as well wear a t-shirt that proclaimed her doomed feelings.

'It was fun,' she said lightly. 'But I don't think I'm cut out to be a model, despite Logan's best efforts.'

He frowned, and seemed about to say something, so Eve ploughed on. 'Whereas Selina is clearly a natural,' she said, indicating the nearby picture. 'Don't you agree?'

The agent studied the photograph for several seconds. 'It's very striking,' she agreed. 'You've clearly all been a huge inspiration to Logan and made him very welcome into your lives. I can't thank you enough for everything you've done. I understand it was you who tempted Logan to dive again, Eve. The results speak for themselves.'

Whatever Eve had been expecting from Phoebe, her graciousness was quite disarming. 'Honestly, all I did was swim alongside him,' she said. 'His talent did the rest.'

'But the scenery did the hard work,' Logan observed. 'As I believe I've mentioned before, there's nothing ordinary about Ennisfarne.'

Selina raised her eyebrows. 'It doesn't sound like you're ready to leave.'

He offered her a rueful smile. 'It doesn't, does it?' he said and glanced at Eve. 'Maybe she's cast a spell on me, this island of yours.'

The words made Eve's heart thump a little faster. If he stayed, a little voice in her head whispered, then maybe there was a chance she might one day admit how he made her feel.

'But all good things must come to an end,' Phoebe said, bringing Eve back down to earth with an unpleasant jolt. 'So many places to photograph, so little time!'

And that, Eve thought, was the truth of it. For all he'd enjoyed his time there, Ennisfarne was just a project to Logan — a life-size set to showcase his talent. 'Absolutely,' she agreed in what she hoped was a bland tone. 'Would you excuse me for a moment? I think Freda needs me.'

She flashed what felt like a horribly wooden smile around the group, not quite meeting anyone's eyes, and made her escape. It didn't matter that Freda was conspicuously engaged in a raucous conversation with Warren and clearly did not need Eve for anything – all she could think about was her sudden need to get away from Logan and the incontrovertible reminder that he was leaving in ten days' time. Placing her empty glass on a side table, Eve reached the exit and kept walking, blinking rapidly to keep her burning eyes from giving her jumbled emotions away. No matter how Selina tried to dress it up, Eve knew in her heart that it was unlikely she'd ever see Logan again, unless she went looking among the online gossip pages. Telling herself otherwise could only lead to more heartache and Eve was far too practical to indulge in that. It was time to put Logan Silk out of her mind and now that the launch party was out of the way, that was exactly what she planned to do.

Eve had never been more grateful to be overwhelmed with work. With a little over a month to go before Ennisfest roared into life, there was a mountain of organization still to be done. She left Aiden in charge of the bar's day-to-day running as much as she could and immersed herself in emails and conversations with suppliers, band members, technicians, engineers, builders ... The list was endless. It didn't matter that she'd been arranging the festival for years and had a good team around her with solid, trusted processes to get everything in place by the time the gates opened and the first festivalgoers arrived – it was still a mammoth grind through details and more details to ensure it all got done. And it meant she'd barely seen a soul apart from her brother since the exhibition launch four days earlier, which suited Eve fine.

The downside of working so hard was that she found herself cooped up inside for most of the day, managing an early morning walk with Huxley but little else. 'You need to take your foot off the gas a bit, Eve,' Aiden said on Wednesday afternoon as he brought a cup of coffee to the small box room they used as an office. 'All work and no play is a really bad idea.'

Eve barely looked up from her spreadsheet. 'Thanks. Maybe when I've got all the performer accreditation forms done.'

'Do they have to be finished today?' he asked. 'Surely you can take an evening off and relax a bit.'

A needle of irritation stabbed at Eve's patience. 'I want to tick them off my to-do list. Is that so terrible?'

'No,' Aiden said, his tone reasonable. 'But the world won't end if you tick them off tomorrow. I don't know whether you've checked a mirror today but you look like an extra from *Zombie Apocalypse II* – all puffy-eyed and pale, with a dribble of what looks like brains down your t-shirt.'

That got her attention. She looked down fast enough to hurt her stiff neck and saw he was right – there was a trail of something silvery across the front of her top. And the truth was she felt like a zombie, or at the very least in need of half an hour in the sunshine. 'You're right,' she relented, massaging her aching shoulder muscles with fingers that didn't feel like her own. 'And I haven't even asked how you are, or how the bar's doing.'

He shrugged. 'I'm fine. Tish and Poppy both know what they're doing and Petr's son is back from university so I've drafted him in for a couple of evening shifts.'

Eve was impressed that he'd made the decision to take on new staff without checking with her – that was a big step forward in his responsibilities. 'Great,' she said. 'Sounds like you've got everything under control.'

'We're coping,' Aiden agreed, then paused. 'I don't think the same can be said of Huxley, though. He's missing you, been pacing the house and bar wondering where you've gone.'

A wash of guilt flooded through Eve when she heard the words. She'd assumed the dog would be snoozing the day away, or hanging out with Aiden while she slaved over her phone and laptop but clearly that wasn't the case and the realization made her feel terrible. 'I'll make it up to him,' she said, pushing her chair back. 'Where is he? I'll take him for a walk right now.'

'In the kitchen last time I looked,' Aiden replied, eyebrows raised. 'But drink your coffee first. And maybe run a brush through your hair – I think there's a spider living in it.'

Eve's hand was halfway to her head before she realized he was joking. 'Ha ha.'

But she took the coffee across the landing to her bedroom and redid her ponytail all the same. Aiden was right – she did look half dead. A walk along the beach would do both her and Huxley a power of good.

Except Huxley wasn't in the kitchen. He wasn't in the living room, or any of the bedrooms, and he wasn't in the bar, scrounging for snacks. Eve felt a familiar sense of doom rising up from the pit of her stomach as she checked every room again and questioned the Darling's customers about whether they'd seen the chocolate Labrador. She rang Warren, who hadn't spotted Huxley on his land but promised to keep his eyes peeled, and asked Freda to put the word out that the dog had escaped again. When everyone had been alerted, Eve returned to the beach and scanned the sea and sand around the bar for any sign of a bounding brown dog. There were plenty of others enjoying the incoming tide but Huxley was conspicuous by his absence and Eve couldn't shake the sickening certainty that this time, something awful had happened.

She was just about to jump into her battered Land Rover to start combing the roads when she heard the crunch of wheels on gravel and saw Logan's Hilux edging through the gateway that led to the yard. For a split second, she considered hiding inside her car before realizing he must have seen her. And besides, he might have seen Huxley on the short journey from Dune Cottage, if that was where he'd come from. It was worth asking, Eve decided, and pasted on a polite smile as she approached the now parked vehicle. 'Hello,' she called. 'I don't suppose you've spotted Huxley on your travels, have you?'

Logan opened his mouth to reply but was interrupted by a volley of indignant barking. 'As a matter of fact, I have,' he said loudly, wincing at the silky eared chocolate head that thrust itself between the two front seats. 'Please come and get him before he bursts my eardrums.'

With a cry that was almost a sob, Eve ran forward to open the car door. Huxley bounded out and immediately leapt at her, attempting to lick her face and check her pockets for treats at the same time. 'Down, boy!' she tried to say in a stern voice but her relief made it impossible to muster any authority. 'Where have you been, you bad dog?'

Logan got out of the car and came to stand opposite her. 'I found him on the doorstep of the cottage – he came trotting in with a chunk of driftwood in his mouth that would have sunk the *Titanic*.'

'Sounds like Huxley,' Eve conceded. 'I've just practically mobilized the whole island to look for him. I didn't even think he'd come to you.'

Logan tipped his head. 'It was a surprise to find him there. But I knew you'd be worried so brought him straight back.'

Eve ruffled the dogs ears as he grinned up at her, tongue lolling. 'Thank you,' she said, swallowing another wash of relief that he'd been found unhurt. 'I was starting to panic.'

'No problem,' he replied easily, then paused. 'I haven't seen you much since Friday. Is everything okay?'

'Fine,' she said, and instantly wondered if she'd spoken too quickly. But he couldn't know she'd been deliberately avoiding him. 'Just busy with work. You know how it is.'

He nodded. 'Of course.' Another brief silence stretched between them. 'I'm having a few drinks at the Fisherman's

Arms on Monday evening – sort of a goodbye thing but nothing formal, in case you wanted to come along. No pressure but it would be nice to see you if you're free.'

The reminder of his impending departure was like a punch to Eve's stomach. She dipped her head to Huxley's in case her dismay showed. 'Thanks. I'll see what I can do.'

She felt his gaze upon her but couldn't trust herself to look up, even though she knew he must be puzzled by her stiffness. 'Okay,' he said at length. 'And I'll just leave the keys in the key safe on Tuesday morning, shall I? Or would you rather I waited for you at the cottage so you can check I've left it clean and undamaged?'

Eve sank her fingers into Huxley's soft brown fur, mercifully clean of any kind of disgustingness, and willed herself to meet Logan's eyes. 'No, I trust you,' she said, forcing herself to sound blithe. 'Just leave the keys when you go.'

'Right,' Logan said, and she thought she caught a flicker of something that might have been hurt cross his face. 'Well, hopefully I'll see you on Monday. Any time from seven-thirty.'

'Sure,' Eve said, knowing it was unlikely she'd go. But she did owe him for returning her dog. 'Thanks for bringing Huxley back. I really appreciate it.'

Logan's smile didn't quite reach his eyes. 'No problem. I hope he behaves himself, for the rest of the day, at least.' With a brief wave, he made for the driver's door of his car. 'Take care, Eve. See you around.'

He was starting the engine before she could respond, so

she offered a matching wave and focused her suddenly burning eyes on Huxley, who was only too happy to receive her attention. When she looked up, the Hilux was disappearing along the lane and she was both maddeningly sorry and glad to see it go.

Chapter Twenty-Four

Logan

Monday arrived faster than Logan would have believed possible. He'd begun the process of packing over the weekend and had been surprised by how much he'd accumulated during his three-month stay but by Monday morning, all bar the essentials were stacked and ready to be loaded into the Hilux. He had planned to pack the car that afternoon, rather than clutter up the living room with bags and boxes, but he was overwhelmed by a yearning to visit his favourite parts of the island one last time – the windswept granite beacon that stood in age-old readiness, staring across the sea to its companions on other islands, the desecrated nunnery whose ruins still managed to radiate tranquillity despite their turbulent history, the bustling village harbour with its crusty lobster pots and bobbing boats, alive with the cheerful calls of the men and women who had fished the island's waters since they were old enough to tie a decent knot. And most of all, Logan wanted to walk out of Dune Cottage and pick his way through the spiky marram grass that grew tall and green on top of the dunes until he reached the golden curve of Darling Cove, to admire the shadows of the towering arch that clung to the headland at the furthest end and absorb the endless music of the ocean. But that was a treat he was saving for early on Tuesday morning, so that he could store it up ahead of the long journey back to London. For now, Logan left the boxes stacked in the cottage and went to soak up the beauty of Ennisfarne one final time.

The restlessness he'd thought might be eased by the drive around the island only seemed to worsen when he returned to Dune Cottage just before six o'clock. The living room felt cluttered and empty at the same time, the boxes altering its landscape and taking up too much space while the coffee table and shelves were bare, the way they had been when Logan had first arrived. The kitchen, with its empty fridge and cupboards, had a similarly vacant air. Only the bedroom still felt like his, at least for a few more hours and the awareness that he no longer felt at home in the cottage was something that bothered him very much. After prowling around for twenty minutes, unable to settle, Logan decided to set off early for the Fisherman's Arms before his mood deteriorated any further. The walk would do him good and he needed distraction, something to take his mind off this unaccustomed sense of being off kilter. Perhaps he would check in on the exhibition one last time and then wander round The Nook to kill some time. If Freda's unashamed nosiness couldn't shake him out of his disquiet then nothing could.

In the end, Logan did neither. As he was nearing the rows of upturned herring boats nestling on a long grass verge that stretched from the side of the road down to the vast channel between the island and the mainland, he became aware of a vehicle slowing behind him. Turning, he saw it was Eve's Land Rover. Aiden was in the passenger seat and Huxley's nose was poking through a small strip of open window in the back.

'Heading for the pub?' Aiden called cheerily. 'Hop in!'

Logan had been enjoying the walk, although the wind was nipping around his ears now that he'd reached the channel. But there wasn't really a polite way to say no, he decided, and opened the rear door to climb into the seat behind Eve. Huxley greeted him with a friendly lick around the headrest but stayed in the boot, for which Logan was grateful. It wasn't that he was concerned about smelling of dog, more that the Labrador was likely to try and sit on his lap and Logan knew from experience just how much he weighed.

'How's the packing going?' Aiden said over one shoulder. 'All set for the big drive?'

'I think so,' Logan replied, watching the waves through the car window. 'It's going to be weird waking up on Wednesday morning, though.'

In the rear-view mirror, he saw Eve's eyes flash to him

then return to the road ahead. 'I bet you can't wait to get back,' Aiden said. 'Bright lights, big city, boozy late nights. No more planning your life around the causeway.'

Logan smiled. 'It's not that bad.'

'There speaks a man who's only lived here a few months,' Aiden said with a theatrical shudder.

'Anyone would think you were being held prisoner here, Aiden,' Eve pointed out mildly as she slowed the Land Rover to pull into the pub car park. 'You could always move to London if it appeals so much.'

'Not sure I could afford it,' Aiden said. 'But I wouldn't turn down a weekend away. What do you say, Logan? You, me and Nick Borrowdale – lads on the lash in London.'

Eve snorted as she reversed into a parking space. 'Now that's something I'd like to see. Or maybe I wouldn't.'

Her brother grinned. 'You could come too. The more the merrier.'

'And who would manage the bar?' Eve demanded.

'Tish,' Aiden said, then saw Eve's expression. 'Okay, maybe not for a whole weekend. But we could go after the tourist season's over, close Darling's and let it all hang out.'

He glanced back at Logan in obvious appeal. 'You'd be very welcome,' Logan offered. 'I can't promise Nick will make it but I'd be glad to see you and it's the least I can do after all you've done for me.'

Eve opened the car door and started to climb out. 'Don't encourage him,' she told Logan, rolling her eyes. 'He's full of these bright ideas but they never come to anything.'

Aiden winked. 'Ah, but this time I've got a partner in crime. A contact in the city. Batman to my Robin.'

'Kermit to your Gonzo?' Eve suggested and looked at Logan again. 'No offence.'

'None taken,' he said. 'I'm not sure which muppet Nick would be. Animal, maybe.'

Eve pursed her lips as though considering, then shook her head. 'I think this has gone far enough. Any minute now someone is going to compare me to Miss Piggy and I won't be responsible for my actions.'

Aiden opened his mouth and – just for a moment – Logan thought he was going to pick up the gauntlet his sister had just thrown down. But instead, he nodded towards the pub. 'After you,' he said, standing back to allow Logan to pass in front of him. 'This is your party after all.'

It wasn't strictly a party, Logan wanted to point out, but the argument died the moment he entered the Fisherman's Arms. Someone had gone to the trouble of decorating. Clusters of balloons hung from the ceiling, with more filled with helium rising like moons from the tables and floor. A *Bon Voyage* banner fluttered over the bar and Freda was tending to what looked a lot like a buffet laid out on tables along one of the walls. Hamish hurried over to shake Logan's hand. 'Good to see you. What can I get you to drink?'

'A pint of Thirsty Bishop, please,' Logan said, before aiming an enquiring look at his companions.

'I'll have the same,' Aiden said, without hesitation.

'Just an orange juice for me, please,' Eve said, which earned her a sniff of disapproval from her brother.

'We agreed to leave the car here, remember?' he said. 'So neither of us has to worry about driving back tonight.'

'I do remember,' Eve replied with a mulish tilt of her chin. 'But I'd still like an orange juice, thanks.'

'Coming right up,' Hamish replied, heading back behind the bar.

'Maybe you can talk some sense into her,' Aiden grumbled at Logan. 'I've been telling her for days she needs to ease off on work and let her hair down from time to time.'

Unbidden, an image of Eve at the exhibition launch popped into Logan's mind. Eve had literally let her hair down then and he'd wanted to reach out and run his fingers through each golden strand. He gave himself a mental shake. Maybe he should be drinking orange juice as well, in case that temptation got the better of him that evening and he made a fool of himself.

'It's a school night,' Eve reminded Aiden. 'Some of us have work tomorrow and that includes you.'

Which was another excellent point, Logan thought. He had a long drive in the morning and it made sense to ensure he was safe to drive. A couple of pints over the course of the evening would be enough. No need to go crazy.

Aiden sighed. 'I try my best but see what I'm dealing with here?' He shook his head in mock sorrow. 'Stick with me, Logan, I'll make sure your last night on Ennisfarne is one to remember.'

He turned and made for the bar, as though to hurry Hamish along with the drinks. Eve watched him go, then gave Logan a sidelong look. 'You might want to rethink that invitation to London.'

'I'm sure he'd be fine,' Logan said, smiling. 'Especially if you came along to keep an eye on him.'

She appeared to have one or two things to say about that, but Logan didn't get to hear them because Freda had made a beeline in their direction. 'Here he is – the guest of honour,' she said, beaming at Logan. 'I know you weren't expecting so much fuss but we wanted to send you off in style.'

'You've certainly done that,' Logan said, appreciative of the effort. 'It looks like there's a feast laid out over there.'

'Just a few bits and bobs,' Freda said modestly and looked around. 'I know it seems a bit empty now but it'll fill up soon enough, don't you worry. You've made a lot of friends here.'

'I'm honoured,' Logan said, and meant it. 'Thank you.'

'No need to thank me,' Freda replied. 'Just promise you won't forget us when you get back to the big city.'

'How could I?' Logan said, grinning. 'I'm going to be pining for The Nook before I'm halfway home. You'll have to send me a survival package.'

Freda had been right about Logan's popularity; the bar started filling up just after seven o'clock and was soon standing room only. He spent a whirlwind couple of hours chatting, laughing and joking with the people he'd come to count as friends over the previous three months, promising over and over that he wouldn't be a stranger. Freda jostled him towards the buffet and made sure he ate; too many people wanted to buy him a drink that he was glad to have the excuse of a long drive the next morning – his liver would have hated him otherwise. He did allow himself to be cajoled into a third pint by George, who wouldn't take no for an answer, and reasoned that he could always set off a little later if he needed.

As the night wore on, the air in the bar grew stuffy, heady with the fumes of alcohol. More than once Logan found himself throwing longing looks at the door that led to the smoking area and recalled someone – maybe Amy Winehouse – telling him that the smoking area was always where all the coolest people hung out. And there was certainly a large group spilling out from the Fisherman's Arms, standing around in small groups as they chatted. But Logan didn't want to get pulled into another conversation. What he wanted was a few minutes of silence – the extraordinary, listening silence he'd only ever encountered on Ennisfarne – and so he circumnavigated the smokers and vapers and made his way to the dimly lit harbour across the road.

The stars seemed brighter than ever overhead. That was another thing Logan would miss once he returned to London – the lack of light pollution that made the night sky come alive. Some of the stars seemed to have tumbled down to float on the blackness of the water, making the twinkling even more spectacular as it danced on the gently lapping tide.

He almost didn't see Eve. She was tucked away at the base of the jetty steps, her phone in her hand. At first, he couldn't make out who it was silhouetted by the light from the small screen but then he caught a flash of gold hair. Frowning, he walked closer. 'Everything okay?' he called, stopping a metre or so back so that she had time to see and recognize him.

'Fine,' she said, raising her phone a little. 'Just catching up with a few emails. Don't tell my brother.'

At her feet, Huxley lifted his head to give Logan a curious once-over but the dog didn't get up, which Logan supposed was something to be relieved about. He didn't fancy being accidentally knocked into the harbour waters.

He waited to see if Eve would invite him to join her but her attention was fixed on the screen of the mobile phone so he stayed where he was, wondering whether he was imagining the sense that he'd somehow managed to annoy her again, perhaps with this intrusion. But she surprised him a moment later. 'Do you know much about the stars?' she asked suddenly. 'The ones up there, I mean, rather than celebrities.'

Logan squinted upwards. 'I did a photoshoot in New Zealand with their leading professor of cosmology and became fascinated by the science. But there's nothing more magical than gazing upwards on a clear night, is there?'

Eve nodded. 'They're always bright here. When we were young, my dad used to take Aiden and me out on midnight sailing trips to teach us how to navigate by starlight. He had a story about each constellation and why it moved the way it did through the night.'

Recalling his tale that the natural blowhole in the harbour

wall was really a dragon, Logan could believe that. 'That sounds brilliant.'

'It was,' she said with a fleeting smile. Then she pointed up to the brightest pinprick of light. 'The first thing you need to do is find the North Star. It stays above the North Pole so once you've got that, you can use it to work out your position relative to the constellations around it.'

She made it sound simple but Logan was well aware there was a lot of skill to navigation, whether by day or by night. 'And what story did your dad tell you about the North Star?'

Eve hesitated for a moment, then seemed to arrive at a decision. She patted the ground beside her. Logan sat. 'He used to say that it was thrown into the sky by the first of the gods, so that their pack of hounds would have something to chase. The clusters of stars surrounding it are the dogs, each trying to beat the others to the prize.'

Logan grinned. He'd expected a more classical take – one of the Greek myths, perhaps – but this fitted Eve much better. 'I'm not sure who I feel worse for – the beleaguered gods, not getting anything done because their dogs want to play all the time, or the dogs, who will never have the delight of finally catching the ball.'

She offered him a rueful look. 'As a child, I was firmly on the side of the dogs. Now, perhaps a little less.'

Her gaze returned to the sky, where the North Star shimmered forever just out of reach of the chasing pack, but Logan's attention was caught by her upturned face, at the way the light from the nearby street lamp created shadows and secrets, lacing silver through her hair and making her seem half made of starlight herself. He wished he had his camera and then fixed his own eyes on the sky before she caught him staring. 'I think I'd have liked your father.'

She looked at him then and the ghost of a smile curved her lips. 'I think so too.'

Logan wasn't sure how long they might have sat smiling in companionable silence, Huxley sitting contentedly at their feet, if Aiden hadn't loomed somewhat unsteadily out of the darkness. 'Hamish is about to call last orders, if you're interested,' he said, the words only very slightly slurred. 'George is getting the shots in – who's up for it?'

To Logan's surprise, Eve nodded. 'I'm in,' she said, climbing to her feet. 'It might keep me warm on the walk home.'

It seemed she'd abandoned her plan to drive, Logan observed, and decided he was glad. Aiden was right – everyone needed a night off every now and then. Of course, Logan had known he'd have to find a way of getting back to Dune Cottage – he would never have presumed Eve would give him a lift – but he'd hoped there would be at least one village taxi to ferry people home. Not so, it seemed. Unless Eve preferred to walk, which was also a possibility. He'd never met anyone quite so fiercely attached to their independence as her.

Standing up, he followed them back to the warmth of the pub. He had no intention of getting involved in any shots – he'd done that too many times in the past and it had always rewarded him with a fuzzy head the next day and only patchy memories of the night before. He'd save that kind of behaviour for London, he resolved, when he was less likely to embarrass himself.

But it soon became apparent that George was not prepared to take no for an answer where Logan and shots were concerned, and he had a pair of willing accomplices in Aiden and Hamish. It didn't matter how many times Logan protested that he needed to be fit to drive.

'One for the road,' George cried with a bleary-eyed insistence that gave Logan the distinct impression this would not be his first shot of the evening. 'Vodka, Sambuca or good old tequila?'

Eve gave Logan a pitying look. 'Don't let them bully you. Keep saying no if you really don't want one.'

He looked around the bar, filled with laughter and chatter, the air warm and even more fugged with alcohol. It was his last night on the island, he reminded himself. Where was the harm in pushing the boat out a little? And as Eve had already pointed out, there was the walk home to sober himself up. Considering for a moment longer, he gave in. 'Vodka, then. But only one.'

A ragged cheer went up from Aiden and George, while Eve just shook her head in amusement and ordered a tequila. When the drinks arrived, George held his glass up in solemn salute. 'To Logan Silk, a gentleman and a scholar and a bloody good bloke. I'm glad to have known you, sir.'

Aiden and Eve raised their glasses. 'To Logan.'

Wordlessly, Logan lifted his own drink and tapped it

against theirs. The four of them drank, the vodka burning a fiery trail all the way to the pit of Logan's stomach. Almost instantly, a mellow buzz radiated outwards. It had been a while since he'd drunk vodka – probably not since arriving on Ennisfarne, where his tipple of choice had been wine, to go with Freda's excellent cheese suggestions from The Nook, or the occasional dram of whisky – and he'd forgotten how seductive that sudden hit of alcohol could be. And that was why shots were never a good idea, he reminded himself sternly. They so very rarely ended at one.

Hamish rang the bell, signalling last orders, and Logan was surprised to see how late it was. 'Time to start saying goodbye,' he said to Eve, who nodded.

'Unless you want to be nursing the hangover from hell when you drive to London. This lot will be here for a while yet – Hamish is famously lax at kicking people out.'

Logan grinned. He'd enjoyed one or two lock-ins courtesy of Hamish in the past and they had indeed resulted in a sore head the next day, although the pain had been very much worth it. He almost wished he could stay one last time but he knew he'd only regret it in the morning. 'Shall we walk back together, since we're going the same way?'

The suggestion was born from utter practicality but it was only after the words were out that it occurred to Logan he might have put Eve in an awkward position. She eyed him for a nanosecond, then seemed to take the offer in the spirit it had been intended. 'Sure,' she said, with a nod. 'You start your goodbyes and I'll remind Aiden he's got work tomorrow.'

Some fifteen minutes later, Logan had worked his way round the remaining drinkers, wishing them farewell and promising to stay in touch. George had been especially emotional and it had taken a sympathetic but stern intervention from Hettie to prevent him from following when Logan finally left the table. Eve was waiting by the door, watching his thwarted efforts to extricate himself with undisguised amusement. 'You've made quite the impression on George. I hope you're ready for him to turn up your doorstep along with my brother.'

'It would be good to see him,' Logan said stoutly. 'Hettie too, since I doubt she'd let him go without her.'

Eve's mouth quirked. 'Very generous of you. We'll need our own coach at this rate.'

At first, the cool night air was a welcome change from the stuffiness of the pub but it wasn't long before Logan was glad of his jacket. In London, May evenings could be sweltering, especially if a journey involved the Tube, but Ennisfarne's summer temperatures still dipped at night. He wasn't surprised to see Eve was more than adequately prepared too, with a cosy-looking puffer jacket that she pulled on as they made their way to the paved footpath that ran alongside the road out of the village. 'Not regretting the decision to leave your car here, are you?' he asked, as Huxley trotted between them.

'A bit,' she admitted. 'But it's only a thirty-minute walk and there won't be many cars to dodge. It'll wear Huxley out too.'

Logan regarded the Labrador's enthusiastic snuffling of the grass verge. 'I didn't think anything wore him out.'

'It's been a busy evening full of fuss and ill–gotten snacks,' she said equably. 'He'll sleep well once we get home.'

'Me too,' Logan said. 'Although I think the vodka will help there.'

She laughed. 'I find it sometimes keeps me awake but I'm not much of a party animal.'

They walked in companionable silence for a few minutes, until Logan realized the road they were taking was about to run out of streetlights. 'Do you walk this way in the dark often?'

Eve rummaged in her coat pocket and produced a pair of headtorches, each with a thick rubber band to attach to the wearer's head. 'Not often,' she said, offering one to Logan. 'But the roads are usually quiet enough this late at night, even in tourist season, and Darling's will have closed ages ago. It's safe enough.'

He didn't like to think of her navigating the pitch black-ness alone and was glad he'd offered to walk back with her. And then he adjusted his thinking, because this was Eve who knew Ennisfarne inside and out, and was perfectly capable of looking after herself. In fact, if anyone needed looking after on the dark road, it was him. 'Thanks for this,' he said, and pulled the torch into place. 'Won't Aiden need it?'

'All part of the service,' she said, as her own torch threw a pool of light at their feet. 'I wouldn't want to have to tell Phoebe that you'd fallen head first into a ditch.'

Logan regarded her illuminated face with wry amusement. 'Again, thanks.'

'No problem. Aiden will find a sofa for the night so he won't be needing to navigate his way home.' She sighed. 'He's ended up in a ditch once or twice in the past so it's all for the best, as long as he's back in time to open the bar in the morning.'

Logan grinned as the affectionate resignation in her voice, which seemed to sum up her relationship with Aiden perfectly. They walked a little further, the silence punctuated by sniffs and snorts from Huxley. 'Did Phoebe really enjoy the exhibition?' Eve asked at length. 'It's quite different from your usual work.'

He thought back to his agent's glowing comments in the car as he'd driven her back to Dune Cottage after the party, including another reminder that she could sell photographs like those on display in a heartbeat. 'She loved it, maybe because it's so different. I think she was a bit smitten with the whole island, to be honest. She said she wanted to come back, anyway.'

Eve nodded, her lamp bobbing up and down with the movement. 'And how about you?' she asked, not looking at him. 'Do you think you'll ever come back?'

It was a natural enough question – one that had been posed several times that evening, in different guises – but there was something in Eve's voice that made Logan look at her as they walked, an indefinable sliver that slipped away when he tried to catch it. 'I certainly hope so,' he said. 'I'm going to miss being here very much, the beach and all the people and—'

He stopped, suddenly aware he'd been about to blurt out that he would miss her very much too. Clamping his lips together, Logan cursed the weakness that had led him to down that shot of vodka. Mixed with three pints of Thirsty Bishop, it seemed to be more effective than a truth serum.

'You could always rent the cottage again,' she suggested. 'Although it's not available now until the winter.'

Again, he got the impression there was something more behind the words, something not being said that he couldn't decode. Perhaps Eve had one eye on her income once the tourist season had died down and was trying to pin him down for another extended stay. 'That's an option,' he agreed. 'Although I suppose a lot depends on work. If things get crazy again . . .'

He trailed off, aware that the thought of returning to his old working life still held no appeal. It would come, he told himself. He just needed to give it time.

'Ah, I'm sure you'll forget about us soon enough,' Eve said. 'Once the supermodels start lighting up your camera again.'

Brows knitted, Logan didn't answer immediately. There'd been a subtle edge in her tone and he wasn't sure why. 'I don't think I'm ever going to forget Ennisfarne,' he said, after a moment or two of thoughtful walking. 'It's an incredible place. I can see why you've never wanted to leave.'

'Yes,' she said, but didn't offer any further comment, seeming to withdraw into her own thoughts. Logan gave up trying to work out what she wasn't saying and let the silence stretch, attempting to guess how far they'd walked instead. The herring boats were just visible on the other side of the road, their hulking forms distinguishable only because they were a shade darker than the night itself. The light from his headtorch caught occasionally on a door handle or lock, flashing briefly like a beacon. From the boats, the road would soon fork left and right and then they would be on the road to Dune Cottage, and Darling's beyond that. It was perhaps a fifteen-minute walk although it might feel longer if they had run out of things to talk about.

'How's the festival preparation going?' he asked after a minute or so.

'Not bad,' she said. 'There's always too much to do and not enough time but everything seems to get sorted in the end.'

He glanced at her. 'Because you make sure it does. Have you thought about getting someone else in to help?'

'From time to time,' she admitted. 'But as Aiden will tell you, delegation isn't my strong suit. I like to know everything has been done, and done properly.'

Logan grunted in recognition; he'd been guilty of that in the past too, on jobs where the crew hadn't been known to him. 'The trouble with always doing everything yourself is that sooner or later, you'll run out of steam. Believe me, I know.'

Suspicion flickered across her face. 'Did Aiden put you up to this?'

'No. I just recognize the signs.' He regarded her steadily.

'Just because you can do it all doesn't mean you should. And getting someone good in to help might mean you enjoy Ennisfest more. I've watched you run around after other people for three months, Eve – you're always doing things to help, fixing problems, supporting your friends and family. Even when you dive, you're looking after everyone else.'

She started to object but he held up a hand. 'It's not meant as a criticism,' he said, his tone placatory. 'It's just – well, if there's one thing I've learned in the past few months, it's that it is okay to say no every now and then, to put yourself first. I think it's been a while since you did that.'

Eve made a sudden gesture, a restless wave. 'Easier said than done. Besides, it's how things work here – we help each other, you know that.'

'I do,' Logan replied. 'But if you spread yourself too thinly, you won't be much use to anyone.'

She said nothing, causing Logan to wonder if he'd gone too far. But then she puffed out a long slow breath. 'You sound like Selina.'

He nodded, because Selina had once told him she worried about her best friend's tendency to take on too much. 'I'll take that as a compliment.'

'You should,' Eve said, then gave a defeated shrug. 'You're probably both right. I could do with a bit of help. Thank you.'

It wasn't exactly an acknowledgement that she worked too hard but it was a start, Logan thought. 'Any time,' he said, tipping his head.

'So, what's next for you?' she asked, after a few more steps. 'Apart from a long drive, I mean.'

Now it was Logan's turn to shrug. 'Settle back in to life in London and see what happens, I suppose. I don't really have a plan.'

Eve shuddered. 'I don't know how you can sleep at night. I need a to-do list just to get from one hour to the next.'

'That's because you're overcommitted,' he reminded her. 'Besides, I've had three months of doing nothing, so a few more weeks won't really make a difference.'

'You've been on a break, totally disconnected from your old life,' she observed. 'I expect it'll be hard not to get sucked back in once you're home.'

It was a fair point, he thought, but it was a bridge he'd have to cross when he got to it. At least he and Phoebe seemed to have reached an understanding; there'd be no pressure there. 'All the more reason to escape to Ennisfarne every so often,' he said, smiling. 'Now, tell me which bands you've got coming next month.'

Whether she realized he was trying to change the subject or not, Eve did as he asked and reeled off an impressive line-up of acts she'd booked for the festival. There were many he'd never heard of, which was entirely to be expected at such a comparatively small event, but it appeared Ennisfest punched well above its weight. 'You've got Infinite Monkey Dance headlining?' he said, impressed. 'They're huge – how did you manage that?'

'I booked them eighteen months ago, before they went

stratospheric,' Eve explained. 'And their manager is a friend – I book a lot of her bands when they're just starting out, offer them the chance to build up paid gig experience – so when one of them hits the big time, she makes sure they honour the booking with us.'

Logan didn't know why he was surprised – Eve had proved over and over how smart and capable she was. But yet again he was struck by her competence. He was beginning to think there was nothing she couldn't do.

With a start he noticed they were approaching Dune Cottage and the realization brought with it a dilemma. The gentlemanly thing to do would be to suggest he walked Eve all the way home, then double back to the cottage, but he was wary of once again coming across as patronizing. The alternative was to part company now, outside Dune Cottage, and let her finish the journey on her own but that didn't sit well with him either. It didn't help that this was probably the last time he would see her, at least for a while, and now that the time had come he found himself reluctant to say goodbye. Ten more minutes in her company seemed very appealing, even if it meant risking her wrath and a longer walk for him.

Perhaps she'd had the same thought because she slowed a little as they reached the gate. 'Here you are, safely delivered,' she said. 'No ditches were disturbed.'

'Thank you,' Logan said, and threw caution to the winds. 'Will you be okay getting back to Darling's? I don't mind walking with you.'

She shook her head. 'That's kind but I'll be fine, thanks. I've got my ferocious hound to protect me, remember?'

Huxley chose that moment to cock his leg against the gate post. 'Ah yes,' Logan said. 'So I see.'

The silence that followed was so tangible Logan felt he could reach out and snap off a chunk. He wanted to thank her for everything, from fixing the leaking tap to chasing off an intrusive reporter and introducing him to the hidden wrecks off the coast of the island, but it seemed like such a measly sentiment to cover all she'd done to make his time on Ennisfarne so pleasurable. Words jumbled in his head but he struggled to marshal them into sentences and he was suddenly aware he had so much to say but had somehow squandered the time he'd had to say it.

'Have a safe journey home,' Eve said with a briskness that suggested she'd picked up on the awkwardness too and was trying to prevent it getting worse. 'I hope London isn't too much of a shock to the system.'

He gazed at her fully then, which caused her to squint in the beam of his torch. Reaching up, he removed it and clicked the off button, holding it out for her to take. Now she was lit by the light from her own torch and it seemed to Logan as though she was an angel, bathed in the glow of her halo. The thought brought with it a sudden realization, one that had been nudging at his mind every time he'd looked at her for weeks: he wanted to kiss her. She would taste of the sea, wild with the tang of salt, because for all her practicality there was something also untamed about her. His camera had caught it time and again, in the picture on the boat and during the photoshoot on the beach. It called to him, snared his imagination and drew him in. It was why he didn't want to say goodbye.

'Eve—' he began, but she stepped sharply back.

'Don't.' Her wide-eyed gaze met his and he saw she'd guessed what he was going to say. 'Nothing good will come of it. You're leaving tomorrow.'

'Not for ever,' he said. 'I could come back.'

'You could,' she said, slowly. 'But what happens then? We see each other when you have time, and gradually you'll get busy. It's not like our lifestyles fit together, is it? You're a celebrity and I run a bar.'

Her voice was flat, so matter of fact, that he knew in a flash this was an argument she'd had with herself more than once and it was a realisation that inspired hope and hopelessness in equal measure. 'There are worse combinations,' he offered.

Grimacing, Eve shook her head. 'You know what I mean. We live in different worlds, Logan, and I'm not a model or pop star or anything remotely close to the type of woman you date. So let's not ruin things by doing something we'll both regret tomorrow.'

The use of 'regret' almost made him wince but then a memory floated into Logan's mind, of Aiden telling him Eve would never choose her heart over her head, and here was the evidence. She was practical to her core and she only gambled when she knew she could win – Logan had understood that much from the way she played poker. The real surprise was that she'd been attracted to him at all, in spite of her determination that it would inevitably lead to heartache. He wanted to disagree, to convince her she was wrong, that being utterly different to Suki was one of the things that drew him to her, that they could make it work. But he knew from the bullish set of her chin that she'd made up her mind. To press his point would be disrespectful, when she'd clearly made her decision. And so he did the only thing he could – reluctantly, with a heaviness that dragged his heart to the ground, he accepted the rejection. 'Understood.'

She let out a long breath, making him wonder whether she'd been expecting him to argue. 'And one more thing, Logan,' she said, with a wobble in her voice that suggested her emotions weren't entirely unscathed, despite her pragmatism. 'By all means come back to Ennisfarne when you're ready. Just not too soon, okay?'

Again, there was only one possible response. Taking a step back, he inclined his head. 'Okay.'

Turning on her heel, she walked away. And Logan let her go.

Chapter Twenty-Five

Eve

No matter how many times Eve told herself she'd done the right thing, it didn't make her feel any less wretched. In the days that followed, she forced herself to remember who he really was – not the funny, introspective, generous Logan she'd come to know and like, but Logan Silk, playboy photographer to the rich and famous. In some ways it felt like a dream she was misremembering – the surreal thump of realization that he felt the same attraction she did couldn't have actually happened, could it? But deep down, she'd known it was coming. It had been building from the moment they'd sat side by side on the edge of the harbour, staring at the starlit sky. She wasn't sure if that knowledge had made it harder or easier to ignore the treacherous voice in her head telling her to give in when the moment had finally come. She'd only known it would be a thousand times harder to say goodbye once she had kissed him.

Selina made no attempt to hide her frustration when Eve confessed what had happened over pizza and wine. 'Let me get this straight. The guy you've been mooning about over for three months – don't argue, you have – admits that he has feelings too and you shut him down without a second's hesitation.' She gave Eve a pitying look and leaned back against the sofa. 'You're insane.'

'I'm sensible,' Eve countered but she had to admit it sounded ridiculous when Selina put it like that. 'Anything else would have been an exercise in futility.'

Her best friend folded her arms. 'Futility is pretending you don't feel something when you do.' She paused for a second or two, considering. 'Or that you feel something you don't. Which is how I knew it would never work between me and Logan. But you are different. You've got it bad.'

Eve shook her head stubbornly. 'It wouldn't work, Sel. Wasn't part of the reason you stopped seeing him was because he was going back to London?'

'Not at all. I said I couldn't see a future with him but that's not the same thing.'

'Isn't it?' Eve stared at her in confusion.

'No, it isn't. But we're not talking about me.' Selina eyed Eve over the top of her wine glass. 'This is about you being a coward. You're afraid of getting hurt.'

Heat bloomed in Eve's cheeks. She started to frame a denial but gave up before the words were fully formed. 'Okay, maybe a bit. But that doesn't mean I'm wrong.'

Selina's expression softened. 'Do you know what went

345

through my head when my boat sank and I was scared I'd drown before anyone found me? It wasn't all the things I'd tried that hadn't worked out, it was the stuff I'd never get to do. The people I'd never hug again.' She sighed, her eyes moist. 'That's what matters, Eve. Being able to look back at your life and know that you bloody lived it.'

Tears stung the back of Eve's eyes too. 'Oh, Sel.'

Her best friend threw her a lopsided grin. 'Pack it in, I'm still here. But the point stands. What are you going to regret more – keeping your heart locked away so it never gets played, or giving it to someone else so they can make it sing, even though the music might not last for ever.'

Eve stared at her, feeling the prickle behind her eyes intensify. 'But how could I ever be enough for someone like him? I'm not beautiful or glamorous – I can't even put mascara on without poking myself in the eye.'

Selina held up a hand. 'Rubbish. There's a photograph hanging in the exhibition that says different.'

'That's Logan's skill,' Eve said firmly. 'Nothing to do with me.'

'Partly,' Selina conceded. 'But he can't capture what's not there. And here's something else to think about. If the pictures Logan takes are how he sees the world, and the photos he takes of you are beautiful, doesn't that mean he finds *you* beautiful?'

It took Eve a minute to work out exactly what her friend was saying. Could it be true? Could it be that Logan saw something in her that she couldn't see herself?

'Do yourself a favour,' Selina went on, refilling both their glasses. 'Next time you're in the village, go and stand in front of that photograph. Put your insecurities to one side and really look at it. I think it'll tell you everything you need to know about how Logan sees you.'

For a moment, Eve was almost convinced, then reality came rushing back in. 'But it doesn't matter,' she said. 'It's too late, he's gone. Best to forget him and move on.'

Selina shrugged. 'If that's what you really want to do then fine. But I reckon he'd come back in a heartbeat if you asked him.' She gave Eve a meaningful look. 'And I know you never gamble on anything less than a dead cert but ask yourself this. What have you actually got to lose?'

It wasn't that Eve purposefully pushed Selina's question to the back of her mind in the weeks that followed, more that the whirl of organization demanded by Ennisfest made it hard to think about much else. Her days were filled with phone calls, paperwork, logistics and site visits, leaving her no time for anything else other than Huxley. She saw Aiden briefly at breakfast, usually as she was leaving the kitchen having gulped down some toast, and then rarely saw him again before the bar closed, when they exchanged weary notes about their day. It was only in the quiet moments before sleep that Eve allowed herself to think of Logan, and it was never long before sleep claimed her.

It wasn't until the middle of June that Eve found herself in the village with a bit of time to kill. It was Sunday morning and she was due to meet Hamish and Warren at the pub to go over final plans for the festival but she'd arrived early. She sat in the car park, answering emails and messages, occasionally being distracted by the steady flow of visitors to the village hall. She already knew from Freda that the exhibition had been a phenomenal success, raising much needed funds for the hall. Plans were already underway to refurbish the building once the tourist season was over. Eve had to hand it to Logan – his photographs drew people in even when they had no idea of the famous name behind them.

She tapped at a few more emails, her gaze straying once more to the hall. What was it Selina had said – stand in front of the photograph and look at it if she wanted to know how Logan saw her? What harm could it do, Eve asked herself and stowed her phone in her coat pocket. It wasn't as though Logan would know.

There was a gentle buzz in the hall, the sound of murmured conversations and hushed observations. Eve nodded to Petr, who was manning the entrance and drawing the visitors' attention to the transparent donations cube, and wandered through the crowd until she found the picture of herself.

Not for the first time, she felt a peculiar jolt of disassociation when she looked at it. This was an ocean spirit, ensnared by the sun in the act of transformation. It couldn't possibly be her – ordinary Eve Darling – and yet she recognized elements of herself, the turned-up tip of her nose, the tilt of her chin. She supposed that was part of Logan's magic, taking the everyday and making it exceptional. How many times had she driven past the herring boats and never been struck by their collective majesty? But it didn't necessarily follow that Logan saw her as anything more than a subject for his art, she reminded herself. No matter how beautiful that art was.

A middle-aged couple came to stand beside her, the woman plump and jolly in her padded tweed jacket and the man ruddy-cheeked beneath his flat cap. They both gazed at the photograph for a few seconds, then the woman leaned towards the man. 'Calypso, I think – goddess of the sea. She lured Odysseus to her island and enchanted him so he would never leave.'

The man grunted. 'Looks quite enchanting to me. I'd stick around for a beauty like that.'

The woman batted him on the arm in mock outrage. Eve felt warmth colour her cheeks and dipped her head suddenly in case either of them glanced sideways and recognized her. The irony of the couple's whispered conversation was not lost on her; if she was Calypso, she'd done a terrible job of enchanting her Odysseus.

Hamish and Warren were waiting when she entered the bar, their heads bent over a newspaper on the table in front of them. They both looked up when she came in and froze, as though she'd caught them in the act of doing something incriminating. 'Morning,' she said, frowning as she walked towards them. 'Hope I'm not interrupting anything.'

Hamish swept the paper aside and cleared his throat. 'Not really. We were just catching up on the news.'

Warren nodded. 'Nothing interesting, though. Just the usual rubbish that wouldn't interest you.'

Perplexed, Eve glanced from one man to the other, taking in their too earnest smiles and air of wide-eyed innocence. 'Right,' she said slowly. 'Well, shall we get down to business? We've got a lot to get through.'

'Absolutely,' Hamish said, with an enthusiastic nod. 'Can I get you a coffee?'

'Tea, please,' Eve replied and took a seat at the table.

The landlord nodded and reached for the newspaper, which drooped half on, half off the table's surface. 'Oh, leave that,' Eve said pleasantly. 'It's always good to know what's happening in the world.'

Hamish darted a look at Warren, who shrugged. 'Best let her see it.'

She knew instantly what they'd been reading. Dominating the front page of the most scurrilous Sunday tabloid was a blown-up picture of Logan and his ex-girlfriend, Suki Simpson, falling out of a London nightclub. SUKI'S TOUCH OF SILK, the headline bellowed.

The blow to Eve's stomach was almost physical. She stared at the photograph, not quite able to take it in, then forced her gaze to travel to the small print underneath.

Fashion's power couple Suki Simpson and Logan Silk looked the picture of loved-up happiness outside Lola's nightclub in London last night. See Page 5 for full details.

Eve sat very still, trying not to betray herself while her mind raced. Her first reaction was disbelief; Logan was free to do whatever he chose with anyone he liked but *Suki*? How could he have gone back to her after she'd tried to destroy him? Hot on the heels of her incredulity was an unpleasant surge of humiliation, because for all his talk of coming back to Ennisfarne, he'd clearly been looking for an easy conquest that final night. At least she'd denied him that. And finally her jumbled emotions coalesced into anger, a searing white-hot fury that she struggled to keep a lid on, even as part of her wondered why she was so enraged. Yes, Logan was a fool for taking Suki back but it had stopped being any of Eve's business the moment he left the island. And yes, it stung that he'd seen her as easy but that too was in the past. But an altogether more basic explanation was unfurling in Eve's mind. She was angry and disappointed but that wasn't what was causing acid to burn through the pit of her stomach. It was jealousy.

'You can't believe everything you read in the papers,' Hamish ventured, setting a steaming cup of tea on the table in front of Eve.

Warren let out a disgusted snort. 'That picture, though. I thought better of him than this.'

Slowly, Eve stirred her tea, and it occurred to her to wonder why the two of them had been so keen to hide the newspaper from her. Did they suspect she had feelings for Logan? *Did everyone know?*

The thought was enough to set her stomach roiling again

but she forced the sensation to one side. 'Shall we get on?' she asked, doing her best to dredge up a smile that she felt sure must be brittle. 'The stage build starts tomorrow and there's still a lot to do.'

Hamish dropped the newspaper to the floor and nodded. 'Sorry, Eve. But you're right, let's not waste any more time.'

Fixing her gaze on her notes, Eve forced herself to breathe in and out, pushing the thought of Logan and Suki further from her mind with each exhalation. In the end it didn't really matter what she did or didn't feel, she told herself as Warren went over the schedule for the festival's construction phase. She was never going to see Logan Silk again.

Chapter Twenty-Six

Logan

Logan awoke on Sunday morning with a thumping head and a sour taste in his mouth that told him he'd had too much whisky the night before. He lay in bed for a few minutes, watching the sunlight play across the ceiling, waiting to see if more sleep might be an option. He remembered going to O'Halloran's in Soho – Nick had heard good things about the mixologist and wanted to sample the cocktail list. Then there'd been champagne at Bob Bob Ricard – too much champagne, Logan decided as he touched his throbbing temples. Eventually they'd ended up in Lola's, despite his better judgement, and that was where things got hazy. There'd been a bottle of very good Orkney whisky, a decent DJ and plenty of laughter ... Logan frowned as he squinted upwards, wondering why he had a sudden feeling of doom. There'd been an argument, he suddenly recalled – had it been with

Nick? No, not Nick – a woman. And then a face swam into his memory and he knew exactly who the argument had been with. Suki.

With a groan, Logan started to piece things together. He'd refused to talk to her but that had only made her try harder. Then, when it had finally dawned on her that he really wasn't going to play, she'd become incandescent, hurling insults so shrilly that they were asked to leave. And then, to crown it all, there'd been a paparazzi on the street when they'd tumbled out. Suki had seen the camera first and made a grab for Logan, wrapping herself around him just in time for the tell-tale flash. Her triumphant smile as he'd pushed himself free had made Logan feel sick. It was a sensation he felt again as he reached for his phone now.

The first message was from Nick: You made the front page.

There was a screenshot attached. Logan didn't need to zoom in to know the photo was in total contrast to the truth but when had that ever stopped a newspaper from running with a story? He wouldn't have been surprised if Suki had called the paparazzi herself, tipping them off about where she'd be, and with whom, to generate a nice juicy front page and a few more precious column inches.

Scowling down the message list, Logan saw a slew of unfamiliar numbers. Most appeared to be journalists, asking him to confirm he and Suki were back together. Some invited him to tell his side of the story, for a generous fee, and a few mentioned rumours of a heated altercation. Logan didn't need to check his missed calls to know it would be riddled with unknown callers. Slumping back on his pillow, he closed his eyes. He'd been in London less than three weeks and he already wished he hadn't come back. Why had he given in to Nick's insistence that what he needed was a good night out? He should have known it would only lead to trouble.

Leaving his phone half buried by the bedsheets, he trudged to the kitchen and made coffee. It wasn't Nick's fault the night had ended so badly, Logan reflected as he carried the cup to the living room; he'd simply been trying to help. He'd known Logan was finding it hard to settle back into his old life and had suggested a night on the town as a way to remind him of the good things about living in the city. And Logan had enjoyed himself – it had been good to hang out with Nick, to laugh and forget his troubles for a while. It was Suki who'd soured things, with her spiteful determination to cause him trouble. He couldn't understand what he'd ever seen in her.

A hot shower washed some of Logan's irritation away but it couldn't soothe the sickness in his stomach. Reluctantly, he checked his phone and saw Phoebe had tried to ring him. Bracing himself, he called her back.

'Please tell me you haven't done what I think you've done,' she said the moment the call connected.

Logan allowed himself a humourless smile. His agent was nothing if not direct. 'That depends on what you think I've done. I assume you're referring to Suki.'

'Of course I am. I'm not telling you how to live your life

but I thought we'd agreed Suki Simpson was bad for you in every conceivable way.' She sighed. 'And yet here the two of you are splashed across the front page. Again.'

With a grim sense of déjà vu, Logan explained. When he'd finished, Phoebe let out a huff of frustration. 'That woman is so toxic, not to mention borderline narcissistic. She just can't let go, can she?'

'Apparently not. But it's just one photo and the papers will move on when it becomes obvious we're not back together after all.'

'At least it shouldn't affect you professionally this time,' Phoebe said. 'I know you're not interested in working the fashion scene right now but there were raised eyebrows after the last stunt she pulled. She's fast getting a reputation as a troublemaker and no amount of beauty will help if photographers refuse to work with her.'

The news should have pleased him but instead Logan just felt tired. The days when he'd been invigorated by drama were long behind him – now what made him feel alive was peace and constancy; the brush of the wind on his cheeks as it blew in from the sea, the bubbling of the waves as they lapped the shore, the cries of the birds circling overhead. It came as absolutely no surprise that they were all things he'd experienced every day on Ennisfarne. Perhaps the time had come to face the truth: London was no longer where he wanted to be.

'There is something else I wanted to run by you,' Phoebe said after a moment. 'I put some informal feelers out about a more nature-themed direction for your work and a couple of editors seemed interested. Do you want me to send you more details?'

Work was the last thing on Logan's mind but he supposed he could use the distraction. 'Sure. It can't hurt to take a look.'

'That's the spirit,' Phoebe said encouragingly. 'And you never know, you might be pleasantly surprised. Hang in there, Logan. This too shall pass.'

She rang off, reminding him unnecessarily to ignore any further contact from the press. Logan sat for a moment, remembering the last time she'd warned him in the same way, after Suki's previous effort to derail his life. He'd been on Ennisfarne then and the whole island had unexpectedly rallied to his defence. Fleetingly, he wondered what Freda thought of the headline, or worse, Eve, and his mood darkened even further. With another scowl at his phone, he tapped out a curt reply to Nick and switched it off. What he needed was to surround himself in the blues and greys of the sea, and while there were plenty of beaches within a few hours' drive of London, he knew they would be a poor substitute for the coastline he wanted. For a moment, he contemplated getting in the Hilux and driving north but there was a good chance the causeway would be covered by the time he arrived. And if by some miracle he had timed it right, what would he do once he was across it? Stare at the sea and come away, more bereft than ever? He couldn't run away to Ennisfarne every time something went wrong.

After prowling restlessly between rooms for some time, he settled on a compromise. He might not be able to go to Ennisfarne but that didn't mean Ennisfarne couldn't come to him. Grabbing a pair of sunglasses and a cap, he made for the front door.

The Wolffson-Cutler Gallery occupied a prime piece of London real estate on the South Bank of the Thames, just along from Waterloo Bridge. It boasted an eclectic mix of paintings, sculpture and interactive installations by some of the best-known modern and more traditional artists, and Logan had been there a number of times. There were several JMW Turner seascapes in the Water Gallery that he was keen to view again, wondering if perhaps some of them might have been painted on Ennisfarne, but what had really drawn him in was the discovery that three of Morag Chester's paintings hung there too.

The Turner pictures were as breathtaking as he remembered. The textured nature of the oil paints gave each scene a three-dimensional quality; Logan found himself almost holding his breath, waiting for the towering, white-tipped waves to be released from their suspension to crash and flow into the churning seas below. But it was the light he admired the most – subtle rays of gold and silver breaking through the bulbous dark clouds to dance upon the sails of a storm-tossed ship. He'd seen that light for himself and done his best to capture it, although he had to concede Turner had been the master.

He found Morag's work in a small room off the main

galleries. Their composition could not have been more different from Turner's work – there was no life-or-death drama in them, no desperate hope for divine intervention and no demand that the audience cower in awe before the ocean's might. Where Turner's seascapes made Logan want to hold his breath, Morag Chester's art encouraged him to gently exhale. It helped that he recognized the setting immediately – one looked out to sea from behind the beacon near her cottage, another featured the arch of Darling Cove – but it was more than familiarity. The ocean in the Turner paintings was an adversary, the scenes a battleground, but Morag portrayed the sea as a gentler, more harmonious entity. Her use of light was every bit as extraordinary as Turner's and Logan found gazing at these paintings just as fascinating as the stormy scenes in the main gallery.

He ambled through several more arched rooms, admiring the works that hung there without pausing too long at any. By the time he reached the last painting he had come to see, the weight of the morning had almost fallen from his shoulders and his mood was significantly improved. He stopped in front of the picture and gave it his full attention.

It was another perilous seascape, pitting the might of the storm against the frailty of mankind. A small wooden boat strove to crest the waves, dwarfed by their magnitude and surely about to capsize at any moment. Its destination was a foundering wreck, barely afloat and pinioned to the rocks, and a desperate huddle of survivors clung to the remains. This was Grace Darling and her father, saving the lives of nine men and women and becoming national heroes in the process.

The artist had done an exceptional job, Logan thought as he stepped nearer to study the gilt-framed painting. Spray flew through the air, spattering the faces of William and Grace as they strove against the storm. Sinews stretched in William's arms and terror shone from the eyes of the survivors as they reached out to Grace. Her dark hair glimmered beneath her bonnet, the pale skin of her face clear and luminous before the black clouds, and Logan could see why she had received proposals of marriage from strangers once her part in the rescue became well known. While Logan knew only too well that what he saw was the product of the artist's imagination, he had captured Grace's strength and bravery in a way that sang from the canvas. And perhaps inevitably, Logan couldn't help being reminded of Eve. He'd tried not to think of her in the weeks since leaving Ennisfarne, pushing her cool, pragmatic rejection to the back of his mind. But now, gazing at her famous ancestor, it was impossible not to think of her and a small bubble of suspicion began to form that it was a subconscious desire to see Eve that had drawn him to the South Bank in the first place.

An email from Phoebe was waiting when he returned home and switched his phone back on. True to her word, she'd included more information on potential work and one of the possibilities caught his eye. The UK's leading diving magazine was interested in commissioning a series of underwater shoots based on recently discovered wrecks dotted around the British Isles, some in dangerous waters – was that something he might consider? Logan didn't have to think twice – if nothing else, it would get him out of London and he'd rather face a shark than run into Suki again. The sooner he was out of her reach, the better.

'What are you doing right now?'

It was just after nine o'clock on Saturday morning and Nick was standing at Logan's front door, a look of suspiciously wide-eyed enquiry on his freshly shaved face. Giving his own unshaven chin a rub, Logan stepped aside to let him in. 'Hello to you too. I'm not doing anything now, which is just as well since you've turned up unannounced.'

Stepping inside, Nick dropped a bulging rucksack to the floor, where it thudded against the wooden floor. 'Good. And how about the rest of this weekend – got any plans?'

Logan's gaze slid from the rucksack to his best friend. 'No. Why?'

'Because I've had a brilliant idea and you're going to love it. But we're going to have to leave in the next twenty minutes if we want to beat the tide so you'd better start packing.'

'The tide?' Logan echoed, thoroughly bewildered. 'Are we going kayaking?'

Nick grinned. 'Better than that. We're going *dancing*.'

And then the penny dropped and Logan understood exactly what Nick had planned. He glanced once more at the rucksack. 'You don't have a tent. Or a sleeping bag.'

'That's because we're not camping,' Nick said, clearly

pleased with himself. 'Or even glamping, for that matter. But we can discuss this once we're on the road. Get packing!'

There was no arguing with him when he was in a mood like this, Logan thought as he headed to his bedroom to dig out a rucksack of his own. But the truth was he didn't really want to argue; if he was honest, he'd been looking for a reason to go back to Ennisfarne almost from the moment he'd left. And like the meddlesome best friend that he was, Nick had made it his business to provide one.

'I assume you do actually have tickets,' he called, as he passed the living room en route to the bathroom. 'You're not just planning to flash the famous Borrowdale smile to get us in.'

'Of course I've got tickets,' Nick replied airily. 'VIP, Access All Areas, as a matter of fact. All it took was a little call to the lovely Freda.'

Logan didn't believe that for a second. 'What did she demand in return – your first-born child?'

There was a slight pause. 'I might have agreed to record an audio guide to the nunnery.'

Folding t-shirts and placing them into his bag, Logan grinned. Freda drove a harder bargain than anyone he knew and to get a hot property actor like Nick to voice the audio guide was definitely a coup. 'Well, thank you,' he said once he was standing in front of Nick again. 'It was good of you to sort it out.'

Nick shrugged. 'I'm flying to Vancouver next week to start

filming a new Netflix series. I thought it would be rude not to have some fun before I go.'

And it would be fun, Logan decided as they made their way downstairs to climb into the Hilux, although he couldn't actually remember the last time he'd been to a festival purely as a punter. There'd always been a commission to complete – cover images for a band's new album or a multi-page spread for *Rolling Stone* magazine – that meant he never truly relaxed. At Ennisfest, he would have no professional responsibilities whatsoever. Unless—

'You didn't agree anything on my behalf, did you?' he asked Nick, eyebrows raised.

'Of course not,' Nick said, sounding injured. 'I wouldn't dare. Although . . .'

He trailed off and Logan said nothing, waiting for him to finish the sentence.

'I might also have suggested you'd take a few photos here and there,' he said with a laconic wave. 'Nothing too oner-ous, just a few shots they can use in next year's PR materials.'

'Right,' Logan said, dragging the word out. But he wasn't angry – how could he be when he would almost certainly have taken photographs anyway?

'I didn't think you'd mind,' Nick said. 'But the main pri-ority is to have fun, okay?'

Starting the engine, Logan had to dampen down a sudden surge of untamed happiness at the thought of going back to Ennisfarne. 'Okay.'

Nick fixed him with a solemn look. 'It's three hundred

and sixty-eight miles to Ennisfarne, we've got half a tank of petrol, no cigarettes, it's not dark and we're wearing sunglasses.'

Logan revved the engine and met his best friend's gaze with a grin. 'Hit it.'

Chapter Twenty-Seven

Eve

The Saturday morning meeting before Ennisfest began always felt like the calm before the storm to Eve. Everyone knew what lay ahead, plans had been made, contingencies devised, risks assessed – even the weather looked set to co-operate, with the forecast set to be warm and dry all weekend. At this point there was nothing more to be done, apart from opening the gates, and Eve tried to keep the tone light. The kitchen would act as the committee's HQ for the duration of the festival and she made sure it was well stocked with sandwiches, cakes and fruit to get them through the weekend. There was still a frisson of tension in the air, however, and even Huxley seemed to recognize something was going on, lying beneath the kitchen table with his head on his paws, although Eve suspected it was a strategic position in case anyone dropped a doughnut.

'Any problems on the campsite overnight?' she asked Warren, who shook his head.

'Nothing major. A few people who'd had one too many drinks but that's usual. And one lad who reported his tent had been stolen but it turned out he was just in the wrong field.'

Grins broke out around the table. Genuine cases of crime were almost unheard of but tent amnesia was common. 'What's the situation across the bars?' Eve turned to Aiden, who she'd promoted to hospitality manager. 'Everything set?'

'Good to go,' he replied. 'I don't think there's any chance they'll drink us dry but I've got back-up supplies on order in case we have a particularly thirsty crowd this year.'

'Cleaning and litter pick teams are already on site,' Hamish reported, before Eve could ask. 'But hopefully the *Leave No Trace* message will help keep things manageable.'

'It was a quiet one for security, too,' Shona chipped in. 'No unauthorized attempts to get to the beach last night. But today will be the real test – fingers crossed the extra fencing and late-night patrols will do the job.'

'That's great,' Eve said, nodding her thanks. 'Sounds like we're all set. There are no changes to the running order yet, so providing the evening acts make it over the causeway on time then we shouldn't have any issues.' She gazed around at her team and felt adrenaline start to fizz in her veins. 'This is where all our hard work comes together. Let's make it the best Ennisfest yet!'

The five of them fist-bumped and the meeting broke up as each team member went off to get on with their responsibilities. Eve stood for a moment in the empty kitchen, breathing in and out, steeling herself for the roller-coaster ride to come. All would be well, she silently told her jangling nerves. The bands would play, the crowds would dance and Darling Cove would bounce with the kind of unbridled joy only music could bestow. And afterwards, when the final notes had been played and the last camper had gone, Eve would sit on the beach with a hot cup of coffee and make some time for herself. The festival had kept her distracted but she was aware of a restlessness in her soul, something she couldn't quite pinpoint, and she knew the time was coming when she'd have to face up to whatever it was. But not today, she resolved, and squared her shoulders. Today she needed to be sharp and focused.

'Come on, Hux,' she said and the Labrador jumped to his feet. 'Time to get this show on the road.'

The morning passed in a blur. Traditionally, the stage opened at midday with a local band, often one who had previously played the monthly music night at Darling's and this year was no exception. Ferris Wheel were an up-and-coming group from Alnwick who played a mixture of original songs and inventive covers that had the crowd tapping their feet from the moment they began. Eve had watched from the side of the stage, enjoying the energy and enthusiasm of the musicians even as her mind was on the next scheduled act. Perhaps one day she'd be able to relinquish her stage management role to someone else and experience the festival more fully, she'd thought as she checked her phone for new messages. She had delegated more responsibility than ever this year, after all. But she wasn't sure she'd ever trust anyone enough to pass on this job. It was the heart of Ennisfest – if the stage fell silent, there was no festival.

Ferris Wheel's set closed to amiable applause and as they cleared their equipment, the next act appeared right on cue. Byker Grove were a spirited trio from Newcastle whose upbeat melodies went down well with the growing audience. In some ways, Eve preferred this part of the festival, when the area in front of the stage was dotted with picnic blankets and camping chairs, the playground full of face-painted children while their parents took a moment to soak up the chilled-out vibes. By evening, they would be gone and the space would be jammed with ever-increasing bodies, their elated faces fixed on the stage. Hearing them sing along to the headline act was always a magical moment but Eve was proud that Ennisfest was so family-friendly.

During a break after the fourth band, she headed off to check in with Aiden. The committee were in constant communication via radios, so she wasn't expecting to find anything wrong, but she much preferred to see for herself how things were going. Predictably, the bars were mobbed but the queues were orderly and moving well.

'How's it going?' she asked her brother when she tracked him down in the Thirsty Bishop tent. 'Anything I need to know?'

He shook his head. 'Nope. The cider pumps went down

around two o'clock but Hamish was on it pretty quickly and it's all fine now.'

'Good. Any trouble with Think 25?'

'There's always one or two chancers who'll try it on without ID so we've turned a few people away,' Aiden said, shrugging. 'But the staff are well trained, if I do say so myself.'

Eve gave him an admiring glance. 'You should say it. I'm really impressed with everything you've put in place since taking this job on. You've worked hard and it shows.'

He winked. 'Turns out I can be trusted after all. Who knew?'

She accepted the jibe in good grace. 'Okay, I admit it. You might be finally growing up.'

'Let's not go that far,' he said with a shudder. 'How are things your end – any problems?'

'So far so good,' she said, crossing her fingers. 'Only another six sets to go.'

Aiden smiled. 'I'm hoping to join you for Infinite Monkey Dance. I reckon they're going to smash it.'

'Hopefully,' Eve said, aware that the headliners had been a big part of the reason Ennisfest had sold out so fast this year. 'They haven't actually arrived yet.'

'They'll be here,' Aiden reassured her, checking the time. 'Look, the causeway will have only just cleared. We've never had a no show yet.'

He was right – of course he was – but Eve couldn't shake the tight feeling in the pit of her stomach. Until the band was checked in and standing in front of her, she wouldn't be able to relax.

'I know,' she sighed. 'I'd better get back, anyway. Worm Asylum are on in five minutes.'

By the time the dance duo from Edinburgh had finished their set, Eve was starting to get seriously worried. There was no sign of the Infinite Monkey Dance tour bus and calls to their manager were going straight to voicemail. Anxiety swirled around Eve's mind as she picked her way to the Accreditation bell tent, hoping to discover the band had just arrived. Lifting the flap, she stepped inside and came face to face with Logan Silk.

She felt her jaw drop, knew she was gaping but was power/less to close her mouth. 'You!' she gasped after what felt like an hour. 'How did – what are you doing here?'

He raised his hand, showing her the jumble of wristbands that gave him the same no-holds-barred access she had. 'Nick wanted to come and I thought it sounded fun. Is that okay?'

Utterly bewildered, Eve glanced over his shoulder to see Nick Borrowdale waving at her from beside the Accreditation desk, where Nancy the admin assistant was looking as though Christmas had come early. 'He – you –' She took a deep calming breath and let it out fast. 'Of course it's okay. Just unexpected, that's all.'

She stopped then, suddenly aware that her stomach was churning for a whole new reason, one that had nothing to do with her missing headline act. Logan was here. Logan was *here*, and her body was wasting no time in reminding her how he made her feel. She scanned his face, taking in the stubble on his chin, the lines of tiredness around his eyes, the uncertain pinch to his lips and she wanted to tell him how glad she was to see him. But she couldn't focus on that now – he was also a distraction she didn't need, not when disaster was looming in her immediate future.

Pulling herself together, she summoned up a brisk smile. 'It's great you're here – enjoy the festival. You too, Nick – let's catch up for a drink later. But right now, I've got some urgent business to attend to.'

She stepped around Logan, and hurried towards Nancy. 'They're still not here?'

The younger woman shook her head. 'Sorry, Eve. But Logan and Nick just came over the causeway. Maybe they passed the bus on the way?'

Hearing his name, Nick glanced back at them. 'What bus?'

'The Infinite Monkey Dance tour bus,' Eve explained. 'They're headlining tonight but I can't get hold of them. I'm starting to worry they're not going to turn up.'

Logan frowned. 'Didn't we see a tour bus at the services near Durham? We wondered if they might be heading here.'

Eve's heart leapt. 'Did you recognize any of the band? Could it have been them?'

Nick pursed his lips doubtfully. 'Hard to say. It was big and flashy and instantly recognizable for what it was but I didn't see anyone get on or off. Sorry.'

The look Logan offered was similarly apologetic. 'Nor me.' He checked the time. 'But if it was them, they can't be far behind. We stopped off at Morag's old cottage to drop our bags before heading here so it's possible the bus is on the causeway right now.'

'*If* it was them,' Eve echoed and shook her head in frustration. 'There's just no way of knowing.'

Nick was gazing thoughtfully at the canvas ceiling. 'Infinite Monkey Dance – who's their lead singer again?'

'Flora Enderby,' Eve said promptly. 'The guitarist is Sim Cockcroft and the drummer's name is Dan Piper.'

'Enderby,' Nick repeated slowly, narrowing his eyes. 'She's not related to Jonas, is she?'

'The actor?' Logan frowned too. 'His sister, I think. Why?'

Nick pulled his mobile from his pocket and smiled. 'Because we were in a show together last year and I've still got his number. Want me to call him?'

It was all Eve could do not to snatch the phone out of Nick's hand. 'Yes. Yes, please. Please call him and ask if he knows where his sister is.'

Tipping his head, Nick pushed back the flap of the tent and went outside, the phone pressed to his ear. Resisting the temptation to follow him, Eve strained to listen but the thud of an insistent bassline from the stage made catching any part of the conversation impossible. Instead, she waited with Logan, aware of the awkward silence but unable to shake off her anxiety long enough to fill it.

'You look well,' he ventured, after a minute had ticked by. 'Stressed, obviously, but well.' He paused. 'It's good to see you.'

The words made Eve's stomach swoop again but she was conscious of Nancy's presence behind the desk, riffling through paperwork and doing her best to pretend she wasn't listening. 'Thanks,' she said and ran a self-conscious hand across her scruffy ponytail. 'It's – erm – good to see you too. How's London – been making up for lost time?'

She hadn't meant to load the question with unspoken disapproval but her self-control seemed to have been undermined by the stress of the last hour. The sentiment wasn't lost on Logan, either. He winced. 'I suppose you mean Suki. Look, it's not what—'

'Success,' Nick announced, bursting back into the tent with a satisfied grin. 'I spoke to Jonas, who wasn't thrilled about being woken up but what can you do, and he confirmed his sister is on her way to a gig.'

Eve stared at him. 'Which gig, did he say?'

Nick shook his head. 'He didn't know.'

Eve couldn't help herself; she groaned. 'Then we're no better off than we were!'

'Hold on, I'm not finished,' Nick said mildly, and Eve had the definite impression he was enjoying himself. 'He didn't know where Flora was but he said he'd find out. I just got a message with the answer.'

'And?' Both Eve and Logan spoke at exactly the same time.

Nick waved his phone like a magician and studied the screen. 'She is – and I quote – "headlining at some festival at the arse end of the universe". Which, no offence, describes Ennisfarne to a t.'

The relief Eve felt was almost palpable. 'Oh, thank you. Thanks so much, Nick.' She glanced from him to Logan to Nancy. 'That has to mean she's on her way here, doesn't it?'

Logan's mouth twisted in wry amusement. 'I think so, yes. So you can relax. They'll be here.'

Nancy nodded. 'Why don't you leave it with me, Eve? I'll let you know the moment they turn up.'

It took her a moment to process what the assistant was saying. 'Yes,' she said, suddenly recalling there were several other bands due to play before Infinite Monkey Dance. 'I'd better get back to the stage.' She made for the door, then turned to grip Nick's hand. 'Bloody hell, Nick Borrowdale, I'm glad you're here.'

She found Selina waiting for her at the side of the stage, singing along to Tall Oaks' final song. 'Where've you been?' she said, when Eve arrived. 'You've missed most of these guys and they've been brilliant.'

'Emergency,' Eve said and explained what had happened. When Selina heard Logan's name, her eyes widened so fast Eve thought they might pop.

'No way! He's here?'

'Yep,' Eve said. 'And not only Logan – Nick Borrowdale too. But that turned out to be quite useful.'

Again, Selina was agog. 'Blimey, these celebrity types really do know everyone, don't they?'

'Apparently,' Eve allowed, applauding as Tall Oaks took their final bows. 'Luckily for me.'

Selina nodded, then gave Eve a sidelong look. 'But never mind that, what did Logan have to say?' She hesitated. 'Oh god, he didn't bring Suki, did he?'

'No,' Eve said gratefully, because she wasn't sure how she'd have reacted if he had. 'He didn't say much. I was distracted by the Monkey business, to be honest.'

'They can't be that close, if he didn't bring her,' Selina mused. 'Didn't you ask where she was?'

Eve felt her patience starting to slip. 'No, I didn't. Believe it or not, I don't actually care and anyway, he said it was Nick's idea to come so I guess Suki wasn't invited.'

'Liar,' Selina said, smirking. 'You absolutely do care.'

'I do not,' Eve insisted, folding her arms.

'Deny it all you want but deep down you know it's true,' Selina continued. 'There's something else to think about too. He's here, when you were so sure he'd never come back. And I bet it's not just Ennisfest that lured him here. I bet he's come to see you.'

It was such a preposterous idea that Eve didn't know where to begin. 'Read my lips, Selina. I. Don't Care. I don't care that he's here, I don't care why and I certainly don't care about Suki Simpson.' The radio attached to her belt crackled and she heard Nancy's voice. 'I've got more important things to worry about, like making sure this festival runs like clockwork.'

Selina held up her hands in surrender. 'Fine. Don't let me get in your way.'

Lifting the radio, Eve spoke into it. 'Nancy, it's me. What's happening?'

'Infinite Monkey Dance have just arrived.' Nancy's voice was crisp and business-like. 'I'm just sorting their wristbands now.'

The irritation Eve had felt at her best friend evaporated instantly and she fired a triumphant grin her way. 'Understood,' she told Nancy. 'I'm on my way.'

After all her earlier stress and anxiety, Eve still couldn't quite believe it when Infinite Monkey Dance took to the stage. Flora had been apologetic, explaining that one of their roadies had been taken ill while they were travelling, which had forced them to make an unscheduled stop on the way. 'I didn't think it would take as long as it did,' she'd finished, rolling her eyes, and Eve was happy enough to accept her apologies, if only to be spared any further details.

She kept her eyes fixed on the band, admiring the light show and doing her best to ignore Logan to her right. It was a task that was made much harder by the meaningful looks Selina kept tossing her way and in the end, she had to hiss at her best friend to stop it. Being backstage with the bands, seeing their brilliance close up, was one of the things that made all the hard work worth it and she wasn't going to let anyone take that away from her.

'Amazing, aren't they?' Aiden yelled as Flora launched into another set of incredible vocals. 'How are you going to top this next year?'

It was a question Eve had no idea how to answer. She'd got lucky in booking Infinite Monkey Dance before they became huge – the chances of doing the same thing again were slim. But perhaps she wouldn't have to rely on luck, she thought, allowing herself a sly peek to where Logan and Nick were tapping their feet in time to the beat. Maybe she could take advantage of Nick's celebrity connections to bring a little more star quality to Ennisfest. It would always showcase local talent, first and foremost. But it wouldn't hurt any of them to be on the bill with a few bigger names. It was definitely something to think about, once the dust had settled on this year's festival.

'How you doing, Ennisfest?' Flora bellowed into the microphone, eliciting a roar of approval from the crowd. 'Are you ready to sing with me?'

Again, the response was instant. A shiver of anticipation ran down Eve's spine. As well as a raft of crowd-pleasing floor-fillers, the band had a few quieter songs that suited Flora's smoky vocals perfectly. Was she about to lead the Ennisfest revellers in a rendition of Eve's personal favourite, 'Moon and Stars'?

Sim, the guitarist, stepped forward with an acoustic guitar and began to pick out a haunting melody that Eve knew well. Unexpectedly, she felt her eyes prickle; she hadn't been sure whether the band would play this song. It was about love and loss and letting go, about lives well lived and the loneliness when love left – in short, it was not a standard festival choice.

'I wrote this song for my mum,' Flora said, as the melody floated softly through the still night air. 'It helped me make sense of her loss and if you've lost someone too, I hope it helps you.'

A moment later, she began to sing and Eve almost forgot where she was.

> *'There's a star so bright, there you are, second to*
>   *the right,*
> *Through the darkest night, how you shine, radiant*
>   *and bright.*
> *That's where you live now, so far away,*
> *Hate that you leave me, day after day.'*

Flora's voice rose and fell, gliding effortlessly through the words and weaving a spell across everyone who listened. Gazing past her to the crowd, Eve saw a handful of twinkling lights appear in the darkness as people held up their phones. More joined them until the night glittered like a black velvet dress strewn with a thousand diamonds. Eve felt her throat catch as Flora reached the chorus and the audience began to sing along.

> *'I'd be the moon to your star, if I could,*
> *Keep you warm with the beam of my heart,*
> *We'd be the moon and the stars, yes we would,*
> *And nothing could keep us apart.'*

The sound was so beautiful that the hairs on the back of Eve's neck stood on end. These were the moments when live music was everything, she thought, as Flora fell silent and let the crowd sing alone. Eve shook her head in wonderment, aware that magic was being created on the stage and beyond. How amazing must it be to hear your own song reflected back at you?

Seamlessly, Flora came back in and led into the second verse. By the time she reached the chorus again, Eve thought every voice joined in and sang until the last melancholy refrain died away. For a heartbeat or two, nothing happened, then Flora raised a fist to the sky and a tumultuous cheer reverberated all the way to the back of the stage. The band basked in the adoration until it began to die down and then launched into another big hit, a disco-themed anthem that was impossible to resist.

Eve wasn't sure how they managed it but every song seemed better than the last. By the time they reached the end of their set, it didn't seem possible that they could lift the crowd any higher but then they came back on and smashed out their biggest hit of all. When the last beat died away, the roar was so loud that Eve half expected it might break the sound barrier. It took several long minutes before the audience would let them go but eventually the stage went dark, indicating the show was over. Once the band members were safely backstage, Eve hurried up to them to offer her congratulations. 'You were incredible! Thank you so much!'

Smiling, Flora dipped her head. 'Thanks, we had a blast. They were the perfect crowd, weren't they?'

'Pretty good,' Eve agreed. 'But it helps when the band is just brilliant. Thanks again for coming all this way.'

'No problem,' Flora said, then cocked her head to listen

as one of the roadies murmured something to her. 'Listen, I hate to sing and run but we're playing Glasgow tomorrow and I've just been told if we're not on the road by 11.30 we'll be stuck here all night so—'

'Go,' Eve said, stepping back and holding up her hands. 'And if you ever want to headline again, just let me know!'

For all the entertainment was over for the night, there was still plenty that required Eve's attention. She stopped briefly in front of Nick, mostly to thank him again for his help, waved at Selina and then hurried off to check in with her fellow committee members around the festival site. Reassuringly, everything seemed to be in hand; the security patrols were enforcing the no-swimming rule on the beach with iron determination, there had been no repeat of the cider pump issue and Warren reported the campsites were getting busier as people returned to their tents but everything seemed under control. Eve was on her way back to the kitchen for a much-needed cup of tea when she got the message from Selina.

Got something we need to discuss. Meet me on the balcony at midnight.

Eve read it several times, wondering what could be urgent enough for her best friend to summon her to a meeting, but not urgent enough to warrant an immediate phone call. But she had too much on her mind to give it any real thought. She simply tapped out a thumbs up emoji by way of response and continued on her way to the kitchen.

Warren and Aiden were both tied up keeping an eye on their responsibilities but Hamish and Shona were already there, munching on pastries and animatedly discussing the day's triumphs. Both congratulated Eve when she came in, although she tried to deflect the credit. 'I just book the bands,' she said modestly as she reached for the kettle and placed it on the Aga. 'It's up to them to knock it out of the park.'

'Credit where credit is due,' Hamish insisted. 'You'll be getting headhunted by Worthy Farm if we're not careful.'

Eve pulled a face. Glastonbury might be the granddaddy of all music festivals but she couldn't think of anything more stressful than managing tens of stages across such a huge site. 'No thanks,' she said fervently, topping up her milk with tea. 'I'll leave that to the experts.'

It was just before midnight when she slipped through the darkened bar of Darling's and made her way up the stairs to the balcony. Her tea plumed steam into the air as she waited for her best friend, enjoying the sound of the waves hitting the beach. A perfect crescent moon had risen, inviting the stars into an endless silent waltz. Behind her, the bright lights of Ennisfest were starting to dim and the sound of the crowd was fading as the site closed down until morning. Taking a seat, Eve wrapped a blanket across her legs, laced her fingers around her mug and waited, letting the sea's unchanging ebb and flow soothe her racing mind.

She didn't turn around when she heard the balcony door slide open. 'Don't say anything,' she called softly over one shoulder. 'Just come and listen to the waves for a while.'

There was a brief pause, then footsteps crossed the wooden floor and stopped behind Eve's back. Closing her eyes, Eve allowed the stress and worry of the day to ease from her weary muscles. She'd sleep well that night, she thought, as long as her head didn't go crazy. 'Is there a better way to relax than this?' she asked Selina. 'What do people do when they don't live by the sea?'

'They listen to apps that have recorded the sound,' Logan said. 'But you're right, it's nowhere near as effective.'

Eve jerked to her feet so fast she almost spilled her tea. 'You!' she gasped as she spun around to face him. 'What are you doing here?'

He raised an eyebrow. 'I might ask you the same question. I'm looking for Nick, he asked me to meet him here at midnight.'

'And I'm waiting for Selina, because she told me to meet her here at – oh.' Eve broke off and glared at Logan. 'Is this your idea of a joke? Because I'm tired and my bed is calling me.'

'No, this wasn't my idea,' Logan said, his voice maddeningly reasonable. 'I think it's fair to say we've been set up by our best friends, Eve. They clearly think we need to talk.'

'Then they're wrong,' she snapped, outraged at Selina and Nick's conspiratorial meddling. 'There's nothing we need to discuss.'

Logan's gaze met hers. 'You're angry with me.'

'I'm angry with our so-called friends,' she retorted and then the truth of his words caught up with her. 'And yes, since you mention it, I'm angry with you too.'

If the admission surprised him, he didn't show it. 'Do you mind if I ask why? I know we didn't part on the best of terms but I don't think I behaved too dreadfully, did I?'

Eve stared at him. 'What? No, of course you didn't. That's not why I'm angry. I'd have thought it was perfectly obvious what the problem is.'

Logan's forehead creased in confusion. 'Not to me it isn't.'

Could he really be this thick-headed, Eve wondered. With a strangled growl of frustration, she turned to face the unseen ocean. 'You getting back together with Suki sodding Simpson, after everything she did to you. That's the bloody problem, Logan.'

There was a long, thoughtful silence. 'You care if I'm with Suki?' he said eventually.

'Of course I care,' Eve huffed, noting the hint of surprise in his tone but deciding to ignore it. 'She might be one of the most beautiful women on the planet but she treats you like rubbish. And I can't believe you went back to her, after all she put you through.'

She broke off, startled to feel tears pressing the back of her eyes. She swiped them furiously in case Logan saw the shimmer of tears and got the wrong idea.

'I'm not with Suki,' he said quietly. 'I know what it looked like in the picture but I promise you it wasn't a happy reunion. Nick and I ran into her at Lola's, she picked a fight and got us thrown out. She grabbed me on the street to make it look like we were back together but that's the last time I saw her.'

She didn't believe him. 'Don't lie.'

'Why would I lie?' he said. 'Ask Nick if you don't believe me. Or ask Phoebe – she's the one who's currently rearranging my professional life so I never have to see Suki again.'

For a moment, all Eve could focus on was the roar of the ocean. Could it be true? Had the photo simply been Suki's final throw of the dice to get Logan's attention? 'But the article said—'

'Lies,' Logan said calmly. Placing a gentle hand on Eve's shoulder, he turned her round to face him. 'I promise you I am not in love with Suki. Does that make you less angry with me?'

It did, she realized. Now all she had to contend with was the horrible jumble of other emotions slugging it out in the pit of her stomach. She sighed and placed her now tepid tea on a nearby table. 'I didn't think you'd come back.'

His gaze was steady. 'I told you I would.'

'But you're only here for the weekend, then you'll be gone again.' She stopped talking, horribly aware she sounded like a petulant child. 'Which you're perfectly allowed to do, obviously.'

Logan nodded. 'I do have to go back to London. I only brought enough clothes for two days.'

She wasn't surprised by the news but it did cause a jagged slash of disappointment to scythe through her insides. Seeing him again had raised all manner of confusing thoughts and half-thoughts and chief among them was that she was glad he'd come back. Her heart had leapt with unmistakeable joy when she'd seen him in the tent, although her head had immediately overruled it. And now he was telling her again that he was leaving. She wasn't sure she could bear it twice.

'But I realized something while I was away,' he went on, taking a step nearer to her. 'I don't like living in London any more. I missed the sea, I missed the silence.' He glanced up at the sliver of moon hovering above the shadowy arch. 'I missed staring at the stars, being able to actually see them and hearing the stories your dad used to make up when you were young.'

Eve watched him, her mouth suddenly dry. Was he saying what she thought he was saying?

'But most of all, I missed you.' He took a deep breath and looked away. 'And I know you think we're too different, that it could never work between us, and if you still feel that way, it's fine. But I tried leaving you and this beautiful island and what I learned was that I can't do without either.'

The breath caught in Eve's throat as she blinked once, twice, three times, trying to take it all in. He couldn't mean it, she thought unsteadily. He just couldn't. 'But I'm—'

Logan gave an impatient shake of his head. 'If you're about to say, "not a model" then I'm going to have to protest.' She blushed and he let out an exasperated huff. 'Firstly, you're perfectly right – I do have a weakness for models. Secondly, you're far more accomplished, smarter and altogether more brilliant than anyone I've ever met, model or otherwise. And thirdly, what makes you so sure you're *not* a model?'

She gaped at him, then closed her mouth fast in case a tiny bubble of hysterical laughter escaped. 'But . . .'

'I've photographed you more than anyone in the past few months – your picture is the jewel in the crown of the exhibition,' he said, and his eyes rested warmly on hers. 'All of which makes you a model, albeit a reluctant one.'

And now she did laugh. 'You're mad.'

'Almost certainly,' he agreed. 'Us creative types often are.' Reaching out a hand, he brushed the skin of her cheek. 'Which brings me back to my first point, the one about the weakness for models.'

He was so close that Eve could hardly breathe. Her cheek burned from his touch. 'It turns out I have a weakness too,' she said, placing both hands on his chest. 'For grumpy photographers who drive me up the wall.'

'Is that so?' Logan breathed, running his thumb ever so gently across her bottom lip. 'Then I have to say, I think we're a perfect match.'

Eve reached up to tangle her fingers in his dark hair, the way she'd wanted to for so long. 'I think,' she whispered, standing on tiptoes so her mouth hovered next to his, 'you might be right.'

His lips, when they finally found hers, were so soft and sweet that her legs almost turned to jelly. Instinctively, Logan caught her, pulling her into his arms and deepening the kiss so that it was all she could do not to lose her sense of who and where she was. Her head spun but somehow it didn't matter, not when she was cocooned in the safety of his love. It seemed to last for ever and was still over too soon, and when they parted Eve could only wonder why they had waited so long.

'I'm going to buy Morag's cottage,' he murmured. 'Maybe start an underwater photography school.'

She nodded breathlessly. She didn't care what he did, as long as he was near her and happy. 'Good idea. And maybe one day, once it's established, if we ever have time ...' She paused to smile hesitantly up at him. 'We could take a trip to the Great Barrier Reef.'

Logan gazed at her for a long moment, then returned her smile with one of his own so tender that she melted all over again. 'I can hardly wait,' he said, and kissed her again.

Acknowledgements

My first shout of appreciation goes, as always, to Jo Williamson of Antony Harwood Ltd – thanks for being there when I need you. Next up is my super lovely editor, Molly Crawford, whose kindness, support and patience know no bounds. I am very happy to have you in my corner – thank you. I count myself so lucky to be published by Simon and Schuster UK – the team is second to none. Many thanks to everyone on the Books and the City team but a special mention to Pip Watkins for bringing Ennisfarne so vividly to life, and to the wonderful SJ Virtue for being so bloody brilliant.

I owe a debt of thanks to John Davies of the National Coastwatch Institution at Boscastle, who dealt very helpfully with my vague questions about potential small boat disasters at sea and saved me hours of plot wrangling.

Twitter followers will know that Luna the golden Labrador puppy bounced into my life while I was working on this book. Although she tipped my life upside down and irretrievably deleted a big chunk of the story along the way, I could not be without her now. And it turned out I didn't need the bit she cut anyway – maybe she should edit all my books in future. Many of the dogs dotted throughout this book are real and I would never have met them without Luna.

All my love to T and E, as ever my heart is yours. And finally, thank you to my readers – as the sun sets through the arch of Darling Cove one last time, I hope you enjoyed the serenity and magic of your visit to Ennisfarne as much as I enjoyed mine.

If you enjoyed *Escape to Darling Cove* you'll love…

The Little Shop of Hidden Treasures

When Hope loses her husband, she fears her happiest days are behind her. With her only connection to London broken, she moves home to York to be near her family and to begin to build a new life.

Taking a job at the antique shop she has always admired; she finds herself crossing paths with two very different men. Will, who has recently become the guardian to his niece after the tragic death of her parents. And Ciaran, who she enlists to help solve the mystery of an Egyptian antique. Two men who represent two different happy endings.

But can she trust herself to choose the right man? And will that bring her everything she really needs?

Available now…